D0379183

Old World
Murder

ALSO BY KATHLEEN ERNST

Nonfiction

Too Afraid to Cry: Maryland Civilians in the Antietam Campaign,
Stackpole Books, 1999

A CHLOE ELLEFSON MYSTERY

Old World Murder

KATHLEEN ERNST

MIDNIGHT INK
WOODBURY, MINNESOTA

First Edition
First Printing, 2010

Book design and format by Donna Burch
Cover design by Kevin R. Brown
Cover illustration © Charlie Griak
Editing by Connie Hill

Midnight Ink, an imprint of Llewellyn Worldwide Ltd.

Library of Congress Cataloging-in-Publication Data

Ernst, Kathleen, 1959–
Old world murder : a Chloe Ellefson mystery / by Kathleen Ernst. —1st ed.
p. cm.
ISBN 978-0-7387-2087-6
1. Women museum curators—Fiction. 2. Old World Wisconsin (Museum)—Fiction. 3. Murder—Investigation—Fiction. 4. Robbery investigation—Fiction. I. Title.
PS3605.R77O43 2010
813'.6--dc22 2010017284

Midnight Ink
Llewellyn Worldwide Ltd.
2143 Wooddale Drive
Woodbury, MN 55125-2989
www.midnightinkbooks.com

Printed in the United States of America

DEDICATION

For the interpreters and curators I knew,
with respect and affection;

and for Sergeant Robert J. Bord,
with thanks.

AUTHOR'S NOTE

Old World Wisconsin is a real place. I had the pleasure and privilege of working there for twelve years, starting in 1982. However, this book is a work of fiction. All characters, including Chloe Ellefson, were born in my imagination. I freely fabricated events to serve the story. For example, although most of the historic structures mentioned do exist, Mr. Tobler's cobblestone cottage does not. To learn more about this very real and fascinating historic site, visit the website:

http://oldworldwisconsin.wisconsinhistory.org/

Perhaps only one thing has remained constant: like most museums and history-related institutions, Old World Wisconsin relies upon public support. Please help sustain your local historic site!

ONE

As Chloe Ellefson walked from 1982 into 1870s Wisconsin, a white frame church emerged from the trees, prettily framed against a cloud-studded blue sky. The view alone was enough to make most visitors pause, appreciate the simple elegance of the restored church, perhaps even wonder about the lives of those women and men and children who had first worshiped within its walls.

For Chloe, the historic site's newest employee, the scene represented a fresh start.

A cadence in her mind kept time with her steps: *Must – make – this – work. Must – make – this – work.* Dr. Eberhardt could no doubt have written a thesis about that obsessive little drone ... but Dr. Eberhardt was still in North Dakota with his white pills and his spiral notebook and his guttural grunts that had reminded her all too often of Markus' father. Visiting a psychiatrist who reminded her of the people she was trying to escape seemed counter-productive, but Solomon, North Dakota—population 793 on a good day—hadn't offered many options in low-cost mental health care.

Anyway, Chloe had come to Wisconsin to stand on her own two feet. Although, she thought as she reached the church gate, it would be more accurate to say she'd come *home* to Wisconsin. The last thing she'd ever expected to do. But she was here now. A new job. A new life. And she was determined to make it work.

After all, her chosen field was all about façades. Curators at living history sites presented impressions of the past. The bustles and bonnets (or braces and boots) that interpreters wore hid more than modern clothes and hairstyles. Well, she thought, nothing wrong with a good façade. In fact, a huge historic site intended to create and present illusions wasn't a bad choice for someone wanting to rewrite her own history.

Chloe had visited the outdoor museum during open-hours only once, the day before her interview almost a month earlier. As she'd wandered the sprawling grounds that day, her spirits had unexpectedly begun to rise. Over fifty historic structures had been restored among the Kettle Moraine State Forest's woods, prairies, and kettle ponds. Interpreters in period clothing brought the farmsteads, homes, and service buildings to life by telling tales and churning butter and making shoes and weeding gardens, and giving visitors as many participatory and sensory experiences as possible. Old World Wisconsin, the state's newest historic site, was spectacular.

Now, she was hoping to recapture some of that good vibe. It was a late Monday afternoon. The last group of shrieking school children had tramped from the site, quickly followed by the interpreters' stampede toward the parking lot. Chloe's first day on the job, a blur of paperwork, staff meetings, and behind-the-scenes orientation, was winding to a close. This was the best time of day to visit any historic site. And having after-hours access was one of the true perks of becoming an employee.

Chloe knew it would take a long time to become truly familiar with Old World Wisconsin. She planned to visit a building or two after-hours each day. Starting with … she consulted her map … St. Peter's Church.

She mounted the steps and, feeling important, used her new master key on the lock. Once inside she paused, letting impressions of the place come. St. Peter's Church offered nothing too striking. Good.

Next, she took a quick curatorial survey: plain wooden pews, a pump organ, painted stations of the cross hanging on the walls. Most of the window panes were thick and distorted—original, amazingly enough. The altar cloth needed cleaning, and she scrawled a note on her pad.

Outside, tires screeched on gravel. A moment later heavy steps thumped up the stairs and a stocky, white-haired, red-faced man burst into the sanctuary. "Who are you?" he demanded.

Chloe blinked. "Who are *you*?"

He scowled. "Look here, lady, the museum closed at four o'clock. You can't be in here!"

Belatedly Chloe noticed the vague uniform: dark brown trousers, tan shirt, patch of some kind duly sewn on his sleeve. His official attire contrasted sharply with the non-uniform she'd mustered for the day: tan chinos and a royal blue cotton shirt, long blonde hair captured in a single braid and coiled behind her head.

OK, Chloe told herself, time to get one more working relationship off to a good start. "My apologies. I should have introduced myself. My name is Chloe. I'm the new curator of collections."

The security guard rubbed his chin. "Marv left something in the log about a new curator starting … but that's not the right name. It was something Scandihoovian. Inger? Ingrid! Yeah, that was it. Ingrid—"

"I go by Chloe. But I *am* the new curator."

"Well …" He still looked suspicious. "You can't come out on the site after hours without letting us know."

Chloe mustered her brightest smile. "I'm really glad to know that site security is so tight. But I'll need after-hours access on a regular basis. Can we consider some other solution, um … what did you say your name was?"

The guard hesitated. "Hank," he said finally. "Well, just be sure to check the alarm before you go barging into buildings. The Village buildings have been switched over to the new security system. Did Marv give you the access codes?"

Had Marv given her access codes? She couldn't remember. She couldn't even picture Marv. The day had been full of too many names and too much information. "I'm not sure, to be honest. I'll have to look through my notes."

Hank showed her the security touchpad hidden behind a door, and gave her an access code. "That'll work for every building in the Village," he told her. "There are different codes for the German and Finn-Dane areas. The Norwegian buildings are still on the old microphone system, so you'll have to call. You'll be outta here within the hour?"

"Less," she promised. "I've got a five o'clock meeting in the restoration area. I'll probably just visit one more building here before heading out for the night."

Hank made a big show of seeing her out of the church. Lovely, Chloe thought, as she watched him get back into his car and drive slowly away. Day One, and she'd already annoyed a security guard.

"Just keep trying," she ordered herself softly. She had a new position—and a permanent one, which was hard to come by in the mostly seasonal world of outdoor museums, complete with benefits and a salary that actually covered rent with enough left over for a bit of food each week. "I will," she announced, "stay positive."

That resolve fled as soon as she oriented herself on the visitor guide and map. The next building was a small cobblestone cottage across the road from the church. She'd skipped the Tobler House on her earlier visit, but the new curator of collections couldn't ignore one of the exhibits just because its first occupant had happened to come from Switzerland.

Chloe knew that her Swiss connection had helped land the job. "I see you spent five years at Ballenberg," Ralph Petty, the site's director, had said during her interview. He'd tilted his head to peer at Chloe over the half-glasses that perched on his nose. "The Europeans have so many excellent outdoor museums. Did you enjoy living in Switzerland?"

"Oh, yes," Chloe assured him blithely, as her fingernails dug angry red trenches into her palms. "I *adored* Switzerland."

"We're currently restoring the home of a Swiss immigrant in the Crossroads Village," Petty said. "Aldrick Tobler emigrated from Switzerland to Green County, Wisconsin, in 1872. We were able to get our hands on the small structure that served as both his carpentry shop and living quarters."

"Will—will I be expected to furnish the Tobler building?" Chloe stammered. If so, they might as well end this interview right now. No way was she up to that.

"Unfortunately… no. We want to open the building to the public later this year, and we couldn't wait for your position to be filled. I hired a freelancer last winter to develop a furnishings plan." And Director Petty had rattled on enthusiastically about the project for at least another ten minutes. Chloe had tried to nod in appropriate places.

She could skip the Tobler house today. Just mosey on down the path to the Hafford House. Mary Hafford had been an Irish laundress, and Chloe was eager to visit her home.

But … no. Just check the place out and be done with it, Chloe told herself. She let herself inside and quickly punched in the access code on the security box hidden behind the door.

As she turned, Chloe paused to get a feel of the century-old building. She got a brief glimpse of half-papered walls; a worktable covered with tools. Then the impression came. It was not the distant jumble she'd felt in St. Peter's Church. Instead, a sense of palpable unhappiness crackled in the air.

Chloe clenched the doorknob. The sensations grew stronger, although she couldn't quite define the root emotion: Frustration? Discontent? When her skin began to tingle, she bolted from the building.

On the front step she wiped her forehead with suddenly trembling fingers. What the hell was *that?* After a lifetime of absorbing impressions of old buildings, she'd learned to take the occasional flash in stride. But that sensory barrage had been unexpectedly strong. Chloe pulled the door tightly shut and snapped the lock.

It probably wasn't even the house, she thought, as she hurried away. Poor old Mr. Tobler had probably lived a hum-drum life and died without leaving any bad ju-ju behind. Surely her own bad ju-ju had caused her reaction. It had been a mistake to enter the Swiss exhibit alone. She'd come back some day when the site teemed with hyperactive fourth graders. That energy would dispel bad vibes of any vintage.

Chloe checked her watch. Time to head out, anyway.

Once she retrieved her green Pinto from the main parking lot, she drove down the site's twisting entrance road. The village of Eagle lay to the left, but Chloe turned right onto Highway 67. She passed the

1940s-era house that inconveniently held Old World Wisconsin's administrative offices. Another right turn onto County Highway S took her past a tree-lined prairie that marked, if she remembered correctly, the edge of the museum's German area. The huge historic site warranted several access gates for staff use.

A mile or so later she slowed and turned right again onto a gravel drive with a fading sign that proclaimed "Restoration Area." In front of her was a long, low building that housed the maintenance staff. A pole barn held a few large artifacts and two of the big trams used to haul visitors around the site.

Two ancient trailers squatted off to the left, almost hidden in a grove of pines. The words "Celebrate The Bicentennial! Visit the History Mobile!" were barely legible in peeling paint on one. The other, an ugly pinkish-gray rectangle on cinder blocks, gave no hint of its lineage. Both trailers had been pressed into temporary service for collections storage, and were crammed with shelves of artifacts.

Chloe climbed rickety steps to the pink monstrosity. The tiny kitchen area had evidently provided desultory office space to a curator who, in a whirlwind of energy, had furnished the exhibit buildings before Old World's grand opening six years earlier, in 1976. The burned-out curator had soon after joined the Peace Corps and moved to New Guinea. State-imposed budget cuts had left Old World Wisconsin without someone to oversee its collections ever since.

The office held a miniscule table and two chairs. It was cramped and dusty, and smelled of mice. Chloe had been aghast that morning when the museum's receptionist had handed her a note with the meeting arrangements on it. "You told a potential donor to meet me at the *trailer*?"

The receptionist—what was her name?—had shrugged. "Look, once this lady heard you'd actually been hired she called half a dozen times, wanting to know when your first day was. She was determined to come out today."

Chloe turned on the ancient faucet. After several moments of agonized burbles and clanks, a dribble of rust-colored water reluctantly emerged. She used the tap water and a few paper towels to wipe down the yellow Formica table and two wooden folding chairs. She jumped when a phone rang. She hadn't known she *had* a phone in here. By the fifth ring she'd located the ancient rotary-dialed monster—an artifact in its own right—behind a stack of black notebooks.

"Chloe? Listen, are you expecting a Mrs. Lundquist? She ended up over here at Ed House by mistake."

Chloe mentally fast-forwarded through a filmstrip of her morning. Ed House ... yes, she remembered. *Education* House. Another of the empty homes left behind when the state bought out the few properties that infringed on the projected Old World Wisconsin site, now used by research and interpretation staff. If she wasn't mistaken, this male voice belonged to the curator of interpretation.

"Right," she said. "I'm waiting here at the trailer."

"I'll send her along."

"Thanks ..."—she went for broke—"... Brian."

Small silence. "It's *Byron*."

"Byron. Right. Sorry."

"I'll send Mrs. Lundquist over."

"Thanks," Chloe began, but a dial tone already rang in her ear. Evidently Byron was a tad touchy about his name.

Day One. She'd annoyed a security guard and irritated the curator of interpretation.

A few minutes later car tires crunched slowly over gravel, and Chloe went outside. The big Buick dwarfed the elderly woman who emerged. She wore Easter Sunday-best—a pale yellow linen dress, white pumps, matching handbag. Chloe winced, picturing what the trailer's dust would do to *that* outfit.

"Mrs. Lundquist?" she asked. "I'm Chloe Ellefson. I'm so glad to meet you."

The hand that clasped hers seemed fragile, like wrapping paper stretched over a toothpick model. Mrs. Lundquist's carefully permed white hair framed a thin face with anxious blue eyes. "How do you do?"

"I'm well, thank you," Chloe said, as she led the way into the office. "Please forgive the dust. It's my first day, so I haven't had a chance to tidy up."

"I understand." Mrs. Lundquist settled gingerly on one of the chairs, put her purse on the table, and folded her hands in her lap. "It was kind of you to see me so quickly."

Chloe sat down with legal pad and poised pencil. "The phone message I got didn't contain much information," she began. "You're interested in making a donation?"

"Oh, no!" The tiny woman sat up straighter. "I need to get one of my family antiques back."

"Um … back? Back from where?"

"From here!" Mrs. Lundquist pulled a piece of paper from her handbag and presented it.

Chloe read the faded photocopy. It was an acquisition form confirming the accepted donation and legal transfer of an item described as a "Hand-painted Norwegian ale bowl with cow heads, nineteenth century" to the State Historical Society of Wisconsin. At the bottom was a neat signature—Berget Lundquist—and the date: November 10, 1962.

"Well … it seems this item was transferred to the Society twenty years ago," Chloe said. "This is your signature?"

"Oh, yes. I made the donation. My son had died, you see. My only child. I didn't see any point in hanging onto family heirlooms."

"But . . . now you want it back."

"Yes."

Chloe studied the paper again. The donation had been made when Old World Wisconsin was no more than a gleam in some architectural historian's eye. "Ma'am, I think that you need to contact one of the curators at the Historical Society headquarters in Madison."

"I've already done that, weeks ago. And I was told that my ale bowl was transferred here when this site opened."

Shit. "Mrs. Lundquist, I'm new, so I'm not familiar with Society collections policies yet—"

"I'm sure you're doing your best, dear." Mrs. Lundquist patted Chloe's hand. "You seem like a sweet young woman. And with that hair . . . you must be Scandinavian also?"

"Norwegian. But—"

"Just like me!" Mrs. Lundquist awarded Chloe a delighted smile. "So you understand."

No, I don't! Chloe insisted silently. "Mrs. Lundquist, once a donation has been made, it can't be undone. It's a legal transfer of ownership."

"But I must get it back! It's very important!"

Chloe pinched her lips together. She genuinely liked old people. She liked their stories, their memories, their hard-won experience. Their mementos, their refuse, even their homes—these things comprised Chloe's chosen profession. Mrs. Lundquist didn't need to beg, or to cajole; Chloe truly wanted to help her.

"The best thing I can do is check with the chief curator in Madison," Chloe said. "I can call her tomorrow, and get back to you."

Mrs. Lundquist's face crumpled. "But... I had hoped to take the ale bowl with me today."

"I'm afraid that won't be possible."

"May I at least see my bowl? Make sure it's alright?"

"The thing is..." Chloe massaged her temples with her fingertips. "Did I mention that it's my first day? I don't know where the ale bowl is. It could be in storage, or on exhibit in one of the Norwegian houses. Have you toured the Norwegian area on site? Do you know if it's on display?"

"Old World Wisconsin is so big... I've been told that I'd have to climb in and out of a tram to even reach the Norwegian houses. I'm afraid that's too much for me." The elderly woman lifted one fragile hand in a helpless gesture. "But surely there are records? Can't you look it up?"

"Mrs. Lundquist, I'm truly sorry, but I don't even know *how* to look it up. I don't know what system the former curator used. The collection here includes thousands of objects. And—" Chloe took a deep breath. "It's my *first – day*."

The other woman looked stricken. "Would you mind if... if I looked for it?" she asked, her voice quavering. "I recall the ale bowl well. I'd know it if I saw it."

"I'm afraid that's not possible," Chloe said again, as gently as she could. "May I keep this acquisition form? Good. I will talk with the chief curator in Madison about your... situation. And—"

"Miss Ellefson, *please!*"

"—I will get back in touch with you as soon as I can."

Mrs. Lundquist looked down at the table, but not before a telltale sheen of tears appeared in her eyes. "I see."

Chloe felt wretched. "I promise you, I *will* find the ale bowl."

The elderly woman gently patted Chloe's hand again—a feeble, papery gesture that made Chloe want to cry herself. Then Mrs. Lundquist got to her feet, wiping her eyes. "Thank you for your time."

Chloe made sure she had current contact information, then helped Mrs. Lundquist down the trailer steps. Mrs. Lundquist walked slowly, her thin shoulders bowed. The Buick's door seemed too heavy for her. Once seated, it looked as if she could barely see over the top of the steering wheel.

Didn't I switch from interpretation to collections to avoid people problems? Chloe wondered, as the Buick crept from the parking lot. What on earth had prompted Mrs. Lundquist's sudden change of heart so many years after the original donation was made?

Day One: she'd annoyed a security guard, irritated the curator of interpretation, and disappointed a sweet old woman. Not the promising start she'd wanted.

"Time to am-scray," she muttered. She'd confront this donation imbroglio tomorrow. Right now she had a mountain of moving cartons waiting at her newly rented farmhouse.

She locked up the trailer, threw her bag on the Pinto's backseat, and headed for home. She tried to forget Mrs. Lundquist, but as she turned onto County S, the irritating drone crept back into her brain: *Must make this work. Must make this work—*

The incantation died abruptly as Chloe crested a rise. Below her, at the foot of the hill, was the big Buick which Mrs. Lundquist had driven from the restoration area parking lot five minutes earlier: in a ditch, upside down, and partially wrapped around a tree.

TWO

PATROLMAN ROELKE MCKENNA HANDED the man in the red Volvo his ticket. "Here you are, sir."

"I know Chief Naborski personally." The driver's tone was peevish. "I think I'll make a phone call about this."

Roelke smiled pleasantly. "Be sure to mention that I clocked you doing fifty-seven in a school zone, sir."

The man tossed the ticket on the empty passenger seat. Roelke had no more than stepped away from the car before the man furiously cranked up the window and pulled away.

"And have a real nice day," Roelke added, before walking back to the squad car. Was the guy a long-time local? Roelke didn't know. His old buddies from the Milwaukee Police Department, who often skewered Roelke for "fleeing to cow country," assumed he was on a first-name basis with everyone. But although he'd been an Eagle cop for almost a year, he didn't recognize everyone in the village.

Roelke noted the stop on his daily activity report while the radio chattered. Almost all of Waukesha County's calls were routed through a centralized communications center, which kept the frequency busy. He was putting his clipboard aside when the dispatcher called his ID. "George 220. Respond to S & 67 for possible 10–50."

An accident. Roelke snatched up the radio. "I'm three minutes from S. On my way." He turned on siren and flashers and headed west, cutting through the swath of the state forest that bordered Eagle. As he turned left on County Highway S he took several deep breaths, steeling himself for … whatever.

When the cruiser crested the final hill on County S, Roelke saw a white Buick, flipped and crumpled against a massive oak. A thin blonde woman was on her knees by the broken passenger-side window. Roelke parked behind an old Pinto on the shoulder, slid from his car, and scrambled down the embankment. "What happened?"

"I think she's dead." The blonde sounded dazed. "I think I killed her."

"*What?*"

"I didn't try to move her. I'm just holding her hand. But I really think she's dead."

"Let me see," Roelke commanded. "And you—don't go anywhere. Get in my car and wait for me there." The woman scrambled out of the way as he knelt beside the Buick.

The elderly woman's seatbelt tethered her to the seat. Roelke snaked his hand past the jagged splinters of glass and crumpled metal, feeling for the driver's pulse. A Hardees cup had spilled, leaving brown stains on the victim's dress and the champagne-colored upholstery. The woman's small purse—white leather, expensive—rested on the ceiling. One white shoe had fallen beside it.

Roelke turned away, and frowned. The dazed blonde woman sat on the ground at the edge of the road, leaning against the Pinto. She didn't look like a flight risk, but Roelke took note of her plate number before radioing dispatch for assistance. "George 220. This is a probable J3." Roelke knew the old woman was dead, but the medical people didn't like patrol cops calling it.

He needed an ambulance, an accident reconstructionist, a coroner, and a wrecker. While he finished with dispatch, the growing wail of another siren sliced the soft spring evening. A county car braked to a shuddering halt, sending a little spray of gravel across the road. Waukesha County Sheriff's Deputy Marge Bandacek emerged.

Roelke stifled an inward groan. Sheriff's deputies provided him backup in Eagle, and he provided them backup outside the village limits. All in all everyone got along, helped each other out. But Marge was a pain in the ass.

He went to meet her. "Hey."

"What we got?" Marge was a big-boned woman, with gray hair cut in a straight line just below her ears.

Roelke gestured. "Just the driver."

"Fatal?" Deputy Bandacek said, too loudly. Roelke saw the blonde woman wince.

"Yeah. No skid marks, no sign of other trauma."

More keening wails scarred the stillness as the emergency squad approached. Marge jerked her head toward the blonde woman. "That a witness?"

"I don't know yet."

Marge hitched up her pants. "I'll talk to her."

Highway S was just barely out of the Village of Eagle limits, which put Marge in charge. "I already got started with her," Roelke told Marge, keeping his tone friendly. "She's pretty upset. I'll finish up there."

He turned away before Marge could object, leaving her to deal with the EMTs. An old VW bus zoomed over the hill and pulled to a stop—a good Samaritan or gawker—followed closely by a Department of Natural Resources patrol car. Good. Marge could give orders to the DNR guy, and they'd both be busy with crowd control.

Roelke approached the blonde woman. She still sat on the ground, knees up, staring at the wreck. She was probably somewhere in her early thirties. Her pallor evidently came from genetics as much as shock, for she had the look of a classic Wisconsin Scandinavian. The eyes that finally looked up at him were chicory blue.

"I need to ask you some questions." Roelke pulled a pad and pen from his shirt pocket, and crouched beside her. "What's your name?"

"Chloe Ellefson. Um, Ingrid Ellefson." A rosy flush stained her cheeks. "Ingrid Chloe Ellefson."

"How did you know the victim?"

"I didn't know her. I mean, I *did* know her." Ms. Ellefson stared at her hands, which were trembling. "I'd just met her. Her name is—was—Mrs. Lundquist. Berget Lundquist."

Roelke kept his tone even. "How did you kill Mrs. Lundquist?"

She jerked. "*What*?"

"You said, 'I think I killed her,'" Roelke reminded her.

"I did?"

"You did."

"Oh, God." Ingrid Chloe Ellefson swiped at her eyes. The wrecker arrived. Roelke waited. It was a pleasant day, which didn't feel right, but there it was. The state owned the land on either side of County S, and bits of prairie remnants and oak openings still buffered the rigid rows of pines planted three decades earlier in much of the land southwest of Eagle. In between the sporadic metallic moans emanating from the wrecked Buick as the rescue team bullied the car into releasing Mrs. Lundquist's body, a meadowlark sang. The spring air smelled damp and fresh.

"She needed help," Ms. Ellefson began finally. "And I wasn't able to help her."

By the time she'd haltingly reconstructed her meeting at the Restoration trailer, Roelke was satisfied that she hadn't committed murder. "Did Mrs. Lundquist appear to be ill?" he asked. "Did she seem breathless? Flushed?"

While the blonde woman struggled with those questions, the coroner arrived. He'd examine the body and decide if an autopsy was indicated, or if the local funeral home should be called to collect the body. The tow truck driver was getting to work with winch and chain. Two more passersby had stopped to rubberneck. The DNR officer kept them in check while Marge Bandacek oversaw operations by the wrecked car.

"No," Ms. Ellefson said finally. "I mean, I don't think so. She was just upset about her family heirloom."

"Thank you," Roelke said. "I've got all the information I need for now."

She nodded, wrapping her arms around her knees.

"Is there someone we can call to drive you home?"

"No." She lay one cheek on her knees. "But I'm fine."

She didn't look fine. Roelke turned away. "Hey, Denise," he called.

Denise, a short, plump mother of two, had been an EMT for years. She looked his way as Roelke walked toward the truck. "What's up?"

"Give her a quick once-over, OK?" Roelke jerked his head toward Chloe Ellefson. "Make sure she's fit to drive herself home."

"Sure."

Roelke checked in with Marge. She would wait for the accident reconstructionist, finalize things with the coroner.

"Looks clear-cut to me," the young DNR officer said. "The old lady's time was up."

“Yeah,” Roelke said. After six years in the huge Milwaukee Police Department, he was still getting used to the assortment of backup that often responded to calls in and around Eagle. Sometimes it was overkill. Mostly it was reassuring.

He got back in his squad and started his report, waiting as Denise cleared Ms. Ellefson to drive home. He watched her slide slowly into the Pinto and drive away. He didn’t know which image was more sad: Berget Lundquist, undignified in death, or Chloe Ellefson, stunned in life.

By the time Chloe turned into the gravel drive circling her farmhouse in La Grange, bats were swooping over the alfalfa field across the road. She let herself into the kitchen through the back door.

Ignoring the cartons stacked on the counters and floors, she headed straight to the bathroom. She rummaged in her little bag of toiletries. The prescription bottle was on the bottom—orange plastic, directions printed neatly on the label, with Dr. Eberhardt’s name and phone number in one corner. It was almost full of little white pills, round and innocuous. For a long moment the afternoon dissolved into that plastic container.

“*Damn* it.” Chloe jerked open the medicine cabinet over the sink, put the container on one of the empty shelves, and slammed the mirrored door.

Back in the kitchen, she rinsed out the lone cup in the sink. The second-hand refrigerator installed the day before, which was now rattling ominously, offered a liter of diet soda and a half-eaten package of string cheese. She reached for the soda, poured some in the glass, added a few ice cubes and a liberal splash of rum.

She paced through the first floor, glass in hand. The faint hum of a tractor drifted through her living room window. Her landlords lived within hollering distance, but they were little more than strangers. Her parents? She could call them, or drive to their house, but ... no. No solace there, either.

After several more minutes of agitated circling, Chloe dropped into a faded armchair rescued from her parents' attic. She reached for the phone and dialed a familiar number.

She heard the reassuring signal of distant ringing. Then a familiar voice, warm and low: "Hello?"

"Ethan?"

"Chloe? Good God, girl, is that you? Where are you?"

"La Grange, Wisconsin." Chloe clenched the phone receiver and closed her eyes. "I rented an old farmhouse about twenty minutes from the museum. The garage door is broken, and the living room carpet is mustard-colored shag, and the whole place needs paint. But you'd love it. You really would. The property backs up against a state forest."

"Yeah?"

"I just moved in over the weekend. I've got a bit of settling-in to do. You know, unpacking. Stuff like that. But I think I'm really going to like it here."

Ethan blew out a long, audible breath. Then, "What happened." Ethan was so sure of his trans-wire assessment that the statement was flat, with no hint of questioning inflection. Damn the man for knowing her so well. Bless the man for knowing her so well.

"Well ..." Chloe took a sip from the glass. "It was my first day on the job today, you know? And the thing is ... I think I was ... sort of responsible for an old lady getting killed."

That stopped him. Chloe took another sip. Soda pop and rum: inelegant, but effective.

"You what?" Ethan asked after a moment.

Chloe told him what had happened. "So there really wasn't anything I could do for her."

"Then why are you taking responsibility for the crash?"

"Because—because she was a sweet old lady. For some reason, getting this ale bowl back had become incredibly important to her. People kept putting her off, saying she had to wait until I got hired. But no one ever told her you can't just undo a legal donation. So she comes today, thinking *I'll* help her, and all she gets is *more* runaround. She was really upset when she left."

"And you think that's why she wrapped her car around a tree?"

"Well . . ."

"Maybe she got stung by a bee. Maybe her brakes failed."

Chloe pulled her heels up to the edge of the seat. "Maybe. But I can't help feeling responsible."

"I hope you didn't phrase it quite that way to the cops."

"I might have." Chloe slid sideways in the chair. "This cop from Eagle questioned me. He can't be more than late twenties, but he had this boss-man air about him. And he wore mirrored sunglasses like some motorcycle cop in a bad movie. He kinda freaked me out."

"What happened was horrible," Ethan said firmly, "but you can't take any responsibility."

She shrugged. It wasn't that easy. "Well, enough about me. Tell me about you. What's going on in Idaho?"

"The beginning of the fire season. Environmentalists and lumber companies chewing on the same bone. Lost campers. Dumpster-diving bears. Same old, same old." Ethan worked for the United States Forest Service.

"How's Chris?"

"Chris is good."

"I wish you lived closer."

Ethan laughed. "Wisconsin is a hell of a lot closer than Switzerland."

"I suppose."

"Hey, Chloe." He'd stopped laughing. "Are you OK?"

"Yeah." She got up and stood by the front window, the receiver still tight to her ear.

"Should I be worried about you? I mean, really worried?"

Chloe stared out at the last streaks of sunset staining the sky. "No. Really, Ethan. It's not like last winter. I'm better now."

"You're sure." He didn't sound convinced.

"It's weird, you know? Last winter the thought of death seemed like a comfort. Seeing that sweet old lady dead, though—it was horrible." A shudder twitched over her skin.

"I can imagine."

"I truly am better. I think." Chloe sighed. "I just—I just still miss Markus sometimes."

"Do you ever talk to him?"

"Talk to him? God, no." Think about him—yes, every day. His quick laugh and knowing hands. His lanky stride on hikes to high hidden lakes. The smudges under his eyes when he'd been up all night at lambing time. The way his dark hair grew in a tiny cyclone whorl from a spot on the back of his head—

"Chloe? You there?"

"I'm here." She swallowed down the sudden lump that had formed in her throat. "And I know it's stupid to still feel this way. It's been almost a year since we broke up." Since Markus dumped her.

"It's not stupid. It just is."

"I miss school sometimes, too. The good old days." Forestry school at West Virginia University. Backpacking trips with the Outings Club. Feeling completely at home in a place she'd never been before. Meeting Ethan, who'd become her best friend.

"Me too," he said. "But now is good, too."

Chloe realized she was exhausted, and that her glass was empty. "Listen, thanks for lending an ear. I gotta go unpack some boxes. Let me know if you get called out on a fire, OK? I'll give you my new number." She waited until he'd found a pencil before dictating the digits.

"Got it."

"Hey, Ethan?"

"Yeah?"

"Are you still gay?"

He chuckled softly. "'Fraid so."

"Just checking."

After hanging up, Chloe resisted the temptation to mix another drink, and returned the glass to the sink. She located a small carton in the bedroom, conspicuously marked with a Magic Marker asterisk. She dug beneath a photo of her parents, a tissue-wrapped pinecone from an exceptionally wonderful back-country campsite at Dolly Sods, and a small stuffed dog so battered it had no fur left around the middle. She finally found a framed snapshot of herself and Ethan, bulging backpacks visible over their shoulders, dirty and sweaty, posed on a rock outcrop in the southern Appalachians.

Chloe set the photo on one of the empty bookshelves in the downstairs bedroom. The only other signs of life in the room were a sleeping bag and pillow on the bed, a suitcase worth's of clothes in the closet, and a battered paperback copy of Jack Finney's *Time and Again* on the nightstand. "I'll unpack tomorrow," she promised herself, and got ready for bed.

THREE

When Chloe drove to work the next morning her stomach, acknowledged that morning only with coffee, clutched in protest as she turned onto County Trunk S. Aside from the tire tracks left in the vegetation beside the gravel shoulder, there was little to mark the accident scene. No one had left flowers, or banged a hastily constructed cross into the ground.

Did Mrs. Lundquist have a family? Had that young Eagle cop called them with the news? Or did cops still do things like that in person? Chloe wasn't sure. The policeman who'd questioned her didn't seem a likely candidate for delicate duty. His uniform had been a solid, grim black, not friendly blue like on TV. And his manner…

Her thoughts trailed away as she pulled into the restoration area lot and saw a patrol car with "Eagle Police" stenciled on the side. The subject of those thoughts appeared around the corner of the pink trailer.

Lovely. Chloe got out of the Pinto. "May I help you…" She checked his name bar. "Officer McKenna?"

"I need to ask you a couple of questions, Ms. Ellefson."

Chloe had promised to meet Byron at Ed House in ten minutes. Besides, it rattled her to find the policeman waiting. Couldn't he have called or something? "Sure," she said.

He pulled his pad free and uncapped a pen with his thumb. "First—"

"Let's go inside." Chloe turned away. Anything to get him to take off those damn sunglasses.

She immediately regretted her impulse, for it was unsettling to walk into the tiny galley where she'd last seen Mrs. Lundquist alive. Embarrassing, too, to have more company before she'd had a chance to scrub and air the place. "I just started working here," she said, propping the door open with a rock.

He leaned against the sink and—thank God—removed his sunglasses. "I'd like you to tell me again what transpired between you and Mrs. Lundquist."

Chloe rubbed her palms on her trousers. "I told you everything yesterday."

"I know. But I'd like to hear it again, now that you're not quite so upset."

Chloe eyed him, wondering if there was more to the request. Officer McKenna was about her height, five-foot-ten inches. He was perhaps four or five years younger than her own thirty-two, lean, well-muscled. He looked like a recruiting poster for the Marines, with dark hair clipped close to his head, a too-strong jaw, and direct brown eyes. There was something unsettling about his demeanor—a muscular tension, a sense of perpetual watchfulness. His inscrutable gaze made her long for the mirrored shades.

"Is there a problem?" she asked. "Do you know what caused the accident?"

"It was probably a heart attack or stroke. Is this where you met Mrs. Lundquist?"

"Yes." Chloe stared through the doorway at the pines and replayed the conversation for him.

He made notes in a tight scrawl. "And you have no idea where this particular antique might be?"

Chloe sighed. "As I *said*, yesterday was my first day on the job. There are thousands of artifacts on this site. Some are on exhibit, in fifty-odd buildings that are open to the public. Some are stored in these trailers, and in that pole barn over there, and probably half a dozen other places I haven't even seen yet. Some were donated specifically to Old World Wisconsin, and some were originally donated to the State Historical Society and transferred here. There hasn't been a curator of collections on staff here for six years, and—"

The archaic rotary telephone jangled. Chloe snatched the receiver. "Hello? Um, Collections area. This is Chloe."

"Chloe? It's Byron."

Byron ... Shit. "Right. You're probably waiting for me."

"You said you'd meet me here by eight-fifteen so I could take you to the interpreters' morning briefing." The accusation in his tone slid through the wire.

"Right. I'm sorry. I ..." She glanced at the police officer. "I got detained. I'll be right over." She glanced at Officer McKenna again. "Well, in a couple of minutes—"

"I have to leave right now. We've got seven hundred school kids coming today. You can meet the interpreters tomorrow."

"That'll be fine," Chloe tried, but she was—once again—speaking to a dial tone. She replaced the earpiece and looked back at the officer. "Is there anything else you need?"

"May I see the accession form you mentioned?"

"Sure." The form still lay on the counter where she'd left it the evening before. She handed it to him.

He squinted at the blurry printing, then handed it back. "That address is the same one we have on file from her driver's license. The sheriff's department hasn't identified any family members yet."

"All she mentioned to me was a son. She said he died years ago."

"One of her neighbors told the sheriff that he didn't think Mrs. Lundquist had any relatives."

Chloe's shoulders slumped. The whole thing was horribly sad. Everything was so sad…

Officer McKenna cleared his throat. Chloe snapped back to the morning, and for a moment they stared at each other. He was frowning slightly. Chloe felt stupid. "Is that all? I've got to get to work."

He nodded. "That's all I need. But if a relative should happen to contact you about that artifact, please give me a call. Here's my card."

She took the card. *Village of Eagle Police Department, Roelke McKenna, Police Officer*. "Rell-kee?" she asked, checking the pronunciation. "Is that German?"

"Roelke was my mother's maiden name."

"Birth name."

He frowned again. "I beg your pardon?"

She gave herself a mental shake; this was not the time for a feminist lecture. "I'll call you if I hear from anyone about the ale bowl."

"Thank you." He nodded.

Chloe watched him descend the steps, then suddenly bolted after him. "Wait! I was wondering—do you know anything about a funeral?"

He paused, hand on his car door. "No."

"Well, please let me know if you hear anything."

"OK." He nodded again, got into his car, and drove away.

After he was gone, Chloe picked up the old accession form again. All she needed to do was file the form away—when she figured out the filing system—and forget the whole episode.

Still, she stood for a long moment, staring at the mimeographed page. Like many decades-old records she'd seen at various museums and historical sites, this one was frustratingly short on details. *Hand-painted Norwegian ale bowl with cow heads, nineteenth century. SHSW 1962.37.3.* Hand-painted, Norwegian, nineteenth century—that meant rosemaled. Rosemaling—or rose painting, as it was sometimes called—was a highly decorative style of embellishing that had become synonymous with Norwegian folk culture. The cow head reference seemed odd . . . but then, she was hardly an expert.

Shouts from two of the teenage boys on the summer maintenance crew drifted through the open door. A truck door slammed. An engine roared to life. A fly buzzed at one of the dirty windows.

Finally Chloe slipped the accession sheet under the metal edge of her clipboard. She needed to find the ale bowl, as she had promised. There were only two places it could be: on display in one of the restored Norwegian farms, or in storage. If the bowl wasn't already on display, she'd put it out for visitors to enjoy. It will be a silent memorial for Mrs. Lundquist, Chloe thought, and felt a tiny bit better.

Chloe spent the rest of the morning assessing the overall condition of the two trailers. Some artifacts crowded their shelves. Others were packed into boxes, or layered into bags. The benign neglect would have overwhelmed most curators—at least any sane curator, Chloe thought sardonically. But this—*this* she could do. These artifacts needed cleaning, better storage conditions, perhaps cataloging. But they waited silently, without reproach or complaint. And she was the person to improve their lot.

One thing did give her pause. She immediately noticed a few recent smudges in the fur of dust on the shelves. Who would have been in here prior to her arrival? She frowned, fingering one of the clean streaks. Director Ralph Petty? Byron, looking for something for one of the historic homes? She'd have to make sure that no one felt free to disturb the artifacts in storage without her permission. Some of these items were extremely fragile, and even well-intended handling could cause damage.

She'd mention that to the director the next time they talked. When she'd met with him yesterday, the need for permanent, environmentally sound collections storage had been number one on his agenda. Actually, Ralph had talked *at* her for half an hour, but she certainly agreed with his assessment. She'd made a cheery promise to start considering plans for a collections storage building.

That would take time. For now, she made a list of items she wanted to order immediately: cotton gloves, masks, mountains of archival tissue and acid-free boxes. She'd have to learn the state procurement system, no doubt an overly complex process. Still, it was satisfying to take even the first tiny steps toward providing good care for these artifacts.

When her list was complete—at least for the moment—Chloe searched the trailers for Mrs. Lundquist's ale bowl. She found a number of rosemaled Norwegian artifacts, but the painted designs she could make out fell into the floral or curlicue categories. One had handles carved as dragon heads. Not a cow head in sight.

Next she poked through the big pole barn. She found some abandoned office furniture shoved into one corner. Side storage stalls were full of large antiques—antique plows and cast-iron cookstoves and a *schnitzelbank* or two. No smaller items. No ale bowls.

By eleven-thirty she was hot, hungry, dirty, and ready for a break. Years of wilderness camping hadn't prepared her for the trailer's neglected bathroom—no one was *that* hard core—so she walked across the parking lot to use the bathroom facilities in the maintenance shop. She found a little front hallway that boasted a soda machine and three mismatched chairs. "Hello?" she called, but received no answer.

The garage, storage rooms, and a desk area were also deserted. She had a vague memory of meeting the maintenance supervisor the day before. He was a red-haired man in his mid-thirties, wearing blue cowboy boots, gold chains, and a distinctly smarmy air. What was his name? Stanley something... Stanley Colontuono, that was it.

Chloe passed his desk, which was overflowing with files, boxes of bolts, and the various other detritus of a man whose position straddled administration and hands-on maintenance work. The wall calendar hanging above Stan-the-Man's telephone featured a naked blonde woman leaning on a motorcycle. D-cup.

Lovely. Chloe pulled the calendar from the wall, ripped each page in half, and stuffed the dreck into his trashcan.

Five minutes later, she emerged from the maintenance building just as an old white Chevette rattled into the lot near the trailers. When the door opened a young woman popped energetically from the car. She was slim and lithe, with milk-chocolate skin. She strode forward, hand outstretched. "You must be Chloe!"

"Yes!" Chloe agreed brightly, allowing her hand to be pumped. "And you are...?"

"Nika." She was perhaps five inches shorter and ten years younger than Chloe, with fine-boned features and slightly slanted eyes, like a cat's. A headband striped with yellow and green and blue kept a curtain of shoulder-length braids swept back from her face. "Tanika Austin," she added, when Chloe didn't respond.

Tanika Austin, Tanika Austin? Chloe spread her hands.

"Your intern."

She had an intern? Chloe tried to hide her dismay. Had Ralph Petty said anything about an intern? Perhaps she should have listened. So. She had an intern—

"Is there a problem?" Nika asked, her eyes narrowing.

"Of course not," Chloe said. "I'm afraid I'm on overload. Still sorting out names."

Nika eyed her a few seconds longer before saying, "No problem. I interviewed with Mr. Petty during spring break. I actually started last week. I'm sorry I wasn't here on your first day, but I took a long weekend. My fiancé's parents were celebrating their thirtieth anniversary. I told Mr. Petty it would probably be just as well to give you some time to get your bearings, anyway." Nika's voice was quiet but decisive, her posture full of self-assurance.

Chloe wondered if Nika expected her to have those bearings magically aligned after a day and a half. "I was just about to go out for lunch," Chloe said, groping for a reprieve. "Care to join me?"

Nika hesitated, then nodded. "All right."

"I'll drive," Chloe added. Maybe eating lunch would buy her enough time to figure out how she was going to keep an intern busy. After they'd slid into the Pinto, she tried to postpone the inevitable by turning on the car radio. A reporter was cheerily chattering about President Reagan's trip to discuss the Falklands War with Prime Minister Thatcher. Chloe turned the radio off again.

"Not many places to eat in Eagle," Nika told her, as they came into town. "Best is Sasso's." She directed Chloe to a tavern near the railroad tracks that bisected the village. Chloe pulled the Pinto in line on the gravel lot on the far side of the tracks. The three-story building had a vaguely Western motif. Peeking over the roof was the steeple of a church, and a yellow water tower painted with a huge smiley face. A typical message from small town Wisconsin: *Welcome to Eagle. Drink, repent, be happy.*

Inside the tavern, half a dozen tables clustered near the front windows. An L-shaped bar ran the length of the north and east walls. A crowd at the bar watching a television mounted in one corner began wildly cheering for race cars circling some track in a maniacal pack.

Chloe had never understood the appeal of watching cars drive in circles, wasting gas and spewing fumes and noise. She picked a table farthest from the bar. A waitress appeared quickly, gave the red-and-white checked plastic tablecloth a swipe, and handed them menus. "Anything to drink?"

Chloe suppressed the urge to order a cocktail; surely guzzling booze on state time was *verboten*. She ordered diet soda and talked the young waitress into asking the cook for a grilled cheese sandwich.

Nika ordered a cheeseburger and a side of fries. "Don't eat meat?" she asked.

"Nope." Chloe leaned back in the wooden chair. "So. You started last week? What did you do?"

"Well, not much." Nika made a dismissive gesture with elegant fingers. "Byron gave me a quick tour of the site. Then I spent most of the rest of my time in the exhibit buildings. I made some notes about objects that need attention. Some need actual repair, but most of it would be minor cleaning. Whenever you have time, we can go over my notes."

"We'll do that this afternoon," Chloe promised. Maybe this intern thing wouldn't be a total disaster. "You're in museum studies? I apologize, but I haven't seen your records. What's your focus?"

The waitress arrived with their drinks. Nika took a delicate sip of root beer before answering. "I got a BA in History from Marquette, and now I'm finishing up the graduate program in museum studies at Eastern Illinois."

"Why did you apply to Old World for your internship?" Chloe was curious why a black woman would choose to work in a museum focused on white history.

"I have formal museum experience, so I wanted to work at a living history site to round out my resume. I'm particularly interested in racial and ethnic expression manifested in material culture. My fiancé's in the pharmacy program at UW-Madison, but he'd gotten a summer job in a lab in Milwaukee, so I wanted to be in southeast Wisconsin."

Chloe blinked. Had she ever been so focused? She doubted it. She certainly couldn't remember it.

"I plan to get my Ph.D. in women's studies," Nika added coolly. "And I may do some extra course work in museum administration."

Chloe wondered if she would find herself working for Nika one day. There seemed to be a challenge in the younger woman's eyes: *You better prove yourself, because I'm right on your tail.*

The arrival of their lunch eased the moment. Chloe took a bite of her sandwich—American cheese. Tolerable at best.

"How about you?" Nika asked. "Mr. Petty hadn't even done interviews for your position yet when he hired me."

"I have a Bachelor of Science from the School of Forestry at West Virginia University. *My* particular interest is the historical interaction between people and their environment."

"How ... intriguing."

"I did seasonal work as an interpreter for a couple of years, then did graduate work at Cooperstown," Chloe added.

"Oh!" This met with more approval. The two-year New York program, the oldest in the country, led to an MA in History Museum Studies. "And somebody told me you worked in Europe?"

Chloe should have been expecting the question. She wasn't. "I, um ... yes. I worked in the education department at *Freilichtmuseum Ballenberg* for five years. That's in Switzerland."

"Oh, I know! What was it like?"

"It's similar to Old World," Chloe said, hoping the conversation wouldn't digress into a long Q&A about Switzerland. "They've got about a hundred historic buildings, all dismantled, moved to the site, and restored. The biggest difference is that there, buildings are grouped together based on the area of origin, instead of by ethnic group like we've got."

"Five years at an open-air museum in Europe." Nika looked wistful. "I'd *kill* for a chance like that."

It damn near killed *me*, Chloe thought, but she pasted on her artificial smile. "I learned a lot. Then I moved back to the States. Took a curator of interpretation position at a small site in North Dakota last September."

"Why'd you come here? I mean, most people don't switch from education to collections mid-career." Nika nibbled a French fry.

Chloe shrugged. "I suppose not. But I've had basic training in collections care. When I interviewed here, Ralph probably thought my experience at Ballenberg was a big advantage. And I'm a Wisconsin native." Chloe hitched her chair closer to the table as three men in paint-stained coveralls squeezed past. "How about you?"

"Oh, me too." Nika took a bite of her cheeseburger and dabbed at her mouth with her napkin. "Wisconsin born and bred."

"Where did you grow up?"

"Milwaukee."

"Where in Milwaukee?"

Nika picked up another French fry. "Near the lake."

Well, Chloe thought, that narrows it right down. The entire city of Milwaukee, it could be argued, squatted near Lake Michigan.

"Where are you from?" Nika asked, before Chloe could ask for more details.

"Stoughton."

"Settled by Norwegians, right? Between my coursework at Marquette and the prep I did for this internship, I have a pretty good handle on Wisconsin's nineteenth-century settlement patterns."

"Yep. I'm fourth generation, but pure Norwegian." At least in the States, Chloe thought. Her European friends were baffled by American tourists' proud insistence on referring to themselves as Norwegian or German or French.

"So this job brought you home."

"I suppose, although that's not why I applied for the job." Chloe chewed the last bit of her sandwich. The conversation felt strained, with unspoken undercurrents running beneath.

She tried for a brighter tone. "I was ready for a change. Supervising interpreters is exhausting. Classic middle-management, getting complaints from two directions. I guess I thought objects would be easier to handle." She made a derisive noise. "Little did I know…"

Nika stiffened, almost imperceptively alert. "What?"

The waitress slapped a check on the table. "Pay at the bar," she called over her shoulder.

"I'll get that." Chloe picked up the check.

"Well… thanks." Relief flashed in Nika's eyes. That, Chloe understood. Her own financial situation was precarious, but the younger woman was planning a wedding, and no doubt staring at college loans, all while likely working for minimum wage.

Nika brought the conversation back. "What were you about to say?"

"I had a bit of a rocky start in collections work. An elderly woman came to see me yesterday about an artifact. And as I was heading home ... I came across her car. She'd crashed into a tree. She was dead."

"Oh my God! That's—that's awful!"

"Yeah." Chloe left a couple of dollars on the table for the waitress, and shoved her chair back. "Let's head back, OK?" She didn't want to talk about Mrs. Lundquist anymore.

FOUR

Chloe and Nika seized possession of a wooden picnic table under the pines near the trailers. Nika fetched a briefcase from the trunk of her car, and produced a notebook and some files. "I made copies of those notes I mentioned. You can have these."

"Thanks." Chloe glanced at the photocopies: neat tables, with columns labeled "Exhibit Building," "Artifact," "Accession Number," and "Notes." Impressive. "I have to figure out where we can even claim a workspace—"

"I have a plan for that."

Chloe raised her eyebrows. "Oh?"

"Just a suggestion, of course." Nika met Chloe's gaze calmly. "I'm not trying to do your job or anything."

Right. "Did you go into the trailers?" Chloe asked. "I could tell that someone had been in there recently."

"I took a quick look."

"Do you have a key?"

Nika shook her head. "No, Stanley let me in. You know, the maintenance guy?" The barest hint of distaste—a narrowing of her catlike eyes, a slight tightening of her mouth—made her opinion of Stanley clear. "I didn't do anything but look around, though."

"So . . . ?"

"Well, I think our best option for expanded storage is the basement of St. Peter's Church." Nika began talking quickly. "I know it's not ideal, especially since the church is in the public area. *But*, the basement does have a separate door, near the back of the building. We could fit a fair amount of shelving and storage cupboards down there. And I don't think it would take more than a dehumidifier or two to control the environment. The basement already has its own temperature system."

"It does?" Chloe was struggling to keep up. "Why on earth does the church basement have its own temperature system?"

"The first year Old World Wisconsin was open, visitors received their orientation down there." Nika smiled at Chloe's look of disbelief. "Yeah, I know. Byron said it was the only space available. A slide projector, a few rows of folding chairs, and an interpreter to give directions. The visitor center didn't exist yet."

"Well, what do you know." Chloe considered. She didn't want to confront her intern's unmasked ambition on an hourly basis. "Nika, we've got you for what, three months? How would you like to make designing and setting up our first controlled storage area your project? Assuming we can scrounge basic storage supplies."

"That'd be great." A satisfied smile lit Nika's face. "We can move the woodenware."

Chloe shook her head. "Textiles are most vulnerable."

"But . . . the thing is, I started making plans already. Based on moving the wooden pieces."

Chloe met her intern's gaze. "I want the textiles tended to first."

Nika shrugged, and gave a palms-up gesture of compliance. "Textiles it is."

"I'll talk to the division curator in Madison, and let her know what we're planning. Evidently the historic sites division's curator in Madison provides some kind of oversight to the curators at each of the State Historical Society's historic sites."

"Right."

Nika clearly knew as much as Chloe about the historical society's organization. Probably more. Chloe got to the point. "Once you get the proposal together, I'll add that to my 'needed supplies' list."

"I brought a bunch of catalogs with me, so I can get cost estimates." Nika began scribbling notes on a legal pad. "I'll call around to see if we can get shelving donated, too." She stared thoughtfully at a chickadee darting among the pines for a moment, then focused her direct gaze back on Chloe. "I'd like to ask a favor. I want to get published before applying for a doctoral program. I—I really need financial aid, and publication credits might help a lot."

The admission of need was clearly not an easy one for Nika to make. "You're right," Chloe said. "Pub credits do count."

"As you familiarize yourself with the collection, could you let me know if you happen to find any artifacts with a particularly strong ethnic story, or a story to tell about a woman, or any pieces documented to African-Americans? There might be an article in it."

Chloe thought of Mrs. Lundquist's ale bowl—it's story would never be known, now—then forced herself back to the moment. "Sure, although I doubt we'll find many artifacts from early African-Americans. Anything like that is probably held in Madison. The history presented at Old World is pretty much white bread European."

"It is *now*. That needs changing."

Chloe couldn't hold back a tiny smile. "Fair enough. If I find any tidbits, I'll pass them along."

"Thanks." Nika stood and gathered up her things. "I'll head over to the church now and get started."

When she was alone again, Chloe sat for a moment, collecting her thoughts, appreciating the stillness and the way the sunlight filtered through the pine trees. Nika was too driven for Chloe's tastes, but at least she was a self-starter.

So, what now? Chloe's previous museum jobs had all involved supervising interpreters and meeting tour groups and planning special events and the myriad of on-site tasks that kept each day humming. She wasn't used to the change of pace. She really should start on that proposal for the new storage building.

"Later," Chloe promised herself. She got into her car and drove back on County S. Her fingers tightened involuntarily on the steering wheel as she passed the crash site. Would she ever pass this spot without seeing the dead woman in her mind? Without feeling those fragile fingers patting her hand? Probably not.

After turning onto Highway 67, she drove slowly until she saw a large sign: "Norwegian Area—School Bus parking only." Plus staff, surely? Chloe pulled in the open gate and parked her car as unobtrusively as possible among the trees.

Although most Wisconsin children in 1982 could celebrate more than one racial or ethnic branches on their family tree, there had been a time when "old world Wisconsin" was a mostly-apt description. Now, Old World Wisconsin celebrated a heritage that was quickly disappearing. And a big part of that heritage had come from the women and men who had once traded Norway's fjords and soaring mountains for the upper Midwest's unknown prairies and pineries.

Old World Wisconsin's Norwegian area was the farthest from the site's visitor center. A public restroom and picnic area had been placed discreetly in the trees near the highway. The historic structures were a five-minute walk away. Holding her clipboard—the universal emblem of officialdom—Chloe headed down the gravel lane toward the old buildings.

When Chloe reached a junction in the road, she checked her site map. From this spot she could see the Raspberry School, brought from the northern tip of the state; the 1845 Fossebrekke farm, a tiny log cabin nestled between trees and corn patch and pig pen; and the more substantial Kvaale farm, restored to its 1865 appearance. Two interpreters in period clothing walked down the Kvaale lane, baskets over their arms. A farmer attacked weeds in the Fossebrekke corn patch with a hoe. The air smelled faintly of wood smoke. The sound of the schoolteacher questioning a class drifted through the open windows of the school. A sandhill crane's faint rattling call floated earthwards.

For a moment Chloe forgot Markus and Switzerland. She forgot the depression that had almost consumed her during the long, bleak North Dakota winter. She forgot that she'd pissed off a security guard and the curator of interpretation. She forgot that her intern probably had more to offer Old World Wisconsin, this summer, than she did. She forgot that she'd seen a sweet old woman in the last moments of life and first moments of death. Chloe allowed herself to simply soak in the intangible pleasures and sensory delights that compensated historic site workers for long hours and low wages.

Then one of the open-sided trams used to haul visitors around the huge site roared from the trees. With a screech of brakes the tram driver pulled into the tram stop and used a microphone to give directions to the visitors spilling from the vehicle. Half of the tourists headed toward the rest area, and most of the others trooped toward the school. Chloe hurried down the long driveway toward the Kvaale farm.

The hewn-timber farmhouse was small, furnished with both Norwegian artifacts—rosemaled pieces, several tapestries, one chip-carved box—and obviously American-made furniture. The curator who'd furnished the building had clearly intended to convey a well-settled Norwegian family, blending old world and new. Chloe paused in the doorway, allowing impressions of the layers of life in the old building to present themselves. Nothing too strong here in Kvaale, just the common jumble … good. She stepped inside.

In the sitting room, a young woman sat behind a spinning wheel. She wore a faded blue dress, a stained apron, and a brown headscarf tied European-style over her hair. She was frowning at the spool, picking at the strands of newly spun yarn. Chloe guessed she was learning to spin wool, had treadled too hard, and had lost the end of her yarn when it whipped around the spool.

"Welcome to the Kvaale farm," the interpreter said, still poking at her yarn.

Chloe quickly introduced herself. "Don't mind me. I'm just getting oriented." She homed in on a high shelf near the kitchen door, where several rosemaled pieces were displayed at a safe distance from children's grasping hands. One lovely tankard was painted orange with blue, green, yellow, and black floral designs. One carved but unpainted ale bowl featured two squarish heads—horses, or possibly dragons, but definitely not cows. No painted bowl with cow heads.

"Do you want to go talk to Delores?" the interpreter asked.

"Um …" Chloe spread her hands. "Who is Delores?"

"Delores is the Norwegian area lead. Lead interpreter. She's with a group in the stabbur. Out back."

Outside, Chloe wandered on toward the back of the farmyard . . . and stopped, rock-like, when two tiny Cotswold lambs cavorted across the pasture toward the fence to meet her. Living and working with Markus, whose great driving passion had been the preservation of historic livestock breeds, ensured that Chloe recognized many of those breeds herself.

She quickly turned away from the lambs. Markus had nothing to do with her life, now. It was time—long past time—to move on.

The stabbur, a small two-story building of weathered-gray logs, was so crammed with school children that Chloe got no further than the steps outside. ". . . So, can anyone guess why the Norwegians built their stabburs up on posts?" an unseen interpreter was asking—Delores, no doubt.

No one could.

"Do you remember what I said the farmers used this building for?" Delores asked. Finally a boy retrieved the answer: food or grain storage. "Exactly!" Delores said. "Do you think the farmer wanted to store his grain in a place where mice and other critters could get at it easily?"

"Come on, come on, come on!" Chloe muttered. She walked past the stabbur to explore a two-bay barn nearby. Two squealing hogs raced across their pen behind the barn. Chloe stopped at the back of the barn's breezeway, contemplating them.

This time she forced herself to stand still. She had to get used to being around livestock—even these damn Ossabaw hogs, with their familiar rough coats and long snouts. They were likely half-feral. Chloe took care to stand well back from the fence as they rubbed against it, grunting. And when she felt ready she walked back to the stabbur, congratulating herself on her composure.

Delores was winding down. "Who remembers visiting the 1860s Yankee house? Did the lady there do a lot of farm labor? So why do you think the Norwegian women were responsible for the cows and milk and butter?"

Once the kids had bounded from the stabbur, Chloe went inside and introduced herself. Delores Timberlake sat at a four-harness loom upon which a few inches of cream-colored wool cloth had been woven. She was perhaps a decade older than Chloe, with gray-streaked brown hair pinned neatly behind her head. She wore a russet-colored dress and a stained and patched apron.

"I'm glad to meet you!" the lead said, so fervently that Chloe felt a twinge of apprehension. "Your timing is good. That was our last school group of the day."

"I caught the tail end of it, but decided I'd do better to wait outside," Chloe confessed.

"The kids get squirrely this time of year," Delores agreed cheerfully. She set a shuttle aside and emerged from behind the loom. "I need to check on Cindy, the interpreter in the house. She's new this spring, and Ginny is still on lunch break." Delores led Chloe back into the sunshine.

"Have you worked here for long?" Chloe asked.

"Since Old World opened."

"In the Norwegian area all that time?"

"I've been the Norwegian lead for three years." Delores stepped onto the Kvaale porch. "Before that I worked all over. Let me tell you, we have *really* been looking forward to having a collections curator on site! We have these reproduction request forms to let someone know what we need for daily programming. We keep turning them in to Byron."

"I'm sure Byron's got them all waiting for me," Chloe said quickly, wanting to stem a potential side trip into several years' worth of queries. "I'll go through them as soon as I can. Actually, today I'm looking for a rosemaled ale bowl."

"Those are the only rosemaled pieces we've got." Inside the main room, Delores pointed to the shelf Chloe had already examined.

"I'm looking for an ale bowl with cow head decorations."

Cindy, still valiantly hunched over the spinning wheel, looked up. "That's funny," she said. "You're the second person looking for an ale bowl with cow heads."

"What?"

"Some visitor asked me about ale bowls with cow heads. I think it was the first weekend we were open." Cindy fussed with the tension knob on the spinning wheel. "Delores, are you sure you want me to keep going with this bobbin? Your yarn is so even, and mine is so lumpy. I feel like I'm just wasting wool."

Delores laughed. "We've got plenty of wool."

"What did they say?" Chloe asked.

"About the ale bowl? Just that!" Cindy shrugged. "Somebody asked me if we had one. I said we didn't. I work Fossebrekke too, so I know."

"A woman? A man?" Chloe's voice sounded sharp, and she tried to tone it down. "Was the person young, old? Try to think back."

Cindy sighed. "I really don't remember. That was probably a thousand visitors ago."

Chloe forced herself to swallow her frustration. "OK, thanks. If anyone else asks about a rosemaled ale bowl with cow heads, could you ask them to contact me? Or—maybe just see if they'll give you their name and phone number."

"Sure. Whatever." Cindy began to work the treadle. The yarn whipped from her fingers, wrapping itself—again—among the coils already on the bobbin. "*Delores!*"

"I'll let the other interpreters know," Delores told Chloe, then turned back to the younger woman. "You just pushed too hard, that's all. Find the end and I'll show you . . ."

Chloe stepped outside. The lambs cavorted in the sunshine. Above her head, a red-tailed hawk circled on a thermal. She barely noticed. It seemed odd that someone had visited the Kvaale farm in search of a rosemaled ale bowl decorated with cow heads just two weeks before Mrs. Lundquist showed up, wanting to reclaim that very item. Too odd to be a coincidence. Mrs. Lundquist had said plainly that *she* had not visited the site.

So . . . what the hell was going on?

FIVE

Roelke slowed his pickup truck and checked the fire number he'd written on the slip of paper. He was driving on a state-designated "Rustic Road." Nothing more than a tourism official's propaganda, but the scenery was admittedly classic Wisconsin: stately old farmhouses, hay and corn fields, pastures of placid Holsteins, and nary a speedy-mart or factory farm in sight. Roelke didn't have the barn gene, even though three generations of his maternal German-American forebears had farmed Wisconsin soil. Still, he appreciated the legacy.

He found the number he'd been looking for posted by a gravel driveway that looped behind a tired two-story frame house in desperate need of a fresh coat of paint. Cow pastures bordered the house on the east and south, with a huge garden and second farmhouse on the west. New alfalfa rippled green in a field across the road.

Roelke pulled into the driveway, got out of the truck, and walked across the lawn to the front porch and door. His cousin Libby's voice echoed in his head as he knocked: *This isn't your problem, Roelke. Leave it.* He ignored the voice.

The inner door swung open. "Oh!" Chloe said. "Officer… McKenna. I didn't… that is, um, would you like to come in?"

"Yes, if I may."

She held open the door, and frowned slightly when she noticed his truck. "You're not on duty?"

"Just finished my shift," he told her. "Parking police cars in peoples' driveways sets off all kinds of speculation. This isn't official business."

"Oh."

Roelke stepped inside. Cardboard cartons were stacked in the bedroom he glimpsed to his left. In the living room she led him to, also. Bare walls. No sign of personality. No sign of life.

She noticed his perusal and shrugged. "I just moved in. Can I get you something to drink? I'm having a rum and soda."

"Nothing for me, thanks." He perched on the sofa, and watched her sink back into a deep chair by the window. She had traded her casual work attire for shorts. God, she was thin. Too thin. She'd left her glass on the table by her chair, but he saw no evidence of a book or television set.

Abruptly he realized she was waiting for him to explain his visit. "Mrs. Lundquist was a member of the Lutheran church in Daleyville. The minister is planning a service for ten A.M. Friday morning."

Chloe narrowed her eyes in thought. "Daleyville… that's west of here, isn't it?"

"Probably about an hour away. Eastern Dane County."

"Have any relatives come forward?"

He shook his head. "No. Her neighbor said she attended the church, so the county guys checked with the minister. He wasn't aware of any relatives, either. Mrs. Lundquist had been a widow for years."

Chloe picked up her glass and took a sip. "Did they figure out what caused the accident?"

"Heart failure. She was seventy-four. These things happen." His words sounded clipped and brusque in his own ears. He wasn't any good at this stuff.

"I see." Chloe used one finger to poke at an ice cube.

Roelke leaned forward, elbows on knees. "Did you find that antique she was looking for?"

"Does it matter?"

He shrugged. "I was just curious. Wrapping up loose ends."

"I haven't been able to find it."

He got the distinct impression that she had something more to say. He waited, giving her plenty of space to spit out whatever was on her mind. She evidently decided against it. "I'll keep my eyes open, though," she said. "And I left a message for the sites division curator in Madison, to see if records on that end are more complete."

Roelke watched her. Should he press for more? No. He didn't have any reason to. He didn't have any reason to even be here, since she'd given him her telephone number.

He stood. "Since Mrs. Lundquist didn't have any legal claim to the antique, I think the issue is closed."

"Yes, I guess so." Chloe padded after him to the door. "Thanks for letting me know about the funeral."

Roelke drove north through the Kettle Moraine State Forest, thinking about the woman sitting alone in a sterile farmhouse, nursing a drink, surrounded by moving cartons that showed no signs of being unpacked.

He felt too restless to head home. Fifteen minutes later, without conscious decision, he pulled over in front of an old farmhouse built from the locally common "cream city" yellow bricks. Shrubs had grown up over the house's lower windows, and a garden plot visible in the side yard was choked with burdock and dandelions. The weathered barn showed no sign of animal life. Once, though, Holsteins had filed in and out of stanchions, filling the barn with the warm smells of milk and manure.

And once, Roelke had milked those cows in that barn. After high school he'd left the farm behind, moved to Milwaukee. And if he'd sometimes thought about his maternal grandparents—both dead, by then—he'd given little thought to their farm. But since he'd moved back out from the city... well, sometimes he felt the impulse to drive by the old place.

God knew why, though, he thought. He checked for traffic, put the truck in gear, and did a tight U-turn on the road.

Ten more minutes and he was back in Eagle. He pulled into the space at the village parking garage that he'd vacated before driving to Chloe's house.

The Eagle Police Department employed half a dozen officers. All but one of those were part-timers, most trying either to break into a police career or to ease out of one. Roelke was officially part-time as well, although the chief gave him extra hours when he could, and had recommended him for pick-up shifts in nearby Palmyra and North Prairie.

Chief Naborski had a private office. Marie, the clerk who entered citations and filed reports and prepared everything for court, had her own desk in the small squad room. The officers shared workspace and a typewriter, a necessity that generally worked out but sometimes got on Roelke's nerves. Skeet Deardorff, who'd come on as Roelke went off, was out on patrol. Now would be a good time to catch up on paperwork.

He had a lot of paperwork waiting. Chief Naborski liked being able to show the taxpayers exactly how his officers spent their time. In addition to Mrs. Lundquist's accident and the usual speeding citations and a report of property damage, Roelke had also arrested a drunk driver the evening before.

For some reason, though, he had trouble concentrating. He got up and opened his locker. On the top shelf sat a small photograph of a pretty young woman, smiling from a simple gold frame. His muscles tensed. He'd met Erin Litkowski only once, and weeks went by without him really seeing the photo. Sometimes, though, her smile chided him. Like now. He picked the photograph up, stared at it, put it back in place. When he sat down again he turned back to the DUI report he needed to complete, looked at it, and put it down, too.

When the phone rang he snatched the receiver before it could kick over to dispatch. "Eagle Police, Officer McKenna."

"For cripes' sake, Roelke," a woman complained in his ear. "If I needed help, your tone would scare the crap out of me. When are you going to lighten up?"

"When are you going to stop calling me when I'm working?"

"You're not working. You went off duty over an hour ago. I tried your place first, and when I didn't get an answer, it didn't take a Ph.D. to figure out where to find you."

He leaned back in his chair, stretching the phone cord as far as it would go. "I'm staring at a stack of paperwork that would—"

"Why don't you come over to my place? I've got bratwursts simmering in beer and I just lit the coals."

"I went by the farm this afternoon."

"You—why? Why do that?"

"I don't know. I just did."

Libby exhaled audibly. "Roelke, put away whatever you're doing and come by. The kids want to see their favorite uncle."

"I'm their second cousin."

"See you in ten." She hung up.

The wall clock ticked noisily as Roelke replaced the receiver, contemplating an evening with his cousin and her two kids. Libby had never lost her I'm-older-than-you attitude. She'd scold him for faults both real and imagined, jab the hot buttons she'd identified by age seven, and then make him scrub the grill after dinner.

He grinned. The reports could wait.

SIX

Chloe made it to work the next morning in time to attend the interpreters' briefing with Byron, held on-site in the basement of the Four Mile Inn. Byron was somewhere in his late twenties, of medium height, and thin. His shaggy brown hair, tiny goatee, and wire-rimmed glasses reminded Chloe of early Russian revolutionaries. He led the morning briefing efficiently, reviewing the tour schedule and last-minute staffing changes. The program assistant who helped Byron announced that she hadn't finished the next month's staff schedule yet, so there was no point in asking her about it. One of the historic farmers, already sweat-stained and smelling of manure, asked who needed milk for the day's cooking. Then Byron introduced Chloe, and had each of the four lead interpreters wave as he pointed them out to her.

"I'm glad to be here," Chloe said, with her warmest smile. "I'm eager to help ensure that the material culture in each exhibit provides helpful tools in your interpretation." She looked at the ring of faces, suddenly wondering if any of them had worked in the Norwegian area in the 1970s. If so, they might know if Berget Lundquist's ale bowl had ever been displayed in the Kvaale house.

Then she saw Byron glance pointedly at his watch. "Thanks," she concluded. The interpreters stampeded toward the steps.

Chloe was heading toward the state sedan when someone called her name. She turned to see the village lead, a stout, gray-haired woman in a blue bustle dress.

"Got a minute?" the woman asked.

Chloe nodded. "Sure." Byron hadn't emerged from the basement yet.

"I know you'll be coming to our weekly leads' meetings—"

She would? Had Byron told her that?

"—but we have a lot of questions about the artifacts in Tobler—"

Tobler? Shit.

"—and all we've gotten is a list of facts about the furnishings. We usually get an interpretive plan that helps us understand main themes for each exhibit—"

Of all the personal requests she could have gotten, why did the first one—the very first blinkin' one—involve the Swiss carpenter's cottage?

"—and on top of that, the wallpaper is already curling at the seams," the woman concluded. "You need to look at the paste job."

Byron bounded up the steps. "We've got to get the car out of here," he barked at Chloe. "There's an early tour."

Chloe gave the village lead a rueful gesture: *I'd love to do it now, but I can't. Darn.* "I'll check it out next time I'm in the village."

"Let's go!" Byron started the car. Chloe managed to jump in and slam her door before Byron took off.

Byron drove the way he talked—impatiently. He whipped down the village hill, slowed briefly to skirt the German area, and left a wake of dust as he flew along the gravel road toward the gate at Highway S. "You know you can't drive on the site during open hours, right? But we're OK until nine o'clock."

"Got it." Chloe eased a hand to the seat and hung on.

"And never drive into the farmyards, even after-hours. We don't tolerate modern intrusions like tire tracks."

"No tire tracks. Got it. Listen, Byron, I was wondering if any of the original interpreters still work here."

"Me."

"You?"

Byron swerved wildly to avoid a maintenance truck that appeared around a corner. "Yeah, me. I started here as an interpreter."

"Oh. Did you ever work Norwegian?"

"No. Just the village shops. And that reminds me, we've got this great new guy who wants to make a wagon. I think he can do it, but he needs tools. Can you stop by the wagon shop and take a quick look at our jack? It's an original, but I think it's sturdy enough for use."

"Sure, I'll look at it."

"You and I need to talk about record collection items—those are reproductions, or artifacts that you designate, that the interpreters can actually use in the foodways and gardening and craft programs."

"OK—"

"I can't today, I'm booked solid. You've got the dates for the summer interpreters' training down, right? It's too bad you weren't here for spring training, but I'll encourage the veterans to attend your presentations. And ..."

Chloe hadn't managed to steer the conversation back to her ale bowl by the time they got back to Ed House. "Byron!" she said finally, before he could bolt from the car. "I've got another question for you. I'm trying to find a Norwegian ale bowl—"

"Great!" Byron awarded her a look of approval for the first time. "I'd love to see a couple more ethnic pieces put on display. There's a great tankard in the pink trailer that would work. Acculturation is a big theme in the Norwegian area, and—"

"No, *wait.* Please. I'm looking for one particular ale bowl. It's not on exhibit, and it doesn't seem to be in storage. Is there a place interpreters bring items that are damaged, or need attention? Anything like that?"

"Come inside," Byron said.

He was inside the building, rummaging in the top drawer of an ancient metal filing cabinet, before Chloe caught up. He began extracting bulging file folders and piling them on his desk. "First, I've saved all the collections-related catalogs that have come in. Some are for archival supplies, some for repros."

"OK," Chloe said dubiously, eyeing the towering stack.

Byron continued to pull folders from the cabinet. "And these are reproduction request forms. Six years' worth. There you go."

Chloe glanced inside the top folder, riffled through the pages, and saw a bewildering assortment of handwriting, pencil and pen, some with a few printed words and some with lines and lines of cramped cursive.

"I'm glad to get all this stuff out of here," Byron said. "I need the filing space."

So do I, Chloe thought, picturing the tiny galley/office/mouse hole of a workspace in her trailer.

"As for damaged items, the interpreters bring them to me. I put them upstairs. Come on. I'll show you."

Most of the second story of Ed house was a single, long room running under the eaves. Low metal shelves lined two of the walls, and someone had covered half of the floor space with sheets. These were covered with dozens and dozens of objects in need of attention: cracked china cups, rusted iron ware, books with loose bindings, rag rugs starting to fray… Chloe stared with dismay at the graveyard. She shouldn't have been annoyed to learn she had an intern. She needed an army of interns.

Byron gave her a satisfied look. "It's all yours."

"Gee, thanks."

"Most of these things are repros, if that makes you feel any better," he added.

"Not much."

Byron smiled. "I'd appreciate it if you could get these things moved out of here as soon as possible."

"Well, don't get too excited. I have to make a lot of progress in the trailers before I can start moving anything else in there."

"I'm sure you'll do your best." Byron glanced at his watch. "I gotta head over to the visitors' center and meet some Swedish dancers. Planning session for Midsummer. One of our big special events."

"Mind if I stay and look these things over?"

"Suit yourself. Just lock up when you leave."

Chloe listened to Byron bolt down the stairs, then slam the exterior door. A moment later she heard the sedan start and roar away. Only then did she draw a deep breath. Byron was acting like a royal jerk, dumping all of this on her so smugly. Chloe replayed their conversation in her mind, feeling self-righteously indignant—then suddenly hit pause.

Byron had mentioned a tankard in the pink trailer. Evidently Nika hadn't been the only person in the trailers recently.

Chloe searched carefully, but the rosemaled bowl was not among the casualties. One more dead end.

She gathered the files Byron had given her, made the short drive back to the restoration area, and settled down at the picnic table to take a closer look. She flipped through the reproduction requests quickly, reading a few random samples:

June 12, 1977. We need another tin washbasin in Schulz.

September 14, 1979. The hoe handle at Pedersen cracked. Next time you order hoes, get stronger ones.

May 3, 1981. Any chance we can get a reproduction cookstove at Benson? The stove we have heats really uneven.

Chloe glanced up, grateful for any diversion, as a blue Mustang pulled in and parked on the far side of the lot. Stanley Colontuono burst from the maintenance building. "You're late!" he bellowed at the young man who emerged from the Mustang.

"Geez Louise," Chloe muttered, watching the teen slouch toward his boss. The two met halfway across the lot. The offender, a lanky boy with too-long bangs and tight blue jeans, stood silent, shoulders hunched. Stanley dropped his voice but launched into a tirade that included finger pointing and even one hand chopping into the other palm. After several minutes Stanley turned and stalked back toward the maintenance building. Chloe wasn't surprised. She knew Stan's type, all false charm that hid an explosive and controlling temper. What a jerk.

She looked back at the files in her lap, then shut her eyes, suddenly exhausted. Perhaps she'd given up the anti-depressants too soon. She thought of the orange plastic bottle waiting all by its lonesome in her medicine cabinet.

Then she opened her eyes. No, dammit. She'd either make it on her own or cash in her chips. She wasn't going to live some half-life of psychiatrists and drugs.

So. Chloe glanced at her watch, considering. She really should head back to the Village. She should stop down at the basement of St. Peter's Church to see how Nika was doing with her retro-fitting plan, and then stop by the Tobler House to assess the furnishings and look at the problematic wallpaper. And she would do both of those things, Chloe promised herself. Just not right this minute. Right this minute what she needed to do was get these frickin' reproduction request files out of sight.

Leaving the files in tidy stacks, she walked to the maintenance building. The young man who'd come late to work was loading flats of sodas into the back of one of the state trucks. "Hi," Chloe said as she passed. "My name's Chloe."

He looked startled. "Uh, hi. I'm, uh, Rupert."

"Nice to meet you, Rupert." She smiled. There. She'd done her bit to even out someone's bad karma for the day.

She found Stanley leaning back in his chair, feet on his desk, laughing into the telephone. When he saw Chloe he planted his cowboy boots—black today—back on the floor. "I'll talk to you later," he muttered into the phone, and hung up.

"Sorry to disturb you, Stan," Chloe said.

He grinned in a manner she suspected he hoped was sensual. She resisted telling him that his boots and red curls made her think of Howdy-Doody. "You're not," he said. "In fact, I've been meaning to ask you about something. It seems like somebody took a dislike to my calendar. You know anything about that?"

"Not a thing," she lied calmly.

"I figured it must have been someone who wasn't gettin' any."

Chloe had to unclench her teeth before speaking. "I need some empty cardboard boxes. You got any around here?"

"Sure, doll. Big stack out back."

She smiled sweetly. "You may *not* call me 'doll.' 'Chloe' works just fine."

Stan shrugged and laced his fingers over his big belly. "Well, saw-ree."

"I'll go grab those boxes, then," Chloe said. "Thanks." Asshole.

After stuffing the reproduction request files into two cartons, she folded the flaps in and dumped them into the trunk of her car. They could wait until she had the time and energy to tackle them.

Inside the pink trailer, she shuffled through her orientation file until she found the phone list she'd been given. Then she dialed a Madison number.

Old World Wisconsin was only one of a handful of historic sites owned and maintained by the State Historical Society of Wisconsin. The historic sites division consisted of a division administrator and a collections curator. The division curator, a woman named Leila, answered her phone on the first ring.

"I'm sorry I haven't called or been out to welcome you," she said when Chloe identified herself. "We had some flooding at Villa Louis, so I've been helping out there."

"That's all right. I did want to check in, though. I'm compiling quite a list of supplies I need. Also, my intern is creating artifact storage in the basement of St. Peter's church. It'll be a stop-gap, I know, but a good start until we get a permanent collections storage facility."

"Mail me your list," Leila said promptly. "I've been holding a pot of money aside for you, and I have some basic supplies earmarked too."

Chloe raised her eyebrows, pleasantly surprised. "Will do. Can I fax the info?"

"From the site?" Leila hooted with laughter. "Oh, that's rich. We just got our first fax machines here at HQ. They have to become obsolete before any drift out to the sites."

Well, no surprise there. "OK. Second, what can you tell me about Old World Wisconsin's collection records?"

"There should be a stack of big black ledgers somewhere in those trailers," Leila said. "The former curator bound the collections records in those. One book for each year, and one page for each item donated to Old World or transferred to the site from the main collection here."

Chloe tapped her pen against the kitchen counter. "One more question. Who should I talk to about a specific artifact transferred here from the main collection there in Madison?"

"The registrar here will have duplicate records. Need her number?"

Chloe took down the name and number. Before hanging up, she and Leila agreed on a date for Chloe to come to Madison for orientation.

Then Chloe dusted off one of the heavy black ledgers piled on the counter and opened it gingerly. Sure enough, the site's accession records were arranged in chronological order. She hauled the notebooks back outside and planted herself at the picnic table.

It took over two hours to page through them. She justified the time by telling herself that she was acquainting herself with the collection. She *did,* after all, see a lot of information about artifacts donated and transferred to the site. What she did *not* see was any mention of a rosemaled ale bowl with cow heads transferred from the main state collection to Old World Wisconsin.

She headed back inside to call the registrar. The woman who answered sounded brisk and efficient, welcome traits common in a profession that depended upon extreme order. "You're looking for one record in particular?"

"That's right." Chloe looked at the accession form Mrs. Lundquist had given her. "I'm trying to find out the date of transfer—"

"Give me the accession number."

"SHSW 1962.37.3."

"OK ... hold on ... got it. Norwegian ale bowl."

Chloe's fingers tightened on the black plastic. "That's it."

"That was transferred to Old World on July 17, 1977. You should have a record of it."

"I'm sure I do," Chloe said. "But it's my first week—I haven't had time to get straight on everything yet." She was already mourning the fast-approaching time when she couldn't fall back on that "I'm-just-the-new-girl" excuse.

"Call me if you need a copy of the transfer form."

"Will do," Chloe said. "Thanks."

She grabbed the 1977 ledger and sat on the trailer steps. Perhaps she'd flipped past the transfer form on her first pass through. She thumbed through the July entries. No record of a Norwegian ale bowl.

Frowning, she looked again. The accession numbers jumped from 1977.13 to 1977.15. In between those two pages, she spotted something she'd missed. A tiny triangle of paper with ragged edges protruded from the binding. Someone had torn a page from the book—the transfer form for Mrs. Lundquist's ale bowl.

Chloe hugged the book to her chest. First an unknown visitor had asked about the bowl. Now this. Strange. And disturbing.

So, what should she do with that information? Talk to Leila in Madison again? Leila didn't even have time to call a new staff member and welcome her on board. Ralph Petty, the site director? She chewed that over.

Then she went back inside, called the director, and gave him a brief summary of events: Mrs. Lundquist's visit and accident, the visitor looking for an ale bowl, the missing accession form. "So I was wondering if—"

"This woman is dead?" he asked.

"Yes," she said cautiously.

"So why are you wasting time looking for her donation? You didn't think you could return it, did you?"

Chloe rolled her eyes. "Of course not. It's just that—"

"Stop worrying about things that don't matter. Are you making progress with the collections storage building plan?"

OK, calling Ralph had been a mistake. "I'm working on it," Chloe said. "Thanks, Ralph. I'll let you go."

She hung up and stood for a long moment, debating. Then she dug through her bag, found a creased business card, and dialed another number.

"Eagle Police Department." A woman's voice, cool and competent. She'd make an excellent registrar

"I'd like to speak with Officer McKenna, please."

"Is this an emergency?"

"Um . . . no."

"Officer McKenna won't be in the office until noon. May I take a message?"

"No, thank you," Chloe said. She hung up and stared at the phone. She was probably being silly.

Then she remembered Mrs. Lundquist, very dead.

Chloe locked up the trailer at 11:50, and drove to Eagle. She realized belatedly that she should have asked directions, but she had no trouble finding the police station, which shared a roof with the village hall.

Once in the entryway Chloe opened the appropriate door and stopped. She'd vaguely imagined a reception area guarding private office space. Instead she'd stepped into a cramped, narrow workroom. The counters were topped with manuals and stacks of papers and cubbyholes holding an array of forms. Shelves crowded with more manuals and cardboard cartons covered one wall.

A middle-aged woman who'd been clattering away at a typewriter looked up enquiringly, as did a very young officer sitting at the counter. Roelke McKenna stood at a line of lockers in the opposite wall, buttoning his uniform shirt. A framed photo of a pretty young woman perched on the shelf in his locker. She had long red hair, a fair complexion—probably of Irish descent—

"May I help you?" the woman asked.

Chloe flushed. "Um . . . I was hoping to see . . ." She looked at Officer McKenna.

He closed his locker. "Is there something I can do for you, Miss Ellefson?"

"You said I should contact you if—if anything came up about Mrs. Lundquist." Chloe tried to sound matter-of-fact. She was acutely aware of the clerk and other officer.

The patrolman seemed to catch on. "The chief is out. Why don't we use his office." He opened a door in the back wall and led her into a private office. Two chairs faced the desk; he took one and gestured to the other. "Please, sit down."

"Thank you." Chloe looked away from his penetrating stare and made a mental note to break no laws in the Village of Eagle.

"Did a relative contact you?" Officer McKenna asked.

"No. I just—well, I've been looking for this ale bowl, you know, and I haven't been able to find it. But a couple of odd things have happened." She told him about the visitor who'd asked about a rosemaled ale bowl with cow heads, and the transfer page torn from the ledger.

He listened in silence. "Do you think someone stole this antique from Old World Wisconsin?"

Chloe spread her hands. "I don't know."

"Would this be a valuable piece?"

"I suppose so. Lots of collectors want nineteenth-century ethnic pieces in good condition."

"Nothing about this piece in particular, though?"

Chloe shifted her weight. She was getting annoyed—whether at him or herself, she wasn't sure. "I don't know that either. I'm not an expert."

"You must know an expert though, eh? Someone you could contact who knows Norwegian antiques?"

"Why, because I'm of Norwegian descent? Do you think we all sit around eating *lefse* and painting woodenware?"

"No," he said carefully. "Because you work for a museum."

Chloe ordered herself to get a grip. "Yes, of course. I do. I will. My original point, though, is that any rosemaled piece is valuable, and there are dozens of them at the site, both on display and in storage."

A phone rang in the outer office, and the clerk's voice cut through Officer McKenna's thoughtful silence. Then he asked, "Do you happen to have that piece of paper you showed me the other day? The one Mrs. Lundquist gave you?"

She pulled it from her bag and handed it to him.

He stared at it for a moment, then leaned forward and turned the paper sideways. "What does this number mean?" He pointed to the accession number, 1962.37.3.

"Well … the '1-9-6-2' means the ale bowl was originally donated in 1962. Mrs. Lundquist was the thirty-seventh person to donate something to the historical society that year. And the '3' indicates that she donated at least three objects, and that the ale bowl was the third piece the registrar numbered and marked."

"What about the other two objects?"

Chloe blinked. "What?"

"What about the other objects she donated?" he repeated. "Were those first two transferred to Old World along with the ale bowl? Are they missing too?"

Chloe felt herself flush again. A pox on her Scandinavian features. A pox on Officer Roelke McKenna for making her feel like an idiot. "I don't know," she admitted. "I didn't think to check on that. The registrar in Madison will be able to tell me."

"Perhaps that should be your next step."

"Yes." Chloe took the accession form back and stood up. "I apologize for taking your time."

"Just a moment."

Chloe sat back down and waited. The cop's mouth formed a tight line. He stared blindly at the wall, one thumb tapping a staccato beat on the arm of his chair. His tension was palpable. He was a young cop in a sleepy village. What had wound him up so tight?

He looked back at her. "You don't have any evidence that a crime has been committed."

"No," she said curtly. "I don't."

"Old World Wisconsin is a state property. If you do decide that a crime has been committed, your director needs to file a report. It'll go to the Capitol police first, and probably on to the county. In any case, law enforcement can't get involved until you make a report."

"No, I didn't expect . . . that is . . ." Shit. Just what had she expected? She didn't know. "I just wanted to tell you what I'd found. That's all."

She stood again. This time he didn't stop her.

—

"What was that about?" Marie asked, rolling a piece of paper from her typewriter.

Roelke finished his quick check of his duty belt: everything in order. "Just a follow-up from that fatal accident on Highway S."

"What about that fatal?" Chief Naborski walked into the room through the side door, from the village municipal offices, just in time to hear Roelke's remark. "Some problem there?"

"Not really."

Chief Naborski was a solid man of medium height with a craggy face, tired eyes, and gray hair buzzed in a flat-top that may have been a holdover from his service during the Korean War. He looked at Roelke a moment longer than casual courtesy required, then cocked his head toward his office. "Come in for a minute."

Roelke followed and dropped into the seat he'd recently vacated. The chief was a plain-spoken and fair man—except during deer season. Chief Naborski's annual calendar revolved around his week at deer camp, much to the annoyance of some of the younger cops who wanted to take vacation at the same time. Roelke didn't ask for vacation time during deer season. He and the chief got along fine.

"Anything I need to know?" Naborski asked.

"I don't think so. An employee from Old World Wisconsin stopped in a few minutes ago. She'd met with the victim just before the accident, and was first on the scene. She's been trying to find an antique the victim donated, years ago. It hasn't turned up."

"If they think something's been stolen, they need to file a report."

"That's what I told her."

"I've got something else for you." Chief Naborski tipped back in his chair. He had a habit of leaning back so far that Roelke, during his first weeks on the job, had lived with the distracting fear that he was about to watch his boss fall on his ass. It hadn't happened yet.

"Yes, sir?"

"Ginger Herschorn stopped by my house last night. Ginger Herschorn is very unhappy."

The image of a pinched, disapproving face nudged Chloe Ellefson's lovely troubled one from Roelke's mind. Ginger Herschorn, a long time village trustee, routinely campaigned to eliminate the village police force. It would be "free," she argued, to simply rely on the county for all calls. No one had been able to convince Ginger that one way or another, her taxes paid for law enforcement. Roelke was pretty sure that the first time she faced a real emergency, she'd be glad to have a local cop two minutes away.

"Ginger says her nephew lost seven hundred dollars on a Brewers game last week," the chief was saying.

Seven hundred dollars far exceeded the scope of a friendly wager. "Where did that happen?"

"The Eagle's Nest." The chief picked up a pencil and let it slide through his fingers until the eraser end bounced from his desk. "Evidently somebody's taking bets on craps or NASCAR or anything else that moves."

The Eagle's Nest was a new bar on the outskirts of the village. "Hunh," Roelke said.

"You been in there yet?"

"I did a few walk-throughs the first week they were open. Found a couple of underage drinkers. A couple more with fake IDs. I've mostly been on first shift."

"Pick up a couple of later shifts, then. Switch with Skeet." Naborski bounced the pencil off its tip, turned it over, and let it begin another slide.

"Did the kid provide any names? Any other details?"

"Not to Ginger. He only 'fessed up to his parents because he needed to come up with the money. His father forked over the cash so his kid could walk away, then called his sister, the village board member. You can talk to the kid yourself. See if he'll tell you anything else." Naborski handed him a piece of paper with some notes scrawled on it. "How do you want to play it at the bar?"

Roelke considered. Up-front, in uniform? Hanging out in street clothes first, trying to blend in, keeping his eyes and ears open? "Up-front, to start," he decided. "I can make it clear that we've had a complaint. That might be all it takes."

"Do it," Naborski said. "We need to shut this thing down fast. It's probably some bookie moving out from the city, thinks he can fly under the radar out here."

"Right."

Roelke left the chief in his office, wished Marie a good afternoon, and headed out to his patrol car. But before signing in with dispatch he allowed himself one last thought of Chloe Ellefson. He knew she'd been irritated and frustrated by the time she left. There's nothing you can do about it, he told himself, which didn't make him feel even a little better.

SEVEN

CHLOE RETREATED TO BED that evening with Jack Finney's *Time and Again* and a glass of wine. Her mind kept drifting, though, from the novel's plot to the missing artifact transfer record. Who could have taken it? Nika had admitted to being in the trailers recently. And Byron had mentioned a specific artifact in the pink trailer, so he'd been inside recently as well. But why would either one care about one ale bowl? Other people on staff had access, too. Maintenance chief Stanley Colontuono, for one. Director Ralph Petty, for another.

The bedside telephone's ring startled her. She checked her watch—almost eleven—and eyed the phone with suspicion. Only two people were likely to call at this hour: Ethan or her mother. Quite a gamble. She took a sip of wine. The phone rang again, and kept ringing well beyond the point of politeness. Decision made. "Hello?"

"Hey."

She sighed and relaxed, snuggling farther down on the pillow. "Ethan. Hi."

"I called to see how you were doing."

A lump rose in her throat, and her eyes welled with unexpected tears. "Thanks," she said simply. "OK, I think. I feel like I'm underwater. I always seem to be a step or two behind everyone else. But OK."

"Everyone feels like that when they start a new job."

"I guess. How are you?"

"Good. I'm likely to get called out on a fire and I wanted to talk to you before I left."

Chloe clutched the receiver as if it were his hand. "Where?"

"California. Didn't you see it on the news?"

"I must have missed it." Since Chloe hadn't bothered to plug her television in yet, that wasn't surprising. "You know, most of the people we graduated with took nice, safe jobs with nice, destructive, paper companies."

His low laugh rippled through the wire, over the miles. "Yeah. Go figure. So. Are you getting to know some of the people you'll be working with?"

"A little. It's quite a crew." She curled on her side and told him about Byron and Stan, Ralph and Nika. "There are only ten or twelve permanent employees, so I'll get to know the others. Most of the work is seasonal."

"Yeah." Ethan knew all about seasonal work. "Well, give 'em a chance, Chloe. I worry about you being isolated out there."

Chloe looked around the bedroom—empty shelves, empty bureau, stacks of cartons—and on to the dark, silent rooms beyond. She was living alone in a nine-room farmhouse on a lonely rural road. Yep, pretty isolated. And so different than the small house she'd shared with Markus, which had squeezed European-style between two others in Brienz, within walking distance of almost everything they needed. That little house had overflowed with life: music drifting from the stereo, two collections of books tumbling from over-crammed shelves, the aroma of baking cheese and fresh bread spilling from their tiny kitchen, window boxes dripping with flowers each summer.

God, she missed Markus.

"Chloe?"

"I was back in Switzerland," she admitted. "It was just so damn easy there, you know? Markus and I—the day we met, it was like we'd known each other for years." While Chloe and Markus lived together they'd spent some vacation days touring other outdoor museums and historic sites, interviewing elderly people on remote farms, attending conferences. Other days they laced up hiking boots and disappeared into the mountains with nothing in their daypacks but bread, cheese, and a bottle of wine. Markus and Chloe belonged to a folk dance group. She encouraged him to submit his account of his efforts to stabilize populations of two rare goat breeds, *stiefelgeiss* and *fauengeiss*, for publication. He encouraged her to pursue her long-held, mostly secret wish to write an historical novel. She—

"Chloe?" Ethan asked again.

She reminded herself that although Ethan was gay and oblivious to the charms of historic sites, he was one thing Markus was not: an ever-faithful best friend. "Sorry," she said. "I'm here."

"You need to get out of the house. Go do something cheerful. Remember that bluegrass bar you took me to that Christmas I came home with you?"

"The Green Lantern. It's near Fort Atkinson."

"Go listen to some music this weekend."

"Maybe I will," she said, knowing she wouldn't.

"You feeling better about that car wreck thing?"

She hesitated. Her bedroom window was open, and a cow in the pasture just beyond the driveway snorted and stamped. "Well... There's something going on here that I don't understand."

"Why are you worrying about it?"

"I promised Mrs. Lundquist I'd find the bowl." She flexed her toes. "She came to me for help. I can't help wondering if someone was bullying her about that ale bowl, somehow. Pressuring her to get it back. What if that's what caused her heart attack?"

"If that's the case," Ethan said, "then I *really* don't think you should get involved in it. You can't bring her back. You have a new job to get a handle on, and your health to take care of."

He was right, of course. The Old World collections, the interpreters and their artifact-related needs—she had overwhelming responsibilities. There was no time for unnecessary side trips.

"... so don't try to take this on by yourself, too. You need to get out with other people more. Join a club or something."

"A club?"

"There must be some kind of adult sports league or something around there. Get on a softball team. Didn't you pitch on your dorm team?"

"That was a million years ago." Another person, another life.

"Well, look into it, OK? And get a dog."

"*What*?"

"Get a dog. They're great companions."

"I can't get a dog," she said slowly.

"Why not?"

"They're—it would be too much responsibility."

"What responsibility? You feed it, you take it out for walks. In return you get exercise and company and unconditional love."

"I'll think about it," Chloe lied. A dog implied commitment. She couldn't get a dog.

"Listen, girl, I should let you turn in. It's late."

"OK." Chloe stared at the photograph of her and Ethan perched island-like on the empty bookshelf. She loved Ethan for loving her, through good and bad. She also cherished the living link to her life before her gradual unraveling. Ethan reminded Chloe of her old self—energetic, focused on growing a career, passionate about hiking and paddling and skiing into wooded hills. Content. Normal.

"Thanks for calling, Ethan," she said. "You be careful on the fire line, you hear? Call me when you get back."

"I will on both counts."

"Ethan?"

"Yeah?"

"Are you still gay?"

He laughed. "Good night, Chloe."

Chloe got lost on Friday morning while trying to find Daleyville, but she'd been so sure of getting lost that she still arrived fifteen minutes early for Mrs. Lundquist's funeral. The old stone church stood on high ground, overlooking farm fields rolling piously into the distance. The string of homes that comprised the village seemed inadequate to fill the imposing church. Chloe's Pinto brought the total of cars in the parking lot up to a mighty three, and the minister and organist presumably accounted for the other two. Evidently very few people mourned Mrs. Lundquist's passing.

Once inside, she felt obligated to slide into a pew near the front. A simple white coffin was positioned in front of the altar rail—closed, thank God. Chloe sent a private nod to Mrs. Lundquist, wherever she was: *I'm so sorry I wasn't more helpful. I wish I'd asked you more ques-*

tions, learned why you were so upset. I'm trying to find your ale bowl, and to figure out what was troubling you.

Three elderly ladies walked silently down the aisle and took seats together a few pews in front of her, all wearing proper black or navy blue dresses. Two wore hats. It hadn't occurred to Chloe until that morning that she shouldn't show up at a funeral in chinos and a polo shirt, and a frantic scramble through suitcases had resulted in a wrinkled denim skirt and dark green cotton blouse. She had no idea where her iron was—did she even still own an iron?—so she'd laid the clothes over her kitchen table, dribbled water on the worst of the creases, pressed them flat with her fingers, and pulled them on.

She was grateful for a quiet moment to gather her thoughts. Dust motes danced in a stream of light pouring like molten gold through a window. Sober organ music filled the air. Chloe tried to remember when she'd last been inside a Lutheran church. As a child, she'd attended Sunday School and worship services with her family at Christ Lutheran Church in Stoughton. Markus was an agnostic, but that hadn't mattered to her—not living in a place where Lake Brienz sparkled on one side, and the Alps soared heavenwards on the other—

"Hello."

Chloe jumped; she hadn't even noticed the elderly man who'd taken a seat in the pew beside her. "Good morning," she murmured back.

He was very thin, and wore an old but tidy black suit. He removed his fedora with fingers that tremored with a slight palsy. A fringe of white hair circled his head just above ear level. "Who are you?" he whispered.

"Just a . . ." Just a what? "I only met Mrs. Lundquist recently," Chloe told him. "Were you a friend of hers?"

"We were next-door neighbors for twenty-seven years. Years ago me and my wife and Berget and her husband used to get together every Friday night to play Sheepshead." The man waved one trembling hand in a gesture part resigned, part helpless. "No more card games, now. I'm the only one left."

Chloe pressed his hand briefly. There were too damn many lonely people in the world. "I'm sorry," she said, and introduced herself. "I work at Old World Wisconsin. I only met Mrs. Lundquist once."

"I'm Bill Solberg." He gave her a searching look with blue eyes that looked pale, as if age was leaching even that color from him. "It was good of you to come."

"I wanted to. She—she came to see me the day she died."

"About that ale bowl." He nodded. "She'd been fussing about that for weeks."

Chloe sat up a little straighter. "Do you—"

The minister, who had stepped unnoticed to the pulpit, chose that moment to begin the service. Chloe forced herself to swallow her questions.

The service was brief and, with the exception of mentioning Mrs. Lundquist's dependable presence at Sunday service, impersonal. After the organ postlude, the funeral ended.

Mr. Solberg sat immobile, staring at the coffin. The three elderly women followed the minister down the aisle. Chloe glanced after them, wondering if they had been friends of Mrs. Lundquist … and was startled to see Officer McKenna standing by a back pew. He caught her eye and nodded.

The old man sighed heavily. "I'll miss her."

"I'm glad she had a friend like you," Chloe said. "When I met her, she seemed very distressed about that ale bowl. And then the police told me they couldn't find any relatives. I've been very sad about it all."

"Were you able to help her?" Mr. Solberg said.

"I'm afraid not. It was my first day, you see, and..." Chloe took a deep breath. "The form she showed me said she had legally donated the ale bowl to the State Historical Society in 1962. I'm afraid that kind of thing really can't be undone."

"I told her so, but she was determined to try. I can't recall seeing her so worked up about anything since her husband died."

"Do you know why she was so upset?" Chloe asked. "What made it so important for her to get that ale bowl back?"

Mr. Solberg shook his head. "She never said. She was a classy lady, never talked much about personal stuff. Not like most nowadays."

"Mr. Solberg, I haven't been able to find the ale bowl. It was transferred from the state collection in Madison to Old World Wisconsin in 1977, and it seems to have disappeared. I'd really like to find that ale bowl, and to learn why Mrs. Lundquist was so worried about it. If you can think of anything she ever said about it, anything at all, it might be very helpful."

He turned sideways in the pew, a frown creasing his forehead. "Why do you care so much?"

"Because I feel badly that I wasn't able to help your friend when she came to see me. I promised her I'd find the bowl. Even though she's gone... I'd like to honor that promise, and to put the bowl on display in one of the Norwegian houses." That much was true. Chloe chose not to mention her fear that someone might have been pressuring the old lady to produce the artifact.

His forehead smoothed out again, and he turned to stare thoughtfully out a window for a few moments. Then he shook his head. "Sorry, Miss Ellefson. I can't think of a thing. I don't know why she wanted it back so much. She had one son, but he died in Vietnam. Pretty early in the war—he was one of the first."

Nineteen sixty-two, Chloe thought, remembering that Mrs. Lundquist had donated her heirlooms after her son's death. "Did she mention getting a phone call or visit that distressed her within the last month or so?"

"No. And I kept a good eye on that house, let me tell you. I did it for her husband. I know he'd have done it for my wife if things had been different."

"I'm sure you did." Chloe gave him a sympathetic smile. "I'm sorry for your loss, Mr. Solberg. I won't take up any more of your time."

She stood up, and he did too. But he didn't step into the aisle. "I suppose you could look around," he said slowly.

"Look around?"

"Her house. I suppose that would be all right."

"Look around her house?" Chloe repeated stupidly.

"I have a key. I don't know what's going to happen to her things, but nothing's happened yet. We can go right now, if you want."

Chloe considered. She *really* should start that storage building proposal. Still, her afternoon was clear—she'd actually gone through her orientation notes the evening before, checking for any scheduled meetings. Nika had somehow badgered the restaurant staff into giving up two tables, and the maintenance staff into hauling them down the narrow stairs to the basement of St. Peter's church. With her own portable typewriter in place, already hard at work, she wasn't likely to even notice that Chloe was gone.

Mr. Solberg stood waiting patiently. "Sure," she told him.

"I'll just be a minute." Mr. Solberg walked slowly to the coffin and stood, head bowed.

Not wanting to intrude, Chloe turned away. Roelke McKenna still stood near the back of the sanctuary. She joined him. "Good morning. I didn't expect to see you here."

"When people die on my shift I always attend their funerals, if I can."

"Oh." Chloe stared back toward the casket, wishing Mr. Solberg would hurry.

"Did you check into the other donations?"

Chloe blinked at Officer McKenna. "I beg your pardon?"

"The other donations," he said patiently. "You were going to call Madison."

"Oh. Right. Yes." Shit. Why did she always stutter like an idiot in this man's presence? "I called the registrar yesterday. She said the ale bowl was the only artifact from Mrs. Lundquist's donation that was transferred to Old World."

He nodded. "Well, I need to get to work."

Me too, Chloe thought, but she felt no inclination to tell this uptight cop that she was about to poke through the dead woman's home and belongings.

Mrs. Lundquist lived—had lived—in a tiny frame house just off the main street. Lace curtains hung in the window, and a wicker rocking chair waited on the small front porch. Crimson geraniums blossomed cheerfully in half-barrels on either side of the front walk. Life goes on, Chloe thought, but it all seemed strange.

Mr. Solberg unlocked the front door. Chloe stepped inside and automatically paused, taking in the feel of the place. The house was forty, maybe fifty years old. It held a distant jumble of sensory energy, but the strongest sensation was one of calm quiet. That made sense; Mrs. Lundquist had lived alone for a long time.

Pocket doors to the right of the entrance hall led to an eat-in kitchen. Mr. Solberg turned left. "If there's anything to find, I think it'd be in here," he said.

Chloe scanned the tidy living room. The furniture was old, worn but not dingy. A recliner waited in front of a television set, holding a half-done crocheted afghan in cheery purple and yellow. Mr. Solberg picked up the project, smoothing the zigzag pattern with his fingers. "Berget always was one for crochet. She'd make blankets and donate 'em to the hospital in Madison for new babies."

Chloe murmured something sympathetic before turning away from the sadness in the old man's eyes. Bookshelves lined two walls. Mrs. Lundquist's reading tastes had ranged from James Michener's novels to presidential biographies, but evidently did not include Norwegian history or antiques.

A montage of photographs formed a square on one wall, and Chloe stepped closer for a good look. Mr. Solberg joined her. "There's Berget and Jack. Jack died young. Bad ticker." He pointed to a black-and-white wedding photograph of a beaming couple. Mid-1930s, Chloe guessed, judging by the gown style. She stared at Berget as a young bride, trying hard not to juxtapose the lovely image with a lined face, slack in death.

The other photographs were older and of still, stern people, stiffly posed. Mrs. Lundquist's parents, grandparents? "Do you know if both of the Lundquists had Norwegian ancestry?" she asked.

"She did, that's for sure. She was proud of her people. 'I'm from good Norwegian stock,' she always said. But Jack was Swedish. Berget used to say how open-minded she was, marrying a Swede."

Ah! It was an old jest, but helpful. The sketchy accession form specifically noted a *Norwegian* ale bowl. If Jack Lundquist had been Swedish, the ale bowl had almost certainly come through Mrs. Lundquist's family, not his.

"We should take a look at her desk," Mr. Solberg told her. He led Chloe to a small desk in a back corner, painted white. A tiny, almost thread-bare stuffed rabbit rested against a mug holding pens and pencils. Her son's? Chloe touched the toy with a finger.

In the top drawer they found neat stacks of bills and canceled checks. "Were you aware of any financial difficulties Mrs. Lundquist was experiencing?" Chloe asked, uncomfortably aware that she sounded more like Officer McKenna than herself. "Property tax payments, a medical problem, anything like that?"

He waved that idea aside. "No. She wasn't rich, but Jack's insurance policy left her provided for. She took pills for arthritis, but that's it. Not like me. I take seven different medications."

"Then I don't think we'd learn anything helpful by examining her finances," Chloe said. The idea of pawing through the dead woman's bank records felt just too intrusive.

The second desk drawer held packets of yellowed thank-you notes, half-used boxes of faded Christmas cards, one unopened package of elegant writing paper.

"Did Mrs. Lundquist have many friends?" Chloe asked. "Other than you, I mean?"

"She lived pretty much in Jack's shadow when he was alive. A lot of the gals did, back then. After he died, I think most of their friends drifted away. Jack was orphaned young, so there's no family there. And then Berget's son got killed in Vietnam. Now, that was a nasty war."

"So Mrs. Lundquist never had any grandchildren?"

"Nope. She was a loner, I guess you'd say. She was a regular down to church, and helped out with the altar guild. Those three ladies at the service this morning are altar guild. But Berget was reserved. Always was. Didn't make friends easy, I'd say. And did just fine on her own."

Chloe sighed and closed that drawer. Crouching, she pulled out the bottom one. It was heavier than the first two, and revealed two leather-bound photograph albums. Chloe pulled out the first. The most recent photographs were already decades old; evidently Mrs. Lundquist hadn't taken a picture since her son died. Chloe flipped back through blurry snapshots that documented Christmases, a family picnic, a trip to the Grand Canyon, color portraits of a young man in uniform. Mrs. Lundquist looked perpetually happy.

The second album held more heirloom photographs—cabinet cards and *cartes de visites*. "Do you suppose this is Mrs. Lundquist?" Chloe asked, pointing to a lovely girl in white. "It looks like confirmation day."

Mr. Solberg peered over her shoulder, and tapped the photo with a trembling finger. "Oh, yes. That's Berget."

"This must be her and her parents. But who's this?" Chloe stared at a studio-posed cabinet card. A very young Berget stood at her mother's elbow. A boy stood beside the man Chloe assumed was Berget's father. "A brother?"

He squinted at the photo. "Perhaps. Whoever the boy was, he must be long dead. I heard Berget say more than once that everyone had died on her. She didn't have any family left."

"That's so sad." Something began to ache in Chloe's chest as she stared at the sweet girl Mrs. Lundquist had been—not knowing she was destined to bury her parents, her brother, her husband, her child.

"Ooph." Mr. Solberg straightened with a little grimace of pain. "Knees don't work the way they used to. Don't get old, Ms. Ellefson. It's no fun. Although, as they say, consider the alternative."

I have, Chloe wanted to say. Suddenly she'd had enough. She put the photo albums back carefully, shut the drawer, and turned to her host. "Thank you, Mr. Solberg, but I don't think we're going to find anything to tell me more about that ale bowl."

EIGHT

After pulling his squad car into The Eagle's Nest parking lot that evening, Roelke surveyed his surroundings. The bar occupied the lower level of a small, two-story frame building. It had stood empty for most of Roelke's time in Eagle. In the past he'd occasionally made a pass through the parking lot while on patrol, checking for kids huddled behind the building to smoke cigarettes or pot. Now, half a dozen cars and pickup trucks were parked in front of the bar, and three motorcycles waited for their drivers in the glow of a pole-mounted security light. Low gray clouds threatened rain, and made the neon Miller and Bud signs blinking in the front windows seem welcoming.

Somewhere inside, according to Ginger Herschorn's nephew, a nameless bookie had pressured the underage kid to bet a lot of money on a baseball game. The boy had been half defensive and half surly. "I wagered on a ball game," he'd said with a shrug, slunk down low on the flowered sofa in his parents' living room. "I lost some money. No big deal."

Roelke parked around the corner to keep the car accessible without being blatantly visible. He pulled his nylon jacket on when he got out of the car. The air felt damp and cool as he headed across the parking lot. The shrieking vocals of AC/DC's "You Shook Me All Night Long" pulsed from a jukebox and into the night. Blues, he thought wistfully. Just once I'd like to do a bar check and hear some good blues.

A wall of smoke and noise greeted him inside, accompanied by the odor of fried mushrooms and onion rings. The bar itself stood island-like in the middle of the room. A horseshoe of small wooden tables sat along the front and side walls. A waitress sporting bottle-blonde hair and tight black jeans was delivering a tray of beer mugs to a noisy group in one corner. She glanced at Roelke when he came in, but didn't stop moving.

Two pool tables sat behind the bar. And in the wall behind them, three closed doors. One no doubt led to a kitchen. One room was probably an office. And the third?

Roelke approached the bartender, a cadaverous-looking man perhaps in his fifties. The barkeep stopped sliding clean glasses into overhead wooden racks, looking wary. He had thinning gray hair combed away from a narrow face. The overhead light's yellow glow wasn't kind to his sallow complexion, or to the dark circles under his eyes.

"How's it going?" Roelke asked, his tone pleasant but not jovial. Finding the friendly-balance in a bar was a knife-edge thing. If he was too friendly, regulars would come to expect chit-chat, slowing him down whenever he did a bar check while on patrol. Not friendly enough, an empty beer bottle might just come sailing from some dark corner next time he stopped by.

"Ah, Jesus." The barkeep put both palms on the bar. "You got some problem in here?"

“As a matter of fact, we have had a complaint. Underage drinking and underage gambling.” Out of the corner of his eye, Roelke saw the waitress slide quietly through one of the closed doors. “Are you Joe Pagenkampf?” One Joe Pagenkampf had filed a request for the tavern’s liquor license.

“Yeah.”

“You know anything about those things?”

“Nope.” Pagenkampf shook his head. “I run a clean place.”

“That’s good to know,” Roelke said politely, holding the man’s gaze for an extra moment. Message delivered.

Before leaving he strolled around the room, nodding hello at the patrons. Most looked to be nothing more than tired men and women enjoying a cold one on their way home. He didn’t see anyone who looked young enough to card. He checked the bathroom. A bookie might not operate in the john, but drug dealers often did. This one was empty. In need of scrubbing, but empty.

As Roelke emerged from the bathroom a red-haired man wearing work clothes and cowboy boots burst through the door. “Is he here?” he demanded of the bartender. “Is he back there?”

“*Stan!*” Pagenkampf cocked his head infinitesimally in Roelke’s direction, then lowered his voice. “Sorry, Stan. Haven’t seen him tonight.”

Roelke had gone very still, watching.

Stan glanced at the policeman and shed his anger like a lizard shedding his skin. “Hey,” he said with a friendly nod, and slid onto a barstool. “Get me a draft Miller,” he told the bartender.

Roelke returned the greeting and headed out to the squad. After calling back in to service he sat, staring at the bar, thinking. Who had this Stan guy been looking for? The bookie?

Raindrops began a tentative sprinkle against his windshield. Roelke tapped a rhythm against the steering wheel with his thumb. He'd done all he could do tonight. The chief would probably send one of the young guys in wearing street clothes, one of the part-timers, not likely to be recognized. The EPD's newest hire was fresh from the academy, still in the John Wayne phase. He'd leap at the chance to try to make nice with the bartender, and see if he could sniff out any hint of whatever was going on.

But Roelke would quietly talk with a few people in Eagle as well, see what else he could uncover. If a bookie was operating out of the back room at The Eagle's Nest, the cops would need a warrant to nail him. And to get a warrant, they'd need more than a sullen teen's vague admission.

His ear caught a call among the radio chatter, just as rain began a torrential timpani on the car roof. "George 220. Respond to a 10-45, northbound lane of Highway 67, approximately one mile north of junction with Highway 59."

Great. Ju-u-ust great. "George 220. On my way."

He started the car and pulled out of the lot. If he was a gambling man, he'd have put a lot of dollars on his guess that no one—not from Waukesha County, not from the DNR, not from any of the surrounding municipalities—would show up to offer assistance on this call. His unseen colleagues would no doubt judge Roelke competent enough to move an animal carcass from the road in a downpour, all by himself.

"Protect and serve," Roelke muttered, and headed north.

NINE

AFTER WAKING UP THE next morning Chloe lay in bed for some time, hands on her flat belly, feeling empty and alone. Markus had been an early riser, and often woke her with cups of steaming hot chocolate. Other days he'd plop down on the bed, full of ideas for the day. "We're out of flour—we need to go to the market," or, "Let's take the steam cog up the Rothorn!" Chloe loved the Appalachian mountains, but the Alps … oh, the Swiss Alps, with their steep paths hiked to the music of cow bells and songbirds, were like no place else on earth…

"*Dammit.*" She abruptly scrambled out of bed. Enough of this. If she didn't get moving, she'd likely crawl back under the covers. Not good.

After padding into the kitchen, she opened her refrigerator. The shopping fairies had not magically filled it for her. In fact … she sniffed, then stuck a hand deep inside. Lovely. Her brand-new used refrigerator had died. She wouldn't get her first paycheck for weeks. Fridge repairs were not in the budget. Chloe shut the door again.

It was Saturday, and her mother was expecting her at the old homeplace in Stoughton. Chloe had mixed feelings about going home. Still . . . she could eat there, and do a load of laundry too.

The drive to Stoughton took less than an hour, winding through small towns and rolling farmland. Her parents still lived in the two-story colonial on South Prairie street where Chloe had grown up. When she pulled up in front of her parents' house that morning, she cut the engine and sat staring at the sign hanging by the front door: *Velkommen til vårt hjem.* Petunias and sweet potato vines spilled from rosemaled window boxes. A flagpole in the front yard hosted both American and Norwegian flags. Mom and Dad avoided Norwegian cute—no little ceramic elves peeking around garden plants, no stumps carved like trolls. Still, in a town that had turned its Norwegian heritage into a bankable tourism phenomenon, Chloe's parents were part of a dwindling minority: the real deal, both born of families that had not married outside the Norwegian community.

Mom met her at the door. "Oh, come in, dear! My, you look wonderful."

"Not really," Chloe said.

Her mother blinked, and for a moment Chloe thought she might actually respond. Then Mrs. Ellefson turned away, heading toward the kitchen. "I still have the coffeepot on. Want some?"

"Sure. And granola or something too, if you've got some."

"I'll scramble you some eggs."

As her mother bustled about the kitchen, Chloe settled into her old chair. Blue curtains, a blue teapot on the stove, and blue dish towels livened up the white walls and appliances. A wall calendar featuring Norway's scenic fjords hung above the sink, and a *krumkakke* iron hung above the stove. A high shelf circling the room displayed a variety of rosemaled bowls and boxes and trays. Her mother's work, all of it. Chloe remembered her irritable outburst in the police office—"You think we all sit around eating *lefse* and painting woodenware?"—and felt her cheeks warm all over again. The truth was, when Officer McKenna had prodded her about finding an expert on rosemaled antiques, she'd known she wouldn't have to look far.

"Are you getting all settled in?" Chloe's parents had helped her move into the farmhouse the week before.

"Sure." Chloe took a sip of coffee. "Where's Dad?"

"He's bowling." Mom slid the eggs onto a plate already graced with a sticky bun. "Here."

"Thanks." Chloe had skipped supper the night before, and she dug in.

Mom sipped coffee from her own mug. She was a tall woman who had recently bobbed her hair after decades of wearing yellow braids in a coil behind her head. Silver had overpowered the blonde, but her eyes still shone Scandinavian blue. "So," she said finally, when Chloe put her fork down. "When you called last night you said you wanted to ask me a favor?"

"I'm hoping you might have time to do a little research for me." Her mother knew a lot about local history resources and genealogical searches. And she was cronies with every reference librarian in Dane County.

"Why, of course, dear. What do you need?"

Chloe felt an ache in her chest. Why hadn't her mother been able to ask that question when her daughter had been struggling last winter? When her personal life was in the crapper, Chloe had wondered just how much to confide in her mother. She'd made one or two hesitant attempts. And Mom simply did not want to take delivery—

"Chloe?"

Chloe started. "Right. Here's the thing. On my first day at Old World I talked to an artifact donor about a Norwegian ale bowl. Unfortunately, she passed away before I could get any of her family history." Chloe poured herself another cup of coffee. "And you know how it is," she said vaguely. "It would be really helpful for our records if we had a better idea of the ale bowl's provenance. I don't have time to do that kind of legwork."

"What fun!" Mrs. Ellefson leaned forward on her elbows. "Tell me about this ale bowl!"

Chloe pinched off a corner of the sticky bun and popped it into her mouth. "Mrs. Lundquist—the donor I met—originally gave it to the state historical society years ago. It got transferred to Old World, but I haven't been able to find it. I'm trying to figure out if it might have been more valuable than most other Norwegian pieces, for some reason." Chloe told her mother what little she knew about the ale bowl.

"Cow heads?" Mom looked thoughtful. "That's unusual."

"I thought so," Chloe said, impressed with herself.

"We're probably talking about *kjenge*—"

Chloe held up a hand, palm forward. "English, please."

"A *kjenge* is a type of bowl carved or turned from a single piece of wood, with handles carved as animal heads. Horse heads and lions are common motifs. And dragon heads." She smiled. "Those go back to Viking days. You can see them adorning old churches in Norway. During the era when Christianity was overtaking the old religion, people evidently wanted to hedge their bets."

"The reference to cow heads was probably a mistake," Chloe said morosely. "The original accession record is sketchy. The curator probably didn't even realize what she was seeing." She chewed her lip for a moment. "Mom, what else would make a rosemaled ale bowl particularly desirable to a collector?"

"Well ... the obvious things. Age and condition of the piece. The artist's skill with design and execution and color."

"I want to look at your collection." Chloe ate the rest of the sticky bun and washed her hands before following her mother into the living room.

Her mother was a superb rosemaler who had won a coveted gold medal a decade earlier. Her handiwork was displayed in every room in the house. But a glass-fronted cupboard held pieces she'd collected.

"I haven't bought an antique in years," Mom said. "The prices have really shot up."

"I assume some collectors look for pieces from certain regions." Chloe knew that styles of rosemaling were distinct enough to be identified.

"Sure. Telemark and Hallingdal are best known, of course. Serious collectors might focus on one region, or even one artist." Her mother picked up an exquisite bowl, painted orange and decorated with an intricate design of green, white, and black flowers and flourishes. "This one's from Hallingdal."

Chloe carefully took the bowl from her mother. She shouldn't handle the piece without wearing cotton gloves, but she hadn't brought a pair with her. "Are the pieces signed?"

"It's very rare to find a signed piece, but the best artists developed unique characteristics."

"Were all these pieces painted in Norway?" Chloe eased the bowl back onto the shelf.

Her mother nodded. "Almost certainly. Immigrants brought painted pieces with them. Lots of painted trunks, but also smaller pieces. Rose painting was starting to decline in Norway by the time of peak immigration to North America, though."

"Didn't any of the painters immigrate?"

"Some did. But most weren't able to support themselves with rose painting here. A few might have done some painting for family and friends, I suppose. But the real renaissance didn't begin until the twentieth century."

"So ... a nineteenth-century piece actually painted in Wisconsin might be more valuable than a piece painted in Norway, since they're more rare."

Her mother considered. "I suppose so. A few men may have kept the tradition alive, but in general, the immigrants soon took pride in American styles. You've seen those Andreas Dahl photographs, haven't you?"

"Um ... I don't think so."

"Dahl was a Norwegian-American who took dozens of photographs in Dane County during the 1870s. Lots of them show immigrant families posed in front of their homes, with sewing machines and farm equipment and whatever else they were most proud of. Modern American things, factory-made. I've got copies of a few of Dahl's photos somewhere. We used them in a Daughters of Norway display."

Chloe stared at the bowls and tankards and plates on the cabinet shelves. What did the missing ale bowl *look* like? Was it from Telemark, Hallingdal, somewhere else? Was it one of those rare pieces made in America, or did it show the delicate brushstrokes of a sought-after Norwegian master? Without more to go on, how could she ever know?

I should quit this nonsense, Chloe thought that afternoon, as she drove east from Stoughton. Ethan was right; Mrs. Lundquist's missing ale bowl is none of my business. I have plenty of things to worry about instead. I have no way of *ever* finding out what Mrs. Lundquist was so upset about, not with the shreds of information I have. For all I know she was a senile old bat.

Immediately, the image of the widow's face swam accusingly into her memory. Beseeching Chloe for help in life. Still and staring in death.

"I'm sorry," Chloe whispered. "Truly. And I'm trying hard to keep my promise."

In Whitewater, Chloe made a last-minute decision to turn north on Highway 59 instead of continuing east to her farmhouse. She might as well go to work. She had yet to so much as visit the museum's German, Finnish, and Danish farms. Byron had scheduled her to help provide training to the college students and teachers who'd be augmenting the interpretive ranks for the summer. Ralph Petty had scheduled a meeting to discuss a plan for permanent collections storage. And God knew she'd have to keep on her toes to stay one step ahead of Nika.

The restoration area was quiet. Chloe parked her car under a pine tree. Maybe she should spend the afternoon on site, mingling with visitors, getting to know the place. She hadn't checked out that wallpaper problem at Tobler, either. She'd just pick up her clipboard and—

She stopped halfway up the trailer steps. The door was closed. But its heavy padlock glittered from the ground beside the steps.

Dammit! Chloe yanked the door open and plunged inside. "Hey!" she yelled. The trailer was empty. The intruder was gone. She stared helplessly at the crowded storage shelves. She didn't have an inventory, so she had no way of knowing if something had been taken.

She picked up the phone receiver, but the site phone list she'd left beside it was gone. She put the receiver back down, and took a hard look at her workspace. Her papers had been moved. So had the black ledgers.

Who had messed with her stuff? And why?

She finally found her phone list, and dialed the security office number. A woman answered on the seventh ring. "Hello." She sounded out of breath.

"Is this a security guard?"

"No, it's the gift shop. Hank got called out to German. A visitor twisted her ankle and needed a ride. I can leave a message for him."

Lovely. "Well, this is Chloe Ellefson. The new curator. I'm at the collections trailers in the restoration area. Could you tell him I think there's been a break-in? I'll wait here."

"Sure." The receiver slammed down.

Chloe retreated to the picnic table outside to wait, wishing she'd asked for more information. Hank was giving an injured visitor a ride—to where? The parking lot? The hospital in Waukesha, forty minutes away? She nibbled her lower lip for a moment, then headed back inside to the phone.

TEN

Roelke realized that it was too late to chase the driver who'd just blitzed past the speed trap. Second one, too. His bad mood was distracting him.

He should have been in a good mood. He'd spent the previous night in Milwaukee with some of his old buddies, drinking beer and playing poker. Roelke didn't care about poker. Spending time with other cops, though—that was good. He had a standing reservation on Rick Almirez's sofa in Wauwatosa. Rick and Roelke had gone through the academy together.

"Next time bring more salsa," Rick had said that morning, as they lingered over store-bought cherry kringle and bad coffee in Rick's cramped apartment kitchen.

"Yeah, I will," Roelke had agreed. He wasn't much of a cook, but he made kick-butt salsa.

Rick Almirez was smart, a fast thinker, and even faster on his feet. He also smoked like a stovepipe. "You coming back out for practice?" he asked, reaching for a pack of cigarettes.

Rick, Roelke, and two of their friends from the force played in a bad garage band called The Blue Tones. "If I can get somebody to switch shifts with me," Roelke said. "I'll stop at the PD and check the schedule."

"For Chrissake, do not go in this afternoon just to check the schedule." Rick glanced at the ceiling as if searching for divine counseling: *Lord, what am I to do with this guy?* "You got to get out of that two-bit town. When are you going to transfer back out here?"

Roelke shrugged.

"You said when you left MPD that it was temporary. Helping out your cousin. How long can you drive in circles around that village before you go nuts?" Rick blew a plume of smoke over one shoulder. "You're not even full-time."

"The only full-time guy is out on medical with a bad back. He'll probably take early retirement. I might be in line for that." Or Skeet might. One or the other.

"You're gonna lose your edge, man." Rick got up to get a carton of milk from the refrigerator. "When I went on shift on Friday night there were seventy-nine calls waiting. God, what a night! The only way I could grab a bite was to swing through George Webb's before calling back in service."

"Small towns do have crime too," Roelke said irritably. Although it would probably take the EPD several weeks to rack up seventy-nine calls.

Rick had eaten another piece of kringle, and licked his fingers. Then he'd said, "You're screwing your career out there, Roelke. But I guess we'll let you hang out with us anyway. The band needs you."

Now, Rick's observations echoed in Roelke's ears. He shifted grumpily in the seat. All right, that was it. Next speeder he clocked was getting pulled over, and no amenities given.

Then dispatch came on the radio. "Possible break-in and entry at Old World Wisconsin restoration area, off County S."

Roelke grabbed the radio. "George 220. I've got this one."

He drove a bit faster than usual as he headed out of Eagle. The historic site's security vehicle pulled out of the main entrance and turned onto Highway 67 in front of him. Roelke followed it to the restoration area.

Chloe was sitting on a picnic table near the trailers. "I guess the cavalry is here," she said, getting up to greet the two men.

Hank DiCapo cast a sidelong glance at Roelke. "Hello, McKenna. Didn't realize you'd gotten a call too. I could've saved you a trip."

Roelke made a *no big deal* gesture. Old World's three security guards worked for a private security company—all conscientious men, as far as he could tell. But DiCapo was possessive about his turf.

"What's this about a break-in?" Hank asked Chloe.

She held up a padlock. "I found this on the ground, there by the step. Someone broke in."

"You sure you didn't drop it when you left last time?" Hank asked.

Her face tightened. "Quite sure. And when I looked inside, I could tell that someone had been going through my things."

She looked? Roelke felt the muscles in his jaw tense. Before he could respond to that, another car pulled into the lot. He turned to see County Deputy Marge Bandacek climb from her car. "What we got?"

Great. Roelke swallowed more irritation as he introduced Chloe and brought Marge up to speed.

Marge hitched her pants up. "Is something missing?"

Chloe spread her hands. "I don't have an inventory of the artifacts stored here. All I can say is that some things were messed up in the kitchen." She led the way inside.

The galley was so small that the three officers had to proceed one at a time. Roelke went first. The space didn't look any better than it had on Tuesday—dark, cluttered, worn. Depressing. "What's different?" he asked.

"These ledgers were shoved farther over on the counter than I left them." Chloe pointed. "And some of my papers were shuffled."

They convened back outside. "So basically, you aren't aware of anything that got stolen," Hank said.

Chloe gave him a level look. "No. But finding a padlock on the ground is cause for concern, I'd say."

Marge shifted her weight from one foot to the other. "When were you last inside there yourself?"

"Yesterday afternoon. I locked it up about five, before going home."

"Are you sure you didn't forget to hook the lock?" Marge asked. "Maybe you just *thought* you did. Maybe it didn't quite catch."

"I locked it," Chloe snapped. "And even if it hadn't caught—which it did—it would still be hanging here, wouldn't it? Not on the ground?"

"Maybe your hands were full, or you were in a hurry, and you dropped that lock yourself," Hank said.

"Hold on a minute," Roelke told Hank and Marge firmly. He had no real authority here, but he wanted to intervene before Chloe started throwing punches. "Who else has a key to these trailers?" he asked her.

She looked startled. "Well … the head of maintenance. Stanley Colontuono."

Stanley? Roelke took a mental note and filed it away.

"And Ralph Petty, the site director," Hank added. "He's got a master for everything. Have you called them?"

"No. But—they wouldn't have cause to be here without letting me know," Chloe pointed out. "And that wouldn't explain why the lock was on the ground, anyway. I can't believe any employee would be so careless."

For a moment no one spoke. Then the radio clipped to Hank's big belt crackled. "VC to Security."

He pulled it free. "Security here."

"We've got a family in the parking lot, locked out of their car. Can you give them a hand?"

"I'm on my way."

"It's a Jeep Cherokee, Illinois plates, third bay. VC out."

Hank replaced his radio with an air of authority. "What we've got here is, not a whole lot." He nodded at Roelke and Marge. "Sorry you got called in for nothing."

As Hank drove away, Marge pulled at her belt again. "It seems to me if someone was *really* trying to break in, he would have taken a carload or two of those antiques."

Chloe folded her arms over her chest.

The deputy caught Roelke's glance and jerked her head toward her car. "Nothing here to follow up on," Marge said as they walked away from Chloe. "I think the security guard is probably right."

"Perhaps."

"I'll do some extra drive-bys." Marge opened her car door. "Isn't that the woman from the car wreck? She seems high-strung."

"I think she's just trying to do her job."

"Aren't we all." Marge shrugged. "Catch you later, McKenna."

Roelke walked back to Chloe, who watched the deputy drive away with her lips pressed into a tight line. "It seems the mounties think I overreacted," she said.

"You did the right thing to call. What you *didn't* do right was charge inside an isolated trailer when you saw the missing lock."

"I thought someone might still be inside!"

"Exactly. You should have called for help, let one of us do the looking."

"These trailers and the artifacts inside are my responsibility," she snapped.

A tiny bird serenaded them from a pine branch overhead, *chickadee-dee-dee*. Roelke waited.

"Oh, shit." The tension left Chloe's posture and she sat down on the trailer steps abruptly. "All I could think when I saw that door unlocked was that someone came here searching for that blasted ale bowl."

"Do you have a reason to think that someone might break in with that in mind?"

"Nothing concrete. But I locked that door properly yesterday," Chloe said stubbornly. "I *did*."

Roelke leaned against his squad.

She sighed. "Look, I know you can't help me. I don't have any evidence of a crime."

"No. But I do agree that finding the lock on the ground is cause for concern. If something like that ever happens again, though, don't touch anything."

"You mean … so you could look for fingerprints?" She looked even more chagrined. "I didn't even think of that. Sorry."

"I'll write up what happened, and let the other guys know. We can keep an eye out for a while."

"I'm pretty sure someone messed through the records in the kitchen, but . . ." She rested her cheek on one palm. "Hank was right. I can't be positive, because I've spent more time in the last week looking for that ale bowl than doing my job and starting a proper inventory." She gave a mirthless laugh. "And I'm a state employee. That's your tax dollars at work."

"Would you like to come to a cookout tomorrow afternoon?" Roelke asked.

"Would I—*what*?"

He had no idea where that invitation had come from. "I'm going to my cousin's house to eat with her and her two kids. You're welcome to come with me."

She looked bewildered. "Um . . . OK."

"I'll pick you up," he said, feeling stupid. "Does three o'clock work for you?"

She nodded.

He got in his car and drove away before she could change her mind.

ELEVEN

"WHAT WAS I THINKING?" Chloe muttered. She stood in front of the bathroom mirror, braiding her hair. Why had she agreed to go to a cookout with Roelke McKenna?

She heard his knock as she was tying a ribbon around the bottom of her braid. Squaring her shoulders, she went to greet him. "Come on in. I just need to put on shoes."

He waited politely, looking only slightly less cop-like than usual in jeans and a plain blue T-shirt. The man definitely lifted weights. He did wear scuffed hiking boots, though, which was oddly comforting. They reminded Chloe of hours spent lounging in the lobby of WVU's Percival Hall with college buddies, waiting for the next forestry class to begin.

"Still have a bit of unpacking to do, I see," he said, gazing about at the untouched boxes.

"I've been busy." She laced up quickly. "OK. I'm ready to go."

It felt strange to climb into the cab of this man's pickup truck. She gave him a quick glance as he pulled out of her driveway. Was this a date? Surely not. He barely knew her. She'd turned thirty-two in March; he was maybe twenty-eight, tops. He probably thought she was a nutcase, obsessing about a problem that had nothing to do with her. And he kept a photograph of a pretty redhead in his locker.

OK, enough of that. "I'm a vegetarian," she said into the silence.

"That's all right."

"I should have mentioned it earlier."

"It'll be OK. Libby always overdoes on food."

Chloe searched for another pleasantry. "Um, what does Libby do?"

"She used to work for the DNR, but she quit so she could be at home for the kids. She freelances now. Articles for magazines, press releases for local businesses. That sort of thing."

"Yikes." Chloe tried to imagine taking care of two kids as a freelance writer, never sure where the next paycheck was coming from. "That can't be easy."

"She seems to do OK with it. She's always liked to write." He glanced in her direction. "What do you like to do?"

What did she like to do? Chloe's brain froze. She wanted to say, I write too. I enjoy folk dancing. I play the dulcimer and the recorder. But she hadn't done any of those things in a long time.

"All I can think about at the moment is getting settled," she managed. "I lived in Switzerland for five years, then moved to North Dakota last fall. Then on to here."

"What were you doing in Switzerland?" he asked.

Getting my heart broken into glittering shards, she thought. "I worked at a huge historic site there. How about you? Have you always worked in Eagle?"

"I worked for the Milwaukee PD for six years. I decided urban crime wasn't my thing, so I moved back out. My mom grew up on a farm not too far from there."

"Oh."

More silence. Chloe looked out the window. "I wanted to ask you about something," Roelke said finally. "You mentioned the maintenance chief yesterday. Stanley something."

"Stanley Colontuono."

"Can you spell that?"

She did.

"All right. Thanks." He flicked on his blinker, checked his mirror, and passed the car ahead of them.

"So ... why did you want to know?"

"I ran across a Stanley in an Eagle bar the other night. He wasn't doing anything wrong. I was just curious. What does your Stanley look like?"

"He's not *my* Stanley." The thought gave her the willies. "Howdy Doody with a beer gut."

"What?" He shot her a perplexed glance.

Oh, Lord. Was this guy so young he'd never watched Howdy Doody? "Mid-thirties. Curly red hair. Cowboy boots."

"Hunh." He nodded thoughtfully. "Sounds like the same guy."

They rode a few more miles in silence. "I have to ask," Chloe said finally. "Why did you invite me to come with you today?"

He kept his gaze on the road. "You're new in the area. You had a rough week. I think you'll like Libby. She's good people."

Fair enough. Chloe settled a little more comfortably into the seat.

Roelke drove north through the Kettle Moraine to Palmyra, a village wrapped around Lower Spring Lake about six miles west of Eagle. His cousin lived in a brick ranch-style home on a quiet side street.

The grass needed cutting, but baskets of pansies gave the place a welcoming air.

As Roelke pulled into the driveway a boy of perhaps six barreled around the corner of the house. "Roelke! Roelke!"

"Hey, Justin!" Roelke greeted the boy with a warmth Chloe wouldn't have guessed possible. Justin wore glasses and an earnest, eager air. He launched a breathless flow of words that circled from finding a turtle to maybe going to a Brewers game with his dad to hoping he could have frozen custard that afternoon.

His mother joined them with a smaller girl in tow. "Catch your breath, buddy," she told Justin. She flashed Roelke a grateful look before turning to Chloe with hand outstretched. "Hi. I'm Libby."

Libby had frank eyes and an open smile. Short chestnut hair, prematurely shot with gray, framed a thin face. Cutoffs and a purple tank top displayed a runner's physique, and her feet were bare. Chloe sensed a woman at home in her own skin.

"Come 'round the back." Libby led the way to a fenced backyard. A flagstone patio spilled from the back wall, furnished with planters and deck chairs, and the biggest grill Chloe had ever seen, something akin to a metal drum tipped on its side. From the patio, Libby could keep an eye on a sandbox, a plastic wading pool, and one of those colorful slide-swing-jungle gym-fort things. Perennial beds provided the yard with a riotous border of reds and blues and yellows. Several birdfeeders hung from a river birch near the back fence.

"This is lovely," Chloe said.

"I live out here in the warm weather," Libby admitted. "Can I get you something to drink? Beer, wine, soda?"

Chloe accepted ginger ale served in a "Phone Home E. T." glass, and settled into a chaise lounge. It felt surprisingly good to sit in the sunshine, watching mourning doves pick at the safflower seed in one of the feeders, letting conversation flow around her. Justin grabbed a handful of taco chips and retreated to a game that involved tossing small beanbags at a target. Dierdre, Libby's three-year-old, settled placidly into the sandbox with a plastic shovel and stack of Tupperware.

"I think I'll start the charcoal," Libby said finally. "We tend to eat early around here because of the kids, Chloe. Hope you don't mind."

"Not at all." All Chloe had eaten that day were two granola bars and a piece of rhubarb cobbler her mother had given her. It belatedly occurred to her that polite people brought hostess gifts when visiting. Flowers or candy or something. Shit.

Libby tore open a bag of charcoal and poured some briquettes into the grill. "So, Chloe. Roelke said you're a curator at Old World. What exactly do you do?"

"Well, I'm responsible for all the collections," Chloe said. "I try to support the interpreters by providing what they need in their buildings."

"Interpreters? Do you have to speak a second language to work there?"

Chloe shook her head. "No. We call the guides 'interpreters' because they interpret the past for visitors. It's really a very demanding job."

"Are the interpreters all pure German or Norwegian or something?" Roelke asked. "People trying to learn about their own background?"

"No! You don't have to be 'pure' anything to work there. Besides, cultural identity is more than racial and ethnic genetics. People can choose what aspects of their background they want to explore and celebrate." Chloe reached for her drink. And that's enough, she told herself. Don't preach.

"I always thought Old World must be a fun place to work," Libby said. Then she turned to her cousin. "What's new on the beat?"

He sipped his beer. "Same old. Speeders. A domestic. A few DUIs. I hate DUIs." His voice tightened and his face took on that granite edge that probably, Chloe thought, scared drunks sober. "Then there's that gambling deal I was telling you about—"

Libby interrupted him with a low, inaudible curse. "There he goes."

"I'll get him." Roelke jumped to his feet as Justin nailed his sister with a hurled bean bag. Libby scooped up Dierdre as she began to wail.

"Justin!" Roelke barked. He reached Justin before the boy could let loose again, and grabbed his wrists. Justin's voice rose in a petulant whine as he stamped his feet, trying to break free. Roelke crouched in front of him, unmoving. As both children's cries subsided, Chloe heard Roelke's low, patient tone.

Once Dierdre was settled back with her toys, Libby rejoined Chloe. "Sorry for that bit of drama. Justin has some issues with misplaced anger."

"That must be difficult for everyone."

"It is." Libby squirted lighter fluid on the coals. "Hardest on him, though." She struck a match, lit the coals, and sank into a lawn chair. "Thank God for Roelke. He moved back out from Milwaukee just as things with my ex-husband were getting really bad. He's been a rock."

"I can see that." It was a revelation.

Libby smiled. "You don't know Roelke very well, do you?"

"I barely know him at all." Chloe sipped her soda. "I, um, happened upon a car crash last Monday. My first day on the job. The driver had just left my office. I found her. Dead. Roelke was the next person to get there."

"So you've experienced his tough cop routine?"

"Is it a routine?"

Libby stretched tanned legs out in front of her. "Yes and no. Do you watch *Hill Street Blues*?"

"Um … what?"

"That cop show? No?" Libby shrugged. "OK, you know the old cliché about the 'good cop, bad cop' thing? Sometimes I think Roelke's both. His dad was a tough old guy—" her face hardened briefly—"but his mom was really sweet. She died before Roelke graduated from high school, though. It was really hard on him."

Chloe looked at Roelke. The discussion concluded, he was pitching balls for Justin, who swung valiantly with a huge red plastic bat. She wasn't sure she wanted to learn these things, personal things, about Roelke McKenna.

OK, time to change the topic. "Roelke said you're a freelance writer?"

"I am. I did it on the side for quite a while, then finally felt ready to jump off the cliff and try it full-time." Libby pulled a Corona from the nearby cooler and poked a wedge of lime into the bottle. "Always something new. And it lets me stay home with the kids."

Chloe watched as Libby put her thumb over the opening and tipped the bottle until the lime floated to the bottom. "I like to write," Chloe said, "but I've wondered if it would stop being fun if I had to actually earn a living at it."

"Hey, Lib?" They were interrupted by a brunette woman opening the gate. She was very young and very pregnant. "Oh—sorry, I didn't realize you had company."

Libby gave her a calculating look. "Lordy, Therese, haven't you had that baby yet?"

"Any day now. Just like Princess Di. Wouldn't it be cool to have a baby the same day the royal prince or princess is born?" Therese smiled, then held out several envelopes. "Here. I got some of your mail in my box by mistake."

"Thanks." Libby inspected the mail, then tossed it on a chair. "Nothing but junk and bills. Want to join us for dinner? You know Roelke, and Chloe here is a friend of his."

"Not tonight, thanks. Jim'll be home soon and we're going over to his parents'. Nice to meet you, Chloe." Therese waved and waddled away.

Chloe picked up her glass, put it down. Wine. That's what she should have brought, a nice bottle of wine. Yes. Wine would have been good. Scotch would have been better.

"Back in a sec." Libby disappeared into the house, then returned with platters of skewered shrimp and veggies. She arranged them carefully over the coals. "So," she said, adjusting the grill lid. "Did you lose a baby?"

For a moment, Chloe forgot to breathe. She realized her fingers were clenching the arms of the chaise lounge, and she carefully softened her grip, watching each finger flush pink as blood began circulating again. Justin connected bat to ball with a resounding *thwack*. "Nice job!" Roelke called.

"Sorry," Libby said. "None of my business. I have a bad habit of saying whatever comes to mind."

"How did you know?"

Libby shrugged. "The way you put your hand over your stomach when Therese was here. The look in your eyes. My best friend lost a baby at eleven weeks. She still gets that same look."

"I had a miscarriage last July. The baby was nine weeks."

"I'm really sorry. My friend miscarried over a year ago, and she's still grieving."

"I'm not grieving." Chloe felt her cheeks flush. "I mean—I didn't even know I was pregnant until I had the miscarriage. You can't mourn a baby you didn't know you had."

Justin and Roelke trooped onto the patio. Chloe was grateful for the interruption. Ethan was the only person in North America who knew about her miscarriage. It was over and done.

"Hey, mom! Is supper ready?"

"Just about." Libby got up to check the kabobs.

Roelke nudged the boy with his knee. Justin looked annoyed, but rattled what was obviously expected: "Mom-I'm-sorry-I-made-a-bad-choice-this-afternoon."

"Thanks, buddy." Libby ruffled his hair. "Go wash up."

Libby had marinated the kabobs in an apricot-curry sauce, and she pulled the skewers of portabella mushrooms and peppers from the glowing coals at exactly the right moment. A course of grilled pineapple and pound cake topped off the meal.

Justin behaved well as they ate, and Libby rewarded him by suggesting a walk to the local frozen custard stand. Chloe treated everyone to a cone, and felt at least somewhat absolved for arriving empty-handed.

Then Roelke and Chloe said their goodbyes.

"Thank you," she told Libby. "I can't remember the last time I ate so well."

"Come back any time, with or without this guy. And listen, I get together once a month with a couple of other writers. We pretend to critique each others' work, but mostly we just drink wine and bitch about the industry. You'd be welcome to join us."

Chloe blinked, absurdly touched. She had missed being in a critique group; had even looked for one when she moved to North Dakota. But being in a crit group meant writing, which seemed as impossible as tap-dancing on the moon, just now. "Thanks," she said again. "I'll let you know."

Roelke didn't speak as they drove south toward La Grange. "I like your cousin," Chloe said.

"Me too," he said simply. "And she's had a hard time of it. Her ex is an ass of the first order."

"That must make it tough, with the kids so young."

His hands tightened on the steering wheel. "Yeah."

"You're obviously a big help with Justin." Was that an OK comment to make? Or too personal? Chloe looked out the window.

"I'd be happy if Justin never saw his dad again, but Dan has custody every other weekend." Roelke slowed to pass two bikers, then accelerated again. Then he asked, "Did you ever talk with an expert about that ale bowl?"

"I talked to my mother." Chloe flushed again. "She knows a lot about rosemaling, past and present."

"Anything interesting come of that?"

Chloe shrugged. "Not really."

Roelke slowed the truck as he approached her driveway. "And you still don't know who might have known about that antique."

She shook her head. "Nope."

"So, is that the end of it?" He parked the truck and turned to look at her.

"Well, I asked my mother to do a little genealogical research on Mrs. Lundquist's family. I only know her married name, so she'll have to track back to the wedding records. But who knows? Maybe when she gets far enough in she'll turn up some tidbit that will suggest something." Chloe spread her hands. "I'm going to keep looking for that piece, and for whatever it was that made that poor old lady so desperate to get it back."

"Why?" His tone was quiet, but his gaze was piercing.

Chloe stared at her landlord, cutting hay in the field across the road. "Because I owe Mrs. Lundquist that much."

Roelke pulled his wallet from a pocket, extracted a business card, and scribbled something on it. "Here. Call me if you find anything new. This one has my home phone."

Chloe accepted the card. "Well … thanks again. I really enjoyed meeting Libby and the kids." She put her hand on the door handle.

"My schedule is irregular, but would you like to go out again sometime? Maybe listen to some music?"

Chloe felt a spasm of panic. Then a flicker of hope. It would be good, really good, to go hear live music. "I know a great bluegrass place near Fort Atkinson."

"Bluegrass?" Roelke's expression implied she had suggested listening to a fingernails-on-chalkboard band. "How about jazz?"

"Southern rock?"

"Blues?"

They stared at each other. Chloe didn't know whether their standoff was funny or sad. "Thank you," she said finally, "but I don't think this is going to work."

—

Well hell, Roelke thought, as he drove away from Chloe's house. Maybe he should have given the bluegrass place a try. But what would be the point? He hated twangy music. Always had.

So. Maybe he should just forget all about Chloe Ellefson.

If only there wasn't that—that *something* about her. Something that made his stomach muscles tighten. Something that made him see her behind his eyelids when he went to bed at night. Something that made him want to stand between her and all the trouble in the world. Something that made him yearn to make her laugh, to say something to bring that rarely-seen spark of heartfelt enthusiasm in her blue eyes. Something that made him want to twine his fingers in that incredible yellow hair, and to trace the hollows in her cheeks ....

The truck lurched as the right wheels fell from the road to the gravel shoulder. "Jesus!" Roelke yelped, jerking the vehicle back into the lane. He gave the mirror a quick glance, relieved to see empty road behind him. No witnesses to his erratic driving. That kind of thing could bite a cop in the butt.

When he got back to Palmyra he swerved onto a side road instead of heading to his own apartment. Two minutes later he parked beside the town's tiny municipal airport. He got out of his truck and leaned against the hood, feeling the sun and breeze on his face, feeling his nerves settle. He'd flown in and out of Palmyra a couple of times when he'd been working on his pilot's license, practicing take-offs and landings as he hopped between airstrips within a quick flight's distance of Milwaukee's Timmerman. The runway here was turf. There was something elemental and immensely satisfying about landing on a grass strip.

The field was quiet at the moment, but a couple of planes were tied down near the hangar. One was a bright yellow Piper Cub. A sweet little canvas-topped tail-dragger.

Roelke wanted it, bad.

He'd been saving money to buy a plane for a long time. He'd gotten some after his parents died; the rest he'd tucked away himself. He didn't earn a lot of money as a cop—especially in Eagle, when he couldn't even count on forty hours a week. But he lived simply, didn't spend a lot, and picked up extra shifts whenever he could. It added up. For a while he'd lusted after a Cessna Cardinal, one of the prettiest planes ever built. They were much more expensive, though, unless he wanted to buy a share. But a Piper ... he probably had enough money in the bank to start looking around for one.

Roelke couldn't remember when he hadn't wanted a plane. The dream may have been born when, as a very young boy, he'd watched old World War II movies of pilots soaring, shooting, almost single-handedly winning the war. Or it may have been born one particular September day when he was a few years older, and his father's temper had driven Roelke outside. He remembered sitting against the side of the house, watching an airplane cross the sky and thinking, *That's* what I want. That had probably happened not long before his mother took him to her parents' farm for good....

As the image of the tired old family farm popped into his head Roelke folded his arms and sighed. He wanted a plane. But inexplicably, stupidly, he wanted the farm, too.

He pressed one knuckle against his forehead, willing away the memories of his ancestors working those acres. He hated farming. He loved flying. Farms were dead weight. Planes were freedom. It should be simple.

It wasn't.

What would Chloe think? Despite its current decrepit condition, she'd surely like the farm. That's what she did, right? Look at old stuff and see its value? An ale bowl, a farmhouse, it was likely much the same. But did she like to fly? He didn't know. And whether he ever owned a plane or not, the sheer joy of *flight* was part of who he was.

Roelke shook his head in disgust. As if it mattered. He and Chloe Ellefson seemed incapable of easy conversation, much less anything more.

He gave the Cub one last look. Then he got back into his truck and drove home.

TWELVE

Chloe spent much of Monday sitting at the picnic table in the restoration area, reading about the site buildings so she had at least a vague clue about how she could help the interpreters do their jobs. Chloe would be making presentations to the summer interpreters in each of Old World Wisconsin's areas—the Crossroads Village, German, Norwegian, and Finn-Dane.

She was reading about a Finnish family that afternoon when a shadow fell across the page. Chloe looked up to see Stanley Colontuono standing by the table. The maintenance chief wore snakeskin cowboy boots today with his tan pants and work shirt.

Chloe closed the research report. "Hey, Stan. You need the table?"

"Naw." He waved a generous hand: *You may stay*. "I just saw you sitting here all day and figured you must be getting lonely."

"Well … not really. I'm catching up on the research reports for each exhibit."

"You want to go out sometime?"

"I—what?" she stammered inelegantly. She got to her feet.

"You and me." Stan gave her a grin that might have been wicked if she didn't keep flashing on the image of a marionette dangling in Buffalo Bob's capable hands. "We could stop for a drink at Sasso's one night after work."

"I don't think so, Stan," Chloe said, as pleasantly as possible. "Thanks anyway."

For a split second, the confident leer on Stan's face wavered. Then he gave an exaggerated shrug. "Sure thing, doll," he said, with a smile that made Chloe's knee long to make contact with his nether regions. "Oops. I mean, *ma'am*. I guess some women like being lonely. My mistake." He walked away, climbed into his truck, and roared off.

Chloe leaned her butt against the table. How would her refusal to visit Doodyville impact any help she might need from the maintenance department?

Then Nika's Chevette rattled through the gate and parked near the trailers. Nika emerged and walked toward Chloe with lithe grace, looking especially trim in snug jeans and a tailored black blouse. Nika had pulled her cornrow braids back and secured them behind her neck with a vibrant green ribbon. They'd made a date to move the textile collection from the storage trailers to the church basement as soon as the site closed that day.

"What's up?" Nika asked.

Chloe gave herself a mental shake. "Just waiting for you."

"Look at that." Nika scowled at one of the maintenance vehicles, evidently parked for the night on the far side of the lot. "I asked Stanley if we could borrow a truck, and he said nothing was available."

"Stanley is a jackass," Chloe said. "Never mind. We can get it done. It'll just take a lot of trips." Neither her old Pinto nor Nika's old Chevette had much cargo capacity.

Nika waved that away. "No, my fiancé is meeting us here to give us a hand. His car's got a big trunk. It just pisses me off that Stanley wouldn't help."

Chloe and Nika were hauling boxes of textiles outside when a gleaming silver Eldorado pulled into the parking lot. A genuine smile softened Nika's face as she went to greet the young white man who got out. He was thin, almost gangly, and stood a head taller than Nika. He framed her face with both hands, his face glowing, before leaning down for a long kiss. Chloe turned away and fumbled with a bag of quilts.

Then Nika led the young man forward. "This is my fiancé, Joel Carlisle."

Joel wore horn-rimmed glasses and a Chicago Bears cap. Chloe wondered what punched the most hot buttons in rural Wisconsin: dating a black woman, driving a Cadillac, or rooting for the Bears. "You're a life saver," Chloe told him.

"No problem." Joel shrugged. "I know Nika's eager to make progress with the textiles." The pride in his smile twisted Chloe's heart.

It took several trips, but the three of them got all of the textiles transported to the new storage area before dusk. "Well, it's a start," Chloe observed, wiping grubby palms on the seat of her pants. Boxes and bags of quilts and bonnets, blouses and tablecloths, were piled on Nika's table.

Joel looked at his fiancé. "You've got your work cut out for you."

"Yes I do," Nika agreed placidly.

At least *someone* was doing serious collections work that summer. "You guys up for dinner at Sasso's?" Chloe asked. "I'm buying."

The tavern was busier than she'd expected for a Monday night. After washing up, she and Nika and Joel settled at the bar to wait for a table. Chloe ordered a Pabst for Joel, and glasses of Zinfandel for her and Nika. Chloe could see why the Old World staff loved Sasso's. The crowded tavern had a friendly vibe that reminded Chloe of her favorite pub in Brienz. That one served the best *rösti, raclette,* and *äelplermagronen* in the canton, though. Vegetarian heaven. But no surprise; Markus had delighted in finding restaurants that served food she could actually enjoy.

Well, no *raclette* tonight. Chloe was glad when their drinks arrived. She lifted her glass. "Here's to a good start." She had to shout to be heard above the din of chatter and laughter and the TV over the bar. "Thanks again, Joel. Nika and I would be lugging textiles by flashlight if you hadn't helped out."

"My pleasure." He grinned, leaning one elbow on the bar. "From what glimpses I got, we hauled a lot of white stuff. Linen, cotton. Those pieces should clean up pretty well, right?" He looked to Nika.

"Right," she said. "A good soak, a little sunshine—they'll perk right up."

Chloe smiled at Joel. "You've obviously absorbed some tricks of the trade."

"Hard not to, living with this lady. She tends to bring work home, figuratively if not literally." He bumped his shoulder into Nika's affectionately. "I don't mind. I've always been a history buff."

Chloe really wished these two didn't quite so clearly adore each other. You're being petty, she told herself, but there it was. She and Markus had once been like that, playful and openly affectionate. Hadn't they? "I understand you're studying to be a pharmacist?" she asked, trying to focus.

"That's right. Not sexy, but necessary nonetheless."

Nika put her glass down. "Excuse me. I see the German lead over there. Jenny asked me a question about the tealeaf china in Schottler, and I looked it up for her."

Chloe sighed as she watched her intern slide through the crowd to a warm welcome. "I don't even recognize the woman she's talking to," Chloe said, "much less know her name. I've told everyone their questions will have to wait until I get my feet on the ground. I don't know how Nika keeps it all straight."

"She's something," Joel agreed, that proud shine in his eyes again.

"So, how did you two meet?"

"In the Marquette library. I was doing some genealogical research and she was researching nineteenth-century black quiltmakers for a class paper. The focus knob on her microfilm reader wasn't working right. I gallantly offered her the use of my machine." He grinned at the memory. "She was all fired up. Her professor didn't think she'd find enough information to satisfy his requirements."

Chloe swiveled back and forth on her barstool. "And did she?"

"Oh, yeah. After working through the standard archival materials and collections, she contacted all the black churches in the city. Conducted a bunch of interviews. She ended up with over a dozen documented examples. Got an A on the paper *and* curated an exhibit at the county historical society."

Chloe watched Nika across the room, chatting with Jenny. "That young woman is going to go far."

"I know."

"I keep trying to remember if I ever had that much energy." Chloe sipped her wine, feeling old and tired.

"She is driven." Joel's gaze was on Nika too. "There's a lot she wants to accomplish, and a lot she wants to leave behind." He turned back to Chloe with a lopsided smile. "I'm so glad you gave her the chance to take on the textile project. She can handle it, and maybe she'll find a piece or two worthy of further study."

"Well, I don't know what she'll discover among the textiles. But she's doing important work for the site. We're lucky it worked out for you to live nearby."

"My parents invited us to stay with them this summer, but we decided to rent a little place in Eagle. I thought it would be easier for Nika. My hours at the lab are flexible, and I don't mind the drive."

"Did you grow up in Milwaukee too?"

"Whitefish Bay."

Chloe worked hard to keep her eyebrows, which itched to shoot skyward, in neutral position. She didn't know Milwaukee well, but she'd heard of the exclusive suburb.

"Nika works long hours as it is," Joel was saying. "If she's not here, she's at some library or another. If we had to add a long commute to that, I'd never see her."

"Oh, it's not so bad as all that." Nika had returned in time to hear his last comment. "If I didn't work evenings I'd be twiddling my thumbs while you fall asleep over an organic chemistry textbook."

Ah, young love, Chloe thought. Fortunately, pharmacists were needed everywhere. If Nika pursued her museum career as doggedly as she seemed to do everything else, Joel would be moving—often.

"Hey, hi!" Delores Timberlake, the Norwegian lead, stopped beside them. She still wore her period clothing, with the unconscious ease of someone who spent as much time in costume as she did in modern dress. After being introduced to Joel, she looked from Chloe to Nika. "You're coming out to Norwegian to do training tomorrow, right? Is there anything you want me to do to get ready?"

Chloe shook her head. "I don't think so, thanks. Byron only gave us an hour. It'll go by pretty quickly."

Delores caught the bartender's eye and ordered a soda, then turned back to Chloe. "Any luck finding that missing Norwegian bowl?"

The image of Mrs. Lundquist's eyes—first pleading, then sightless—flashed through Chloe's brain. "No."

"Are we missing an ethnic piece?" Nika asked. Her cat-like eyes narrowed like a tom's on scenting a mouse. "What do you know about it?"

Chloe tried not to cringe, wishing the topic hadn't been raised inside this crowded bar. "Very little, so far. It's the piece that donor came to talk with me about. The woman who died in that car wreck. I'm taking care of it." Chloe spotted a group getting up from a table across the room. She put her empty glass on the bar and stood. "Let's see if we can grab that table."

Sasso's was noisy and hazed with cigarette smoke, and by the time they finished their meal—chicken for Joel and Nika, grilled cheese for Chloe—her head ached. Joel took care of the check, and Chloe decided not to be bothered by that. "It was great to meet you, Joel," she said, as the three of them made their way outside. "Thanks again for your help."

He flashed that endearing grin. "No problem. Holler if there's anything else I can do to get the collections program up and rolling."

They crossed the railroad tracks to the parking lot. "I'll meet you at the church at three to go over the plan for training," Nika told Chloe.

"Right," Chloe said. "Oh—Nika? I need to check on a wallpaper problem in Tobler. If I come by at 2:30 instead, do you want to go with me?"

Nika shrugged. "Sure, if you want."

Nika's no-nonsense demeanor was exactly what Chloe wanted. You are pathetic, she told herself, as she turned toward her car. Your intern is already climbing over you on her way to the top, and you ask her to come with you to check wallpaper. *Wallpaper.* Well, so be it. Tobler freaked her out, and she wanted company—

A wordless cry from Nika pulled her back. Nika and Joel stood staring at Nika's Chevette. Nika's expression was quickly changing from shock to fury. Joel, looking stunned, put a protective arm around her shoulders.

"What's wrong?" Chloe asked sharply.

Nika put her hands on her hips, her face tight. "Some fucking bastard slashed my tires!"

Chloe was exhausted by the time she started driving home. She'd waited with Joel and Nika for the police to arrive. The responding officer—not Roelke McKenna—had been unable to guess why someone would slash the tires on Nika's rust-bucket Chevette while ignoring Joel's luxury vehicle. "Probably just random vandalism," the cop had said.

Had it been random? Or ... had someone done it because Nika was black? Chloe felt sick. Lights glowed from the houses she passed, warm and welcoming. She wished she'd thought to leave a light on at her place.

Then another light caught her eye—this one tiny, and red, and blinking a furious warning from the control panel of her car.

"Oh, no," Chloe groaned. She pulled over and parked beneath a streetlight. She got out, raised the hood, and stared at the motor. No smoke, no flames. No obviously dangling parts.

Back in the car, she flicked on the interior light and retrieved her owner's manual from the glove compartment. Her particular light translated to "See your dealer." Right. She had no idea where the nearest Ford dealership was.

Headlights flashed in her mirror as a familiar blue Mustang stopped beside her. Rupert, the maintenance worker who'd provoked Stan to fury by coming in late, rolled down his window. "You all right? I recognized your car."

"A warning light came on. I'm trying to figure out if I can drive to a garage."

He got out and shoved his hair away from his eyes long enough to fiddle with a couple of caps, check a couple of dipsticks. "Fluids are OK. She making any noise?"

"Nope. Just the warning light."

"You should be all right. I'd take it down to Elkhorn. George's Garage. He's pretty good. First Avenue, near the Fairgrounds."

Chloe decided to believe that Rupert knew what he was talking about. "Thanks for the advice. I really appreciate you stopping."

Rupert headed back to his Mustang, then stopped. "Hey, you gonna be OK? You need a ride from Elkhorn? I could follow you, if you want."

"No, but thanks," she told him. "My parents don't live too far away. I'll call them."

Chloe drove off with her spirits lifted. There were still good people in the world.

She found the garage, parked her car, slid a note under the door for George to find in the morning, and considered. It was almost ten o'clock. George had thoughtfully installed a pay phone on his lot, but she didn't want to bother her parents at this hour. She called a cab instead.

The cab arrived twenty minutes later, and twenty minutes after that, deposited her at her back door. "Thanks again for accepting the check," Chloe told the driver as she got out, hoping it wouldn't bounce. Cab fares were not in the budget.

Then she unlocked the door to her dark, empty house, and went to bed.

Chloe stared into the darkness, wondering what had awakened her. As usual, she'd raised every ground-floor window. Occasionally she heard snorts from the Holsteins pastured just beyond the driveway, but something unfamiliar had disturbed her sleep. She waited. Then she heard the noise again—a hushed *scritch* of sound.

She kicked aside her sleeping bag and got up. She listened. Nothing. She padded silently to her bedroom door and stopped, straining to hear the noise again. The front door to the house was just ahead of her, to her right. Beyond the door was a window which opened onto the porch.

Scri-i-itch.

The noise came from that window beyond the door. Chloe heard another tiny sound, a hushed *thump*. Someone had pulled the screen from the window, and set it quietly on the porch.

Her hand found the light switch by the front door. "*Hey!*" she yelled, flicking it on. In the sudden glare she glimpsed a foot and leg extending through the window. In an instant it was gone. Something thumped again on the porch, much louder this time. Scrambling footsteps pounded over the boards. Then silence.

Chloe flipped the porch light on and jerked at the front door knob. The old door stuck, and she had to wrestle with it before wrenching it open. No one in sight. As she ran across the porch and into the yard, a car with no headlights on roared away.

A sickle moon shed little light. Chloe stood, waiting, feeling the grass cool and damp beneath her feet. Finally she blew out a long breath and turned back toward the house. The window screen lay on the porch. It was inexpensive, the type intended to slide easily in and out, held in place only by the weight of the open window.

Chloe stared at the screen. "Son of a bitch," she whispered.

THIRTEEN

Roelke jerked awake when the telephone rang. His feet hit the floor, his hand reached for the bedside lamp, and his brain switched into gear. One-fifteen A.M. He snatched the phone. "McKenna here."

"Roelke? It's Chloe. Someone just tried to break into my house."

His throat tightened. "Did you call the cops?"

"What? Yes!"

"OK. Unless you have reason to believe that someone is in the house, stay inside and sit tight. Call your neighbors so you're not alone. I'll be right down." He pulled on jeans and extracted his service revolver from the lockbox under his bed, grabbed his truck keys, and ran down his flat's exterior staircase.

He hit Highway 59 at an illegal speed and kept at it as he wound through the state forest toward La Grange. When Roelke pulled into Chloe's driveway, anger pulled his muscles even tighter. Chloe sat on the front porch steps, faintly illuminated by the light spilling from the farmhouse interior. No one else was in sight—no cop cars flashing red and blue, no hovering landlords defending their property.

He jumped from the truck and strode toward the porch. "What are you *doing?* I told you to wait inside!"

"I didn't want to wait inside. I needed air." She stood to meet him. A baggy green T-shirt proclaiming "WVU Foresters Do It In The Woods" almost covered her denim shorts. She was barefoot.

"Did you call your neighbors?"

"I don't want to wake them. They're dairy farmers, for God's sake. The guy is gone. There's nothing here that can't wait until morning."

He glared at her, angry and incredulous and painfully aware of her long blonde hair. He'd never seen it completely loose before, flowing past her waist. "What about the cops?" he demanded. "You *told* me you'd already called the cops!"

"I called *you!*"

Roelke quivered with the effort of keeping his hands from those thin shoulders. He wanted to shake some sense into her. He finally turned and walked away. One deep breath. Another. OK, a few more. Finally he felt ready to try again.

She stood waiting on the steps, arms folded, jaw set.

"Let's start over." Roelke managed the calm, pleasant tone he'd perfected on the beat. "First of all, your home is out of my jurisdiction. I'm employed by the Village of Eagle. You don't live in Eagle. You don't even live in Waukesha County."

She considered that. "Oh. Yeah."

"And second, you didn't call the station. If you had, you'd have been routed to Walworth County."

"Oh."

"You called my home number," Roelke added, feeling a need to make his position crystal-clear.

"OK, I get it." She sighed. "I guess I screwed up. Sorry."

"A local car could have been here in half the time it took me. If you'd been threatened, that might have made all the difference." Roelke ran a hand over his hair, not liking the images flashing through his head. "All right. Tell me what happened."

"Can we go inside? I really don't want to wake up my neighbors."

Roelke ground his teeth together, and followed her into the house.

She gestured to her bedroom door. "I was asleep, and a noise woke me up. I got up to listen. I was standing here in the doorway when I realized that someone was pulling the screen out of that window." She pointed.

Roelke's chest tightened as he looked from her bedroom to the open window. She'd only been a few feet from the intruder. "What happened next?"

"I heard the screen hit the porch. Then I flipped the light switch and yelled 'Hey!' The guy had one leg in the window, but he jumped backwards when I yelled. It sounded like he fell. I tried to get the front door open but it's been humid, and it sticks. You know how old houses can be—"

"Could you please finish the story?" Roelke managed, through gritted teeth.

"So, I finally got the door open." Chloe tucked a strand of that incredible hair behind her ear. "By then he was gone. I ran out into the yard, but I couldn't see anyone—"

"You ran into the yard?" Roelke exploded. "Jesus! Are you incredibly brave, or just stupid?"

"I *beg* your pardon?"

"Two days ago you went into that trailer without knowing if an intruder was inside. I *told* you not to do anything like that again—"

"I don't take orders from you!"

"And now—what possessed you to open your front door, knowing an intruder was on your front porch?"

"I—I wanted to run him off, I guess. Or maybe get a look at him. I don't know! It all happened really fast."

Roelke began to pace. "And then you ran out into the yard! What the *hell* were you thinking?"

"I said I don't know! It was just instinct! Stop bellowing!" She clasped her elbows, arms across her chest.

He paced a moment longer, struggling to rein in feelings that didn't want to be corralled. "You could have been beaten. Or stabbed. Or raped. Or killed."

Chloe rubbed her forehead. "Look, I'm sorry if I didn't follow your rulebook, but I've never had someone break into my house before." She walked into the living room and dropped into one of the armchairs.

Roelke followed and perched on the sofa, leaning forward, elbows on knees. "Let's get back to what happened. You ran into the yard, but didn't see anyone?"

"A door slammed. Then a car drove away without any lights on. I think the guy had left it parked out by the road."

Roelke had talked to many women who'd been victims of one type of assault or another. Too many. He'd never seen a woman so calm. "Chloe." He tasted the word, realizing it was the first time he'd called her by name. "Chloe, do you have any idea who this intruder was?"

"Of course not!"

"Is there any particular reason why a man would want to break into your house? An old boyfriend? An angry spouse?"

"No. Nothing like that."

"Current boyfriend? Anyone you're seeing socially?"

"No."

Was that good news or bad? Roelke wasn't sure. "How about people you work with? Any weird vibes there?"

"Weird vibes? Well . . ." She considered. "Hank DiCapo, the security guard—I ticked him off the first day. Byron Cooke, curator of interpretation—I ticked him off my first day too. Stanley, the maintenance guy—I ticked him off this afternoon—"

Roelke sat back. "How long have you been working there again?"

She shot him an irritated glance. "Well, you asked. And if you want a full list, I should add Ralph Petty, the director." She spread her hands, palms up. "But . . . so what? None of them have any reason to break into my house."

"Let's go back to the moment you turned on the light. Close your eyes and tell me exactly what you saw."

She hesitated, then obeyed. "My eyes squinched up when I turned the light on. But I have this impression of a foot in a white running shoe. White with red styling on the side. And blue jeans above it, just about to the knee. That's all." She opened her eyes again.

"Man's foot? Woman's?"

"Um . . . I don't know."

"Not a lot to go on." He didn't like this. Didn't like it at all.

Chloe nibbled her bottom lip. "I'll tell you what I think. First of all, I left my car at a garage in Elkhorn tonight, so whoever broke in probably thought no one was at home. Second . . ."

"What?"

"Well, maybe someone was looking for that ale bowl. Whoever was pressuring Mrs. Lundquist to get it back. Whoever went out to Kvaale, and broke into the storage trailer, looking for it. Maybe they thought I'd found it."

"Why go so nuts over a particular antique that no one had seen in years?"

"If not that, then what?" she demanded. "Why pick this particular old farmhouse to break into? I don't have anything worth stealing. There's nothing in here but second-hand furniture from my parents' attic and a bunch of cardboard cartons."

But criminals aren't always rational, he wanted to tell her. Sometimes bad things happen to pretty women—things I don't want you to even know about.

He stood up. "I'm going to look around outside."

After grabbing the heavy-duty flashlight from his truck, he searched the yard before going back inside. "Nothing," he reported. "Do you mind if I look at your other ground-floor windows?"

"Go ahead." She managed a tiny smile. "I do appreciate your help, really. It was very kind of you to come."

Roelke worked his way around, living room to kitchen to dining room to bathroom, closing and locking each window. And fighting a new layer of unease. He was used to poking through other people's houses. He'd been called to the homes of the rich and the poor. The slovenly and the tidy. The well-furnished and the cheaply cobbled-together. He'd been in homes that emanated warmth, homes crackling with tension, homes that made the hairs on the back of his neck quiver. He'd never been in a house like this one that exuded . . . nothing.

He checked Chloe's bedroom last. No clutter on the dresser. Shelves empty of books. Nothing but an unzipped sleeping bag on a mattress.

The only memento in the room—in the whole house—was a photograph. He studied the snapshot of a younger Chloe on some mountaintop. She stood bent slightly forward to accommodate a backpack, hands tucked under the shoulder straps as if to relieve some of its weight. Her companion, a bearded man, stood erect beneath his pack. Both, sweat-stained, grinned deliriously at the camera.

Roelke clenched his jaw. I don't know who you are, buddy, he thought. But if Chloe cares enough about you to keep this photograph out, you damn sure should be here making sure she's OK.

Finally he rejoined her in the living room. "I locked all the windows," he told her. "The screens are too flimsy. Talk to your landlord tomorrow about replacing them."

"What about the screen the burglar pulled out? It's still lying on the porch."

"We'll leave it for the Walworth County boys." He doubted they would make much of it, but that was their call.

"OK. Listen, Roelke?" She tipped her head to one side. "I'm really, *truly* grateful to you for coming down. Now … I need to get some sleep."

"Me, too. Mind if I crash on your sofa for the rest of the night? I'm pretty fried."

That was a lie. He knew it, and he was pretty sure she knew it too. He waited.

"Um … sure," she said. "That would be fine."

—

Chloe lay awake, staring at the ceiling, wondering if Roelke was awake, too. She was clearly weirding him out.

Well, so be it. She needed to find out who wanted Mrs. Lundquist's ale bowl so badly. And why. This was no longer some well-intentioned but impersonal diversion. It *was* personal, now.

Mrs. Lundquist may have been afraid of you, she told the unknown culprit silently. But *I'm* not afraid of you. I have nothing to lose, and one way or another, I'm going to figure this mess out.

Chloe heard Roelke stirring a little after six. Groggy, she got up and pulled on a pair of jeans and her favorite dark green shirt. She found him in her kitchen, staring dubiously into her refrigerator.

"I'm not big on breakfast," she said. "The fridge is dead, anyway."

"So I see." He shut the refrigerator door. "I hope I didn't wake you."

"No," she mumbled, stifling a yawn. He startled her by smiling. It made him look even younger than usual. Chloe felt herself smile too.

Roelke glanced at his watch. "If you can be ready to go in, say, twenty minutes, I can run you down to Elkhorn."

She shoved some hair back from her face. "Well ... OK. Thanks. That'll save me another cab fare. Just let me call work and say I'm going to be late."

Roelke's good humor slipped back behind his cop face on the drive. He didn't speak until he pulled up in front of a nondescript diner called the Cloverleaf. "This place serves good food."

Chloe climbed out of the truck and turned back to him before shutting the door. "Thanks again. I'm grateful."

"Get some eggs, and some juice," he ordered. "A nutritious breakfast will do you good. After you get your car, don't forget to stop at the sheriff's station."

"I don't need you to tell me ..." Chloe stared at her double reflection in his sunglasses and swallowed what she'd been about to say. "I won't forget."

The diner was noisy and smelled of fried eggs and baking bread. Most of the customers were farmers and truckers, by the looks of them. Always a good sign. Chloe bought a newspaper and an enormous apple fritter, and settled down at a corner table. Three cups of coffee later, she felt more ready to face the day.

A large check freed her car from George, the mechanic. Car repairs were not in the budget. Chloe was starting to think she'd have to hit her parents up for a loan. Depressing thought.

An incident report freed her from further responsibility at the sheriff's office. A polite young deputy declined Chloe's offer to produce the window screen in question. "Call us if you see any further suspicious activity," he said.

My suspicions are spread over three counties, Chloe thought, as she drove toward Old World Wisconsin. The historic site ... her own farmhouse ... Mrs. Lundquist's home. Maybe she should have searched the dead woman's home more thoroughly when she had the chance. But for *what*?

Roelke sat at the station that afternoon, trying to tune out the music from Marie's radio. Her favorite station played groups like Air Supply and The Little River Band. The bland sugar-pop made his teeth ache.

All right. Focus. He opened his file box of index cards, and spread out his big Eagle street map in front of him. Whenever he answered a call, Roelke either created an index card for the address or added to an existing card. Then he made a tiny corresponding X on the map. Red for domestics, green for drugs, blue for everything else. A line of red Xs marked a house on Hawthorne Drive. The woman who lived there called 911 whenever her husband hit her, but then always refused to press charges. A line of blue Xs marked an elderly widow's house. She lived behind the school, and called whenever she heard kids on the grounds after dark.

Now he penciled a circle around an empty rectangle that represented Stanley Colontuono's house, a nondescript ranch at the end of a quiet residential street. Roelke had checked his record. Two traffic violations in the past three years, nothing more. Nothing more in the county files, either.

Roelke frowned. He didn't have a damn thing to pin on Stanley Colontuono. But the man had been hiding *something*, that night at the bar.

"Watcha looking at?" Skeet Deardorff suddenly loomed over his shoulder. He was a round-faced, ginger-haired man in his mid-twenties who was already married and the father of two.

"Nothing much."

"That's the blue house at the end of Marigold Court?" Skeet leaned close and tapped the spot Roelke had circled. "Did you get another disturbance call?"

Another? Roelke turned his chair to look at Skeet. "What was the first one?"

"I responded to a call ... I think it was two Friday nights ago. A neighbor complained about loud music." Skeet stepped to his locker, opened it, and began unbuttoning his uniform shirt.

Roelke frowned. "Did you write it up?"

"No," Skeet admitted, with a sheepish shrug.

"*Jesus*, Skeet!"

"I was about to go off shift, and I was dog-tired." Skeet said defensively. "It was no big deal. I knocked on the door, the guy answered, I told him to turn the tunes down, he did. He even apologized."

"Hunh."

On the radio, Olivia Newton John was begging someone to get physical. Skeet pulled a polo shirt over his head. "Say, do you know if that uniform allowance got approved?"

"It did," Marie said over her shoulder. She didn't stop typing. "It'll show up two checks from now."

Roelke reminded himself that there was no such thing as a private conversation when Marie was in the building.

"See you tomorrow," Skeet said, slamming his locker. "I've got class."

Skeet was taking criminal justice classes at Waukesha Tech, one at a time, somehow squeezing them in between work and family life. He'd probably get the full-time spot, sloppy reports or not, Roelke thought sourly. He folded his map away. Time to head out.

"Roelke." Marie actually stopped, swiveled in her chair. "You got a problem with that house at the end of Marigold?"

"Not really," Roelke said carefully. "Why?"

"Because my mother lives on Marigold. When I was giving her a perm the other day, she was complaining about all the traffic in and out of that house. She said it had suddenly gotten bad in the past couple of weeks."

"Yeah?" This was getting more interesting.

"Yeah. A lot of kids, mom said." Marie snorted. "Teens, she meant. There's mostly older folks on that street, so it stands out."

"Any pattern? Particular days, or times of day, that she sees people coming and going?"

Marie shrugged. "I didn't ask. Just told her to call it in if she saw anybody breaking any law. Last I knew, it wasn't illegal to have a lot of company. Mom's bored, and she always has to have something to fuss about. I don't pay much attention. You and Skeet just reminded me, that's all." She swiveled her chair back to the typewriter. Conversation over.

That was OK. Marie had given Roelke something new to mull over as he headed out on patrol.

FOURTEEN

"So, WHAT'S THE PROBLEM here?" Nika asked, as she and Chloe approached the Tobler house.

"The wallpaper is already peeling away from the plaster. And the village lead wants some interpretive context for the artifacts in here." Chloe took a long slow breath, and unlocked the door.

The remembered sensations slapped Chloe as soon as she stepped inside. A corporeal sense of unhappiness quivered in the small room.

Nika crouched by one of the wallpaper seams, fingering a puckering edge. "I ran into this problem in grad school. Do you use modern paste, knowing it will be more durable? Or period formulas?"

Chloe's skin began to prickle. She sensed frustration.

"My professor said..."

Enough. Chloe pivoted and stepped back into the sunshine.

Geez Louise. This was going to be a problem.

Chloe couldn't remember the first time she'd felt a presence in an old building. Her memories of family vacations were a blur of long car rides and visits to historic sites. Sometimes these creaking places gave her distinct impressions of emotions: contentment, sadness, loneliness. "This is a happy house, Mommy," she remembered whispering loudly in the middle of a guided tour. Her parents had smiled, the guide had been charmed, and Chloe hadn't realized that she was being indulged, not affirmed. It was only on another trip, when she'd burst into tears at the front door of a homesteader's cabin, that she'd learned that everyone else didn't react to old buildings the way she sometimes did. "Don't go in!" she'd sobbed. "It's a bad house!" Her father had eventually carried her to the gift shop while her mother and older sister Kari took the tour.

Eventually Chloe got used to tuning the sensations out—just as she tuned out background chatter when reading or studying in a crowded coffee shop. She also learned not to speak of her impressions. By the time she'd decided to enter museum work, it took an unexpected whammy to rattle her.

The Tobler house rattled her.

Nika followed her outside, looking cool, collected, and distinctly unrattled. "Hey, you OK?"

"Just a little tired. I was listening, though."

Nika looked dubious, but she shrugged. "Well, as I was saying, I prefer period *everything*—materials and techniques. That way the whole fabric of a building becomes a research tool. Instead of the interpreters being embarrassed by peeling wallpaper, they can explain that we're experimenting. Visitors love behind-the-scenes stuff."

"Yeah." Chloe locked the door, and they headed back down the walk. "But you know, I don't even know if wallpaper falls into my purview. It might be more of a structural issue. I think I need to talk to the curator of research—what's her name?"

"Margueritte Donovan."

Of course Nika would know that. "Come on," Chloe said, glancing at her watch. "We're due in the Norwegian area."

An hour later, Chloe stood on the porch of the Kvaale House, facing a dozen interpreters—some new, some veteran. "How many of you have visited some historic site and found that the entire tour consisted of a docent pointing out one artifact after another?" she asked. "'This settee was made in England... this teapot dates to 1743... that portrait is of Sir Roger himself'... et cetera. That's what I call a furniture tour. If you take just one thought away from our time together today, I hope it's this: artifacts are most important because of what they reveal about the people who made, owned, or used them."

She let that thought sink in before continuing. "Let me show you an example." Chloe nodded to Nika, who held up an 8x10 black and white photograph.

"What do you see?" Chloe asked.

"Some people and a bunch of stuff," one of the college students said.

An older man took the photo from Nika and squinted at it thoughtfully. "Mid-nineteenth-century people sitting in front of a big frame house, with a sewing machine and croquet set and nice furniture. It looks like that one woman has an unusual collar on... maybe ethnic?"

Chloe nodded. "The shape of that woman's collar suggests a Norwegian style. Why do you suppose this family dragged furniture outside for the photograph?"

"Well... they wanted to make a record of it."

"This photograph was taken by a Norwegian-American photographer named Andreas Dahl," Chloe told them. "I think this family wanted to show how far they'd come since moving to Wisconsin. When they moved from their first cabin into a new frame house, they posed with some of the possessions they were most proud of."

"We show that transition here in the Norwegian Area," Delores Timberlake pointed out. "Visitors can learn about a newly arrived immigrant family at Fossebrekke, and a more established family here at Kvaale."

"Exactly!" Chloe nodded at Byron, who had walked up the drive to join the group. "Here at Kvaale, the ethnic pieces have been largely relegated to display status. They're no longer being used; the family has new American-made items instead. Your job isn't to talk about the artifacts themselves, but to tell the broader story."

Cindy, the frustrated spinner Chloe had met on her first visit to the Kvaale farm, raised her hand. "But sometimes visitors ask about specific artifacts," she said. "Are you saying we can't answer their questions?"

"Not at all!" Chloe felt a welcome stir of her old passion for museum education. "Use that piece to help address a bigger interpretive theme. If a visitor asks about the spinning wheel, you can tell them when it was made and how it works. But then go on to tell them about the role of sheep in the Kvaale family's economy, or the agricultural shift from subsistence farming to diversification, or about gender work patterns in Norwegian families. See what I mean?"

Some of the trainees nodded, some looked thoughtful. "If you use the collections to illustrate compelling human stories," Chloe concluded, "what you say will resonate with visitors long after they return home."

Byron stepped forward into the reflective lull. "Excuse me," he said. "I've got copies of the July schedule." He handed them to the nearest interpreter to pass out. "Chloe, may I have a word?"

"Sure. Nika, why don't you tell everyone about your textile project?"

Chloe jumped down from the porch and followed Byron a short distance down the lane. "What's up?" she asked, noticing belatedly that his face was rigid with anger. Shit. What had she done now?

"What was that?" he demanded.

"Um … what was what?"

"Who told you to tell the trainees how to interpret their buildings?"

"You asked me to help with summer training—"

"I asked you to talk about collections! Not interpretation!"

"The two are obviously intertwined," Chloe said carefully. "What did you think I was going to say?"

"I expected you to talk about *artifacts*. I expected you to tell the interpreters what kind of cleaning and care you want them to provide. I expected you to tell them what objects they could use in daily programming, and what objects they shouldn't touch. I expected you—"

"You expected quite a lot," Chloe snapped. "Unfortunately, you failed to let *me* know about those expectations. You told me to show up in Norwegian at four o'clock and talk to the interpreters. That's it. For God's sake, Byron, there are fifty buildings on this site, and I've only been here for a week! I'm not in a position to give specific instructions to the interpreters yet!"

"Well, let me tell you something." Byron jabbed the air with one forefinger. "You're not in a position to provide training about educational techniques, either. That's *my* job. Do me a favor and stick to collections." He turned and stalked back down the lane.

———

"What was that all about?" Nika asked, when the interpreters had trudged back toward the main parking lot.

Chloe tugged on the lock on Kvaale's front door, making sure it was secure. "You noticed, hunh? Did everyone?"

Nika shrugged. "I don't think many of the interpreters caught on."

"Many," not "any." Everyone on the payroll would soon know that the curator of interpretation and the curator of collections had interrupted training to have a major row.

Chloe sighed. "I seem to have stepped on Byron's toes. He evidently expected me to talk about the importance of turning tin cups upside-down to dry, not using collections as a springboard for interpretation."

They were walking toward the small Norwegian area parking lot. The sky was overcast, the air sticky and humid. After a moment Nika said, "That stuff about collections care is important. But the way I see it, an interpreter's most critical job is to engage visitors in a meaningful way. If that happens, visitors will go home and tell their friends to visit the site. They'll sign up as volunteers, and join historical societies, and take their kids to other sites. There isn't a museum in this country that has adequate funding. This one sure doesn't. And nothing here will improve unless we can spark visitors to provide more support themselves, and to demand better support from the state."

God bless the young and idealistic. "Thanks, Nika."

"I thought your use of the photographs was effective, too," Nika added. "Where'd you come up with them?"

"My mom. They're copies from what's evidently a large collection at HQ in Madison."

"I love old photographs, especially of women. So many women left no written record of their life at all."

"You know what they say," Chloe said. "Anonymous was a woman."

"Amen to that." Nika waved one elegant hand. "Listen, don't worry about Byron. He probably didn't get enough sleep last night. His baby's been sick. Once he gets over his snit I'm sure he'll be glad to hear your ideas."

Chloe blinked. Byron had a baby? How did Nika *know* that? Nika had only been on site a week longer than she had, but the intern seemed to already be on friendly terms with everyone, permanent staff and seasonal.

They reached their cars. "Maybe you're right," Chloe said. "But I don't think I'll be making suggestions about interpretation to Byron any time soon."

The farmhouse was stuffy when Chloe got home. She carried her bottle of rum and a warm, flat soda out to the front porch and sank gratefully into one of the old folding lawn chairs her father had left her. After a few sips she tried to focus on her latest problem: Byron. Oddly enough, she liked him. Sure, he was young and sensitive and quick to take offense. He also seemed to care passionately about his job, the site, and the interpretive staff.

She had been like that, once.

She needed to have a strong working relationship with Byron. And, she hadn't had a chance to ask him to identify any interpreters left on staff who had worked there in 1977. Why hadn't she foreseen his possible objections to her training talk?

Well, she didn't have a very good record of understanding men, now did she? Or of spotting trouble before it smacked her upside the head?

She certainly hadn't with Markus. Three days after her miscarriage, Chloe had been curled on the sofa when Markus came home from work. He'd sat down on the floor beside her. "We need to talk," he'd begun. Chloe remembered staring at a shaft of sunlight coming through the window, and noticing that the ivy plant needed watering. "We've had a good run, right?" he'd said in his accented but flawless English. "We never made assumptions, right? Maybe we should look at this as a sign."

Chloe barely remembered packing, saying good-bye to friends at the museum, arranging transport back to the States. With nowhere else to go she landed at her childhood home. Chloe's parents evidently had no idea what to say about her abrupt departure from Switzerland.

"You left Ballenberg without having another job lined up?" Mom had asked. "Well, my goodness."

Her father hadn't done much better. "You've got a lot to offer, kitten," he'd said with fake heartiness. "You'll land the *perfect* job soon."

Neither of Chloe's parents had even asked why she'd left Markus and Ballenberg so suddenly.

Chloe had applied for every museum job available. The first call came from a small historic site in Solomon, North Dakota…

Stop thinking about that time! she ordered herself. You're letting things overwhelm you because you're tired. And you're tired because you got about three hours of sleep last night. It's OK to be down …

But it was no good. She simply wasn't cutting it at Old World Wisconsin. She wasn't making progress with the collections. She'd alienated several colleagues. She hadn't even learned anything new about Mrs. Lundquist and her ale bowl. Chloe's new life, her new start, was an utter failure.

FIFTEEN

Libby closed the spiral notebook she'd been scribbling in as Roelke walked into her backyard. "Hey! What are you doing here?"

"I want to look at your kitchen faucet." Roelke dropped into one of the lawn chairs on his cousin's patio. "I noticed on Sunday that it's leaking."

Libby took a sip of iced tea. "I'll take care of it."

"I was driving by anyway. I've got my toolbox in the truck—"

"Roelke! Thanks, but I can do it."

"I was just trying to help." A dog down the street began barking. Roelke tried to figure out where he'd gone wrong. No telling. "Where are the kids?"

"Went out for pizza with Dan and his parents."

"You OK with that?"

"No. But there's not much I can do about it."

"Maybe I should be here when he comes to pick the kids up next time." Roelke wanted that, wanted to stare into Dan Raymo's eyes with a clear message: *You step over the line, you so much as put one toe over the line, you deal with me.*

"If Dan gives me any more trouble, you'll be the first to know. But I don't want to turn into a woman who can't do anything for herself. OK?"

"Sure, I understand," Roelke said, although he didn't.

Libby traced one finger around the lip of her glass. "I need to talk to you about something."

Roelke was beginning to wish he hadn't stopped. "What?"

"When are you going back to Milwaukee?"

"You mean to work?" Roelke asked, although this time he knew what she meant.

"Yeah. To work." Libby gave him a level look, eyebrows lifted. "Look, you got the heck out of Dodge as soon as you had your high school diploma. You had a career thing going on in Milwaukee. Then stuff got ugly between Dan and me, and suddenly you quit your job and move back here."

"I was tired of the city."

"Bullshit. Listen, you big idiot, I know why you moved. And as much as I hate to say it, I needed you. But things have settled down."

Roelke felt a growl rising in his chest. "Dan is still a—"

"I know." Libby held up one palm. "But the divorce is final, and I got the best custody deal I could."

"I like seeing the kids. Justin needs guy-time."

"Milwaukee's not that far. It's time to go back, Roelke."

Roelke poured himself a glass of iced tea from the pitcher on the table. "You know what? I'm getting tired of everyone telling me how much I want to move back to Milwaukee."

"I don't want to keep you from doing what you wanted," Libby said soberly.

"You're not."

"Just think about what I said, OK?"

He put his tea down untasted. "Did it ever occur to you that I just like being near you and the kids?"

"So drive out on your days off—"

"Dammit, Libby!" Roelke scrubbed his face with his palms. "What don't you get? Everyone else is gone. My folks. Your folks. It's just you and me."

"That not quite true," she said quietly. "Patrick—"

"Patrick doesn't count."

"He's your brother, Roelke."

Roelke leaned over, elbows on knees, and stared at the ground. A headache was starting to pinch the back of his skull.

"You need to deal with Patrick," Libby said. "I've heard you talk about kids you meet on the job. You always say that a person's first encounter with a cop can determine their future, and how that goes is up to the cop. If you can give strangers a second chance, why not Patrick?"

"Because it wouldn't make any difference."

"Maybe Patrick *is* his father's son. But you're Uncle Joe's son, too."

"Yeah," Roelke said, watching an ant hauling a crumb three times its size. "And sometimes that scares the crap out of me."

"You need to work on that."

Right, Roelke thought. Just like that. He hated this know-it-all streak of Libby's. She'd perfected it by age six.

Libby got up and disappeared into the house. A moment later she emerged with a small plate holding several brownies. "I need chocolate," she said, holding out the plate. "Here."

He didn't need chocolate, but he took one anyway. "Thanks."

They ate in a silence. Roelke wished Libby had kept her mouth shut about his job, and about Patrick. Especially about Patrick.

"So." Libby propped her bare feet on the iron patio table. "You said you were headed somewhere?"

Hallelujah, a new topic. "La Grange. Someone broke into Chloe's house last night—"

"*What?*"

"She ran the guy off. But she's pretty shook up." That was a lie, but a believable one. "I thought I'd run down and make sure she's OK."

"A burglar, you think?"

"I'm not sure." Roelke began beating a rhythm on the arm of his chair with one thumb. "Possibly just some punk kid, looking for a stereo or something. Possibly not. Remember that old lady who had a heart attack and crashed her car? She'd been visiting Chloe to see about some old Norwegian bowl-thing, which evidently went missing at Old World before Chloe started. You know how some people get around antiques. There's a chance someone might think Chloe found it." The rhythm increased. "I just want to make sure she's OK," he repeated.

Libby looked at him pensively.

"What?" he demanded. "What now?"

"We-ell," she said slowly, "are you sure you want to get mixed up in this?"

"Mixed up in what? I'm just doing my job."

"No you're not. You've met a pretty lady who's been threatened. That always does a number on you."

"Shut up, Libby." Roelke glared at her. Now he definitely regretted stopping by.

"I worry about you. That goes two ways, eh? You worry about me, I worry about you." Libby pressed her hand over his, stilling his thumb. "Stop doing that. You're making me nuts."

A lawnmower roared to life two or three yards away. "I thought you liked Chloe," he said.

"I do like her. But I think she's got a lot of stuff going on right now. Stuff that has nothing to do with prowlers and missing antiques." Libby squeezed his hand gently. "Just be careful. That's all I'm saying."

Roelke considered that admonition as he backed the truck out of her driveway a few minutes later. Be careful. What did that mean? He was always careful. He was trained to be careful.

At the stop sign, he turned left toward La Grange.

Before Roelke turned into the driveway, he spotted Chloe sitting on her front porch, evidently watching alfalfa grow in the field across the street. She didn't move when he cut the engine, or when he got out of the truck and slammed the door. His senses prickled to full alert.

"Chloe?" he called, and began jogging across the grass. "Chloe!"

He was almost at the steps before she heard him. She jumped to her feet and a glass fell to the porch with a noisy shattering and splash. "What? Oh, God!" She stared from him to the broken glass at her feet.

"Didn't you hear me?"

She looked at his truck. "Oh, God. How long have you been here?"

"I just got here. Sit down. Do you have a dustpan?"

"A dustpan?"

"Sit down and don't move!" he barked. She was barefoot; he didn't want to add a trip to the hospital for stitches to their list of shared experiences. He went inside and looked in the cupboard under the kitchen sink—empty, of course. Finally he tore a piece of paper from a legal pad he found on the table, and used the pad's cardboard backing to carefully brush the shards of glass on the porch into the paper. He deposited the entire mess into the small trash bag he kept in his truck.

Then he brought her sandals outside and handed them to her. "Here. I might have missed a sliver or two."

"Thanks." She slipped them on. Her cheeks were flushed, now. "I'm really sorry about—that. I didn't hear you drive up. Please … sit down." She gestured at the second chair.

Roelke opted for the top step instead. He leaned against the porch rail and stared across the road to the distant mass of the Kettle Moraine State Forest. Shadows were stretching across the landscape. A couple of swallows darted about overhead. Roelke waited.

"Shit," she said finally. "That hasn't happened for a long time."

"What hasn't happened?"

"Have you ever thought about checking out?"

Roelke's heart made a determined attempt to exit via his windpipe. "No."

"Well, I have. Last winter."

He swallowed hard. All right. All right, think. "Are you thinking about that now?" He used his most measured, calming, cop-on-the-job tone.

"Not really. No." She stood up abruptly. "I'm going to get another glass so I can make myself another drink, since I wasted most of the last one. Want one?"

"No. But bring some food out, too, if you're going to drink. And a glass of water so you don't get dehydrated."

She disappeared into the house, and returned a moment later with a box of crackers, a small bottle of water, and a new glass. "Don't worry, I'm not a closet alcoholic." She shook her head. "And listen, forget what I said before. I don't know why I dumped that on you."

"That's OK."

"I'm just tired. I'm fine. Really."

Roelke rubbed his palms on his jeans, choosing his words. "You've been here for over a week, and haven't even started to unpack. You showed no signs of fear when confronted with an intruder—not once, but twice, if you count the missing lock incident at the trailers—"

"Maybe that's depression's silver lining. You don't go through life afraid all the time, because you've already been at the bottom of the well."

"You *need* to be afraid sometimes. The world can be an ugly place." And I've seen things that wake me up at night.

"Why are you here?" Chloe asked quietly.

"Oh. I was visiting Libby, and since I'd come that far—" he'd gotten very good at sliding around the truth—"I thought I'd just stop by and make sure everything went all right with the Walworth County sheriff. You did file a report, right?"

"I did."

"Do I need to call somebody?"

"No. They just told me to contact them if anything else happened."

"And you talked with your landlord?"

Chloe took a delicate sip. "Well, actually ... that slipped my mind."

"It slipped your mind? Jesus Christ, Chloe! What is the *matter* with you?"

"I just told you," she observed mildly.

Roelke felt his face flame. He rubbed it with his palms. While he tried to think of something to say, three bicyclists pedaled past. One of the Holsteins near the side fence coughed and flicked her tail.

Finally Chloe gave a tired, rueful smile. "Don't worry about it."

Roelke stood. "Come on. We're going next door."

Chloe's landlord was a stocky salt-of-the-earth farmer in his forties who left the milking to his sons while she told him what had happened. Roelke offered recommendations for upgrading security at the farmhouse. Standing there in the straw-flecked aisle, with the smell of manure in the air and several kittens tumbling around their feet, Roelke felt a tiny measure of reassurance.

He and Chloe walked back to her house in silence. "I really don't—" Chloe began as she stepped onto the porch, but stopped when her phone began to ring. "I better get that. Come on in."

He followed her into the house, waiting while she grabbed the phone. "Hello? *Ethan!* Are you home safe?" Her thin face lit with true pleasure.

Great, Roelke thought. He'd somehow zoomed from protector to intruder.

Chloe glanced up and said, "Ethan, can I call you back in a little bit?"

"No need," Roelke said. "I've got to get going. Don't forget to lock up tight tonight."

"So," Chloe said to her caller, as Roelke let himself out, "tell me all about …"

He slammed the truck door, and drove away.

"Who was that?" Ethan asked.

"How was the fire? You didn't get hurt or anything, did you?"

"The fire is out," Ethan said. "So, who was that?"

Chloe sighed. "That cop I was telling you about. He just stopped by."

"Oh, yeah?"

"Yeah." Chloe winced, knowing what was coming. "Don't freak out, OK? Last night somebody tried to break into my house—"

"*What*?"

"I scared the guy off, and then I called Roelke. The cop." She didn't go into the fine details of jurisdiction.

Ethan muttered something that was likely a curse. "I *hate* you being alone out in the middle of nowhere."

"Don't go Neanderthal on me, Hendricks."

"I want you to get a dog. I mean it, Chloe. I'm not kidding around."

"I'll think about it." Chloe slid sideways in the chair, hooking her knees over the arm. "I think this is all wrapped up with that missing Norwegian ale bowl. The sooner I find it, the sooner all this will stop."

"Leave it to the police!"

"The police don't have evidence of a crime. If I don't pursue this, no one else will."

He blew out an exasperated breath. "This is crazy, Chloe! If you've searched the historic site without finding the damned thing, what else can you do?"

"I asked my mom to do a little genealogical work about Mrs. Lundquist. And I'm going to the State Historical Society in Madison and poke around there."

Ethan was silent.

"Don't be mad at me," Chloe said. "I truly couldn't handle that. I miss you."

"I wish I could come for a visit. But it's peak season."

"I know. I'm just feeling down tonight. On top of last night's excitement, I had this ugly scene at work..." And she spent the next ten minutes telling Ethan about her exchange with Byron. "Thanks for listening," she said finally. "You're the best. I suppose you're still gay?"

"Get that dog," Ethan told her. "And don't piss off that cop. What's his name?"

Chloe poked at a tiny hole in the arm of her chair. "Roelke McKenna."

"Well, stay on his good side. I'm glad you've got someone out there you can call on."

But I don't want to call on Roelke McKenna, Chloe thought. She'd said too much to him already.

Roelke felt wound too tight to go home. Instead, he drove back at the Eagle PD. Skeet was out on patrol, so the place was empty. Roelke sat down, picked up a pen. Paperwork would calm him down.

He found himself drawing tiny and precise geometric figures along the margins of the form. Finally he crushed the sheet into a ball and tossed it away. Then he got up, opened his locker, and picked up the photograph of Erin Litkowski.

He had met Erin about a month after he started patrolling solo in Milwaukee, the night her husband ignored his restraining order. Erin managed to call 911 as he was kicking in the door. Roelke responded. The husband had already fled. Roelke did what he'd been trained to do. Said the things he'd been trained to say. And then he left, adrenalin buzzing, flying off to the next call.

A week later, he came in from patrol and found Erin's sister Pauline waiting for him at the station. "Erin is gone," Pauline had said, her eyes glittering with unshed tears. "She's not dead. Just terrified that her husband will kill her. Or me, if I helped her. She sent me a card, postmarked New York. She said the only option she had left was to disappear."

"New York," Roelke said slowly. "I'm not sure what we can do, other than sending—"

Pauline shook her head. "I'm not asking you to *do* anything. Erin asked me not to look for her, and I'm honoring that request." She opened her purse. "But I wanted to give you this. My name and number are on the back. If you ever see her, or hear from her... please, get in touch with me."

Roelke stared at the small, framed photograph that Pauline shoved into his hands. Oh, yes. Now he remembered. Erin had been one call in a very busy day, in a very busy week, in a very busy month. "I will," he said.

"Thank you." Pauline stood. "And thank you for trying to help Erin. She said you were kind." She fished a tissue from her purse, blew her nose, and hurried away.

And Roelke had continued to sit still amidst the chaos of a busy district police station, staring at the image of Erin Litkowski. She had the kind of prettiness that came mostly from her smile. And some SOB had made her life so miserable that she had felt compelled to go into hiding.

Roelke had never again seen, or heard from, Erin or her sister. He didn't know what to do with the photo, so he simply kept it. Was Erin

Litkowski alive? Or had her husband traced her, and made good on his threats? He'd likely never know.

He put the photo back on the locker shelf and shut the door. He hadn't done enough for Erin Litkowski. And he couldn't do anything for her now. But he could look out for Libby and her kids, even if she was too damn stubborn and proud to like it.

And he could try to do the same for Chloe Ellefson. That Ethan guy, whoever he was, was doing a piss-poor job of it.

SIXTEEN

A BIG, NOISY, MOTORCYCLE zoomed past Chloe the next morning as she drove to Old World's administration building. By the time Chloe parked, Ralph Petty was taking off his helmet.

"Good morning," Chloe said.

"Morning." The site director pulled a briefcase free from its storage compartment and jerked his head toward the building. "Come on in."

Ralph had summoned her for a meeting. Once inside, Chloe helped herself to a cup of coffee from the percolator on the kitchen counter before following the site director into his office. Something to occupy her hands—not to mention a jolt of caffeine—seemed like a good idea.

"So, are you settling in?" Ralph asked, with a smile that was half cheerful, half solicitous, and totally artificial.

"I'm working on it." Chloe matched his fake smile with one of her own.

"You know you can always come to me if you have questions or problems."

"Thanks." Chloe sipped the coffee, which was wretched. She and Ralph faced each other across a table. He was a compact man of middling height, early fifties, with a short beard he'd probably grown to compensate for a receding hairline. Chloe fervently hoped he wasn't about to ask for a detailed account of her accomplishments to date.

"I wanted to see what progress you've made in terms of developing a plan for a permanent collections storage building," Ralph said.

How much progress had he expected her to make in a week? "My assessment is coming along," Chloe said vaguely. "I'm scheduled to meet with Leila in Madison on Tuesday. I'm sure we'll discuss it."

Ralph frowned. "I doubt that Leila will have time to be of much help. It's important that we get a proposal drafted as soon as possible so I can proceed with fund-raising."

"I'm all for that." Since Chloe hadn't even met Leila in person yet, she wasn't going to offer any opinions on the division curator's priorities.

Ralph picked up a thin file on his desk, and handed it to her. "I've drawn up some rough plans for you to look at."

"I see." Chloe opened the file and flipped through the half-dozen pages inside. Most contained pen sketches of a new facility, with scribbled notations: textile storage, farm implements, ephemera, conservation room. Why was the site's administrator spending time on crude architectural drawings?

"Do you have a written overview of Old World's collections?" she asked. "Something that provides estimates of what we have? I haven't found that kind of breakdown."

Ralph waved a hand. "We don't need specifics for fund-raising."

"But… shouldn't we at least have estimates before we commit to anything? I'll need to spend some time doing an inventory—"

"I did not ask you to do an inventory," Ralph snapped. "I asked you to work on a storage facility plan. Was I not clear?"

"You were clear," Chloe affirmed.

"Do not spend time on an inventory."

That edict made no sense. No sense at all.

Ralph consulted a desk calendar. "I want to see a draft of your proposal in… two weeks. We'll meet two weeks from today."

"I'm not comfortable committing to that," Chloe said. "The collection clearly numbers in the thousands of items, from giant threshing machines to silver thimbles. Nika and I are working on storage issues, but I've got daily needs from the interpreters too."

"We're a huge site with a small staff. Everyone has to work in overdrive." Ralph frowned. "I hadn't expected this negative attitude from you, Chloe."

"I don't have a negative attitude." Chloe struggled to keep her tone neutral. "I'm trying to give you a realistic estimate of what I can accomplish, and when. Nika and I are already making good progress, by the way." Nika was the only one making progress, actually, but Ralph didn't need to know that. "We've moved all the textiles from the storage trailers to the basement of St. Peter's Church—"

"What?" Ralph's frown deepened. "I didn't know anything about that."

Shit. She *knew* better than to volunteer information to an administrator. "I ran the plan by Leila," Chloe said breezily. "I couldn't make progress in the trailers without creating some room. Nika's doing a superb job, by the way. She's a dynamo. I'm really grateful that you hired her."

His phone rang. "Keep me posted," he said curtly. Meeting over.

Chloe drove back to the restoration area, parked, and sat staring at the two horrid trailers. Her relationship with Ralph had obviously skidded onto proverbially thin ice. That took, what—a week? She remembered how hard she had tried, that first day, to get her career back on track.

And she might accomplish that yet, if she did what Ralph wanted her to do. She would need to focus solely on his collections storage building project. Doing a *good* job would mean long days, evenings, weekends. Crawling over the site to get at least a general sense of the collection. Contacting colleagues at other historic sites for comparative plans. Calling vendors for quotes on everything from shelving to climate control systems.

And it would mean pushing everything else aside.

Lovely. She could keep looking for the ale bowl, and risk losing her job; or she could keep her job, but give up on the ale bowl.

You need this job! some inner voice whispered urgently in her brain. Chloe's fingers tightened on the steering wheel. It's what she wanted, right? A collections job, at a superb historic site? She could forget her promise to Mrs. Lundquist. Push aside the guilt. She didn't have a choice. She really didn't.

Chloe let her head rest on her steering wheel. Minutes ticked past.

Then she got out of her car, opened its trunk, tossed Ralph's file on top of the boxed files already there, and slammed the trunk shut. The hell with Ralph.

She was scheduled to provide training to the German-area interpreters that afternoon. Based on yesterday's debacle with Byron, she needed to plan an entirely new talk. Supporting the front-line interpreters was the most important thing she could do for Old World Wisconsin. The interpretive staff was the site's public face. Without them, the historic site would begin a downward spiral fueled by unhappy visitors and declining revenues. The interpreters were not well paid; at the very least they should be well trained.

And when she was finished with the training plan, she would kick back and spend some time considering what the heck else she might do to find Mrs. Lundquist's ale bowl.

Shortly before eleven that night, Roelke parked a patrol car down the street from Stanley Colontuono's house. He'd not yet been able to identify the bookie who'd taken Ginger Herschorn's nephew for seven hundred dollars at The Eagle's Nest. Officer Voegler, one of the new part-timers, had gone to the bar in civvies, tried to strike up a conversation with the bartender, hinted that he was looking for action. Zilch. Maybe the bookie had left town. Maybe the barkeep had been wise to Voegler.

Roelke thought back to the night he'd seen Stanley burst into The Eagle's Nest. Who had he been looking for? The bookie? Or someone who owed *him* money? If Stanley was the one taking bets, he might have moved the operation to his house, where it would be harder for the cops to nail him—

A flash of headlights in the mirror caught Roelke's attention. He'd taken the clean flat-top that night because it had a more innocuous profile than a squad car with roof lights. He waited as the car drew even, went on by. A dark Mustang. The driver parked in front of Colontuono's house. A streetlight illuminated a young man—dark hair, jeans—when he got out of the car. At least it wasn't the Herschorn kid.

The radio squawked. There'd been an accident in the township. Multiple vehicles, injuries reported. As Roelke responded, the young man disappeared into Colontuono's house.

—

Roelke didn't get back to the station until almost one in the morning. He emerged from the can just in time to take a phone call. "Officer McKenna, Eagle Police Department."

"McKenna? This is Marv Tenally, chief of security at Old World Wisconsin. We've had an odd thing happen at one of the Norwegian farms. I didn't want to put it over the wire, and I don't think I need to get the site director out of bed, but can you meet me at the Norwegian gate?"

Roelke reached the Norwegian gate in about eight minutes, and rolled his window down. "Hey, Marv. What's up?"

Marv ran a hand over a white thatch of hair. He was a tall man, scarecrow-thin, a retired accountant from Waukesha. "Something seemed funny at the Kvaale farm. I already checked it out, but I'd like you to take a look."

Roelke gestured. "Hop in."

Marv locked the gate behind them, slid into the squad, and pointed the way to a log home with several outbuildings arrayed behind it. The high beams of Roelke's car caught a raccoon in a moment of shocked stillness before it scuttled into the underbrush. "Stop in the drive," Marv told him. "The interpreters are real particular about modern tire tracks in the farmyards."

Roelke parked as instructed, and grabbed his flashlight before following Marv to the house.

"You know we're in the process of replacing the old security system," Marv said, mounting the front steps. "The old system here monitors noise. Everything looked good when I made rounds this evening—all the buildings locked up, microphones out. But about half an hour ago, I got a buzz from this place." He unlocked the front door.

An open porch and an enclosed storeroom fronted the house. Two rooms comprised the back, a sitting room and a kitchen. Roelke played his light around the sitting room. The guides—no, Chloe called them interpreters—had left an incongruous series of large microphones planted on the floor, with heavy gray cords snaking back to the security box hidden from public view. The building's ceiling was low, the doorways even lower. The combination of wires to trip over, lintels to bang into, and antiques to knock over made Roelke feel large and clumsy.

He planted his feet carefully as he turned to Marv. "So, you had an intruder?"

"Hard to say." Marv rubbed his chin pensively. "A mouse'll trigger the sensor, sometimes. But this … this didn't feel right. First that mike tripped—" he pointed—"and then that one. By the time I'd grabbed my car keys …" he circled through the little house, leading Roelke into the storeroom, "*this* one buzzed."

Roelke considered. The third mike to buzz was placed near a narrow flight of stairs in the storeroom.

"The door was locked when I got here," Marv said. "The windows were secure. And the Norwegian gate was locked, too."

Roelke made his way up the steep stairs. The attic was divided into two rooms—one front, one back. The front room was empty except for a row of lidded buckets probably used as mouse-proof storage, out of public view. The air smelled musty.

Roelke moved his flashlight beam carefully across the floor. A jumble of footprints marred the dust filming the floorboards, marking a clear trail from the stairs to the door of the back room.

"Are these your footprints?" Roelke called.

Marv trudged up the stairs. "Some of them are, from when I checked the place out earlier. Some could have come from an interpreter who came upstairs for some reason."

Roelke squinted at the tracks again. There was no way to isolate any individual prints, but all of the tracks stopped at the door to the back room. He stopped there as well, splashing his light around the room. Empty.

Well, hunh. If an intruder with a flashlight was looking for something specific—say, Chloe's missing antique bowl—he would have known from the doorway that it wasn't there.

The two men clomped back downstairs. Roelke walked through the house again, considering the sequence of buzzing microphones. The side door from the porch to the storeroom provided the quickest access to the second story. But someone unfamiliar with the house would probably enter through the front door and circle through the lower story before finding the stairs. That matched the sequence Marv had heard.

"Can you think of any reason why an intruder would be interested in the second story?" he asked.

In the weird shadows cast by the flashlights, the security guard's expression was hard. "No. And as far as I can tell, everything in the house is right where it's supposed to be. But I read the incident report from the other day, when the new curator found the storage trailer open. I know Hank blew that off, but I didn't like it."

"Yeah. I didn't like it either." Roelke mentally shuffled facts into a row. Someone had left a lock open at the storage trailers—possibly in haste, or perhaps just uncaring. Someone had tried to break into Chloe's house. Someone had now, it seemed, entered the Kvaale house after-hours.

As they left the old home, Roelke realized that his jaw muscles were beginning to ache from being clenched. He'd been wrong to discount Chloe's instincts about an old woman's fears and an antique gone missing. He pictured Chloe, thin and vulnerable and foolishly unafraid, and swallowed a growl. What in the hell had she stumbled into?

SEVENTEEN

REMOVING THE TEXTILES TO the church basement gave Chloe the wiggle room she needed to mount a thorough search of the trailers. She tackled one on Thursday and the second on Friday. She'd held out hope that Berget's ale bowl was small, perhaps hiding behind other objects. No such luck. When the light began to fade on Friday she reluctantly admitted defeat.

She'd searched storage. She'd searched on site. Berget's ale bowl was definitely, officially missing.

"Shit," she muttered. What should she do about it? Report the bowl's status to Ralph Petty, after he'd ordered her not to look for it?

Well, she'd figure that out later. It was time to call it a day. "And a week," she added, tugging on the padlock to be sure the trailer was secure. "It's the weekend. Normal people do normal things on weekends." She was determined not to return until Monday morning. She had managed to finish summer staff training without further antagonizing Byron. She had managed to avoid Ralph Petty since their uncomfortable meeting. Better to leave while she was … if not ahead, then at least not in deeper doo.

As Chloe was uncoiling the chain on the restoration area's security gate, headlights approached on Highway S. She pulled the gate open when she recognized Nika's Chevette. Nika parked beside the trailers.

"You're working late," Chloe said, as Nika emerged from her car.

Nika shrugged. "You too."

"Yes, but I don't have an adoring fiancé waiting at home." Chloe gestured toward the Chevette. "I'm glad to see you back in motion."

Nika scowled. "Four new tires later."

"Ouch."

"Here." The younger woman deposited a small wooden box into Chloe's hands. "Be careful, the joints are loose. When we were all at Sasso's the other night, the German lead told me she was worried about this piece. They're supposed to bring stuff to Byron, but she was afraid to transport it herself, so she put it upstairs in the Schulz house for safekeeping. She wanted me to come get it. I told her she should talk to you, but … " Nika spread slim hands expressively: *What else could I do?* "I figured I'd swing by now in hopes you were still here."

"I'll take care of it," Chloe said. "So, any plans for the weekend?"

"Nothing special." Nika swung gracefully back into her car. "See you Monday."

The intern was gone before Chloe realized she should have asked Nika for a progress report on the textile storage project. It would have been the responsible, supervisorly thing to do. Shit.

She carried the sweet little box inside. It was well constructed, with small dovetail joints. Some long-gone *hausfrau* had probably used it to store sugar or coffee. Chloe filled a plastic tub with water and gently submerged the artifact. The thirsty wood would soon swell, tightening the joints.

"I solved a problem," Chloe announced. This was the way to approach things. Today, she had helped this artifact. On Monday, she would help one more artifact. Maybe even two.

That dollop of tranquility disappeared as a stray thought wormed into her consciousness. What had Nika said? The lead interpreter in the German area was worried about transporting the artifact, so she'd put it upstairs in the Schulz House.

Upstairs. For safekeeping. *Upstairs.* Out of public view, away from even interpreters' hands.

I, Chloe thought, am a complete idiot.

She reached for the phone and dialed an extension. A gruff male voice answered. Lovely. Why did Cranky Hank have to be on duty every time she needed something from Security?

"Hi, it's Chloe Ellefson," she said, twitching the phone cord impatiently. "I'll be stopping by Kvaale in a few minutes. I know the mikes are out, so shall I call you when I leave the building again?"

She heard a long sigh exhaled into the receiver. "What's all the fuss about Kvaale?"

Chloe went perfectly still. "What do you mean?"

"Last night, tonight—"

"What – do – you – mean?"

"Look, don't pop your cork. Marv was on duty last night. According to the log book, the sound system in Kvaale picked up some noise—"

"What?"

"It happens all the time. A breeze blows a branch down on the roof, a mouse gets inside—"

Chloe wanted to reach through the line and smack the man. "Did Marv check it?"

"Sure, sure. Didn't find anything."

"Look," Chloe said. "As curator of collections, I *must* be informed any time there's a possibility of—"

"Keep your shorts on. Marv even called in the Eagle cops. McKenna didn't find any sign of trouble either."

McKenna. Roelke McKenna. Officer Roelke McKenna had been called to Kvaale last night to investigate a possible break-in.

"The next time something happens in one of the exhibits that prompts a call to the Eagle police," Chloe snapped, "I *expect* to be informed. Immediately. Make a note of it." And she slammed the phone down.

Her palm was still stinging as she fished another number from her bag and dialed. Be home. Be home, you jerk.

"McKenna here."

"Why the hell didn't you call me last night?"

Silence.

"It's Chloe." She suddenly wondered if there might be any number of women waiting impatiently for Roelke McKenna's call. "I heard you got called out to Kvaale last night. Why didn't you let me know?"

"Because I didn't see any need to. There was no sign of any theft or damage." His tone was careful, considered, as if he was talking a crazy woman off a ledge. Maybe he thought he was.

"That's bullshit. You *know* I'd want to hear about something like that."

"OK, I do. But you haven't shown the best judgment—"

Chloe clenched the receiver. "I beg your pardon?"

"I'm concerned for your welfare."

“Well, don’t be. And don’t patronize me. I came to you for help about the ale bowl, and you blew me off, remember? And now you think you can decide what to share with me about my own job?”

“I—”

“Don’t *ever* do that to me again.” For the second time in five minutes, she slammed down the phone.

Her hands were shaking, and she pressed them against her thighs. The little wooden box shifted in its tub of water and one lone bubble bobbed to the surface. That might as well be my contribution to Old World Wisconsin so far, she thought. One lone bubble. Pop.

Chloe stared at the artifact sitting in a green plastic tub of water in a matchbox-sized kitchenette in an ancient pink trailer, and tried to laugh. No laughter came. She dropped into a chair, folded her arms on the tiny table, and rested her head.

She *did* deserve to know if a security guard summoned a police officer to one of the historic structures. She shouldn’t have blasted Hank about it, though. There were effective ways to accomplish change in a professional setting. Shrieking ultimatums into the phone didn’t make the list.

And … she *did* feel justified in her anger toward Roelke. She’d gone to him for help, maybe even started thinking of him as a friend. And in return, he’d turned into a pompous ass. Well. He’d never tell her anything, now.

A moth fluttered against the window. The restoration area was silent. Everyone else had long since gone home to their families, their fiancés, their lives.

Chloe stared at the bobbing little box and longed mightily to rest like that, to fill up and sink under and slip away.

The moth beat frantically at the pane. Chloe blinked. In an explosion of action she grabbed her briefcase, banged out of the trailer, and—after locking all locks—headed for home.

The first thing Chloe did when she got home was call her mother. Screw you, Officer McKenna, she thought, as she used a pencil to dial. She, Chloe, had her own *über*-resource.

"Chloe?" Her mother's voice sounded warm in her ear. "I'm glad you caught us, dear. Your father and I are off to Decorah first thing in the morning. I'm giving a workshop at Vesterheim." Vesterheim, a museum in Decorah, Iowa, was a Mecca for all Midwestern Norwegian-Americans.

Chloe had assumed she could visit her parents that weekend, eat some real food, use their washing machine, and find out what her mother had learned about Berget Lundquist. "Mom," she said, trying not to sound pitiful, "I was hoping you'd had time to do that genealogical work I asked you about."

"Haugen."

"... Beg pardon?"

"H-a-u-g-e-n. Your Berget's original surname. Before she married Mr. Lundquist."

Chloe scrabbled for the pencil, which had disappeared behind the chair cushion. "Wait—I need you to spell it again. You're sure?"

"Of course, Chloe. It means 'the hill.' I'd guess that the first Haugen immigrant came from a farm on a hill."

A farm on a hill. That narrowed things right down.

"Berget Haugen married Jack Lundquist in 1934, when she was twenty-two. It was a small, private ceremony, I gather. But of course the Depression was on then, and—"

"Mom!" Chloe rubbed her forehead. "Why didn't you let me know? It's kind of urgent that I learn as much as I can about Berget Haugen Lundquist. Is there anything else?"

"Not yet," her mother said, with a hint of reproach in her voice. "It's only been a week, Chloe. I had three lessons to give, and the scholarship lunch at the high school to help organize, and—"

"OK, OK. Sorry, Mom." Chloe frowned at a bruise on her shin, legacy of an unplanned meeting with a corner of the artifact shelving. "I do appreciate your help. Truly, I do."

"We'll talk again soon, all right?"

"Sure, Mom," Chloe said, and just in time remembered to add, "and have a good weekend."

So. What now? She sat in the gloom, thinking. Finally she dialed information, asked for a number, and waited while the operator put the call through.

The phone was answered on the fifth ring. "Hello?"

"Mr. Solberg?" she said. "This is Chloe Ellefson. We met at Mrs. Lundquist's funeral. I'm terribly sorry to call so late."

He chuckled. "That's all right. I don't go to bed until after Johnny Carson. I don't like that new guy, that David Letterman. I don't think he'll last. And I never turn the darned tube on during the day. But Johnny's always good. He's got Bob Newhart on tonight."

Chloe glanced at her watch, making sure she wasn't encroaching on Johnny's monologue. "I was wondering if I could visit you this weekend. I'm still trying to learn more about your friend's missing heirloom, and I hoped you might take me back into her house." She waited, hoping Mr. Solberg didn't ask what she thought she'd find that she hadn't found the first time.

"Well, let's see," he said thoughtfully. "I've got a boy coming 'round to take out the storm windows tomorrow, and there's a Carol Burnett reunion show on tomorrow night. I'll be ready for bed after that. Then service on Sunday morning. So Sunday afternoon would be best."

Chloe wondered if the storm window operation would take all day, or if the lonely old man simply wanted to spread out his company. "Sunday it is," she told him. "Thank you."

By mid-afternoon on Saturday, Chloe was walking in circles inside her farmhouse. She'd gone to a Laundromat in Elkhorn, and picked up crackers, peanut butter, coffee, and a few other non-perishables at the grocery store. What she wanted to do was head back to Old World to continue her search for Berget's ale bowl. "But I don't know where to look!" she muttered.

OK, she needed a new strategy. And she needed to get out of the house.

She stuffed a towel and notebook into a canvas bag and drove to Palmyra's public beach. Since Libby had mentioned that her kids would be with their dad this weekend, there was little chance of running into anyone she knew. Libby did not strike Chloe as a lay-in-the-sun kind of person.

The beach at Lower Spring Lake was small, with a picnic pavilion sporting a Lions International sign, a couple of grills, and a small playground. A studly young man with zinc oxide on his nose reigned supreme from his lifeguard chair. Toddlers played in the sand with brightly colored buckets and pails.

Chloe staked her claim to a quiet spot well off to one side, settled down, and pulled out her notebook. If she didn't know how to find the ale bowl, perhaps she could figure out why someone else was trying so hard. *Something* made this bowl particularly desirable. What?

She wrote POSSIBLE REASONS across the top of a fresh page, then began collecting her thoughts:

1. *Bowl came from a particular region of Norway.*
2. *Bowl was made in Wisconsin, not Norway—rare.*
3. *Bowl was made by a well-known artist.*

What else? Chloe tried to think. What had she told all of her trainees about valuing artifacts? Artifacts are most important because of what they reveal about the people who made, owned, or used them.

4. *Bowl was owned by a famous person.*

Chloe nibbled her lower lip as she looked over her list. She hadn't written the obvious because it made no sense. But nothing about Berget Lundquist's quest made sense, so Chloe scribbled one more item:

5. *Bowl was a treasured family heirloom that some unknown descendant wants back.*

Mr. Solberg believed that all of Mrs. Lundquist's relatives were dead, but what if he was wrong? Chloe stared over the water, where teen-aged boys dove from a wooden platform anchored well off shore, and teen-aged girls in barely there bikinis bobbed on inflatable rafts, pretending to be unaware of the boys. And suddenly Chloe thought of something new.

Mrs. Lundquist's son had been killed in Vietnam. Could he have had a child before leaving for Vietnam, or while there? If so, perhaps Mrs. Lundquist hadn't known about it. Maybe she discovered late in life that she was indeed a grandmother, and desperately regretted giving away her family heirloom.

It was also possible that some other distant relative—a long-lost cousin?—might have surfaced. And that, Chloe thought, is what I will try to discover when I go back to Mrs. Lundquist's house tomorrow. The photograph albums, buried correspondence, even the untouched financial records—

"Hey! It's Chloe!"

She slapped her notebook closed as Justin ran to greet her, scattering sand. Libby followed more slowly, with Dierdre in her arms.

"Well . . . hi!" Chloe managed.

"What are you doing here?" Justin asked.

Chloe was wondering the same thing about them. "Just relaxing."

Libby let Dierdre slide to the ground. "Sorry to intrude."

"You're not intruding." Chloe tried to smile. Today was not a good day to make small talk with Roelke McKenna's cousin.

"I'm going in the water," Justin announced.

"Stay where I can see you," Libby warned. "And don't go in above—"

"I *know*." Justin ran toward the water. His baggy red swimsuit flapped around his legs, and the strap holding his glasses in place made a funny horizontal line against the back of his head.

Libby pulled a plastic scooper and bucket from a beach bag and handed the toys to Dierdre. The little girl wore a frilly pink bathing suit. Her skin showed a few white traces of recently applied sunscreen.

"My ex didn't show." Libby's profile was tight as she tucked a floppy hat over Deirdre's head. "Again."

"Men can be pigs."

"They can indeed." Libby leaned back on her hands, watching her son.

After a moment Chloe began to relax. This still might be OK.

"So, what do you write?" Libby asked.

It took a moment to make the transition. Then Chloe considered her last project, a work of historical fiction set in Switzerland, burned page-by-page when she'd left Brienz. "Um, well, I—"

"Hey, Libby!"

Libby looked up sharply, cast a quick glance at Chloe, and jumped to her feet. "Therese! Don't tell me you've got that little guy out already!"

Chloe belatedly recognized the approaching brunette. The swell of her belly had transformed itself into a small lump in the middle of a safari-print sling worn across her chest. Chloe sat very still, watching Dierdre shovel sand, trying hard not to listen to Therese's chatter: "Here, Libby, want to hold him? No, it's OK, really! Just keep him wrapped against the sun."

The lump was transferred into Libby's arms. "He's so sweet," Libby murmured, swaying back and forth the way women do when cradling a child. Chloe shifted her gaze to Justin. Someone needed to keep an eye on Justin. After a few more eternities she was aware of Libby easing the infant back to his mother's arms.

Then Therese's attention landed on Chloe. "Oh, hi!" Therese bubbled. "We met last week, remember?"

"Of course. Hi."

Therese dropped to her knees. "I went into labor later that night! Princess Di hasn't had her baby yet. Oh well. Derek's a week old already, see?"

Derek was thrust forward for review. "He's lovely," Chloe said.

"Want to hold him?"

"No, I—"

"It's OK, really!" Therese slid the baby toward Chloe's lap. "Just watch his head."

Chloe felt the soft nap of a thin cotton blanket, and the solid warmth of the tiny life it cradled, being eased into her unwilling arms. The warm weight stirred—an arm moving in sleep, perhaps, or a leg. She smelled *baby*, talcum and milk and something indefinable.

The air seemed to get thinner, less able to satisfy her lungs. "Please—take him," she said. Libby was already scooping Derek up and away.

Tears spilled over as Chloe rose to her feet. "He's beautiful. Congratulations." She tossed the words at Therese as she grabbed her things and stumbled away. She aimed for her car but swerved at the last minute and bolted into the public restroom, a smelly cement-block affair. Chloe dove into one of the stalls, latched the door, dropped onto the john. Curled over her knees, trying hard to be quiet, she sobbed.

EIGHTEEN

Chloe emerged from the stall damp-faced, hiccupping, and slightly nauseated. Libby was leaning patiently against the sink.

"Oh," Chloe said. Her head felt fuzzy. "Where are the kids?"

"I asked a neighbor to watch them." Libby turned toward the door. "Come on. You're coming home with me."

Chloe watched a daddy longlegs walk up the wall. "I don't want to see Roelke."

"Roelke's not there. Come on."

Ten minutes later, Chloe was sitting in a chaise lounge on Libby's patio. "I'm sorry that thing happened with Therese," Libby said, handing her a glass of lemonade mixed with crushed raspberries.

Chloe sipped. The concoction was strong and cold.

"When was the last time you ate a good meal?"

"Um ... the last time I was here."

Libby fired up the grill and moved back and forth from the kitchen with silent, fluid efficiency. Chloe watched a toad hop slowly through a forest of begonias, and sipped her tea, and allowed herself to empty out.

Libby grilled zucchini and cherry tomatoes, and tossed them with cooked pasta shells and almonds and grated Romano cheese. To Chloe's surprise, the food tasted good. "And a peach pie for later," Libby added, setting a foil-covered pan on one side of the grill. She lowered the lid. "So. What did Roelke do?"

"He got called out to Old World to investigate a possible break-in, and he didn't bother to tell me about it." Chloe tipped her glass from side to side, watching ice cubes slide back and forth.

"Sounds like him. My cousin has a Galahad complex."

"A gallant prince?" Chloe tried out that idea, measuring childhood fantasy men against Roelke's reflective sunglasses and tightly clenched jaw.

"Nothing so romantic." Libby poured herself a glass of wine. "His dad could be a mean SOB. He never beat Roelke, I don't think, but he hit Roelke's mother."

"Oh."

"The point is, nothing trips Roelke's trigger like a woman in distress."

"But I … I'm not in distress."

"He told me about the break-in at your farmhouse. He thinks you're vulnerable."

"I don't need him to protect me," Chloe protested. "I don't *want* him to protect me. I never asked for that."

Libby dropped a napkin, pinned it with a toe, then bent to retrieve it. "I didn't either, but it doesn't keep him from trying."

Chloe was silent.

"Let me tell you something else." Libby hesitated, looking unsure for the first time. "Roelke's not always so good at figuring out the emotional stuff. Sometimes I think ... I think the protection instinct gets mistaken for something more."

A breeze whispered in the trees above the patio. The whirring sound of a skateboard on the street out front drew close, then faded away.

"I don't want anyone to get hurt. You, or him. Just be careful. That's all I'm saying."

"I will," Chloe said, because it seemed easiest. She set down her glass of tea. "If you don't mind, I think I'll switch to wine."

"I've got plenty." Libby poured a glass of Chablis, and handed it over. "So. You want to talk about the other guy?"

"What other guy?"

"The father of your child."

Chloe's response formed clearly in her head: *No! I do not want to talk about him!* But somehow what came out was, "I met Markus when he visited a historic site in Virginia where I used to work. Markus Meili. He was looking at hogs."

Libby's eyebrows raised. "Hogs?"

"Markus' thing is the preservation of old livestock breeds. He works at a huge historic site in Switzerland. Ballenberg. A lot of agricultural sites, all over the world, are trying to save some of the old breeds from extinction. I was working at a site in Virginia with a healthy group of Ossabaws. That's a rare hog breed from an island off the Georgia coast, originally brought hundreds of years ago from Spain."

"Um ... that's interesting."

Chloe tried to smile. "I thought so. Anyway, he was at my site for several days, and we ... hit it off. Then we spent every evening of his first month back home on the telephone. I did the math and flew to Switzerland for a week." She sipped her wine.

"Switzerland." Libby considered that.

"Two months later Markus flew back to Virginia. He told me that he was in love with me over *pad thai* in Alexandria. Not long after that, I quit my job and moved to Brienz."

"Wow."

Chloe watched a chipmunk beneath one of Libby's bird feeders, stuffing its cheeks with sunflower seeds. "We lived together for five years. I began volunteering at Ballenberg. I eventually got hired to an education position."

"You speak German?" Libby sounded impressed.

"*Suisse-Deutsch*. A little. I didn't speak any when I went over, but most of the people I worked with spoke pretty good English."

"That must have been hard." Libby shook her head.

"Not at all. I *loved* Switzerland. Ballenberg is a wonderful historic site. And Brienz is lovely. I could walk to the market ..." Chloe let her words trail away. Some of her best memories were simple ones: wandering up *Oberdorfstrasse*, a street lined with old chalets and window boxes of vibrant flowers. Sitting on a bench near a church while the sound of a rehearsing choir floated through an open window. Sipping white wine while Markus puttered in the kitchen, chattering about honeybees and Grison gray cattle ...

Dammit. She had to stop this. Markus had ended their relationship almost nine months earlier. Sure, she'd been hurt. Shocked. Stunned, even. But still *functional*. She'd done what she needed to do: packed her suitcases, come home, found a new job.

It was only months later that she'd realized, belatedly, that a sucking gray depression had crept up from behind. It had come so stealthily that she hadn't realized she was losing herself until it was too late to stop the descent. And she hated being that depressed person. She hated not being able to scrub Markus from her mind. It felt as if some record album in her brain had one deep scratch, and the needle kept jumping back to a chorus she'd already heard *ad nauseum*.

Libby regarded her. "Is there any reason you can't stay here to-night?"

"I guess not, but—"

"Good. I think you should."

By the time the neighbor dropped Justin and Dierdre off, Chloe was already cocooned in Libby's guest bedroom. The small room was painted a cheerful purple. Photographs of the children lined the walls. Shelves overflowed with dog-eared paperbacks and storage tubs labeled "Sewing stuff" and "School papers—J" and "Photographs, 1981." The room wasn't haunted by memories of girlhood dreams, as Chloe's bedroom in her parents' house was. It wasn't a sterile taunt of her failures, as the bedroom in her farmhouse was. It felt calm.

And she felt calm, too. Calmer, anyway. Chloe curled into bed, hearing the comforting murmur of Libby and her children as their evening unfolded. Very soon, for the first time in many months, Chloe fell deeply and soundly asleep.

Roelke sat at his kitchen table while Shirley Horn sang "You'd Be So Nice To Come Home To," and the coffeepot burbled. It should have been a peaceful Sunday morning. It wasn't.

"Well, hell," he muttered. He shoved to his feet, instinctively ducking to avoid braining himself on the low sloping eaves, and restlessly prowled his apartment.

There wasn't much to prowl. When he'd moved to Palmyra, all he'd wanted was a cheap place near Libby and the kids. This tiny flat had been available; he took it. He'd done the basics to make it feel like his own: pictures of the kids on the bookcase, a brontosaurus rex painting Justin had given him for Christmas on the wall, the last quilt his mother had made on his bed. He'd never thought of the flat as more than a temporary place to sleep. Besides, Libby's place—a true home, with canned tomatoes in the basement and perennials in the gardens and inked lines on the kitchen door marking the kids' heights at every birthday—was just a few blocks away.

Except that Libby's house suddenly didn't feel so welcoming. He wished that Libby could admit that once in a great while, she didn't know everything about everyone.

He glared at a snapshot of his cousin. Maybe he *should* just move back to Milwaukee. Let Libby fix her own damn faucet. Get back in line for sergeant's stripes.

See the kids once a month. Go to sleep wondering if their father was going to show up unannounced one night and break their mom's arm.

The stereo switched off. Roelke replaced Shirley Horn with "Brilliant Corners" by the late, lamented Thelonious Monk. After setting the needle, Roelke slid back into his chair. He wanted to think about something else. Index cards were spread on the table before him, and he stared at his notes:

- May—OWW visitor asks about ale bowl with cow heads
- Sometime prior to June—page about ale bowl torn from OWW record book
- 6/5—Mrs. L. visits OWW to ask for bowl; car crash
- C. E. can't find ale bowl
- 6/10—possible break-in at OWW storage trailers
- 6/12—attempted break-in at C. E.'s farmhouse

- 6/15—possible break-in at OWW/Kvaale house; evidence of possible foray upstairs; no sign of forced entry

Roelke sighed. The only concrete piece of evidence was the intruder at Chloe's house, which might have nothing to do with the missing heirloom. Still, the list created an odd sequence of events. Something wasn't right.

He was beating a fierce rhythm against the table with his thumb, trying to think, when the phone rang. "McKenna here."

"Well gee, good morning to you too." Libby's voice was sardonic. "Still working on that pleasant greeting thing, I see."

Her tone held no sign of "my-ex-is-being-an-ass" or "Justin-is-out-of-control."

He frowned. "Why are you calling so early?"

"I want you to come over."

Roelke leaned back in his chair. "Still working on that *asking* thing, I see. What's going on?"

"Chloe's here."

Roelke sat back up straight. "And?"

"And you need to talk with her."

He considered. "Does she know you're calling me? Did she happen to mention that she's royally pissed at me?"

"No and yes. And you know what? You both need to clear the air. You may never see her again, and that's fine by me. But don't leave things like this."

"I haven't even had coffee yet."

"I've made coffee."

"And I haven't eaten."

"I'm baking cinnamon rolls," she said impatiently. "So stop making excuses and get your ass over here!"

Chloe could tell that Justin was in a sulky mood as soon as he emerged from the house. His sulks escalated into a tantrum thrown just as Roelke walked through the back gate. "I don't *want* to be here!" the boy yelled. He hurled a plastic Smurf against the fence before stamping inside.

"I'll get him," Roelke offered, looking downright eager.

"No, I'll get him," Libby said firmly. "Sit. Drink coffee. Keep an eye on Dierdre." Then she followed her son into the kitchen. Dierdre, wearing a Halloween princess costume, was playing on the grass with a turquoise toy pony.

"Good morning," Chloe said. She hadn't been thrilled to learn that Roelke was on his way over. But she was determined to be polite.

"Morning." Roelke poured a cup of coffee from a carafe, stirred in some cream, and dropped into a chair. He wore his scuffed hiking boots, and he sat with one foot resting on its side and supporting the other. Those boots were once again oddly endearing.

"I'm sorry I was such a shrew on the phone," she said. "But I hope you can see how disconcerting it was for me to find out by accident that you'd been called out to Kvaale the night before."

"I would have thought there'd be a daily memo or something to share news like that."

"Apparently there isn't. And that's not the point."

Roelke gulped some coffee. It was evidently hotter than he'd expected; he jerked, and a few drops spilled on his hand. He managed to set the cup down without further disaster. "You're right," he said finally. The sky was threatening rain and Roelke's sunglasses, thank God, were nowhere to be seen. "But I hope that *you* can see that—that I'm the cop here. I don't know what's going on—"

"I don't know what's going on either," Chloe said, "but I deserve to know when something happens."

"I don't want you mixed up in this."

"Excuse me? I'm already mixed up in this, remember?"

"It's police business!"

"It's *my* business!" Chloe retorted, then noticed Dierdre frowning at them. "It is my business," she repeated more quietly. "Wait—are the police really getting involved?"

Roelke tried his coffee again, this time with more care and success. "No," he admitted. "We would if the director of your museum filed a formal theft report. Have you talked with him?"

"With Ralph Petty? Yes. And he told me to forget about the ale bowl. I ignored that, but despite my best efforts, I haven't been able to find the bowl. I suppose I could try talking to Petty again ..." She chewed that over, then shook her head. "All I have is this feeling that something's not right."

"Yeah," Roelke admitted. "When you add everything up ... something's not right."

"So," Chloe said. "I really think we'd get farther if we cooperated. Communicated. That sort of thing."

Roelke stared into his mug as if searching for answers.

"I'm a big girl," Chloe added. She saw again Mrs. Lundquist's pleading gaze. "And I'm the one who didn't ask Mrs. Lundquist enough questions. If I'd only tried a little harder ... I might have learned something that—"

"It's not your fault she had a heart attack."

"She gave me the impression that I was her last hope. I disappointed her. I was too self-absorbed to ask the right questions." Chloe hitched her shoulders. "If I had, we might at least know *why* she was so desperate to get the piece back. And that might tell us if someone was threatening her, and who's trying now to find the bowl."

Roelke leaned over, forearms on thighs, head down as if protecting his thoughts. Dierdre began singing to the pony. A chickadee zipped in to one of the feeders.

Then Roelke straightened, slid a hand into one pocket and pulled out several dog-eared index cards. He put them on the iron table at Chloe's knee.

Chloe felt a spark of satisfaction as she realized what she was reading. She retrieved her notebook, opened it to her page of notes about possible motive, and passed it to him. They both read in silence until one particular line of Roelke's printing caught Chloe's attention. "What's this about upstairs?"

"At the Kvaale house there were footprints in the dust upstairs. They could have been left by one of the guides. But . . . maybe not."

Chloe glared at the page. "I knew it. I looked for that ale bowl at Kvaale right after Mrs. Lundquist died, but it didn't occur to my feeble brain to look on the second story. By the time it did occur to me—*he'd* already been there."

"If it *was* an intruder, I don't think he found what he was after. The line of tracks stopped at the doorway to the back room, as if the person had gone that far just to check."

"Well, it was a long shot." Chloe frowned again at his notes. "It's the 'no-sign-of-forced-entry' that really bothers me. It happened at the trailer, too."

"Remind me: who else has keys to those buildings?"

"A few permanent staff members, that's all. I had to check my set out from the head maintenance guy."

"Stanley Colontuono?"

"Right. He's a jerk."

"Who else would have easy access?"

"Ralph Petty, obviously. He's a jerk, too. And Byron, who is something of a jerk as well."

"Nice people you work with."

"Yeah."

"Tell me what your beef is with those guys."

Chloe gave him a condensed version of her encounters with Stanley, Ralph, and Byron. Roelke pulled more index cards from another pocket, one for each man.

"And I suppose you could add Hank DiCapo to the list," Chloe added. "He doesn't like me."

Roelke tapped his cards on a patio table to even the edges. "Any other workplace encounters you want to tell me about?"

Chloe pulled one heel up to her chair seat and wrapped her arms around her knee. "I don't think so."

Roelke shuffled through his pile of cards, reading slowly. "Hank DiCapo, security guard—insisted open trailer was your fault. Byron Cooke, curator of interpretation—argued over training—"

"Don't roll your eyes," Chloe interrupted.

"I didn't roll my eyes."

"Byron was really pissed, and didn't care who knew it. And he mentioned once that he'd been in the storage trailers recently, where he's got no business being."

Roelke sighed, made another note on Byron's card, and moved on. "Ralph Petty, site director—on your case. Stanley Colontuono, maintenance chief—asked you out." He shook his head. "If there's some connection here to your missing bowl, I don't see it."

"I don't either."

Roelke put his cards away. "OK, one more thing. This ale bowl—what is an ale bowl, anyway?"

"A bowl, carved from a single piece of wood, often very decorative. During wedding celebrations or other special feasts, they'd get filled with ale, and passed around. So I'm told."

"Hunh." Roelke took that in, then picked up her notebook. "All right. So, you've come up with these possible motives." He pointed to the reference about someone famous once owning the bowl. "That's one I hadn't thought of."

"I don't know how information like that would have suddenly come to light, though. Even if that info was in the accession record—the one that got ripped out of the ledger—somebody knew to go *looking* for the record. I can't believe it was random."

"We can't make assumptions."

"OK, OK." Chloe poured herself another cup of coffee. "Well, I'm still digging. My mom is doing some library research—"

"Your mom?"

"My mother has connections in Norwegian circles like you wouldn't believe. And maybe I can find some evidence of a long-lost relative. I'm going to visit Mr. Solberg again today—"

"The neighbor?"

"Right. I met him at the funeral."

Roelke frowned, and one knee began to jiggle up and down. "It's not smart for you to be asking questions so openly."

"I'm going to visit a lonely old man," Chloe said. "That's all." She didn't explain that she'd called Mr. Solberg because she needed action, and she didn't know what else to do.

Libby came out the kitchen door, carrying a plate of cinnamon rolls. "You two OK?"

"Yeah," Roelke said. "Where's Justin?"

"Watching a *Mork and Mindy* rerun. He's all right. He just needs some space."

Chloe surprised herself by eating two of the rolls, which were hot, moist, and not ruined with frosting. Finally, reluctantly, she carried her dirty plate and mug into the kitchen.

"Just leave them in the sink," Libby told her. "I have to empty the dishwasher."

"Thank you," Chloe said. "For everything."

Libby smiled. "No problem."

Back outside, Roelke was waiting for her. "Where's your car?"

"At the beach," Chloe said. "Long story."

"I'll walk you over."

Chloe was grateful that he didn't ask why she'd left her car at the beach. They walked in comfortable silence. Two boys zoomed past on bicycles. A bell chimed from a nearby church, calling the faithful. Chloe thought about the big church in the little village of Daleyville. One less congregant, now.

"Do me a favor," Roelke said when they reached her Pinto. "Call me tonight. Let me know what you find out."

He'd put on his sunglasses, and his favor was inflected as an instruction, not a request. But Chloe didn't want to get tangled in those dynamics again—at least not right away. "Will do," she promised her double reflection, and got into her car.

NINETEEN

When Roelke got back to Libby's house he found his cousin in the kitchen, emptying the dishwasher. "Chloe get off OK?" she asked.

"Yeah." Roelke looked around. "This place got quiet."

"Justin went to play next door. Dierdre's having a tea party with two dolls and a teddy bear. You want some juice? I'm out of OJ, but I've got cranberry."

"Sure." Roelke sat down at the table and accepted the glass without looking Libby in the eye.

"Hey, you," she said. "I didn't mean to piss you off the other day."

He shrugged. "OK."

She leaned against the sink, regarding him as she wiped some hard water spots from a plate. "But I care about you, Roelke. And I can't just not say anything when I think I see you making a mistake. Especially when it's because of me."

Roelke loved Libby, but swear-to-God, there were times he wanted to shake her. "Libby, just *stop*. Stop talking. Stop telling me what to do. You don't – know – everything."

Libby put the plate away. "I do know you. I know how excited you were when you got hired on in Milwaukee. And I know the only reason you're still hanging around Palmyra is me and the kids—"

Roelke's glass shattered against the cellar door. Cranberry juice ran down white paint. In the seconds of stunned silence that followed, Roelke thought he could hear it dripping to the floor.

"Mama?" Dierdre called.

"It's OK, baby," Libby called, managing an almost-normal tone. "I just dropped something."

Roelke shoved his chair back with such force that it clattered to the floor. In two strides he was out the back door. He strode around the house, climbed into his truck, slammed the door.

Then he sat. Jesus holy Christ.

He imagined Libby cleaning up the shards of glass, the angry stain. Four or five minutes passed. Then the front door opened. She walked across the lawn, arms folded, body rigid. When she reached the truck she opened the passenger side door and got inside the cab.

"I won't have that shit in my house," she said.

He studied the dashboard. "I know."

"You think my kids don't get enough of that from their father?"

"I *know*."

A little girl next door wobbled down her driveway on roller skates, the cheap kind that clipped onto the bottom of regular shoes. Roelke and Libby watched her make progress, trip, fall. It took her three tries to get up.

"OK," Libby said finally. "I've got to get back inside. I don't want Dierdre to wonder where I am."

"You're not always right," Roelke said. Something ached inside.

She sighed. "You want to tell me why I'm wrong? Fine. But come back into the house."

She opened the door, got out, slammed it behind her. She was halfway across the yard before she realized he wasn't following. She stopped, then walked back. This time she came around the truck and stood by his open window. "Roelke? Are you going to sit and sulk, or are you coming back into the house?"

"I think it's inside me."

"What's inside you?"

The ache in his chest tightened to a knot, squeezing, cutting off his air.

Libby glanced back toward the house. "Roelke? *What's* inside you?"

"I think … sometimes I think I'm like my father."

Her shoulders slumped. Then she reached into the cab and put her hand on his wrist. "You're not."

"You don't know—"

"Yes, I do," she said firmly. "About this, I know."

Maybe she knew him better than he knew himself. Maybe she didn't. He stared at the little girl on roller skates. She was getting her stride, now. Roelke became aware of a thickening in his throat, the sting of tears in his eyes.

"You are not like your dad," Libby said. "You broke a glass. He broke your mother's arm. Big difference."

"But—"

"Would you ever hit me?"

Roelke finally looked at her. "I swear to God, Libby, I'd chop my hand off before I ever hit you, or the kids."

"That's what I know," she told him. "Yeah, you've got a temper. You've got to deal with that. But I'm not afraid of you, OK? And remember, I do know what I'm talking about. I was afraid Dan was going to smack me long before he ever did."

Toxic, Roelke thought. Men can be so toxic. Women could be too, for sure. But most often, it was men. And the thought that he might have even a trace of whatever—

"Come inside," Libby ordered. "Come on. I don't want you driving like this."

Roelke sucked in a deep breath, exhaled very slowly. He wanted to go inside and pretend that the last half hour hadn't happened.

He put the key in the ignition instead. "I'm sorry," he told his cousin. "I've gotta get out of here."

———

The clouds began to drizzle rain as Chloe drove toward Daleyville, replaying the morning's conversation in her mind. It was freaky to discuss her co-workers as possible suspects. "I hope it's Ralph," she muttered, amused by the mental image of Roelke McKenna putting Petty in handcuffs. He'd actually ordered her *not* to inventory the collection. What sense did it make to raise funds for a storage building without knowing what there was to be stored?

Chloe thought that over, unease growing with every slap of the wipers. Ralph could be erratic and irrational. Was he just an autocratic megalomaniac, or was some secret fueling his volatility? She'd mention all this to Roelke when she called.

Just as Chloe eased her car into Mr. Solberg's driveway, the rain turned torrential. Of course. Since she had not been home since the day before, she did not have an umbrella or jacket along. Of course. After killing the engine she sat for a moment, watching water cascade down the windshield. The front door stayed implacably shut.

"So it goes," Chloe muttered, and plunged out of the car. She trotted across the small yard and up the front steps—which did not, of course, have the protection of a portico—and knocked on the door.

And waited, and banged again, and waited, T-shirt already sodden against her skin, heavy braids beginning to drip. A light burned in the room to the right of the door, visible through drawn curtains. Maybe Mr. Solberg hadn't heard her over the driving rain. Chloe stepped down to the grass. As she leaned toward the window, she heard the sound of a television. She knocked firmly on the glass, then visored a hand above her eyes, waiting to see palsied fingers pull the curtains aside.

No luck.

A passing car sprayed a fan of water over the lawn. Chloe retraced her soggy steps and frowned at the front door indecisively. Should she leave? But what if Mr. Solberg was ill? *I take seven different medications,* he'd said. She suddenly felt a chill that had nothing to do with the rain.

She put a tentative hand on the doorknob. It turned easily. She cracked the door open. "Mr. Solberg?" she hollered. "It's me, sir. Chloe Ellefson."

No answer but rain drumming on the roof. She pushed the door open wider, called again. No response. She imagined him lying on the floor, paralyzed by a stroke or fall, alone and unable to call for help. "Oh, God," she whispered, and stepped inside.

"Mr. Solberg?" she yelled. "Mr. Solberg!" No answer but the muffled raindrops. She quickly scanned the living room: floor lamp burning by an easy chair, a Zane Grey novel left open on the floor, what looked to be a talk show flickering in black and white on a small television.

Chloe hurried from room to room. Dining room: table piled with old magazines and a half-finished jigsaw puzzle. Kitchen: dirty saucepan waiting in the sink, porcelain canisters shaped like Dalmatian puppies. No Mr. Solberg.

Calling his name, her wet sandals slapping, she ran up the stairs. One bedroom: neatly made bed, large photograph of a gray-haired woman on the dresser. No Mr. Solberg. Second bedroom: a lifetime's accumulation of stuff crammed in bushel baskets and suitcases and old beer cartons. No Mr. Solberg. Bathroom: blue towels and shower curtain. No Mr. Solberg.

Don't over-react, she told herself as she slapped back down the stairs. The man probably went to visit a neighbor.

And left his television on? *I never turn the darned thing on during the day,* he'd said when she'd called.

Oh, God.

Chloe plunged back into the streaming gray afternoon. She ran down the steps and across the yard to Mrs. Lundquist's house. Her shorts plastered themselves to her thighs and her bare arms prickled with goose bumps. She slowed to climb the front steps, past the geraniums in their tubs. They were almost dead now, brittle skeletons bobbing angrily from the force of the rain.

Chloe shivered as she put her palm on the doorknob. It too turned easily. She eased it open, moving slowly now, silently. She stepped inside—and staggered backward from the slam of negative energy that had replaced her earlier perceptions of quiet calm in this house. "Oh, God," she whimpered, her heart thumping beneath her ribs.

She took one step and looked first to her right, into the kitchen. Nothing. Then she looked to her left.

It was the soles of his shoes that caught her eye, scuffed and oddly visible. The soles were attached to sturdy black lace-ups, the kind elderly men wear. Chloe took another step and she saw ankles in dark socks. Then gray trousers.

Legs, she told herself numbly. Legs jutted from behind the desk.

Two more steps and she shuddered violently, pressing a hand over her mouth. She closed her eyes, but it was too late; she'd already seen Mr. Solberg lying on the floor, the back of his head a bloody mess.

TWENTY

THREE HOURS LATER, ROELKE found Chloe sitting in the lobby of the Dane County Sheriff's office. She'd pulled her heels up and wrapped her arms around her legs and rested her cheek on her knees. Roelke felt something give way inside, something he'd have to think about later.

"Chloe," he said. She lifted her head. "You're all through here?"

She nodded.

"Then let's go." He took her hand and led her to his truck. The rain had given way to a muggy afternoon.

"Thank you for coming," she said, as he pulled out of the parking lot.

"I'm glad you called."

"My parents are in Iowa, and I didn't know who else—"

"Would you shut up about calling me already? I said I'm glad you called."

Chloe retreated into silence. Roelke inwardly cursed his clumsiness.

For the next few minutes he concentrated on getting out of Madison. When he was finally headed east he tried again. "Sorry. I'm not angry at you."

"OK." Chloe stared out the window, hugging her arms to her chest.

"Tell me again what happened."

Chloe told him.

Roelke's fingers tightened on the steering wheel. "OK, here's why I'm angry at you," he began.

"You just said you weren't angry at me."

"I lied. I *am* angry at you. What the hell were you thinking? Plunging into not one but two houses, alone, in suspicious circumstances? We've been through this before!"

"Stop yelling at me."

"You deserve to be yelled at!" Roelke clenched the steering wheel so hard his hands hurt.

"OK, I get it."

"Do you? Because I have no idea. I truly don't. Bill Solberg was murdered, Chloe. Someone evidently bashed a nice old man in the head."

"Stop it!" She scooted closer to the window.

"It could have been you. I could have just as easily gotten called to the morgue to identify your body. Do you hear me?"

"I think I'm going to throw up," Chloe said in a small, tight voice.

Some of Roelke's fury leaked away. "Seriously?"

"Yes."

He pulled onto the shoulder. Chloe slid out and leaned against the cab, hands on knees, head lowered. *Dammit*, Roelke thought.

After five minutes Chloe straightened. Another five and she slowly climbed back into the cab. "OK," she said. "It passed."

"What have you eaten today?"

"Um ... two cinnamon rolls and about four cups of coffee."

Roelke eased back into traffic. "You need something to eat."

"I need fresh clothes—"

"Fine. Your place to change, and then food."

Chloe twisted her fingers together. "Someone was looking for the ale bowl."

"Maybe it had nothing to do with the ale bowl." Roelke sighed. "But for the sake of discussion ... let's say it did."

"Mr. Solberg might have heard a noise from Mrs. Lundquist's house. Or maybe he saw a light on over there, sometime late last night. Probably while that Carol Burnett show was on."

"If so, Mr. Solberg went over to investigate, surprised the killer, and got—" Roelke caught himself just in time. "And, um, ended up in the wrong place at the wrong time."

Chloe swiped at her eyes. "But why kill that sweet old man?"

Roelke shot her a sidelong glance. "Well, it may have been unintentional. It's not as easy to kill someone by knocking them in the head as they made it look on *Starsky and Hutch*. Maybe Mr. Solberg fell and hit his head, and bled to death. Was there a lot of ... never mind." Asking about the amount of blood she'd seen—which could indicate how quickly Mr. Solberg had died—would be a bad thing to do. "We just don't have enough information now to speculate."

After Chloe had changed into fresh clothes, Roelke headed to his place. Ten minutes later he pulled into the tiny lot behind a second-hand clothing store in Palmyra, and parked beside a dumpster. "This is where you live?" Chloe asked dubiously.

"I rent the second story." He led her up the exterior staircase, unlocked the door, and ushered her into the miniscule kitchen. "Watch your head." Visitors often thumped their heads against the slanting pitch of the ceiling.

Chloe perched in one of the chairs, hugging herself as if chilled. Roelke looked in his refrigerator. What the hell did vegetarians eat? "Are eggs OK?"

"Yes."

Cheese omelets, then. He put a cutting board, knife, and wedge of smoked Gouda in front of her. "Slice up some of that."

She sliced, and he whisked, and soon butter was sizzling in a skillet. He made one large omelet, cut it in two, and slid the halves onto plates.

"Let's eat up front," he said. "More room." Chloe followed him to the living room. He put her plate on an end table by the sofa, and dropped into his own favorite chair.

Chloe studied a model airplane hung from the ceiling with fishing line. "Did you make this?"

"Me and my dad did that, when I was about eight. It's a Lockheed P-38 Lightning."

She looked surprised. "You and your dad?"

"Yeah, why?"

Chloe dropped onto the sofa. "Sorry. It's just that Libby said your dad..."

"Libby talks too damn much."

They ate silently for a moment. Then Roelke heard himself admit, "My dad could be a real bastard. But... but there were some good times, too, especially when I was young. Before he got soured on life."

"I'm glad."

"I see too much crap. Too many men doing stuff they shouldn't." He looked at the model. "I try to remind myself that something made them that way."

"Like something made somebody kill poor Mr. Solberg?" Chloe put her fork down as her eyes glazed over with tears.

"Nothing excuses that. But the killer probably felt that he had his reasons. It's my job to figure out what those reasons were, so we can nail him."

"It's not really your job, though, is it?"

"Well, no," Roelke conceded.

"I told the Dane County detective about the ale bowl." Chloe used her fork to toy with a bit of egg. "He was … polite."

"I'm going to take this to my chief on Monday," Roelke told her. "I should be able to keep current with what the Dane County boys find."

"Good."

Roelke held her gaze. "And *you* are done with this. Got it? Done. This is a murder case now, and you – are – done."

"There was something I wanted to tell you about Ralph Petty," Chloe said quietly. Roelke tried to pay attention but as she talked of inventories and storage building plans, his mind kept straying to an unwanted fact. Because of her job, who she knew, what she worked with, Chloe would *not* be done until the killer was behind bars.

Chloe couldn't finish her omelet. Still, by the time they walked back outside she felt collected enough to face what needed to be done. "I think I've got it together now," she told Roelke. "Can you take me back to Daleyville to get my car?"

He frowned. "I don't think you're ready to drive."

"I have to go to work tomorrow. No way I can take off after two weeks on the job."

"I'll drive you to work."

"I need my own car," Chloe said wearily. "I *want* my car." She could not handle the idea of being trapped at her farmhouse, dependent on him—or anyone—for transportation.

He growled a bit more before driving her to Daleyville. Chloe slid into the Pinto quickly, keeping her eyes averted from the yellow police tape flagging both Bill Solberg's and Berget Lundquist's houses. The police were gone, though, with their cameras and notepads and questions. The tape drooped in the humid air as if ashamed of its role in the whole sad affair.

Roelke and Chloe caravanned back to the farmhouse, with her in the lead. By the time they pulled into her driveway, fireflies were blinking up from the hay field across the street. She and Roelke emerged from their vehicles and stood staring at each other, suddenly not knowing what to say.

"Thank you," Chloe managed finally. "For everything."

"Are you going to be OK here tonight? I could take you to Libby's."

Chloe shook her head. "I can't hide at Libby's. I'll be OK."

"You should get a dog."

"Oh, Lord. Not you, too. I don't want a dog!"

"Why not?"

"It's not a minor thing! When you adopt an animal, it's a commitment."

"And why are you afraid of making that commitment?"

Chloe felt ready to drop with exhaustion. "Look," she said, "I simply can't have this conversation right now."

"I'm concerned for your safety."

"I know." She watched him struggle to accept her message: topic closed, day at an end.

Finally he satisfied himself with an order: "Call me tomorrow."

"All right," Chloe said. "I will."

Alone in the farmhouse, the silence seemed mocking. She paced. She watched the fireflies twinkling. She paced some more.

And she found herself in the bathroom. For a moment she stared at her reflection in the mirror. Her hand opened the medicine cabinet. The prescription bottle still sat in the middle of the shelf like a piece of art, carefully placed. She reached for it, thumbed off the lid, stared inside. The bottle was almost full.

The prescribed dose was four of the tiny tablets. Chloe slowly shook them into one palm. One … two … three … four.

And then the rest of the contents cascaded into her hand. Dozens of innocuous-looking white pills.

Abruptly she clenched her fingers around them. *Shit!*

She moved her fist over the toilet bowl, sucked in a deep breath. But she couldn't do that, either.

Finally she let the pills dribble back into the orange plastic container, capped it, and stashed it back in the medicine cabinet.

"What's wrong?" Ethan asked.

"Nothing." Chloe simply wasn't capable of talking about Mr. Solberg right now.

"You're lying."

"I'm not lying," she lied. "Really. I'm just feeling down and wanted to hear your voice."

"Why are you feeling down?"

Chloe wound the phone cord around her index finger. She had to give him something. "I was thinking about my baby."

Silence stretched across the country as they both digested that unexpected statement.

"I was wondering," Chloe said, "if maybe I did something that caused the miscarriage." She stared at the beige curls of plastic looped around her finger.

"What did the doctor say at the time?"

"He said, 'These things happen.' If there was anything more than that, my *Suisse-Deutsch* was insufficient."

"I don't know anything about that kind of stuff," Ethan said slowly. "But it sounds like something just ... just went wrong."

"Yeah," Chloe said. "Well, enough of that. Tell me what you've been up to."

Ethan talked and Chloe listened, clinging to the sound of his voice. When they finally said good-night she felt ready to try to sleep.

But her dreams were full of accusing eyes—the very old, and the very young.

TWENTY-ONE

"Next item." Ralph Petty glanced down at a sheet of notes in front of him. "Chloe."

Chloe tried to look alert. The Monday morning permanent-staff meeting at Old World Wisconsin was not for the faint of heart.

"What progress have you made regarding the new collections storage facility?"

OK, this one she could punt. "I'm meeting with Leila tomorrow in Madison," she reminded him.

"Very well. Next item. Stanley." Ralph zeroed in on the maintenance chief. "The restaurant trash cans weren't emptied mid-day on Sunday."

"I'll check on that," Stanley said vaguely. "I wasn't on."

"Who was on?"

"Well, let's see . . . I guess it was Rupert. Rupert Engel. One of the summer hires."

Chloe felt sympathy for Rupert, who was no doubt in line for another chewing-out. But it was impossible to care about overflowing trash cans. Not with what she'd seen. Mrs. Lundquist—dead. Mr. Solberg—dead. And now, Chloe had no way of getting back into Mrs. Lundquist's house. No way to check the backs of her photographs for names. No way to search for a letter from a long-lost relative, or a scholar, or anyone else who might have prompted recent events.

"Next item," Ralph said briskly. "Byron."

Byron stopped doodling and looked up warily. "Yes?"

"I've found a source of shoes for the interpreters." Ralph slid a catalog across the table. Chloe, sitting next to Byron, saw a red circle inked around an advertisement for "ladies' costume boots." They were white, with high heels and pointed toes.

Byron stared at the picture. "I'm not sure," he said finally, "that these are practical for our site. Being white. And the high heels—well, a lot of our interpreters are middle-aged ladies."

Ralph's eyes bore into the younger man. "At the very least, order some for the lead interpreters."

Byron shifted uneasily. "The leads walk miles every day. And the costume budget is already strained."

"Four leads, four pairs of boots," Ralph snapped. "Am I being clear?"

The room was quiet. Stanley picked his fingernails with a tiny screwdriver. The historic farmer had become fascinated with his pen. Research curator Margueritte Donovan was staring out the window at passing cars, and the restaurant manager was surreptitiously making tic marks on an order form on his lap. The visitor center manager had claimed that five hundred school children in the gift shop precluded her attendance, and was conspicuously absent.

"I appreciate your suggestion," Byron began, "but I'm a little concerned—"

"Oh, for God's sake!" Chloe slammed one palm on the table.

Silence mantled the room as everyone went very still—fingernails, traffic, pens, and order forms forgotten.

Chloe looked at Ralph. "Very few interpreters could wear these boots all day. The style is all wrong for immigrant farm women, anyway. And—" she flipped the catalog over to double-check the source—"it is *extremely* unlikely that boots offered by a company that caters to theatrical productions would stand up to the wear and tear of our gravel roads." She sat back in her chair, smiling demurely as satisfaction briskly swept away the gray fog in her mind. So there, Ralph Petty, she thought. You have absolutely no power over me.

A phone ringing from the anteroom cut the stunned silence. The receptionist's voice drifted into Ralph's office: "Old World Wisconsin. Yes, ma'am, we're open from ten to five on weekends."

Ralph's nostrils flared. Ignoring Chloe, he pinned Byron with another glare. "I expect you to consider these boots, Mr. Cooke."

"I will," Byron said quickly.

When the meeting adjourned, Chloe left the room at the back of the pack. No one lingered to chat in the kitchen. They all think I'm nuts, Chloe thought. They were probably right. She hardly recognized herself anymore. Old Chloe would never have told the truth to an administrator. Old Chloe had taken a lot of crap, all in the guise of getting good grades, keeping good jobs, making sure she had health insurance and a savings account and a circle of friends.

Well, she was different now. And maybe that was OK. Once she'd hit the bottom of her proverbial well, and wallowed about in filthy black muck for a while, perceptions changed. Old priorities didn't matter. Telling off Petty? It hadn't felt scary at all. New Chloe wasn't inclined to waste any energy putting up with crap. She didn't know how long this new sense of abandon would last. But it was kinda fun.

By the time Chloe reached the small parking lot, most of her colleagues were already spewing gravel as they roared away. Byron stood by his car. "You got time for lunch?" he asked.

"Sure."

"Get in. I'll drive."

Fifteen minutes later a waitress thumped plastic tumblers of water in front of them at Sasso's. "You know what you want?" she asked.

"I want a grilled cheese sandwich," Chloe said. "On wheat, not white. And do you have any real cheese?"

"Real cheese?" The waitress looked confused.

"Mozzarella. Provolone. Anything that doesn't come wrapped in plastic with the words 'cheese food' on the label."

"We've got Swiss for the Swiss-burgers."

Swiss. Of course. "That'll do nicely." Chloe said. While Byron vacillated between a baconburger and a baconburger with cheese, she wondered what Markus was doing, right that moment. Did he ever think of her at all? How would he feel if he knew that she had stumbled over a bloody corpse the day before?

When their order was complete, Byron leaned back in his chair and eyed Chloe. "So. What the hell happened back there?"

"You mean with Petty?" It suddenly occurred to Chloe that she may have antagonized more than the site director. "Oh, please. Don't tell me you're pissed again. Look, I realize I probably shouldn't have jumped into your business like that, but—"

"No, it's OK," Byron said. "But—why did you do it?"

"Because Ralph Petty is an oxen's ass. Those boots were ridiculous. I didn't want the interpreters to pay the price."

"They would have gone ballistic," Byron agreed gloomily. He pulled off his little wire-rimmed glasses, fished a tissue from his pocket, and wiped them off. "We don't provide shoes. It's just too expensive. But if we could, it wouldn't be those fakey white Victorian things."

"Well, I'm not sure that me speaking up did any good."

"Are you kidding?" Byron blinked at her, put his glasses back on, and blinked again. "I expected Ralph to grab the phone and place the order then and there, sizes be damned. Instead I got left with nothing more than a command to *consider* the stupid things. Major victory."

The waitress returned with their plates. Chloe's sandwich looked perfect: toasted a golden brown and pulled from the grill just as the cheese began to drip down the sides of the bread. They ate in silence for a few moments.

"So," Chloe said finally, licking her fingers, "what do they teach in the Administrative track at grad school these days, anyway? How To Be An Autocratic Jerk, 101?"

"Don't ask me. I have no hankering to climb that ladder."

Which said good things about Byron, Chloe decided. It couldn't be easy for this twenty-something guy to supervise a huge staff comprised largely of older women. But he took his responsibilities to heart, and she liked that. "Me either. But seriously, what's Petty's problem?"

"I have no idea."

"He's always been that way?"

"Pretty much."

Chloe took another bite, chewing slowly, trying to think of another approach. "He doesn't want me to inventory the site's collections. He actually ordered me not to. Does that make sense to you?"

"He's from out east," Byron offered. His thin nose wrinkled daintily, as if he'd gotten a whiff of rotten pork. "New York City. And his last job was in Las Vegas, running some historic house."

Ralph Petty might have been God's gift to the museum world, Chloe thought, but with a resume like that, he had two strikes against him in Wisconsin, Harley motorcycle or no. "They have historic houses in Las Vegas?" she asked.

"I don't know *what* they have in Las Vegas." Byron dipped a French fry in ketchup. "Maybe they interpret the history of gambling."

"Weird stuff," Chloe affirmed vaguely. Where had she heard something about gambling lately? From Roelke. Hadn't he mentioned some gambling problem to Libby, that day of the cookout? But ... surely it was ridiculous to think there might be a connection between a director from Las Vegas and a local gambling problem. Wasn't it?

She decided to change course. "Listen, I've been wanting to ask you something. Are there any interpreters left on staff who were working in the Norwegian area in the seventies?"

"Sure. Let me look at the staff list and get back to you."

"I'd appreciate it." Chloe took a sip of her water before moving on to the last item on her Byron list. "Do you have keys to the trailers?"

"The artifact trailers?" Byron looked startled. "Why would I?"

"In case you wanted something for one of the site buildings?"

He shook his head. But he suddenly seemed fascinated with his French fries.

"I wondered," Chloe said, "because someone went in there without my permission last week. And you said something about Norwegian artifacts in the pink trailer that made me think you'd been in there yourself not too long ago."

Byron flushed. "Well ... yes," he admitted. "I did go in there, the week before you started. I got Stan to let me in."

"What were you looking for?"

"Reproductions. I need cookware, and garden tools, and—well, you've seen the requests, so you know. It occurred to me there might be something stashed away in there."

Chloe frowned. "Why didn't you just wait until I got here?"

"We're *desperate* for repro stuff on site. I didn't see any harm in spiriting away anything I could find before you were the wiser. I figured it could take weeks—months—for you to find time to deal with something like that."

"Did you find anything? Take anything?"

"No. I just took a quick look, and I didn't see anything that wasn't accessioned."

Was he telling the truth? Chloe didn't know. But she had confirmed that both Nika and Byron had been in the trailers prior to her arrival. Either could have ripped the accession form page from the ledger.

"I know you need reproduction items," Chloe said finally. "And I'll gladly work with you on that. But you're right about the demands on my time, especially since Ralph wants me to focus exclusively on designing the new storage facility."

Byron leaned back in his chair and regarded her, his eyes sober. "You'll pay for it. With Ralph, I mean. Taking him on in the staff meeting. Maybe you should … you know. Apologize."

I'll lay down in traffic first, Chloe thought. "What's he going to do, fire me?"

"Well … yeah! New hires are on probation for six months. You've got no protection."

Chloe shrugged. "It doesn't matter."

"Don't you care?"

"Nope." She didn't. Her first-day dream of finding normal was long gone—splintered in a car wreck, bashed in the head.

Byron shook his head. But when the waitress returned with the check, he snatched it from her hand. "Give it to me," he said. "I'm buying."

"Well, I'd consider it a courtesy," Roelke told the Dane County detective assigned to Mr. Solberg's murder. "I know Ms. Ellefson's problems are likely unrelated, but you never know… yes, you can reach me here. Thanks." He dictated the Eagle Police Department number before hanging up.

"What was that about?" Chief Naborski asked from behind him.

Roelke had waited until Marie was on break before making the call, and he'd wanted to get as much information as possible before talking with the chief. So much for that plan. He swiveled to face his boss. "It's a long story."

Chief Naborski jerked his head. "Come into my office."

Fifteen minutes later, the older man knew everything that Roelke did. He had listened in silence, his chair tipped back toward the wall. Now he let the chair rest on four legs and put both palms on his desk. "So. You're indirectly connected to a murder in Dane County because a friend of yours found the body."

"I think it might be tied to the events at Old World Wisconsin."

"You've got an unlocked trailer that might have been left that way by the employee. A possible intruder alert from an outdated system that often gives false alarms, at a building that appears to be undisturbed. Still no burglary report from the site director." The chief picked up a pencil and began playing with it.

"Yeah," Roelke admitted. "That's about what I've got."

They heard Marie come back from break and slam her purse into a drawer in the next room. "Let me know if you hear anything from Dane County," Chief Naborski said finally. "But you probably won't. Roelke, this is not your concern. We do not have jurisdiction on state property. You will not involve yourself further."

"Right." Roelke kept his best cop face in place.

"Any luck tracing the bookie who ripped off Ginger Herschorn's nephew?"

"Still working on it. I'm pretty sure we don't have enough to convince a judge we need a warrant. There's one other angle ..."

"What's that?"

"A guy came into the bar that first night, acting squirrely. Stanley Colontuono. Lives at the end of Marigold Court. Neighbors have been complaining about a surge in traffic into his place over the past couple of weeks. Skeet and I have been keeping an eye on it."

"What kind of vehicles?"

"All kinds. More beaters than anything else, but a couple of high-end jobs as well. If Colontuono is our bookie, he might have moved his operation home after he found out we'd had a complaint. Or it could be drugs. Or nothing at all."

The chief nodded. "Keep me posted."

Roelke headed out on patrol, hoping the Dane County detective would call back by the end of his shift. If not, Roelke would get in touch with him later, and leave his home telephone number instead.

Chloe was working in the trailers that afternoon when the phone rang. She glanced at her watch: ten to five. Maybe Ralph had waited until the end of the day to fire her. She answered in her most courteous and professional tone: "Chloe Ellefson."

The voice in her ear was definitely not Ralph Petty's. "I need you to get over here. Right now. Before I explode."

Chloe blinked. "Nika?"

"I will *not* be treated this way. You hear me?"

"What way?" Chloe began, then interrupted herself. "No, wait. You're at the church? I'll come over."

By the time she reached the main entrance the site was officially closed, so Chloe took the liberty of driving out to St. Peter's Church. Nika stood by the fence, rigid.

"What is this all about?" Chloe asked as she got out of her car.

"I'll show you." Nika turned and marched down the basement stairs. With every step the white wooden beads adorning the bottom of each cornrowed braid bounced for emphasis.

In two short weeks, Nika had made amazing progress in transforming the church basement into a serviceable storage facility. She'd gotten some large storage cabinets donated from God-knew-where. Everything was organized and tidy… except for a jumble of baby clothes lying beside an empty archival storage box on the worktable. Baby clothes, Chloe thought. This particular crisis would have to involve baby clothes.

Nika pointed at the offending pile. "I had all these things packed up, and he comes along and does this!"

"*Who*?"

"Ralph Petty!"

"Why on earth…"

"You ask me *why*?" Nika's voice quivered with rage. "There is no *why*! I'm down here working and he walks in and says he wants to see what I'm doing. Next thing I know he's taking everything out of this box. When I asked him what for, he tells me he wants to inspect my work."

Chloe's jaw tightened. That little prick.

Nika jabbed one elegant finger toward Chloe's nose. "I will not take this, you hear me? I will not—"

"*Hey.*" Chloe put her hand over Nika's and pressed down. For a brief moment the younger woman resisted. Then she let her hand drop.

"I want to hear what you have to say," Chloe said. "But I will not be harangued. We clear on that?"

"Yes."

"OK, here's the thing." Chloe ran a hand over her hair. "In a staff meeting this morning I pissed off Ralph. Big time. In fact, when the phone rang I thought it was him, calling to fire me." She exhaled slowly. "Evidently he decided to take his ire out on you instead."

Nika picked up a christening gown and smoothed row upon row of white lace. Her long brown fingers against the lace were so gentle that Chloe had to look away. "I spent *hours* cleaning and packing these things," Nika said.

"I know. I'm sorry. I'd talk to him about what he did, but honestly, it would probably do more harm than good."

Nika gave Chloe a level gaze. "What did you do in the staff meeting? If you don't mind me asking."

Chloe, long past worrying about the subtleties of professional decorum, told Nika what had happened.

Nika shook her head. "And you think he's so small that he'd come down here and give me shit rather than deal straight with you?"

"Well, it's just a theory." Chloe considered. "I didn't ask his permission before we got you set up down here. That didn't help, either. Ralph is a classic micro-manager."

"You think?"

Chloe leaned against the worktable. "Nobody wants a top-of-the-line collections facility more than me. But I intended to get a sense of the collection overall, make some estimates, and come up with a plan that reflects the size and scope of our collection. Ralph decided I was dawdling, so he took the liberty of drawing up his own architectural plan."

Nika raised her eyebrows. "Was it any good?"

"Oh, please. I could do better with a crayon and a cocktail napkin. And you would probably have the whole thing spec'd by now, and fundraising well underway. Listen, try not to let him get to you. Average middle-aged white guys tend to flock toward administrative positions. You gotta get used to them."

"I suppose." Nika looked pensive. "You know, I've processed hundreds of items down here, and to the best of my knowledge, not a single one was worn by a black person."

"I'm not surprised by that." Chloe sighed. "Have you found any good Euro pieces, though? Anything worthy of writing up?"

Nika began re-folding the christening gown around protective rolls of acid-free tissue. "No such luck."

"Don't give up. You'll find the right story somewhere." And that, Chloe thought, is the last piece of banal advice I'm going to spout.

"Thanks," Nika said. "And ... I hope you don't get fired."

As Chloe was leaving, she spotted something truly amazing in the corner: two four-drawer filing cabinets, old but serviceable. "Are these full?"

Nika shook her head. "Not even close. They were surplus, I think. I found them in the pole barn at Restoration. Joel helped me haul them over here, clean 'em up and bang out a few dents. I figured they'd get put to use somehow."

"Well, I'd like to commandeer a drawer or two. Byron dumped a bunch of files on me, and I don't have any place to put them."

"Where are they?"

"In the trunk of my car."

Nika followed Chloe out to the Pinto. Her eyebrows lifted when she saw the overflowing file folders. "What is this stuff, anyway?"

"Repro requests from the interpreters. They need everything from darning eggs to plows." Chloe grappled a box up to one hip. "And Byron thoughtfully saved six years' worth of vendor catalogs for me."

With Nika's help, all of the forms and catalogs were soon down in the basement. "Leave them," Nika said. "I'll put them away."

"Thanks. Offer accepted."

"It's the least I can do, after losing my cool." She held Chloe's gaze. "I apologize for that."

"Apology accepted, too." Chloe dusted her hands on her trousers and headed back up the stairs. "Let's call it a day."

They emerged into a peaceful evening. "You want a ride back to the parking lot? Oh—wait." Chloe sighed. "I promised Byron I'd look at a jack in the wagon shop. I might as well do that while I'm here."

"No problem. I'll walk."

Chloe checked on the jack at the wagon shop, and scribbled a note for Byron. She was plodding back to her car when she remembered something else. She'd planned to ask Nika for an overview of her progress with the textile project before meeting with Leila in Madison the next day. Numbers, analysis—the hands-on stats bosses like. Shit.

Well, she'd take a quick survey herself. That would have to do.

Back in the basement, Chloe took a closer look around. Cabinets were labeled: *Children's. Men's. Ladies, pre-1900. Ladies, post-1900.* Storage boxes were stacked and labeled as well: *Gloves. Aprons. Mourning items.* Rows of hats sat poised on shelves, protected with tissue. A stack of neatly typed forms stood on the old desk Nika had found somewhere. If I just got out of her way, Chloe thought, Nika could whip this whole site into shape.

Chloe carefully moved a stack of folded textiles aside on the desk so she could scribble a few notes for her meeting. An apron string slipped loose. "Can't have that," she murmured, and picked the piece up for refolding. It was a white cotton apron, limp and spotted with age, but lovely nonetheless. White embroidery stitches, almost invisible, created lacey designs and flowers. She touched the stitching with a gentle finger. Some long-ago woman had stitched the apron, perhaps for Sunday best. Or for a hope chest, a trousseau, a gift? Chloe unfolded the apron for a closer look.

And her mouth opened in surprise. Letters had been stitched carefully above the hem. *Vi maa uddanne vaare dötre.*

Chloe's eyes narrowed as she squinted at the white work. *Dötre*... Wasn't that "daughter" in Norwegian? Or possibly Danish. Either way, Nika had discovered a very rare ethnic piece.

Half an hour earlier, Chloe had asked about just that. Why had Nika lied?

TWENTY-TWO

THE NEXT MORNING, CHLOE left the farmhouse at 6:45 A.M. Even with a stop at the Cambridge Bakery for coffee and a chocolate doughnut, she made it to the State Historical Society of Wisconsin headquarters building in Madison ten minutes early for her 8:30 meeting with Leila.

The society building was old and elegant, with mosaic tile floors, worn marble staircases, artifacts displayed in glass cases, and the obligatory portraits of dead white men on the walls. Chloe paused in the lobby, letting perceptions come: layers of quiet busy-ness, varnished with a brittle veneer of frustration. Chloe attributed both to the employees with state-mandated obligations to preserve and protect the past, but insufficient funds to do so. Nothing here to jangle her nerves. Good. Her nerves were jangled enough.

Leila was a plump woman, perhaps forty, with prematurely gray hair cut in a thick bob. Her windowless office on the fourth floor overflowed with piles of stuff, old and new: potato mashers and emergency Management Plans, hog scrapers and plastic cups full of paperclips. Chloe's assumption of chaos disappeared as Leila repeatedly exhibited an uncanny ability to put her hands instantly on whatever she wanted.

Leila talked rapidly, outlining division procedures for everything from handling potential donations to closing up the site for the winter. "I think that covers it," she said finally. "Our next division collections committee meeting isn't until—" she consulted her calendar—"July eighteenth."

Chloe dutifully marked the date on her own planner. July 18th seemed impossibly far away.

"Any questions?" Leila asked. "I know you got dropped into deep water. But the historic sites division is staggeringly understaffed. You learn to tread water pretty fast."

Or sink, Chloe thought. "I do have a question," she said. "Who do I work for?"

Leila looked startled. "Excuse me?"

"Who is the primary person I answer to?" Chloe said. "You, or my site director? Here's the thing." She summarized her difference of opinion with Ralph Petty about the collections storage facility plan.

Leila toyed with a button hook while she listened. "Well, that's tricky. I am responsible for overseeing collections issues at all of the historic sites, though. And I agree that a general assessment of what you've got is a logical first step. I'll talk with the division administrator and let him know that we have a possible scenario." Possible scenario was evidently historic sites division code for "conflict between site curator and site director."

Chloe had assumed that her orientation would consume much of the day, but Leila indicated she had a ten o'clock meeting with a paper conservator. "You can call me any time," she said, as Chloe gathered her things. "And I'll see you on the eighteenth."

"Right!" Chloe said brightly, and left. She didn't mind having most of the day ahead of her. She had projects of her own in mind.

First stop: the microforms room. Margueritte Donovan, Old World's curator of research, had refused delivery of the wallpaper paste problem, explaining kindly that such issues did indeed fall into Chloe's domain. She had also explained that the freelance curator who had researched and furnished the Tobler House had left a furnishings plan with specific information about each artifact acquired, but little contextual material to help the interpreters explain the building to visitors. "Next time you're in Madison, try going through the Green County newspaper," Margueritte told Chloe finally. "You can learn more about the community. And sometimes you get lucky and find some descriptive detail that can make all the difference in understanding how a building was furnished and used."

"I'm pretty swamped," Chloe'd said, trying to look needy.

"Me too," Margueritte had said firmly. "I'm up to my eyebrows looking for a Polish building to bring to the site. That's Ralph's priority."

Chloe knew all about Ralph's priorities. She also sympathized with the interpreters' needs. So after leaving Leila's office that morning, Chloe made her way to a cramped room tucked behind the main library. She found the proper rolls of microfilm and, miraculously, an empty reader. Huddled in the dark among genealogists and grad students, she rolled through the pages of old newsprint as quickly as she dared, squinting, skimming, hitting "print" whenever anything seemed relevant to the Tobler House. Two hours later she paid for her file of smeary photocopies, and left.

The society building was surrounded by the UW campus. Chloe bought lunch from an Asian man operating a cart on the library mall, and munched a vegetarian spring roll while enjoying the sun. Students in shorts and flip-flops sauntered past. Young men played Frisbee with their dogs. Young women sunned themselves on the grass in front of the historical society building. Across the street, beyond the student union, Lake Mendota sparkled invitingly. Chloe considered squandering more time with an ice cream cone, eaten on the terrace overlooking the lake. Then she remembered her main goal in coming to the society today, and the events behind it. She headed back into scholarly gloom.

The iconographic collections—photographs—were housed in another small windowless room. "Be sure you sign in," a student worker said impatiently, indicating a clipboard by the door. She was pencil thin and had a snake tattooed in a coil around one arm. How long did it take to get that? Chloe wondered, as she scribbled her name, address, the date and time of entry, and her topic of interest on the form. Then she told the young woman what she wanted.

"Name files are in those drawers," the worker said, pointing. "I'll have to pull the Dahl stuff for you."

While the Dahl photographs were being fetched, Chloe thumbed through the "H" names file. Harrod ... Hart ... *yes!* She pulled the folder labeled "Haugen" and parked at a table.

"Hey!" The student worker's voice over her shoulder was accusing. "You've got to wear gloves!"

"I haven't touched any photos yet," Chloe observed mildly, but she dutifully pulled on a pair of cotton gloves from the pile left out for patrons.

At first glance, the file appeared to contain only images of one Nils P. Haugen: a ferrotype of Nils as a young student, several *carte de visites* of Nils as a young man, a cabinet card of Nils in middle age, one black and white photograph taken in 1945 of Nils in his living room with his wife and two daughters, the latter in Norwegian folk dress.

Chloe turned that one over and found an inscription: Nils P. Haugen, First Tax Commissioner of Wisconsin.

Chloe leaned back in her chair, considering. As she'd told Roelke, the elusive ale bowl might be especially valuable if it was known to be made or owned by someone famous. Did being the first tax commissioner of Wisconsin qualify as famous? Only to a very select minority, surely. "This is just too weird," she muttered, earning another frown from the tattooed student.

At the bottom of the file she found the only Haugen image that did not belong to Nils P., a poor-quality photocopy of what might have originally been either a retouched daguerreotype or an oil painting. It showed the head and shoulders of a stern man dressed in a black coat and white shirt, with a long gray beard. Late 1890s, she guessed, although she was better at dating women's clothing than men's. Some helpful soul had blithely scrawled "Halvor Haugen" across one corner of the image.

Was Halvor Haugen an ancestor of Berget's? Without full genealogical information, it was impossible to know.

This is a complete waste of time, Chloe thought. Still, she made photocopies of both Halvor and Nils P.'s likenesses before moving on. The girl had wheeled a cart stacked with gray file boxes from a back room ... boxes and boxes and boxes.

"These are all Dahl photos?" Chloe asked.

"All Dahl photos."

Geez Louise. Mindful of the ticking clock, Chloe began quickly scanning the photographs.

Soon her back and her eyes joined her head in aching solidarity. The curator part of her brain was impressed by the rich visual documentation of southern Wisconsin in the 1870s. The other part, the part that desperately wanted to understand Berget Haugen Lundquist's and Bill Solberg's deaths, was completely frustrated. Andreas Dahl had photographed many Norwegian-American families in front of their homes, but the vast majority were posed only with mass-produced, American-made belongings. Women in bustle dresses sat at sewing machines, men stood proudly beside new-fangled reapers, children played croquet. *We are American now.*

Only a handful of images held any hint of the old country: a Norwegian flag flying over a house or excursion boat, a family that had posed for "before" and "after" photographs (one standing in front of a small log cabin, the other in front of a beautiful frame home), and several portraits of women wearing decorative, obviously old-country collars. Chloe photocopied these for Nika, so the afternoon wasn't a total waste. But she'd seen nothing she could identify as an ale bowl, much less *the* ale bowl.

"Thank you," she said to the student. "I'm through with these."

"Be sure you sign out!" the girl called after her, vigilant to the end.

Chloe picked up the clipboard and wrote down the time she was leaving Iconography. It had been a quiet day in the photo archives, she noticed. Only one other person had used the collection, someone who'd marked their interest as "Iron Brigade."

Then Chloe went very still as she registered the neat printing several lines above that, left by someone who had visited on Saturday and spent six hours looking at photographs. She'd marked her interest as "Norwegian/Dahl." And she'd recorded her name: Tanika Austin.

So what? Chloe asked herself, as she headed down the stairwell. So what if Nika came here on Saturday? She's a hard worker, self-motivated, interested in ethnic objects.

But Chloe had asked Nika if she had plans for the weekend, and Nika had said "Nothing special." Not a lie, exactly, but why hadn't she mentioned an excursion to the historical society? Even if the trip had been spontaneous, it seemed a little odd that Nika hadn't mentioned it yesterday.

Chloe had also asked Nika if she'd found any interesting ethnic pieces among the textiles she was cataloging. Nika *had* lied about that.

When Chloe spotted a recycling bin on one of the landings, she stopped long enough to discard the photocopies she'd made for her intern.

Ten minutes later she was dialing a phone in the lobby. She had one more stop to make that afternoon, and the society's collections processing and storage facilities were locked away from public access.

The registrar who came to let Chloe into the nether regions didn't look much older than the student worker upstairs. She was short and petite, with brown hair that hung in a glossy curtain to her butt. "I'm Ann," she said, offering a quick handshake.

"Thanks for this," Chloe said, following her through a maze of narrow corridors. "I'm sure you're busy."

"Always," Ann said.

OK, message received. Chloe didn't mind. She wasn't in the mood for chitchat either.

Ann's tiny office was everything Leila's was not, precisely ordered and sterile. "I never did find the site copy of the transfer form for that artifact I spoke with you about a couple of weeks ago," Chloe began. "It's a Norwegian piece, and—"

"Accession number?"

"SHSW 1962.37.3."

Nine seconds later Ann handed Chloe a file. "Here you go."

Chloe flipped it open. The original donation form Mrs. Lundquist had signed in 1962 lay on top, identical to the photocopy the elderly woman had given Chloe. Beneath it lay a neatly-typed transfer form, officially reassigning the ale bowl to the OWW collection. The ale bowl's new designation was OWW1977.14.1—which fit the numbering sequence in the Old World accession ledger where the page had been removed.

But stapled to that form was a page of hand-scribbled notes, evidently written in 1962 by the curator who had initially accepted the donations: *All three pieces came from Mrs. Jack Lundquist's maternal great-grandmother, Gro Skavlem.*

Chloe shoved aside her instinctive flare of feminist indignation—Mrs. Jack Lundquist, indeed—and stared at the words. Gro Skavlem. She had a name!

"There's a note here," she told Ann, stabbing her finger at the form. "Why didn't you read me this information when I first called you?"

Ann folded her arms. "I recall our conversation quite clearly. You asked me about the date of transfer. I provided it."

Chloe tried to count to ten before responding, and only made it to three. "First, I'd like photocopies of this transfer form and notes. Please."

Ann silently took the folder, disappeared, and returned with the photocopies.

"Thank you. Second, I'd really like to see the other two pieces in the original donation."

"You'll have to talk to Greg about that." Ann sat down at her desk.

"OK, here's the thing. I'm new, I've never met Greg, and I don't know my way around." Chloe scrounged up a smile that she hoped might qualify as congenial. "Could you direct me to his office, please?"

Greg was a plump middle-aged man, completely bald, wearing a Hawaiian shirt printed in vivid reds and blues. "Sure, no problem," he said affably, after Chloe explained her quest.

Chloe refrained from hugging him. Within minutes, Greg gently placed a large wooden plate on a worktable. "Here's the first one."

The plate—what her mother would call a *smorgåsbord*—was painted with swirls of brown and orange and green. Chloe leaned close. "It's stunning!"

"It is," Greg agreed.

"Can you identify the artist?" she asked hopefully.

Greg shook his head, staring at the plate. "No. It has a Telemark feel, though. See the asymmetrical design, and the main C scroll?"

"Yes," Chloe said, although he'd already lost her.

"But there's a unique quality, too. And I don't think the piece is old enough to attribute to one of the Norwegian masters."

Chloe shot him a glance. "Made in Wisconsin?"

"That's quite possible. And definitely before the twentieth-century revival."

"So that makes this plate pretty rare, right?" Chloe felt a flicker of hope.

"It does." Greg nodded. "Let me find the other donated piece."

Chloe studied the *smorgåsbord* while she waited. Who had held the brush that made this flourish, that scroll? Could it possibly have been the gruff-looking Halvor Haugen? She struggled to reconcile this glorious example of creative expression with the man posed so stiffly.

Greg emerged from the ranks of shelves with a second *smorgåsbord* in his gloved hands. It was similar to the first, with flowing flowers and curlicues. But this one had Gothic Norwegian lettering around the edge. Chloe turned her head to make out the words … and sucked in a harsh breath.

Vi maa uddanne vaare dötre.

She pointed. "Can you translate this?"

"Sorry. I don't speak Norwegian."

"Is there anybody on staff here who does?"

"Not that I know of. I'm sure someone at the university could help you. Want a campus phone directory?"

Chloe accepted the offer with a growing sense of urgency, and dialed the listed number. "Sorry," said the receptionist who answered the phone. "No Norwegian classes are scheduled for the summer session. Professor Gulbrandson is in Norway."

Shit! Well, another phone call to good old mom was in order. Chloe hung up the phone and turned to see Greg regarding her with a slight frown. "Is something wrong?" he asked.

"Not really," Chloe lied, scrabbling for a response that wouldn't leave this nice man thinking that the new curator at Old World Wisconsin was nuttier than banana bread. "We ended up with a bowl from the same donor transferred to Old World, and I—I'm just curious about that phrase."

"Ah. I see," Greg said, although his dubious expression said that he didn't—not really.

"My mom's a rosemaler," Chloe added. "I'm familiar with some of the more common expressions painted onto plates. *Takk for maten. Hunger er den beste kokke*. This one is new to me. I'll ask her about it."

Chloe took a moment to carefully copy the lettering on the *smorgåsbord*. If she was remembering correctly, the words painted on this old plate exactly matched the lettering embroidered on the apron Nika had so carefully set aside in the basement of St. Peter's Church.

Chloe puzzled over the day's revelations as she drove out of Madison. She didn't believe that seeing *Vi maa uddanne vaare dötre* on an old Norwegian apron one day and on an old rosemaled *smorgåsbord* the next was a coincidence. Mrs. Lundquist, though, had not donated any textiles to the State Historical Society. Chloe had seen the donor files. One ale bowl, two plates. No question about that.

So, what was the relationship between the apron and the *smorgåsbord*? And what was Nika's role in all this?

When Chloe reached Fort Atkinson, she angled east toward Eagle instead of continuing south toward home. She needed to see that apron again. She would check its accession number, drive back to the trailer, and see what she could learn from the donation form.

She reached Old World Wisconsin's main gate well after closing time. A few vehicles were still parked under the pines—probably visitor center staff tallying the day's ticket and gift shop sales. Nika's car was not among them, and it wasn't parked at St. Peter's Church, either. Good. Nika was gone.

But so was the apron. It was no longer on the desk, or on the worktable, or anywhere else in plain view. Chloe scanned the gray archival storage boxes stacked on shelves, found one labeled "aprons," and pulled it down to the worktable. After pulling off the lid she hesitated, contemplating the textiles packed with extraordinary care. No way could she paw through this box without Nika, if she happened to look, knowing that someone had messed with her work.

"Oh for God's sake," Chloe muttered crossly. "You're her boss. You are allowed." She dug gingerly through the aprons: 1940s gingham and 1880s lace, immaculate and patched, child-sized and tent-like. No Norwegian apron.

After returning the box to the shelf Chloe balled her fists in frustration. She didn't know where else to look. Defeated, she locked up.

As she drove past the empty administration building on her way home, she swerved at the last minute into the small, empty parking lot. She might as well check her mailbox while no one was here. Much better than taking the chance of running into Ralph Petty during regular office hours.

The row of plastic mail holders used by permanent staff was posted just inside the door. Chloe grabbed her handful of stuff and got back into her car before shuffling through it. An ad for window treatments that protected historic interiors from ultra-violet light. An all-staff memo from Byron about July Fourth programming. A letter from a tinsmith, wanting an appointment to show his reproduction wares.

And a special delivery envelope from her mother: "Here's the basic genealogy, as far as I've gotten. I'm just showing the direct line to your donor, but have info on aunts and uncles, etc. if you want it. Still digging."

Chloe ran her finger down the page, following the lines of her mother's careful printing, muttering as she read:

"Nels and Gro Skavlem emigrate from Norway to Wisconsin in 1845, five sons born before their only daughter, Astrid Skavlem (Nelson), arrived . . . Astrid's daughter Brita Nelson (Haugen) born 1888 . . . Brita's daughter Berget Haugen (Lundquist) born 1912. (1914, Emil Haugen born.)"

So much for Halvor Haugen. Halvor was evidently irrelevant, since the bowl's provenance went back further than any Haugens in Berget's ancestral line. Chloe had checked for a "Skavlem" file in Iconography before leaving the historical society, and hadn't found anything. But at least she now had confirmation that Berget was descended from Gro Skavlem.

Curious, that with five brothers, Astrid had ended up owning three rosemaled pieces that had belonged to her parents, and that through two more generations, the family heirlooms had passed from mother to daughter. "Score one for the ladies," Chloe said—

The answer hit her like a *lefse* stick to the head.

Ladies. *Dötre.* An embroidered apron. A rosemaled bowl which incorporated carved cow heads into the design, instead of the more traditional dragons or horses.

Chloe jumped out of her car, ran back to the administration building, wrestled with the lock, dropped her key, cursed loudly, got the door open, and grabbed the nearest phone. She dialed the Eagle Police Station first. It rang several times before she heard a click as the call was redirected to the county line.

She didn't want to talk to the county dispatcher. She hung up and dialed Roelke's home number. No answer.

Well, nothing to do but to try again later. Her thoughts still tumbling, she headed for home.

By eleven P.M. Roelke still was not answering his phone. In desperation Chloe called Libby, who said that no, she had no idea where he was.

Chloe's parents didn't answer their phone, either. In desperation Chloe called her sister Kari, who said that no, she had no idea where their parents were.

Where on earth was everyone? Chloe kicked one of the unpacked boxes before admitting defeat and going to bed. But after a couple of hours of restless sleep she found herself awake again, tossing this way and that, kicking off the sleeping bag she was still using in lieu of sheets, then grabbing it back again. Her body couldn't decide if it was exhausted or buzzed.

Eventually she gave up and got up. Her head was in danger of exploding if she thought any more about Norwegian heirlooms, Mrs. Lundquist, and Mr. Solberg. She needed a distraction, something that would still her mind. She picked up *Time and Again*, put it back down. The book was a favorite. She already knew what was going to happen.

Then she remembered the thick stack of photocopies she'd made in the microforms room that afternoon. At this point, even delving into Aldrick Tobler's oh-so-Swiss life was more appealing than other options. She padded to the living room, grabbed the papers from her briefcase, turned on the floor lamp, and settled down to read.

It was boring stuff, mostly—notices of land sales, advertisements, reports from local social clubs—all reproduced in tiny, blurry fonts. Chloe felt her eyes growing gritty with fatigue. Good.

She kept reading. She knew she was too tired when words began to literally not make sense. She rubbed her eyes and forced herself to read the small business notice in her hand again.

She sat up straight, suddenly wide awake, and read it one more time.

Then she turned off the light and went to stand at the living room window, trying to let the darkness soothe her eyes and her nerves. This simply did not make sense.

Nothing was making sense. Alone in her big dark farmhouse, staring at the still night, she wondered if her tentative grip on emotional stability had truly been strained to the breaking point.

Then the night exploded, in a crashing and tinkling of broken glass.

TWENTY-THREE

Roelke felt an odd sense of *déjà vu* as he roared into Chloe's driveway. This time, though, every light in the farmhouse was on. Chloe was sitting on the front step, her blonde hair shining almost white in the porch light's glare. She wore shorts and a long T-shirt and, he was glad to see, sandals. She didn't move when Roelke got out of his truck, but her landlord emerged from the house and came to greet him.

Roelke was operating in that strange half-buzzed, half-exhausted state that comes from too little sleep and too much adrenaline. He had worked the three-to-eleven shift the night before, and had been about to go off-duty when he spotted a clearly inebriated driver weaving north on Highway 67. By the time he'd made his arrest, taken the asshole to the Waukesha County jail, finished his paperwork, and headed home, it was almost two o'clock in the morning. He heard his phone begin to ring as he trudged up the staircase to his apartment.

When he grabbed the receiver, an unfamiliar man's voice greeted him. "Officer McKenna? It's Gene Holsworth. Chloe Ellefson's landlord? We met that time—"

"What happened?"

"She's OK," Gene Holsworth had said. "But I think you better come down here."

Now Roelke gripped the farmer's hard, calloused hand. "What happened?" he asked again.

"Somebody threw a rock through a window. I was up with a sick calf, and heard it."

He pointed. Roelke stared at the savage hole. The bastard had hit Chloe's bedroom window.

"A county deputy has come and gone," Gene was saying. "I tried to get her—" he cocked his head toward Chloe—"to wait over at our place, but she wouldn't go. She didn't even want me to call you."

"I'm not surprised."

Chloe frowned at the two men. "I can hear you, you know."

Gene Holsworth leaned closer and muttered, "The wife and me, we just didn't think she should be by herself."

"I'm *fine*," Chloe announced.

Roelke decided to ignore her for the moment. He helped Gene cover the jagged pane with a piece of plywood brought from next door. "That'll do 'til I can get the glass replaced," Gene said, stowing his hammer back in the loop on his overalls. "It was probably some kids out drinking beer or smoking dope or something. I don't know why they keep hitting this old place, though. I bet this'll kick my insurance up another notch." He shook his head. "Well, if that's it, I'll head on home. I'll be milking before too long."

When the older man was out of earshot, Roelke planted himself in front of Chloe. "Why the hell didn't you call me yourself?"

"Maybe it's because the last time somebody broke into my house, you scolded me because I *did* call you."

"I didn't—that's not—you know I—*Jesus!*" He glared down at her.

Chloe stood, neutralizing his advantage. "I've already called you twice to come rescue me. Maybe I'm sick of playing the distressed damsel."

Roelke had control of his temper; he absolutely would—*not*—grab Chloe's thin shoulders and shake her. But he really, really wanted to.

"Would you use your brain, then?" he snapped instead. "The person who murdered Bill Solberg may very well be the person who came here tonight, in the dark, and—"

"But he *didn't* hurt me. I think he just wanted to scare me."

I will find him, Roelke thought. I will find him and put him behind bars.

"I was in the living room when it happened," Chloe was saying. "It could have been much worse. I won't say it didn't freak me out." She shuddered. "But I'm OK."

"What you say may be right. But I'm still angry."

"Well, I'm angry too! I'm angry at whoever killed poor Mr. Solberg and probably threatened poor Mrs. Lundquist until she had a heart attack. And if you're done yelling at me, I would like to tell you some things I discovered today." She looked at her wrist; no watch. "Well, no, that's stupid, it's very late, and—"

"Would you stop trying to be so damn rational?" Roelke was aware instantly of how irrational *that* sounded. "Get your keys. Lock up the house."

She looked wary. "Why?"

"I don't want to talk here. Nothing's open at this hour, but we can at least get away from this place."

For a moment he thought she was going to argue, but with uncommon good sense, she refrained. "OK," she said. "Let me just grab the files I was looking at."

Five minutes later Roelke parked his truck in the tiny lot at the La Grange crossroads, usually used by people switching to bicycles to explore the Kettle Moraine State Forest. He felt better ensconced in the cab, on Highway 12, close enough to a street lamp that he could see anything coming. His revolver was in the glove compartment and his tank was full of gas.

"OK," he said. "Start at the beginning and tell me what you learned."

Chloe began to rapidly outline her discoveries. "Wait," he said. The adrenaline rush was fading. "Start over. Leave out words like 'accession' and 'iconography.'"

"Berget Haugen Lundquist donated three rosemaled wooden pieces to the State Historical Society in 1962. Two plates and an ale bowl. In 1977, one of those pieces—the ale bowl—was transferred to Old World Wisconsin."

"Right, got it. Go on."

She told him about the embroidered apron and the rosemaled *smorgåsbord*, Andreas Dahl photographs and Mrs. Lundquist's family tree. "Berget Lundquist's ale bowl was passed down from her great-grandmother, Gro Skavlem. But the odd thing is that it was a straight matrilineal line of succession—"

"Would you *please* try to keep it simple?" Roelke longed for a cup of coffee.

Chloe looked at him triumphantly. "I think Gro Skavlem was the rosemaler!"

"So?"

"*So?* Don't you get it? Rosemaling was not a traditional women's art. All the known rosemalers from the nineteenth century were men. Rosemaled pieces that date to the period between the first wave of immigration and the twentieth-century revival are rare to begin with, but if we can prove that a *woman* painted the bowl—"

"Wait, back up. What makes you think this Gro woman painted the bowl?"

"It's just a hunch," she admitted. "But here it is. First, the curator who talked with Berget Lundquist in 1962 noted that the pieces 'were from'"—she used her fingers to indicate quotes—"Gro Skavlem. Now, that could be interpreted as 'handed down from.' But I think it also could be interpreted as 'made by.'"

"Wouldn't the curator have noted that down?"

"Today, absolutely. But record keeping wasn't always as thorough back then."

A pair of headlights appeared in the west. Roelke watched them approach. A Dodge Mirada. "I don't know," he said, when the car had flashed by.

"Then there's the notation that the ale bowl we're looking for was decorated with a cow head motif." She looked at him expectantly. "Cows! Get it?"

"Obviously not," he growled.

"Historically, in Norwegian families, dairying was *women's* work. It was probably a holdover from Viking days, when men sailed off and left all the chores to them. Women milked, made cheese, tended the cows. See?"

Roelke chewed that over, blew out a slow breath, shook his head. "It's possible, I suppose. But it still feels like a stretch."

"Well, I think Gro made the bowl," Chloe said stubbornly. "I just have this gut feeling. Instinct."

Roelke imagined trying to explain Chloe's line of reasoning to Chief Naborski. "I need facts."

Chloe frowned and looked out the window for a moment. "Well, there's also the Nika connection. Nika desperately wanted to find a good ethnic woman's artifact that she could research and write up."

"But how would she have even known about the ale bowl?"

"She was here for a whole week before I was. She could have gone through the accession books. Somebody tore out that page…" Chloe sighed. "Although it is hard to believe that Nika would get so obsessive about the ale bowl based on just the sketchy information on that accession form," she admitted. "I didn't understand the bowl's significance myself until I saw the genealogy my mom sent, and realized that the rosemaled pieces had passed from mother to daughter for four generations."

Roelke pressed his knuckles against his forehead before speaking. "Even if Nika *did* decide to look for the ale bowl after she started working at Old World, why had Berget Lundquist suddenly decided she desperately wanted the ale bowl back? You said Berget Lundquist had started in on that before you *or* Nika started working at Old World, right? And if Nika had actually found the bowl, and wanted more information from the donor, wouldn't she just have called Mrs. Lundquist and asked? It seems to me that Nika finding the bowl, and figuring out what she could about its history, would be all she needed to write her article or whatever. Someone has been trying to *steal* the ale bowl, presumably to sell. Your Nika theory doesn't add up."

"Well… maybe." Chloe scooched down in the seat and propped her feet on the dashboard. "What doesn't line up for *me* is the apron. It shows up in Nika's workspace, and then it disappears. I don't know where the apron originally came from. But with the same Norwegian phrase as Berget's plate? No way is that a coincidence."

"Is there any way Nika might have seen that plate?"

Chloe's shoulder's drooped. "I don't know. Shit! How stupid is that? I was there, and I didn't even ask the curator! I didn't think of it."

"The curator would have mentioned it though, don't you think? If someone else had recently asked to see those very pieces?"

She thought about that. "Yes. But they have interns up there too, student workers... the person who helped me in Iconography today was probably a work-study student. It is possible that someone other than the curator showed Nika the *smorgåsbord*, especially since she was there on a Saturday. Unless they've got a big exhibit launch coming up or something, museum curators generally work regular office hours. And the artifact storage area isn't public, so they don't keep a visitor log the way they do in Iconography."

Roelke leaned his head against the window. "You've spent time with this woman. Do you think Nika is capable of getting mixed up in something... unethical? Illegal?" Another car came and went on the highway, this one traveling west. A Ford, driven too fast. Roelke reminded himself that he wasn't on duty.

"I've come to like Nika," Chloe said slowly. "And in a lot of ways, I really respect her. But she's lied to me, and she's sometimes evasive. She's got an explosive temper. She's driven. Her fiancé mentioned once that Nika has a lot she wants to accomplish, but also some things to leave behind."

"What's Nika's last name?"

"Her full name is Tanika Austin. She's going to grad school in Illinois, but she grew up in Milwaukee."

"Hunh." Roelke chewed that over. Then he reached across, opened the glove compartment, and pulled out a couple of index cards so he could make notes.

"I think that once Nika sets her mind on something, some goal … she's probably capable of doing whatever she needs to do to get what she wants."

"If nothing else, she may have stolen the apron," Roelke said. "Could it be identified?"

"It would be marked with an accession number. Unfortunately, I didn't write the number down when I had the chance. But the embroidery makes the apron unique. I'd know it if I saw it again."

A murder investigation, Roelke thought, and a missing apron. If there was a link between the two, he couldn't find it. "There's something here we're not seeing. Some incident that started a domino reaction."

"I know." Chloe pushed her hair behind her ears. "Did I ever mention that Nika got her tires slashed in Eagle one night?"

"That was Nika's car? I heard about that at the station."

"I don't know if that has anything to do with anything, but it could." She was silent a moment, considering. "Maybe two different people are hunting the bowl."

Roelke tapped his thumb against the steering wheel. He didn't know how to figure this out. He didn't know how to protect Chloe. He felt powerless. There were few things he hated more.

"I'm just an Eagle cop," he said finally. "You need to talk with the detective handling Mr. Solberg's murder—"

"And tell him what?" Chloe demanded. "That I'm missing an apron now, too?"

"Then talk to your site director," Roelke insisted. "It's time to go on the record with all of this."

"I can't talk to the director." Chloe looked out the window.

"Why not?"

"Long story. Believe me when I say I wouldn't get a thoughtful audience right now."

"Chloe—"

"I think the director's going to fire me, alright? And if I get fired, I'll never be able to figure this out. And I *need* to do this—"

"*Why*?" Roelke demanded. "Why the hell do you need to be the one to—"

"Because Mrs. Lundquist—"

"Mrs. Lundquist is dead!"

She shifted on the seat to face him. In the dim light he could just make out the hard set to her jaw. "Yes, she is. The least I can do is help find out why. And if the son of a bitch responsible for all this is the same person who tried to break into my house while I was asleep, I want to help catch him."

"That son of a bitch may well be a murderer—"

"That's right! And if someone who works at Old World Wisconsin is a thief and a murderer, this could just be the beginning! What if he gets away with it?"

"Chloe—"

"And you know what? I haven't done much in my short time at Old World, but maybe I don't want this going down on my watch. Maybe I want to prove Ralph Petty wrong. Maybe I want to accomplish something worthwhile. Maybe I want to feel good about myself again."

Roelke had no idea what to say to that.

"Look," she said, her voice quieter. "I don't have any reason to think that the detective in Madison will take me seriously, or my own site director either. But I want to find out who thinks they can scare me out of my home. I want to get whoever scared Mrs. Lundquist, and killed Mr. Solberg."

Roelke wished he knew how to make her back down. "Aren't you afraid?" he asked finally.

She regarded him. "I wasn't afraid when I saw that person climbing into my house through the window," she said slowly. "Tonight, when that window crashed—that did scare me. For a minute."

Roelke rubbed his eyes. It wasn't enough.

"I still think someone was only trying to scare me tonight. I just don't know why."

"Somebody knows you're asking questions. Somebody thinks you're getting too close."

"I wish it were true. I don't feel close to anything at all."

Roelke realized he could see smudges of exhaustion beneath Chloe's eyes. He looked at the luminous dial on his watch. Five-thirty. Dawn was creeping over the horizon. Gene Holsworth and his sons were probably already milking their cows, while "the wife" measured coffee and sliced bacon.

"Where do you want to go?" he asked.

She blinked. "You mean, now? Home, I guess."

Not the farmhouse. Anywhere but that damned sterile farmhouse, home to nothing but piles of still-sealed moving boxes, and too easy a target. "That's a bad idea."

"Oh for heaven's sake, it's getting light out. Don't be a Neanderthal. I'll be fine. I can walk from here if you—"

"How about I take you to Libby's place?"

She sat up straight. "With the kids? No way."

"Your parents' place, then."

"No! I'm not taking this to them, either. Besides, it's too far. By the time I got there, I'd have to turn around and drive back to work."

He regarded her. "You're not going to work today."

"Of course I am!"

"Call in sick."

"I don't want to call in sick. I need to go to work and go through the accession books, page by page. I might be able to find the accession record for that apron. If it was removed, I can figure out the missing number and see if the registrar in Madison has a copy. They may not, if the donation came originally to Old World, instead of transferring—"

"That can wait."

She turned on him. "No it can't! If I can find the provenance for that apron, it might tell us something important. Something crucial."

"But you're exhausted!"

"So are you! Are you planning to call in sick?"

He wasn't. For a long moment they scowled at each other. Birds were limbering their vocal muscles now, preparing to chorus the sun up. I'm trying to protect you! Roelke wanted to shout, but he was wise enough—at least he hoped it was wise—to keep his mouth shut on that one.

Chloe suddenly popped a hand to her mouth in an oddly childlike gesture. "Oh, geez! And I have to talk to Margueritte about Tobler!"

"Talk to who about what?"

"Sorry. Work stuff. It's got nothing to do with this Norwegian mess."

Roelke reached for the ignition key, and started the motor. "You make me nuts sometimes," he muttered. "You really, really do." After checking for oncoming traffic, he pulled onto the highway.

"Where are we going?" she demanded suspiciously.

"We are going to get breakfast," he said. Then something else occurred to him, something he'd almost forgotten in the events of the past few hours. "And after I've had some coffee," he added, "I am going to tell you about Stanley Colontuono."

TWENTY-FOUR

Back at the farmhouse, Chloe quickly changed into khaki trousers and a clean red shirt. As she stood in front of the bathroom mirror, brushing her hair, she saw dark blotches beneath her eyes. The shirt needed ironing, too. At least red was a power color.

Fifteen minutes later she and Roelke settled into a corner booth at the Cloverleaf Diner. "I can recommend the apple fritters," Chloe said.

"You need protein."

"Geez Louise, Roelke, would you please lighten up?"

"Would you please start taking things seriously?"

A waitress interrupted their standoff by silently splashing coffee into white ceramic mugs. Roelke ordered a Farmer's Breakfast: two eggs, two pancakes, two sausages. Chloe ordered an apple fritter but, to make nice, added an order of scrambled eggs. "Made with cheese, if possible," she added, then turned back to Roelke. "So, what's this about Stanley?"

Voice low, Roelke told her about the flow of traffic recently observed at his house. "I am trusting you to keep this to yourself," he added sternly.

Chloe put one placating palm in the air. "It won't go any further. But . . . what does it mean? You think Stanley is involved in some gambling ring?"

"I don't know. If he's the bookie, it would have no connection to your ale bowl. But if he's a gambler, it could mean he suddenly has a need for cash."

Chloe pondered that while the waitress slammed their plates onto the table and disappeared again. "But Stanley has access to everything on the site. Why would he home in on one ale bowl? And if Stan *did* steal the bowl, and sell it so he could pay off gambling debts, how did Mrs. Lundquist get involved?"

Roelke dribbled syrup onto his pancakes. "I have no idea."

Chloe frowned. Stan could have been looking for anyone the night Roelke saw him burst into the Eagle's Nest. "I'm going to take a look around his office."

Roelke pinned her with a stare sharp enough to carve diamonds. "No, you most certainly are not."

"But maybe I could just—"

"*No*. Am I being clear? Stay away from Stanley Colontuono. If he *is* mixed up with a gambling operation, it could be bad business. You *will* stay away from him, and from his office. You are not leaving this table until you promise me that."

Chloe could tell he wasn't going to budge on this one. "I promise."

His eyes narrowed. "Are you lying?"

"No," she lied. "I still think the one to watch is Nika, anyway. Maybe I'll see what kind of mood she's in today."

Roelke's frown deepened. "You said she's got a temper. Don't go pressuring her with a lot of questions."

"I won't." Chloe avoided his gaze by focusing on her eggs, which were oozing mozzarella and fragrant with basil. "These are amazingly good."

He picked up his coffee cup and leaned back against the cracked red vinyl. "Any chance a hot meal has convinced you that going to work today is a bad idea?"

"None. I've got too much to do." Chloe dabbed the corners of her mouth with a napkin.

"Well, keep in touch with me. My shift starts at noon today. You can call me at home until then, and reach me through the station after that."

"*OK.*"

When they were finished Chloe wrote a check for their meal, hoping fervently that it wouldn't bounce. The least she could do was treat Roelke to breakfast. The need to ask her parents for a loan was becoming inevitable. Humiliating thought.

"Thanks a lot," she said, when they were back out in the parking lot. "For bringing me here, and—and everything else." She noticed that he looked as tired as she felt. "Go get some sleep," she added. "I'll talk to you later."

Stifling the urge to tail Chloe, Roelke drove home instead. He didn't like the idea of her blithely going back to work, perhaps with the person who had hurled a rock through her bedroom window the night before; perhaps even with the person who had caused Mr. Solberg's death. And he didn't trust her not to do something stupid. But there didn't seem to be a damn thing he could do about it.

Once in his apartment, he dropped into his chair, reached for the phone, dialed a number. After the fourth ring he heard a muttered greeting.

"Hey, Rick? It's Roelke."

"Jesus, Roelke—"

"Sorry to wake you." Roelke stared out the window at a school bus rumbling down the road. "But I need a favor."

Chloe drove to Old World Wisconsin, feeling more jangled than she wanted to admit, buzzing on caffeine and a growing sense of urgency. Someone had tried to frighten her last night. Why? *Why*? What was that person afraid of? She had to figure that out before Ralph Petty fired her, taking her keys and effectively barring her from the site.

It occurred to her that Ralph might be waiting at the trailers, so she swerved away from the restoration area drive and headed to the education building instead. She needed to talk with Margueritte before Ralph fired her, too.

It was just after seven-thirty A.M. and Chloe found both Byron and Margueritte inside, already at work. Byron was on the phone, but he gave Chloe a wide-awake wave. I am a complete slacker, Chloe thought. She considered getting to work by eight a major triumph.

Margueritte beckoned Chloe into her office, which was cramped and lined with floor-to-ceiling bookshelves. The curator of research looked imperturbable and academic in a dark suit with white blouse, pantyhose, and low-heeled pumps. Chloe felt more rumpled than ever.

As if that mattered. Chloe pulled the unwieldy sheaf of photocopies from her briefcase. "These are all from Aldrick Tobler's local newspaper. I need to show you one in particular." She planted a piece of paper on Margueritte's desk. The older woman raised her eyebrows, looking mildly put out, but Chloe tapped a business notice with her finger. "Read this one. It's short."

She watched as the older woman read the notice, frowned, and read it again. Margueritte sat up straighter, planted her palms on the desk, and read the notice for a third time. Then, wide-eyed, she slowly looked up at Chloe.

"I know," Chloe said. "You'll probably want to look into that."

Margueritte grinned. "I *love* my job! What a treasure hunt!"

"Yeah."

Margueritte looked back at the photocopy. "This … this might not be what it seems, though. This could be an error."

"It could be," Chloe said agreeably. "I'll leave it in your hands."

As she headed back up to her car, though, Chloe smiled. She was sure the notice was *not* a mistake. Maybe, in her short tenure at Old World Wisconsin, she'd actually managed to accomplish something good.

———

Chloe was relieved to see that no big motorcycle was waiting at the trailers. Should she try to hide her car? No. She was being neurotic. Still, for once she did pull the trailer door closed behind her.

After throwing her bag on the counter she grabbed the first heavy black binder, labeled "1974." That was the year her predecessor had begun creating an Old World Wisconsin collection in anticipation of the site's grand opening in 1976. Chloe dropped onto the wobbly chair and began quickly paging through the accession forms. Earthenware jug ... coverlet ... butter churn ... froe ...

She was halfway through the first binder, her eyes already glazing over, when her phone rang. She glanced at the clock: two minutes after eight. Maybe Ralph had come to work with firing her first on his agenda.

The phone rang again.

Maybe she could ignore it.

The phone rang again.

Maybe it wasn't even Ralph.

The phone rang again.

"Shit," she muttered, and snatched the receiver. "This is Chloe Ellefson."

It *was* Ralph. "Ms. Ellefson."

Ms. Ellefson. That couldn't be good.

"I'm calling for your report about your discussion with Leila."

"My discussion with Leila?"

"About the collections storage facility," he said impatiently.

"Oh. Yes."

His tone was icy. "Did you go to Madison yesterday?"

She closed her eyes. Yesterday seemed like a year ago, but this was starting to make sense. "Yes, I did, but—"

"And did you meet with Leila?"

"I did, but—"

"And did you discuss the need for prompt action on the permanent collections storage building?"

"I brought it up, but ..."

"But?"

"But we didn't get too far," Chloe admitted. "She had another meeting scheduled." And I had better things to do.

After a long, uncomfortable silence, Ralph finally said, "Thank you, Ms. Ellefson. I think you've told me exactly what I needed to know."

Chloe heard a click and a dial tone. Well. That had gone badly.

Still, he hadn't fired her flat-out. She replaced the receiver and turned back to the binder. She was going to hunt for a record of that blasted apron until someone physically dragged her from the trailer.

It took her almost an hour. By that time, she was overwhelmed with scanning notes of the multitude of *stuff* transferred or donated to Old World Wisconsin. She was two pages past before the word "apron" registered. She frantically paged backward. There it was: *White cotton apron. Condition: excellent. Embroidered in white thread, floral designs, lacey embellishments, with "Vi maa uddanne vaare dötre" stitched near the hem.*

Bingo.

But the form did not list a donor. Instead, it noted only the apron's official transfer from the State Historical Society of Wisconsin to Old World Wisconsin on April 11, 1978.

Chloe scrabbled for her list of staff numbers, grabbed the phone, dialed, and held her breath until the phone was answered. "Hello, Ann? It's Chloe Ellefson. We met yesterday—"

"I remember."

"Good. Listen, I need another favor. I'm looking at another transfer form, and I need to know who donated the piece originally to—"

"Accession number?"

Chloe supplied it. Within seconds, Ann was reading information from the record. "'White cotton apron. Condition: excellent—'"

"Who donated it?"

"I was getting to that." Ann drew an audible breath and started again. "'White cotton apron. Condition: excellent. Embroidered in white thread, floral designs, lacey embellishments, with *Vi maa uddanne vaare dötre* stitched near the hem. Donated to the Society in 1972.'"

Chloe wanted to leap through the phone line. "By *who*? Who donated it?"

Another aggrieved pause. "The accession form was signed by ... it looks like ... Marit Kallerud."

Chloe dropped the phone. It fell with a noisy clunk to the counter. As she picked it up she could hear Ann's irritated voice: "Are you there? Are you there?"

"I'm here," Chloe said. "Could you spell that name?" The registrar did. Chloe rubbed her forehead. "I don't frickin' believe this," she muttered.

"Look, is there some problem? Who is Marit Kallerud?"

Chloe stared out the window, feeling dazed. "Marit Kallerud is my mother."

Chloe listened to her parents' phone ring ... and ring ... and ring. "Answer the damn phone!" she yelled, before slamming the receiver back to its cradle.

OK. She needed to calm down. Breathe in, breathe out. She would catch up with Mom later. Right now, she could go talk to Nika.

As Chloe reached for her keys a car pulled up outside. By the time she got the door open, Byron was climbing from the state sedan.

"Hey, Byron," she called. "What brings you here?"

He stopped at the steps. "I was just at the admin building. I, um, noticed you had these in your mailbox." Without meeting her gaze, he handed Chloe two of the yellow WHILE YOU WERE OUT slips the receptionist used.

"Thanks."

"And I wanted to get back to you about the Norwegian interpreters. Two people who worked there in the 1970s are still on staff. They're both here today." He gave her a piece of paper with the relevant information.

"Thanks again." Chloe tried to read Byron's expression. "But something tells me you didn't drive over here just to hand-deliver these."

Byron finally looked her in the eye. "The receptionist told me that Ralph asked her to set up a meeting in Madison this afternoon with the division curator and the division director." He rubbed his palms on his trousers. "There was only one item on the agenda."

"Me?"

"Yeah."

Chloe took that in. "I think I'm toast."

"I'm sorry." Behind his little wire-rimmed glasses, Byron's eyes were concerned.

Chloe chewed her lower lip. So, Ralph *was* going to fire her. But evidently he needed to let the Madison folks know what he wanted to do. And if that didn't happen until late today, *she* still had a little time to figure out what was going on. Not much time. But a little.

Byron started toward his car, then turned back. "Are you coming to the picnic this afternoon?"

She blinked. "The *picnic*?"

"Didn't you see the flyer? The interpreters are having an end-of-the-school-tour-season picnic in the village after work. Four o'clock, by the Inn. We've still got a few tours scheduled, but we're definitely over the hump."

"I don't think I'm up for a picnic."

"Well, think about it, OK?"

Chloe almost laughed. In the last few weeks she'd seen two dead people. Someone had broken into her home, and thrown a rock through a window and onto her bed in the middle of the night. She had just learned that her mother—her *mother*—was inexplicably involved in the whole mess. Ralph Petty was gunning to fire her. She was broke and exhausted and fending off clinical depression. And Byron wanted her to come to a picnic.

"Really," Byron said earnestly. "You should come."

Chloe couldn't find the words to say no to someone who had turned, surprisingly enough, into an ally. "OK," she said. "I'll be there."

After Byron left, Chloe read her phone messages. One was from a woman who wanted to donate her grandmother's crazy quilt to Old World. That would have to wait for the next curator, Chloe thought, and put the slip aside. The second made her shoulders sag. *Nika called 7:30 A.M. Has to take Joel to Dr. in Milwaukee today. Will be in later if she can—otherwise will see you tomorrow.*

Lovely, Chloe thought. All Nika's likely to see tomorrow is Ralph Petty kicking my sorry ass off the site.

One day left. A clock seemed to be audibly ticking in her brain. OK. She still had a couple of possibilities. Next: search Stanley Colontuono's desk.

Stan's truck was parked by the maintenance building. Chloe waited an hour before she heard an engine starting. After he'd driven away, she hurried across the yard.

Stanley's desk was a mess. Was he a disorganized slob who wouldn't notice if his things were shuffled? Or was he—like Leila—in total control of the chaos? Chloe decided to begin with the desk drawers. One held a row of bulging files, grease-stained and dog-eared. As far as she could tell, all were stuffed with state business. The other drawers held junk: thumbtacks, envelopes, loose change, a spark plug, a pack of cigarettes, a doorknob, and various other bits of hardware.

All right, the desktop. Chloe quickly shuffled through requisition forms for paper towels, a bill from the local building supply company, a request for proposal for a new picnic pavilion. Scattered among these were time sheets and loose washers, pencils showing teeth marks, stray coils of wire. Nothing of any use.

Then something caught her eye. A blotter-sized state-issue calendar lay beneath the clutter. Amazingly enough, Stanley actually used his. Chloe moved piles back and forth so she could quickly scan the terse notes inked onto the dated squares. *Staff meeting—9 A.M. Pick up lumber. Dst appt—2:45. Pay day. Oil change. RFP due. Court.*

Hold on. Court? Why was Stanley due in court at the end of June?

Chloe high-tailed it back to her trailer, shut the door, fished out Roelke's card, and called his home number. "Listen," she said when he answered. "I found something." She told Roelke about the calendar. "A court date! I—"

"I *told* you not to—"

"I know, I *know*. You can yell at me later, OK? Don't you think the most important thing to do right now is find out why Stanley is going to court on June 30?"

"I can do some checking," he said grudgingly. "But I swear to God, Chloe, if you don't stop—"

"Look. I am almost certainly going to get fired tomorrow. So today is what I've got, Roelke. Just today."

"Stay – away – from – Stanley."

"I will," she promised. And since she didn't have any more ideas regarding the maintenance chief, it was a promise she was pretty sure she could keep.

TWENTY-FIVE

After hearing from Chloe, Roelke called a clerk he knew at the Waukesha County Court and asked for a list of scheduled appearances for June 30. "I'm about to head in to work," he told her. "Could you fax the list to me there?" With any luck, he could snatch the fax before Marie spotted it and started asking questions.

He walked in to the office just as the PD's new fax machine began to purr. Roelke grabbed the list, settled in an empty chair, and began skimming. Burglary. DUI. Assault. Vandalism. The court schedule for June 30 brimmed with the usual litany of human malfeasance. Unfortunately, he saw no item or name that he could connect with gambling at the Eagle's Nest, Chloe's missing ale bowl, or Stanley Colontuono.

Not good. Roelke felt ready to explode. He needed to *do* something. And short of driving to Old World Wisconsin and removing Chloe with a fireman's carry, he didn't know what he could do. Rick wouldn't call before three, when his own shift started—

"*Roelke!*"

He started, swiveled, and saw Marie sitting with the phone in one hand. "What?"

"Are you on duty? I've got a lady here who says her neighbor's dachshund dug up all of her daffodils. She wants to talk with an officer."

Roelke glanced at the clock. He was technically not on for another ten minutes, but he didn't seem to have anything better to do. "Yeah," he said. "Tell her I'm on my way."

Chloe sat at the table in her stifling, musty trailer with Berget Lundquist's genealogy in front of her. The ale bowl had passed from Gro to Astrid to Brita to Berget. Mother to daughter. Gro had delivered five sons before giving birth to Astrid. Had those boys received other mementos of their Norwegian heritage? How did they—and Gro's husband—feel about Gro's talents with a paintbrush?

Chloe's mother hadn't noted whether Astrid had sons, but Berget had had a brother, Emil, born in 1914. Chloe remembered the young boy she'd seen in Berget Lundquist's family photographs. Mr. Solberg had said Emil must have died long ago.

But . . . what if Emil had married and had a child of his own, before his death? Once again Chloe tried to run a filmstrip in her mind of all the faces she'd seen at Old World Wisconsin—interpreters, permanent staff. Was one of them somehow descended from Berget?

Chloe grabbed the phone and dialed her parents' number for the eighteenth time that day. And this time, her mother answered. Thank God. "Mom? Where the hell have you been?"

Silence. "I don't like your tone," her mother said finally. "And there is no need to use foul language. Really, Chloe."

Chloe shut her eyes. "I'm sorry. I've just got some startling news about that Norwegian donor thing we were talking about. An embroidered Norwegian apron was donated to the state historical society in 1972, and transferred here to Old World in 1978. And the registrar in Madison says that *your* name was on the accession form."

"An apron? Hmmn. I *think* I remember an apron."

"Where did it come from?" Chloe squawked. "Why did you give it away?"

"I didn't personally give it away," her mother said, the frown back in her tone. "I was acting on behalf of the Norwegian Women's Club."

Chloe vaguely remembered Mom and her cronies gathering for *krumkakke* and slide shows about trips to the fjords.

"By the early seventies our numbers were dwindling. Some felt we were competing with the Daughters of Norway. We decided that we could better serve the Norwegian community by disbanding."

"But how did the club come to own the apron?"

"The club did collect a few items," Mom said slowly. "For a time we were hoping we'd find a permanent display area. In the library, or the town hall—something like that. But in the end we voted to give the pieces to the state historical society. I was secretary that year, so I handled the paperwork."

"What I really need to know is who donated the apron to the club in the first place." Chloe bounced on her toes.

"Well, I wasn't directly involved in that. I think Elaine Bakken handled donations."

"Do you still know her?"

"Of course. Fred Bakken is on your father's bowling team."

"OK, that's great." Chloe paced in a tight circle, tethered by the phone cord. "So, could you call Elaine and ask if she remembers who donated the apron to the club? It's kind of urgent. As in, *very* urgent."

Chloe struggled to find the balance between motivating her mother, and freaking her out.

"Certainly, if it's really that important."

"It is. Let me know as soon as you find out anything, OK? Thanks ... Oh, wait! Mom? Are you still there?"

"I'm here, dear, but—"

"I really, *really* need your help with something else." Chloe vowed to never *ever* again get frustrated by her mother's preoccupation with all things Norwegian. "Berget had a brother, Emil, born in 1914. Do you have any more on him? A death date? Marriage information?"

"Well, I'll have to look. Hold on." After a short eternity her mother came back on the line. "Chloe? I don't have any information about Emil. I didn't pay much attention because you were focused on Berget."

"I was. But now I'm wondering about Emil. If you could dig into that, Mom—and as quickly as possible—I'd be forever grateful."

"I can do that."

"You're a lifesaver. Really. I'll explain it all later. Call as soon as you know anything. Oh—wait! *Wait!* Mom?"

"I'm still here."

Chloe scrabbled through the papers on her table. "I need help with a translation. A Norwegian sentence."

"Written or spoken?"

"Um, written. It's—"

"Old Norwegian or New Norwegian?"

Chloe pounded one fist lightly against her forehead. "I'm thinking Old. Here it is." She spelled the words that had been painted on the plate and embroidered on the apron. "Can you translate that?"

"Of course," her mother said. "It means, 'We must educate our daughters.'"

Roelke handled the dog-vs.-daffodil skirmish, made a loop through the school parking lot, and spent some time cruising Eagle's mean streets Being Visible, which taxpayers liked. He got back to the station at 3:03, dropped into a seat beside a phone extension, and dialed. "Rick?" he asked, when the connection went through. "You find anything?"

"Just this minute," Rick said. "Tanika Austin was arrested in 1975 for shoplifting."

"Shoplifting?" Roelke pictured a teen pocketing cosmetics.

"She lifted something from an antiques store in the Third Ward."

Roelke began tapping his pencil against the table.

"It gets better," Rick added. "When a cop showed up, she resisted arrest. Ended up punching him."

That was all Roelke needed to know. "Thanks, Rick. I owe you."

After disconnecting, he tried to reach Chloe. "I'm sorry, sir," the Old World receptionist said. "That line is busy. May I take a message?"

Dammit. "No thank you," he told her. "I'll try again later."

It didn't take long for Chloe's mother to call back. "I just had a lovely talk about your apron with Elaine Bakken," she told her daughter. "Elaine said the apron was donated to the Norwegian Women's Club by Berget Lundquist! Isn't that an amazing coincidence? Evidently Elaine's cousin attended her church."

Yes! "Thanks, Mom. I really appreciate your help."

After hanging up, Chloe stared blindly out the window, trying to add this new bit of information to the puzzle. In the mid-seventies, after her son died, Berget Lundquist had donated an embroidered apron and three rosemaled pieces to historical organizations. The unusual sentiment incorporated into the pieces—*We must educate our daughters*—implied that all had been made by the same artist. Chloe believed that artist was Gro Skavlem, who had emigrated from Norway with her husband in 1845. Gro Skavlem, female rosemaler. Gro Skavlem, way-early feminist.

And if I'm right, Chloe thought, the missing ale bowl would be of enormous interest to any scholar of Norwegian-American material culture. And very, *very* valuable.

She glanced at her watch. She still had time to run out to the site, check in with the two interpreters Byron had mentioned, and make a token appearance at the interpreters' picnic.

Five minutes later, Chloe felt a flush of relief when she spotted Nika's white Chevette parked in the visitor center lot. Site business first, though, Chloe decided. Then she would stop by the basement of St. Peter's Church and try to get some answers from her intern.

Chloe's trip around the site, however, was fruitless. "I did work in Norwegian for the first couple of years," an elderly woman now working the Hafford House said apologetically. "But only in the schoolhouse." From there Chloe jogged cross-country to the Danish farm, arriving breathless—only to learn that her second potential informant had gone home early. "She wasn't feeling well," the lead interpreter, equally apologetic, told Chloe. "I'm covering the building."

Chloe held in a frustrated shriek. Well, she'd tried.

She arrived at the inn just as the interpreter in St. Peter's tolled the bell four times to announce the site's closing. "Hey, you came!" Byron called. "I'm really glad."

Chloe wasn't. She felt wired and jumpy and completely unsure of her ability to smile and chat.

The picnic tables weren't even set up yet, so she veered off toward a nearby exhibit. She might as well take a moment and check in with Roelke. The white-haired interpreter in the tidy Victorian-era home looked dismayed to see her. "Um, I was about to lock up," she said.

"You can go ahead," Chloe told her. "I just need to make a call."

The interpreter pointed her toward the hidden phone. "Be sure to stay off the carpet," she added. "You can only walk on the runner."

Since I'm the curator, I do know where to walk! Chloe almost said, but didn't. She wouldn't be the curator for much longer. Instead she dialed the police station and asked for Officer McKenna.

"Chloe?" His voice was hushed. "Why haven't you called me? I've been trying to—"

"I'm sorry," Chloe said. "But listen, I've got some new information." She quickly shared what she'd learned from her mother about the apron, and the translation. "So I really think—"

"Have you talked to Nika?"

"I'm about to. I'm in the Crossroads Village now."

"Do not talk to Nika until—" His voice broke abruptly. Chloe heard an inaudible voice in the background. When Roelke came back, his voice was even quieter. "I gotta go. But I can take a break at five. I'll swing into the main parking lot. Meet me there. I've got some new info on Nika." The line went dead.

What was that about? No telling. Chloe checked her watch again. She had some time to kill, now. After dutifully locking up the building, she headed toward the plywood-on-sawhorses tables the lead interpreters had set up in the inn's side yard, with white sheets for tablecloths and a canning jar of flowers as a centerpiece. The interpreters had brought food from their buildings.

"Want some bread?" one of the German interpreters asked. She was hacking at an ash-blackened, crusty round loaf with a knife that obviously needed sharpening. "It's from the Schultz bakeoven, so just break off the bottom crust. And—" she lowered her voice—"I popped it in Tupperware to keep warm."

Chloe accepted a piece of the fragrant rye bread and some fresh-churned butter, then retreated to the inn's front steps. The bread was amazingly good, heavy and seasoned with sorghum and a hint of caraway. European bread. She felt a pang of loss, but let it pass. She didn't have time to mope over alpine picnics shared with Markus.

A few interpreters nearby were telling My Worst School Tour Ever stories. Delores, the Norwegian area lead, waved her hand for attention. "Did you guys have that group from Grimes today?" she asked. "I was showing them how to card wool, and one kid grabbed a carding comb and brained one of the other kids with it. For a minute I thought we were about to have an all-out brawl right there in the stabbur. The teacher said that if the stabbur was such a good storage place, maybe she could store her seventh-graders there for the rest of the day…"

Chloe's mouth turned up in the hint of a smile, remembering her own days in the trenches. Then her smile abruptly disappeared. She sat up straight. Could it really be so simple? *Could* it?

Probably not. Almost surely not.

But it was worth a try.

She jumped to her feet and trotted back to her car. It was only four-thirty. She had time to check this out before meeting Roelke.

She drove through the open site-access gate, past the Village, through Finn-Dane, on toward the Norwegian area. She took the shortest route, driving backward on the site loop. She tried to drive slowly, wary of any farm or maintenance vehicle that might roar around one of the blind curves.

She managed to reach the Norwegian area without catastrophe, and accelerated down the long driveway toward the Kvaale farm. She was almost at the end when she suddenly braked hard. The interpreters would scream if she left modern tire tracks in the farmyard. And rightly so. She parked in the drive.

The farmstead was quiet, all buildings locked up tight. Chloe loped past the house and summer kitchen. The log stabbur sat ahead of her, weathered silver and perched a foot off the ground. The design discouraged rodents and mold. It was a good place to store things. A safe place. The traditional place.

The door to the stabbur's main room, where Chloe had first met Delores, was locked. The upper floor extended out over the lower room, accessed by steps leading up from the porch. Chloe charged up the steps—

Her left foot hit something hard in a place where nothing but air should be. She fell down three steps, landing on her butt and cracking one elbow against the wall. "Ow!" she yelped. She struggled back to her feet, rubbing her elbow, then flexing it cautiously. Painful, but not out of service.

She approached the steps warily this time, and saw the pane of clear Plexiglas used to keep visitors from climbing to the second story. Chloe wrestled it from its brackets, tossed it aside, and stampeded back up the stairs to the loft.

A sprawling, fluffy mountain of fleeces covered the floor. Some tied into tight bales, some sprawled loose. Some white, some gray, some brownish-black. Some clean, some with tips still clotted with dried manure.

Geez Louise. No wonder Delores had told Cindy not to worry about wasting wool as she practiced spinning.

Chloe began pawing among the heavy fleeces. Soon panting, she heaved one aside, then another. Her hands grew greasy with lanolin. Nothing... nothing there... nothing against the side wall.

And then she saw it. In one of the back corners, not covered with wool but screened by it, sat a rosemaled ale bowl.

"Holy Mother of God," Chloe breathed. She waded to the corner, wiping her hands furiously on her shirt. Then she gently eased the bowl from the floor. It was smaller than most but carefully carved, with two cow heads—complete with horns—serving as handles. The rosemaling was an exquisite blend of flourishes and swirls dabbed in blue and orange and yellow. The overall effect was spectacular.

Chloe felt a thickening in her throat, and hot tears in her eyes. Had Gro felt a fierce pride in her work? Had she been happily married, or had she channeled frustration and loneliness into these carved and painted lines? Did she worry about the fate of her daughter, finding her path in a male-ordered world?

Chloe blew out a long, slow breath, trying to think clearly. Speculation could wait. Right now she needed to get the ale bowl to a safe place. She crept down the stairs with the artifact held in front of her like an offering. She eased the bowl to the porch floorboards long enough to replace the Plexiglas barricade, then cradled the artifact back in her arms.

But as she walked around the log farmhouse, she saw a car in the distance beyond the sheep pasture, driving along the site road from the south—a car that had evidently just entered the grounds through the Norwegian gate.

A white Chevette.

Chloe froze as she saw Nika's car approach the Kvaale drive. *Keep going,* she urged silently. *Don't turn left.*

The Chevette turned left.

Chloe darted back behind the house. She didn't want her intern to see this ale bowl. Not yet. Not without explaining some things.

But where could she hide it? If she tried to enter the main house, Nika would see her. There wasn't time to climb back up into the stabbur and re-hide the bowl.

Tires crunched on gravel as Nika drove up the long drive.

"Shit!" Chloe scanned the back farmyard. No time to fish her keys out and unlock the summer kitchen or the corn crib or the barn—

No, wait. *The barn.* Both bays of the structure were locked, but there was a small wooden door cut low into the front wall of the bay nearest the stabbur—probably used to shovel out manure. Chloe raced to the barn, dropped to her knees, scrabbled at the wooden latch, opened the door.

At the last moment she balked. No way was she going to put this holy grail of ale bowls down on a manure-dotted stable floor. She leaned into the opening, arm blindly flailing … and her palm hit something rough and scratchy. Burlap. The interpreters used burlap sacks to camouflage the fire extinguishers kept in every building.

Perfect. Chloe pinched the sack between thumb and forefinger, jerked, and felt the heavy extinguisher fall. Grunting, she pulled the sack free, made a nest, and deposited the bowl inside the stable.

A car door slammed just as Chloe re-latched the little wooden door. She wiped her palms on her trousers, preparing to meet her intern with a smile on her face and a lie on her lips. *Hey, Nika. Delores asked me to look at that fanning mill in the breezeway. What brings you to Kvaale?*

But something stopped her. A twinge of unease, a flicker of intuition, an unheard whisper from Gro—*something* beyond conscious reason took over. Chloe darted back into the breezeway's shadows and crouched behind the fanning mill.

Footsteps pounded through the peaceful afternoon. Chloe stopped breathing. It sounded as if Nika was running straight to Chloe's hiding place … but then the footsteps passed the barn. A few seconds later Chloe heard Nika race up the stabbur steps.

Chloe leaned her forehead against the fanning mill. Nika *knew*. How? How had Nika learned that some long-gone interpreter had stashed the bowl in the stabbur? Chloe felt something cold in her stomach, a sinking sensation.

A minute passed, the stillness broken only by the Ossabaw hogs rooting grumpily in their pen behind the barn. Chloe tried to think. She had to get away while Nika was up in the stabbur. Just grab the bowl again, and make a dash for her car.

Chloe shot to her feet, took one step, stopped. Her car was blocked from behind in the narrow drive by Nika's Chevette.

Footsteps sounded from the stabbur again, pounding back down the steps. "Chloe? Where are you?"

Chloe froze.

"I know you're here, Chloe!"

This was all wrong. She crouched back behind the fanning mill.

"I know you found the bowl! Just come out here and give me the damn bowl!"

Chloe tasted something metallic on her tongue. If Nika had followed her to Kvaale, she hadn't come alone.

TWENTY-SIX

Where was she?

Roelke sat in his squad car, trying to look inconspicuous. He shouldn't be here. He could get away with circling the Old World Wisconsin parking lot while on patrol. But to park here, waiting—no, that was bad. He attracted too much attention.

He glanced at his watch again. Almost five-fifteen. Had Chloe blown off his request to meet? Forgotten about it altogether? Plunged headfirst into trouble?

He flipped again though his index cards. A missing ale bowl. A director who'd worked in Las Vegas. A maintenance supervisor who might, or might not, be involved with a gambling operation. An embroidered apron. A murder in Dane County. An intern with an arrest record, who'd recently had her tires slashed. Jesus! Roelke stuffed the cards back into his pocket. If there was a pattern here, he was too dumb to see it.

Two interpreters walked through the gate and gave Roelke curious looks as they headed toward their cars. He nodded politely, trying to look both unalarmed and unalarming. He needed to talk to Chloe before someone asked why he was here. He needed to talk to Chloe before his radio squawked with a call about daffodil bulbs or road kill or some other damn thing.

So where the hell was she?

Crouched behind the fanning mill, Chloe considered her options. On either side of her, a locked door led into one of the barn bays. If she climbed the fence into the hog pen behind her, the Ossabaws would come running in greedy anticipation, squeals and grunts proclaiming *Here she is! Here she is!* And straight ahead was the farmyard where Joel was waiting.

She had to keep him away from the ale bowl. So: there was nothing for it but to walk out into the yard and try to bluff her way out of this. She stood, and took two uneasy steps.

A gunshot split the still afternoon. Reverberations echoed in Chloe's head. The saliva in her mouth evaporated. An angry blue jay squawked somewhere behind the barn.

"Chloe!" Joel yelled. "I want that damn bowl, and I want it now!"

Calm, Chloe ordered herself. Stay calm. She pressed a hand against her ribcage, trying to send that message to her thumping heart.

"You're pissing me off!"

Chloe felt nausea ball in her stomach.

"You want to play hide-and-seek? Fine. I will find you." His voice faded as he spoke.

Chloe put one palm against the log wall to steady herself. It sounded as if Joel was circling away from her in his search. That was good. And—and he must have come alone after all. You're pissing *me* off, he'd said. *I* will find you. Also good. Maybe she could still get out of there. She could dart across the open yard, make a run for it through the woods—

No. The thought of abandoning Gro's bowl to Joel prompted a fierce burn of anger in her chest. She had to grab the bowl before running. Chloe scrabbled in her pocket with shaking fingers, found her keys, darted to the door on her right. She'd been *stupid* to put the bowl through the pass-through—

A muffled bellow of anger—it sounded like Joel was near the summer kitchen—made Chloe's fingers tremble as she shoved the padlock into her pocket. She cracked the door, wriggled through, and pulled it closed behind her.

"Chloe!" Joel's voice was closer again.

It was already too late. Coming inside had been even more stupid. She was about to be trapped in a one-room stable with Gro's ale bowl.

Maybe she could snatch the bowl and hide in the loft. Two windows lent only dim light to the room. Chloe frantically cast about for a ladder or stairway. Where the hell was access to the loft?

There was no access to the loft. No functioning loft at all. Half a dozen rough log beams ran front to back above her head. Smaller poles lay across them from side to side to form a low hay mow of sorts, but no sturdy loft. *Shit*.

Chloe needed a weapon. If she waited right by the door, maybe she could surprise Joel when he came inside. She hastily checked the three stalls—empty, empty, empty. No shovel to hit him with. No pitchfork to stab him with. What stupid curator had outfitted this place? The room held nothing but a waist-high grain bin, perhaps three feet wide, near the door.

"Chloe!" Joel was approaching the stable. She was out of options.

Chloe threw her weight against the side of the heavy bin. She managed to shove it across the doorway with an ear-splitting screech.

"*Chloe!*" He was right outside.

As Chloe retreated from the door her heel hit something hard. Oh, God. Had she kicked the ale bowl? She spun around. The ale bowl was untouched. But instead—

Joel wrenched the door open. He appeared in the doorway, visible waist-up above the bin. The academic face Chloe had seen glow when regarding his fiancée had settled into hard lines. His dark eyes glinted behind his horn-rimmed glasses. His right hand held a gun. It was pointed at her.

He slapped his left palm on the grain bin. "Move this damn thing."

"Joel—"

He slammed his hip against the bin. It shuddered several inches into the room.

Chloe stooped, came up swinging the fire extinguisher, and banged the canister onto the grain bin for balance. After years of safety training at historic sites, the motions came instinctively. Pull the pin. Aim the nozzle. Squeeze the handle.

Joel's face disappeared beneath a cloud of dry chemical powder. He stumbled backward with an indistinct bellow. And his right hand jerked. The shot deafened her. The glass window in the front wall exploded.

"Shit!" Chloe gasped. Bowl or no bowl, she needed *out*. Climbing over the grain bin would land her in Joel's lap. Jagged shards of glass lined the front window. Last option: the back window.

A wooden peg held the six-pane window closed. Chloe yanked it free and shoved the window up with a thud. Adrenaline fueled her launch and she skidded through the window, scraping her belly, wildly kicking her feet.

She landed painfully in an oozing black slurry of mud that coated her hands, soaked through her pants. She heard the grain bin being heaved aside. Joel was already back on his feet.

Muck sucked at Chloe's shoes as she scrambled to find footing, aiming toward the fence separating her from the breezeway. Joel wanted the ale bowl more than he wanted her. The padlock was still in her pocket. If she moved fast enough, she could lock him into the stable. That would buy her a few more minutes.

But she'd forgotten the two Ossabaws. They reached her before she got to the fence. One knocked against her thigh. She fell again, landing painfully on the same elbow she'd smacked earlier. "Get away, you stupid hogs!" she hissed. "I don't have any food!" One hog stared her down with dark glittering eyes. The second nudged her again, its bristles scraping roughly against her bare arm. She shoved it away and struggled back to her feet.

Joel stood at the fence separating the hog pen from the breezeway. A grayish-white residue was visible in his hair and on his forehead, on his throat and shirt, but he'd wiped his mouth clear. His glasses, now smeared, had protected his eyes from the worst chemical blast. He held his gun in one hand, and Gro's ale bowl—carelessly, by one carved cow head—in the other.

"Could you at least hold the bowl with both hands?" Chloe panted. One of the hogs butted her in the knee. She widened her stance.

Joel jerked his head like a dog trying to shed water. The fire retardant was probably irritating his skin. "Just shut—*up*." He balanced the hand holding the gun on the top of the fence. The muzzle's dark round hole looked huge.

Oh, God. If he shot her now, the damned hogs would eat her.

Chloe did not want to die in a hog pen. "You have the bowl," she said. "Just go. Don't make things worse."

"You already made things worse." Joel coughed, then spat some chemical residue. "I didn't want any of this."

"Then why are you here?" Chloe raised her voice to be heard over the hogs' insistent squeals. "I don't understand—"

"*Shut up!*" Joel snapped. His hand jerked. Chloe closed her eyes. And one of the Ossabaws slammed into her, knocking her to her knees.

No shot came. When Chloe looked up, the gun was still pointed at her. But Joel was looking over his shoulder, toward the farmyard.

Chloe shoved up from the ground with every ounce of strength, lunging for the gun. As she leapt, a sharp pain tore through her right thigh.

"Chloe!" The shout was distant—from perhaps the front of the house. A man's voice.

Joel jerked the gun away just before Chloe landed on the bottom fence board. "Stay where you are!" he hissed. He ran to the front of the breezeway and pressed his body against the log wall.

"Chloe!" Louder now.

One of the hogs tore at Chloe's shoe and she climbed high enough to straddle the top fence board. "Roelke, be careful!" she yelled. "He's got a gun!"

"Shut up!" Joel snapped. He coughed again, then walked from the breezeway. "Stop right there! You take one more step and I kill her!"

The Ossabaw gave the fence one last angry smack before trotting away. Chloe's heart was pounding, her chest heaving. Her leg was on fire.

But something unexpected glinted in her peripheral vision. A pair of sheep shears was hanging on the back wall of the stable. They were old-style, a curve of metal that ended in two heavy, sharp points. One of the farmers shearing sheep in the breezeway earlier that spring had probably hung them there over the hog pen, out of sight of curious young visitors, and forgotten them. Maybe, *maybe*, she could reach them.

Roelke's nerves were taut when he edged around the back corner of the house. When he heard Chloe's shouted warning, he pulled his gun.

A young man separated himself from the shadows of a log barn. "Stop right there!" he cried. "You take one more step and I kill her!" A wooden bowl dangled from his left hand. Something powdery on his face and chest gave him a weird, clownish appearance. But there was nothing clownish about the revolver in his other hand. The gun was pointed toward the ground.

Roelke froze, feet planted firm, both hands supporting his own revolver as he took aim. "Drop the gun!" he bellowed. "You raise that gun and I'll shoot you in the head! *Drop it!*"

The young man's hand twitched. His finger was on the trigger. "Oh, God," he said. "Oh, Jesus."

Roelke was acutely aware of his own right finger, still pressed against his revolver's barrel. But the guy didn't aim. They stared at each other. Roelke felt every second pulsing by. This wasn't working. Chloe was somewhere nearby. And because he had no business driving onto the Old World Wisconsin grounds, Roelke had not radioed his location in to dispatch.

"OK," he said. "Let's talk about this. Nobody needs to get hurt." He edged a little closer. "Put the gun down. All you need to do is put the gun down."

"Just—just shut *up*. Oh, God. This wasn't supposed to happen. I—I have to think."

Roelke took another tiny step. "Come on, buddy. Help me out. I'm trying to make things easier for you. Put the gun down."

The young man stared down at the gun in his hand as if he didn't know how it got there. He still held the barrel pointed down. But he shook his head with a last gasp of bravado. "I'll only let Chloe go after you get in your car and drive away."

Roelke's nerves winched even tighter. "Keep me instead. They'll give you whatever you want if you have a cop."

The guy swallowed—he was close enough that Roelke saw the bob of his Adam's apple. "Chloe," the younger man called. "Come out here."

"*No!*" Roelke yelled. Too late. Chloe crept from the breezeway. Her face looked white. Black mud coated her hands and lower legs. The blood staining one thigh of her tan chinos was a rusty red.

Roelke's anger crystallized into hot rage, sharp and clear. This bastard shot Chloe, he thought. I'm going to fucking plug him. "Chloe, get back behind the wall."

"Don't do it!" the guy cried. And Chloe stayed rooted where she was, about a yard behind and to the right of the assailant.

Roelke shoved down surging adrenalin. "You need to let Chloe walk away," he said, edging still closer. "Look, I'll put my gun away." He forced himself to holster his revolver.

"I need—" The young man coughed, his chest heaving. "I need to ask Chloe a favor."

That hubris almost cracked Roelke's self-control. Then the dispatcher's voice crackled from the radio on his belt. "George 220."

When Roelke had learned to fly, his instructor had once summarized a pilot's priorities during difficult situations: aviate, navigate, communicate. It still made sense. Roelke ignored the radio.

"Joel." Chloe's voice was shaky. "What is it you want?"

Joel? Roelke flipped through his mental stack of index cards: Stanley, Byron, Ralph. Who the hell was Joel?

Joel's breath came in little heaves. "I want you to understand that Nika had nothing to do with this."

"Um … OK." She sounded half frightened, half bewildered.

"George 220," dispatch called again. Roelke eyed Joel, trying to decide if he could make a move.

"No radio!" Joel barked. Then, "It was Emil."

Who the hell was Emil? Roelke took another step.

"Emil? He—he died young," Chloe said.

"No, he didn't. But he married a black woman and changed his last name to Austin."

"You mean … Austin?" she stammered. "*Austin?*"

"George 220!"

"Don't touch the damn radio!" Joel snapped at Roelke.

Roelke didn't. It occurred to him that if he didn't respond, dispatch would sound the tones. And that alarm might be the only distraction he could get.

Joel stared at Roelke, still speaking to Chloe. "I wrote that old bitch a letter. She—Berget Lundquist—wrote me back. It was *hateful.*"

"Hateful …?" Chloe faltered. "So you decided to steal the ale bowl?"

"*Officer McKenna!*" dispatch blared.

"Rupert said—" Joel ended the statement with a dry hacking wheeze. "Never mind."

Rupert? Who the *fuck* was Rupert? Roelke slid one foot a little closer to Joel, shifted his weight.

The radio crackled its final warning: "All county units stand by for the alert tones."

Roelke held his breath, tensing for the spring.

"Chloe—*please* don't fire Nika because of me. She doesn't deserve—"

The radio on Roelke's belt let loose with an ear-piercing scream. Roelke launched. Something whirling and metallic stabbed his shoulder as he grabbed Joel's wrist with his left hand, and clenched the revolver wheel with his right. Roelke jammed Joel's hand back, getting the barrel pointed away from him and Chloe. The thrust broke Joel's grasp. His trigger finger too, most likely. Then Roelke brought his right knee up hard into Joel's crotch.

Joel fell to his knees with a howl of pain. But Chloe was diving *at* them.

"Lie on your belly, you piece of shit!" Roelke bellowed at Joel, as he emptied the chamber of Joel's gun. He tossed the gun out of reach and whipped his own from its holster. "Face down! Stretch your arms out from your sides!"

Joel uncurled slowly, cringing and whimpering. Roelke kicked the sheep shears away. Chloe scooped the ale bowl up from the ground.

"Chloe," Roelke growled, "go get in your car. Lock all the doors." She scurried away with the bowl hugged to her chest.

Keeping his gun trained on Joel, Roelke pulled his handcuffs free. Joel wasn't moving but Roelke knelt on his back, instead of the ground, while he jerked Joel's wrists into the cuffs. He yanked the younger man to his feet and dragged him, stumbling, around the log house to the squad car.

With Joel locked into the back seat, Roelke pulled the radio from his belt. "George 220, 10-78." After providing directions, he stood panting. Trying to come down. Jesus.

Two minutes later, wailing sirens announced backup. A county car roared up the site road and skidded into the farm driveway behind his squad. Deputy Marge Bandacek emerged. "McKenna!" she barked. "What you got?"

"That asshole was holding a woman at gunpoint when I arrived," Roelke said. "I'm taking him in."

Marge frowned. "It's my jurisdiction."

"I have charges on him in the village," Roelke lied. "I've got a municipal warrant. His gun's back beyond the house, though. I tossed it. You could look for it." Marge obeyed without argument.

Roelke found Chloe sitting in her car, clutching the wooden bowl. When he knocked on the window she jumped, then unlocked the doors. He slid into the passenger seat.

"Is Joel all right?" She shuddered violently. "God! I was afraid the shears would go straight into his skull—"

"He'll live to go to prison. You hit me instead."

"I *did?*"

"Let me see where he shot you," he demanded, staring again at the blood staining her pants. "EMT's on the way."

Chloe winced when he tried to look at her wound, still oozing blood. "Joel didn't shoot me."

"Then who did?"

"A damn hog bit me!"

"*What?*"

"Don't worry." Chloe's laugh was tinged with hysteria. "It's not the first time I've been bit in the ass by an Ossabaw."

TWENTY-SEVEN

ROELKE DIDN'T SPEAK TO Joel Carlisle during the drive to Waukesha. He didn't speak while they waited in the ER at Waukesha Memorial, or while a nurse cleaned the fire retardant residue from his eyes, skin, and hair, or while a doctor splinted Carlisle's broken finger, or while he got his own shoulder wound cleaned and stitched. He didn't speak while they drove to the county jail behind the courthouse. He handed the young man over to the deputies and completed the necessary paperwork while processing took place.

By that time Roelke was, he thought, in control. "You got an interview room open?" he asked the deputy on duty. "We've had a lot of trouble with this kid in Eagle. I want to ask some questions." He was more cognizant of the lie, now. He would not be able to tell the chief it had come from pure adrenalin.

He didn't care.

Joel Carlisle was soon waiting in Room 2. Roelke went to the door and stared down at the young man. He looked like some mewling college boy. Carlisle now wore an orange jumpsuit and paper booties.

His glasses were clean, his damp hair slicked to one side. A purplish-green bruise was blooming where Roelke had banged his forehead on the roof of the squad car before shoving him into the backseat. He sat slumped, eyes down.

Roelke slammed the door behind him. Carlisle jumped.

"All right," Roelke said. "You and I are going to have a little talk.

Roelke walked into the Eagle PD at 7:45 the next morning, three hours early for his shift. "You got a few minutes?" he asked Chief Naborski.

"What's up?"

Roelke handed the chief the report he'd labored over into the wee hours. "Things got a little crazy after you left yesterday."

Naborski let Roelke sweat, reading the lengthy report through twice, then staring out the window for a small eternity. Finally he got up. "Marie," he barked. "Hold my calls." Then he slammed the door and returned to his seat.

This was not going to be any fun.

"Officer McKenna," Chief Naborski said. "Were you off duty when you drove onto Old World Wisconsin property yesterday? Was it your dinner break?"

Roelke had too much respect for Chief Naborski to lie. "No sir. I was on duty."

"Were you called there to provide mutual aid?"

"No. I drove there on my own accord."

"Did you deliberately disobey my instruction to leave the Old World problem alone?"

"Yes."

The chief regarded him. "Officer McKenna, you have screwed up six ways from Sunday."

"I know." So much for getting that one full-time position. He'd just handed it to Skeet on a golden platter.

The chief tipped his chair back on two legs, his expression grim. "Why don't you tell me about all the mistakes you made yesterday."

Roelke spent an uncomfortable five minutes on the highlights: ignoring the chief's order, leaving his own patrol to drive onto state property, not letting dispatch know where he was, lying to Marge Bandacek in order to override her authority, lying to the Waukesha deputies so he could question Carlisle himself. He didn't mention the epithets he'd hurled at Carlisle, or the bruises Carlisle was sporting. Most cops wouldn't care. Chief Naborski would.

When he finished, the room was silent. Roelke couldn't even hear Marie's typewriter. She was probably listening at the door.

Finally Chief Naborski let his front chair legs thump back to the floor. "Officer McKenna, you know it is my policy to discourage personal relationships with Eagle residents."

"Ms. Ellefson doesn't actually *live* in—"

"That is irrelevant in this situation," the chief snapped.

Roelke told himself to keep his mouth shut.

Chief Naborski glared at him. "I'm going to write a letter of discipline that will go into your file. If you ever get a second letter, you'll be suspended without pay. A third letter will result in termination."

"Yes, sir."

"Right now, you are going to go out to the squad room and write up a matter of record. Shut my door behind you. When you're done, bring it in here."

Roelke didn't allow his shoulders to slump until he was seated at the typewriter in the next room. This was just round one of the trouble he was facing. But disappointing Chief Naborski was the worst of it.

"You OK?" Marie asked quietly. "You want a cup of coffee?"

Marie had never offered to get Roelke coffee before. He sighed. "Thanks. That would be good."

The big mug she brought him was drained by the time he got his admission down on paper: he'd disobeyed, he'd done things wrong, he regretted his mistakes. It would also go into his permanent file. *You're screwing your career out there,* Rick had said. Rick had no idea.

The chief read the admission through, then put it aside. "I just got off the phone with the DA. I explained that you have some kind of a personal relationship with this curator woman. I don't know exactly what it is—"

I don't either, Roelke thought.

"—and I don't care," Naborski was saying. "But the DA is extremely uncomfortable with the idea of you seeing her socially until the trial is over."

Which could take a very long time.

Chief Naborski planted his forearms on his desk and leaned forward. "I am *ordering* you to stay away from this woman until after the trial. Am I making myself clear?"

"Yes, sir." Roelke realized that his right knee was bouncing like a pile driver. He forced himself back to stillness.

"It will come out that you lied to the deputies. I can't protect you from the consequences of that."

"I understand."

"There's just one more thing." The older man rubbed his chin with thumb and forefinger. "The good news is that you got the SOB."

Roelke exhaled slowly. "Concealed carry and reckless endangerment at least. Probably more."

"Carlisle never aimed?" the chief asked.

Roelke hesitated. He'd always known that he *could* shoot to kill if necessary. When a bad guy points a gun at a cop, the cop shoots. But yesterday, when he'd seen Chloe's pants stained with blood … he'd felt those pulsing moments of anger so fierce that he had *wanted* to shoot. He had willed Carlisle to raise that dangling revolver, so he could—

"Officer McKenna?" Chief Naborski was frowning again.

"Not at me. He aimed at Ms. Ellefson before I got there."

The chief picked up a paperclip and toyed with it. "So. You handled a volatile situation without loss of life. That part was well done."

Roelke didn't quite feel safe saying thank you, so he settled for a small nod.

"I will expect your presence at the next Village Board meeting." Naborski tipped his chair back on two legs again. "Next Thursday, 7:30 P.M. You will receive your citation then."

Before Roelke could do more than blink, Chief Naborski's phone rang. "Marie," he yelled irritably.

The clerk opened the door and stuck her head into the room. "I know, I know. But I think you want to take it."

The chief picked up the phone, made a few noncommittal noises, said "Thanks for the call," and hung up. Then he looked at Roelke. "Carlisle's bail was set at fifty grand, but evidently daddy has deep pockets. Your boy's out on bond."

When Roelke emerged from the chief's office, he sat down and reached for the phone. The county was crawling all over the Carlisle case, now. But he wasn't ready to hand everything over in a gift-wrapped box. Not yet.

The DA had told Chief Naborski which Waukesha county detective was now assigned to the case—someone fairly new, which was good. Roelke got him on the phone and introduced himself. "I'm calling about Rupert Engel. I know the ball's in your court, but if you'd like some help on this end, I'd be glad to question the guy myself." He tried to sound off-hand. The politics of this kind of thing could be delicate.

"Well…" Detective Shuler considered. "It might save me some time."

"I've been watching this kid," Roelke said. Not *quite* another lie, since he had realized while interrogating Carlisle that he *had* seen Engel—entering Stanley Colontuono's house. "I think I can get him to roll. If that wouldn't mess up your plans, of course."

"No, that'd be good," the detective said. "Thanks."

—

Roelke worked late that day. He spent much of that night trying not to think about Chloe as he'd last seen her, waiting for her father in the ER lobby. He had no idea when he'd see her again. If, even.

On Saturday morning, his phone rang before his alarm went off. "Roelke?"

"Skeet? What's up?" For one wild moment Roelke wondered if Skeet had already been promoted to full time.

"I just took a call from county." Skeet hesitated. "And I figured you'd want to hear this."

TWENTY-EIGHT

"No, really, I'm OK," Chloe told Ethan. She was sitting in her old bedroom in her parents' house staring at a hideous purple macramé creation that she'd made in seventh grade. "I'm just going to hide out at my parents' place for another day or so." It was Saturday morning. She wasn't ready to go back to the farmhouse. Wasn't ready to even think about facing anyone at the site.

Ethan muttered something inaudible.

"I've had lots of time to sit and think, though. And I do have some good news. I think I'm finally starting to get over Markus."

"Really?"

"I still miss Switzerland. But I think I miss Switzerland a lot more than I miss Markus."

"An important distinction," Ethan agreed.

She sat up straight as a red pickup truck pulled up to the curb below. "I'm sorry, but I gotta go," Chloe said. "Thanks again for always being there. You're my best friend."

"Always, Chloe," Ethan said. "Always."

Ten minutes later she and Roelke were seated at the round wrought-iron table on the back patio. Chloe's mom had left them glasses of iced tea that neither seemed to want. "So," Chloe said finally. "I didn't expect to see—"

"Joel Carlisle is dead," Roelke said. "He overdosed. At his parents' house. They found him this morning."

It took her a moment to take that in. Truly take it in. She swiped at sudden tears. "He was so young. He had so much—"

"He might have killed you! Or me!"

"He's dead, Roelke. Isn't that enough for you?"

"No. It's not."

Chloe put her elbows on the table and rested her forehead on her fingertips. "Was he telling the truth about Nika? Was she involved?"

"I questioned Carlisle on Thursday night," Roelke said. "Nothing suggests that she had any idea what Joel was doing."

Chloe was relieved to hear it. "I've been thinking about what Joel was trying to tell me. About Emil—Mrs. Lundquist's brother. I couldn't figure out how Joel knew about Emil. Then I remembered that Joel is a genealogist."

"That's it exactly. Carlisle discovered that Nika had a great aunt she didn't know about. Berget Lundquist. He got all excited, and wrote to her. And he mentioned Nika's job at Old World in his letter."

"And?"

"She wrote back and said that as far as she was concerned, Emil died when he got married."

"Because he married a black woman."

"Right. Evidently Mrs. Lundquist called the state historical society and learned that the ale bowl had been transferred to Old World. She was afraid that Nika would somehow get her hands on it when she started working there. She told Carlisle that she wouldn't let that happen."

Fresh tears welled in Chloe's eyes. "Everything is so *sad*."

"Berget Lundquist was a nasty bigot," Roelke said brusquely. "And Joel Carlisle was a weak bully who took the coward's way out."

"People who do what he did aren't necessarily cowards," Chloe said. She dug in her pocket for a tissue, winced in pain, and redistributed her weight to ease the pressure on the stitches in her thigh.

"Did you ever ..." Roelke began, and then stopped. He stared at three girls jumping rope in the next yard. Faint snatches of their jumping chant drifted over the fence.

"Did I ever try?" Chloe asked shortly. "No. But that doesn't mean I didn't think about it, during the worst time."

"What... what happened?" His knee was working like a piston. "If you don't mind me asking."

Chloe sighed. She truly didn't know, not really. Despite everything that had happened with Markus and the miscarriage, she'd arrived in North Dakota with at least some of her professional passion intact. The small historic site there should have been manageable. But somewhere during that dull, gray winter, she'd realized that she simply didn't care anymore. Not about her staff's needs, not about the visitors' experiences. Not about anything.

Chloe took a sip of tea. She didn't have any idea why Roelke had become a cop, but she had a feeling that words like "passion" and "joy" wouldn't enter into the equation. So how could she explain what happened to her?

Finally she said, "It was just a thing with a guy."

"That guy on the phone?"

"... Who? Oh, Ethan. No, he's an old college friend. This was someone I knew in Switzerland." Chloe shifted her weight again.

"Look, Roelke, people don't choose to be depressed. Maybe Joel *did* make a cowardly decision. Or maybe he was clinically depressed and beyond help. Or maybe ... maybe he ended his life so Nika and his parents wouldn't be dragged through the public ordeal of a trial. If so, I'd say that what he did took a certain amount of courage."

Roelke ran a hand over his hair. "It's something I simply don't understand."

"I hope you never do."

For a while neither one spoke. "He saved my ass," Roelke said finally. "I did a lot of things I shouldn't have done last Wednesday."

Chloe stared at him with dawning dismay. "Did you get in trouble because of me?"

"Not much."

I am so stupid, Chloe thought.

"The chief and I had a conversation. We're square. I lied to Waukesha County deputies, though. Twice. That would have come out in the whole trial process. But now ... it'll likely all disappear. Because there will be no trial." Roelke scrubbed his face with his palms. "I wanted to pound the crap out of Carlisle there at the farm. Instead, I did my job. I believed he'd have to answer for his crimes in court. Now I feel cheated. And angry."

"Well ... I'm angry at him too. And I'm angry at Mrs. Lundquist. I thought she was a sweet old lady. I screwed up my job for her sake! And instead—she was a horrible racist." Chloe looked away, thinking, And what about me? She'd wondered if a current employee at Old World might somehow be descended from Berget. But she'd never considered Nika. It wasn't the same thing. Not at all. But still.

The back door opened and her mother emerged with a tray. "I've got *fattigman* and almond cookies," she said, as she deposited plates and forks and napkins.

"Thank you, Mrs. Ellefson," Roelke said.

"Kallerud," Chloe's mother said pleasantly. "I use my birth name. But please, just call me Marit." She beamed at him before heading back to the house.

Roelke watched her go. "I should have seen that coming."

"Don't worry about it. It happens all the time." Chloe began pleating a napkin. "Was Joel really the one behind everything?"

Roelke sighed. "Berget Lundquist mentioned the family heirloom in her letter to Carlisle. Before you started your job, he went out on site to help Nika. He was with her when she took a look around the artifact trailers. She got called away for something, and left him there. Presented with that opportunity, he decided to look for the bowl's accession record. He ripped it out of the ledger before Nika got back. He looked in the Norwegian houses without finding it. Later he got Rupert Engel to 'borrow' Stanley's key so he could take a closer look in the trailers—"

"I was nice to Rupert! And I thought he was being nice to me! He even helped me with my car."

"Rupert and Joel Carlisle were bar buddies. Rupert mentioned your car problems to Joel that evening, but he swears he didn't know that Joel planned to break into your house." Roelke gave her a sideways look. "Rupert is Stanley Colontuono's nephew."

"You're kidding!"

"Nope. The kid has a long rap sheet already—"

"With Stanley egging him on, no doubt."

"It doesn't look that way. Rupert's dad is out of the picture. His mother wasn't able to control him. Last spring Stanley brought Rupert to live with him. He gave him the job at Old World—"

"That's a nice little bit of nepotism."

"Yeah. Of course Stan didn't advertise the fact that Rupert was his nephew. The address on his job application lists the mother's Waukesha address. Rupert didn't show up for work yesterday. A county deputy went to the Waukesha apartment, but no luck. Fortunately I was able to pick him up."

Chloe eyed him. "How?"

"I remembered his car. I'd seen him going into Stanley's place. I'd been watching the house because I thought Stan might be the bookie we've been trying to identify."

"And is he?"

"No. The extra traffic at the house was just friends of Rupert's coming and going. One of whom was Carlisle. But I think Stanley really is trying to ride the kid straight, Chloe."

She shrugged.

"The court date you saw noted on Stanley's calendar was for Rupert. Stanley is planning to attend. He told me all the things he's been doing to keep Rupert out of trouble."

"Good for Stanley."

"When he found out that Rupert was gambling, Stan went ballistic. That night I saw him barge into The Eagle's Nest, he was looking for Rupert. And that takes us back to Carlisle. He was a gambler."

"A *gambler*?"

"It started years ago, when Carlisle's parents took him on some cruise. He got compulsive. It's like that for some people."

Chloe thought about that. She didn't understand gambling's appeal, but she supposed she shouldn't condemn Joel because she didn't understand his addiction.

"Anyway," Roelke was saying, "after he and Nika moved to Eagle, he got in way over his head. He was in debt big time, to the wrong people. He couldn't sell his vehicle or use his tuition money without Nika and his parents finding out. He got scared when Nika's tires got slashed. He figured that was a message to him. These things can get ugly real fast."

Chloe studied a passing cloud. She had never sensed anything in Joel except devotion to his fiancée. How had he managed to keep so much hidden? Why could she sense layers of emotion in old houses, and be so blind and deaf to what went on inside people right *now*?

"I do believe that at first, Carlisle just wanted to get the bowl for Nika," Roelke said soberly. "'Nika's had too many hard breaks already,' Carlisle said. 'She won't accept financial help from me. And that old bitch gave the bowl away. It should belong to Nika. She should at least have first dibs on writing it up.'"

Roelke glanced at Chloe. "That whole thing about getting an article published...?"

"That is important to Nika," Chloe said. "But I'd like to think that she wouldn't have accepted the bowl if it was stolen from the historical site."

"So she says. And I do believe her."

Thank God for small favors.

"But after Carlisle realized that his gambling debts had gotten him into serious trouble, he thought he could sell the bowl. He rationalized that it wasn't *really* stealing because it should have been Nika's anyway."

"That logic is a little twisted."

"Desperate people's logic usually is. Anyway, he broke into the trailer to look for it. Then he thought you might have found it, and taken it home, so he tried to break into your house. He swore that Engel had given him the impression that you'd be at your parents' house that night."

Chloe thought back. "And I assume Joel was the one who broke into Kvaale that night you got called out?"

Roelke nodded. "He said he'd been at Sasso's that evening with you and Nika, and heard somebody say something about storing a damaged artifact in the attic of one of the old houses. He took Nika's key and went out to the Kvaale house to see if someone had tucked the bowl upstairs."

"What about the rock through my window? He must have known by then that I didn't have the bowl."

"He was panicking." Roelke picked up a cookie, put it back down. "Carlisle was trying to scare you into quitting. He said he was just trying to take care of Nika."

Chloe frowned, trying to parse that through. Then, "Oh. I get it. He thought that if I quit, Petty might give my job to Nika." The curator job offered what Nika's internship did not: a reasonable salary, stability, benefits, professional recognition. It wouldn't have been that simple, of course; Nika would have had to compete for the job. *Will* have to, Chloe reminded herself, once Ralph Petty fires me.

Well, she'd face that on Monday. "What about Mr. Solberg?"

"Carlisle denied being there. I think he was lying so he could get out on bail long enough to talk to Nika." Roelke made a palms-up gesture. "The Dane County crime scene guys thought that Mr. Solberg hit his head on the corner of the desk. Maybe Carlisle startled him. Maybe he shoved him. Maybe Mr. Solberg got scared when he saw Joel, and tripped."

"Did Joel say anything about me?" Chloe asked. She wasn't sure what she was hoping for. An apology? Could mere words make up for what he'd done?

"No. All he wanted to do was see Nika."

Chloe's head ached, and her thigh was starting to hurt like hell. "I'm sorry," she said. "I just can't think about this anymore right now."

"I'll get going. I just didn't want you to hear about Carlisle's overdose on the news or something."

Chloe braced her hands against the table and shoved gracelessly to her feet. Roelke put out a hand, but she waved it away. "I'm OK."

"I heard you needed stitches."

"Just three. Are you OK?" Her face grew warm; she should have asked at once. "Where I, you know, hit you with the shears? I was aiming at Joel."

"It was just a scratch."

Thank God for that, too. "Good. But listen, Roelke?" Chloe caught his gaze and held it. "Thank you. I don't know what would have happened if you hadn't come."

"You're welcome."

He matched his stride to her limping gait as they walked around the house. "Where is the ale bowl?" she asked.

"In our property locker."

"I need to take care of it. It's been in the stabbur all these years, and some of that fire retardant stuff might have gotten on it, and Joel dropped it, and—"

"It should get released pretty quickly. No reason to hold on to it, now."

Right. No need for evidence anymore. "Well," she said as they reached the curb, "I guess I'll—"

"Chloe." Roelke's eyes suddenly bore into hers.

She took a step backward. "What?"

"With everything that happened, and Carlisle's overdose, I just wondered… Well, you said you felt sad, and it made me think that maybe ..." A ruddy flush stained Roelke's cheeks. "Are you thinking, or feeling, like—"

"No," Chloe said firmly, finally understanding. "I'm not. I'll be OK, Roelke. Truly."

He looked unconvinced. Two teens on skateboards flashed past, the wheels clicking on every sidewalk seam.

Chloe wrapped her hands over her shoulders. "When I was out at the farm with Joel, before you got there ... I was scared, Roelke."

"Yeah?"

"Yeah. Terrified, really. I almost peed my pants."

For the first time that afternoon, Roelke smiled. "Good."

It was almost midnight before Roelke got home that evening. He'd done no more than remove his duty belt when he heard footsteps on the outside stairs, ascending fast—Libby. He opened the door before she could knock, and she barreled inside. "Oh my God," she said, and wrapped her arms around him.

"What?" he asked finally, although he had a pretty good idea.

She stepped back and glared at him. "Why didn't you tell me? I had to read about it in the paper!"

"It wasn't that big a deal," Roelke said. Although it was.

"You're OK?"

"Yeah."

"God, I *hate* your job sometimes." Libby dropped into a chair. "And Chloe's OK?"

"She's pretty shook up. But not seriously hurt." He reached for his kettle and began to fill it at the sink. "Want some tea or something?"

Libby watched him. "Are you in trouble?"

"I didn't go by the book, so I've got a letter in my file," he admitted. "But a commendation, too. I don't think the chief's going to hold it against me." He fixed her with a look. "And Libby? That's a good thing. Because I'm not going back to Milwaukee."

"Because of Chloe?"

"No. Not because of Chloe." Chloe's career at Old World Wisconsin was evidently over. There was no reason to think she'd stick around.

"Then … why?" Libby asked.

"Maybe I actually like working for the Eagle PD. Did that ever occur to you?"

"Name one thing about a part-time job in Eagle that's better than your career in Milwaukee," she said quietly. "Just one."

"Here's one. The first time I saluted the chief, he told me to cut the crap." Roelke folded his arms. "He talks with me, not at me. Want another reason? I've yet to meet a mother in Eagle who's taught her kids to hate anyone in uniform because cops put their daddy in prison. Want another? When a man calls the station in tears after I've just hauled his wife up to detox for the fifth time, I actually have time to talk with him. To *help* him."

"OK," Libby said.

"So cut the I'm-wiser-than-you bullshit." He pulled the kettle from the stove and poured steaming water into two mugs. "I mean it, Libs. I'm sick of it."

"O-*kay*," she said. "I get it."

"Eagle is a good fit for me." Roelke rummaged in his cupboard until he found a box of herbal orange spice tea. He sat down across from his cousin. The tea steeped in silence.

"It's the little things," he said finally. "I do a lot of little things that no one ever sees, or even knows about, but they make Eagle safer. And if that makes me some kind of a lesser cop in your eyes—"

"I never said that," Libby protested.

"You might as well have."

"Look, I'm sorry." Libby put a hand over his. "I was wrong, OK? I was wrong."

TWENTY-NINE

On Monday morning, Chloe stopped first at Ed House. When she arrived at the trailer, she found the expected summons from Ralph taped to the door: COME TO MY OFFICE. Chloe got back into her car and drove to the administration building.

"Thank you for coming in," Ralph said stiffly, when she knocked on his door. He indicated a chair. She took it.

Ralph regarded her. "Shall I be frank, Ms. Ellefson?"

"You might as well." All Chloe wanted was to get this done with.

"In the short time that you have been an employee at Old World Wisconsin, you have persistently ignored my directives. You have exhibited a complete disregard for my authority. You were disrespectful in the staff meeting."

He waited, perhaps giving her time for rebuttal, but she had nothing to say. It was all true.

"I asked repeatedly for a preliminary plan for a collections storage facility, and you refused to comply. I had a donor waiting. She had money to give, and she needed to give it quickly."

Well hell, Chloe thought irritably, why didn't you share that little tidbit earlier? "I didn't know that."

"You didn't need to know that."

She shifted in her chair, trying to ease the strain on her thigh. So much for getting this over with quickly.

Ralph tented his fingers. "When I went to Madison last week, I met with the division administrator and Leila. I made a clear case for firing you. The administrator authorized me to do so."

Chloe nodded. She wanted to get through this final exchange with some shred of dignity. She had nothing else left.

"If you had not called in sick on Thursday, I would have fired you first thing in the morning."

"I wasn't shirking," she observed mildly. "The ER doctor told me to stay home for a couple of days after—after what happened."

"Yes. 'What happened.'" Ralph's mouth twisted with distaste. "As I understand it, 'what happened' was a direct result of you ignoring my instructions to stop looking for the ale bowl."

Oh for God's sake, Chloe thought. Just cut to the chase. "Look, if—"

"*However.*" Ralph leaned back in his chair. "Your escapade at Kvaale, and the recovery of the ale bowl, has generated a lot of publicity. The division administrator called me Friday afternoon. He is having second thoughts about firing you."

Chloe raised her eyebrows, trying to wrap her brain around that unexpected announcement.

"Ms. Ellefson. Do you wish to remain employed at Old World Wisconsin?"

Chloe thought of the cramped trailers and of sandhill cranes calling as they flew overhead, of the crushing backlog of collections work and of the taste of heavy rye bread still warm from its brick bakeoven. “Yes,” she heard herself say. “I guess I do.”

Ralph’s gaze was stony. “You are still on probation. Is that understood?”

“Yes.”

“I may be able to salvage the storage facility donation. Completing the preliminary plan will remain your primary responsibility. Is that understood?”

“Yes.”

He stared at her, mouth pressed in a hard line. Was he waiting for her to leave? She rubbed her palms on her knees, then stood.

“One more thing.” Ralph pinned her with a look of naked dislike. “If you ever again belittle me in front of other staff members, not only will I fire you on the spot, I will do everything in my power to make sure you never work in the museum world again.”

“I was out of line,” Chloe said. “It won’t happen again.”

An hour later, Chloe unlocked the door of the little cobblestone cottage in the Crossroads Village, formerly believed to be the dwelling and shop of a Swiss carpenter named Aldrick Tobler. She held her breath, eased the door open, stepped inside … and smiled. No more bad ju-ju.

It didn’t take long to pack up the tools the freelance curator had left. “It’s just a start,” she said, to whomever might be listening. “I’ll get the rest later.” She look around, imagining the cottage as it might one day be. “And oo-la-la, am I going to have fun furnishing *this* building.”

Chloe locked the cottage up again and considered the rest of her day. Astonishingly enough, it would be spent doing her job at Old World Wisconsin. Ralph's precious collections storage project? It could wait one more day. She just wasn't in the mood.

As she stood debating, she noticed a light glowing from the window wells at St. Peter's Church. Surely Nika hadn't come to work…?

Nika had. Chloe found her at the table in the church basement, sorting a pile of socks and stockings. She wore a purple silk blouse and sleek black pants. A purple band captured her braids behind her neck, and amethyst earrings dangled against her neck. Nika looked as classy and controlled as ever—until she glanced up. Grief and shock and anger showed beneath a glimmer of tears in her eyes.

Chloe stifled the urge to hug the younger woman, sensing it wouldn't be welcome. "Hey," she said instead.

"Hey." Nika carefully placed a hand-knit and well-darned woman's sock into a gray archival box.

"Nika. You don't have to be here right now."

Nika reached for another sock with a suddenly trembling hand. "Are you firing me?"

"No! But surely… I mean, some time off might be a good idea—"

"I don't *want* time off. Where do you expect me to go? I have nothing left but this job."

Chloe sighed. "I am so, so sorry."

Nika took a deep breath. "I need to talk to you."

"OK." Chloe removed a storage box from a folding chair and sat down.

"I saw Joel after he got out of jail. He told me about the gambling. And that he bought a gun after my tires got slashed."

Chloe opened her mouth, then thought better of speaking.

"Joel also told me about that woman. Berget Lundquist. My great aunt. You know about that?"

"Yes. I swear, Nika, I had no idea." An ache was growing beneath Chloe's ribs. "I just can't believe ... she seemed so sweet."

Nika gave a contemptuous flick of her hand. "That woman doesn't matter."

"How can you *say* that? Her neighbor told me she said she was open-minded for marrying a Swede. I thought she'd been *joking*."

"Do you think she was the first person to judge me because of my skin?" Nika asked harshly. "I knew my grandfather's family had disowned him. I just didn't know their names."

"But Joel figured it out."

"He was very protective." Nika's voice trembled. "He wanted to take care of me."

"I know," Chloe said. "I do know that."

"But he fucked up." Nika clenched her fists in her lap. "Last Thursday, he kept saying that the ale bowl was my birthright. That I'd been cheated out of my family name and I should at least have the bowl. *God!*" Nika stood abruptly and began to pace in the short aisle. "As if I would have consented to theft!"

"He adored you. Sometimes people act stupid when they're in love."

Nika was silent for a moment, letting that in. "I didn't know, Chloe. That's all I can say."

"I believe you." Chloe sighed, feeling old.

"I would have sworn that Joel would never have been able to hide anything from me. But even on Thursday, the last time we talked ..." She wiped her eyes. "I guess he was thinking of suicide even then. And I didn't get it."

Mystery
(Paperback)

Mystery
(Paperback)

Suicide. Nika is the only person strong enough to say it straight out, Chloe thought, remembering how she and Roelke had swerved around the word.

Then she remembered something else. "How on earth did Joel figure out where the ale bowl was?"

Nika went to one of the battered old file cabinets she'd salvaged. She pulled open a drawer, revealing a neat row of folders. "Last Wednesday, Joel came here with me. We got in late because he'd felt sick in the night, and I insisted he go see his doctor. I think now he was just hyped up with worry about the trouble he was in." A tiny frisson seemed to ripple over her skin. "Anyway, he wanted to help me. Just like always. I asked him to organize all those reproduction request files you brought over."

"No." Chloe felt a sinking sensation in her stomach. "Oh, no. Please don't tell me..."

Nika picked up a piece of paper lying on top of the file cabinet and handed it over. Chloe read the penciled scrawl: *Can we get a reproduction ale bowl? It would be great to use on Midsummer. When I was dusting the rosemaled artifacts in Kvaale today I noticed a tiny crack in the bowl with cow head handles. Somebody should look at it. I put it up in the stabbur for safekeeping. Ginny Dunning, August 3, 1978.*

"The answer was in my car the whole time," Chloe whispered. "The whole frickin' time."

Nika sank back into her chair. "Joel found that. He told me he was going to the visitor center to use the bathroom. I started wondering when he didn't come back. Finally I went looking, and found my car gone. One of the interpreters came by and gave me a lift home. I didn't know what was going on until the cops showed up."

"I don't suppose this matters, now." Chloe put the note down on the table.

Nika laid a piece of tissue over the layer of stockings in the box with the precise care of a surgeon, then picked up another stocking to begin again. Suddenly her fingers clenched, crushing it. "Joel told me on Thursday that he was going to tell his father's lawyers not to fight the charges. 'It's time to face the music,' he said."

And what about poor Mr. Solberg? Chloe thought. Did Joel mention him? But Nika didn't say, and Chloe wasn't brave enough to ask.

Nika swallowed. "I knew he was going to his parents' house after he left me. I did not know that he was going to swallow a bottle of sleeping pills." She was crying now, silently, tears rolling down her cheeks. "Mrs. Carlisle called me on Saturday morning, after they'd found him."

Chloe's throat felt thick. The sound of children's voices drifted through the windows, followed by a chaperone's shrill whistle. Nika finally glanced down, noticed the scrunched sock, and smoothed it flat again.

"Look, Nika," Chloe said. "There are a couple more things we need to get out in the open."

"Like what?" Nika asked warily.

"When I went to Madison last Tuesday, I saw your name on the patron roster in Iconography."

Nika looked perplexed. "So?"

"Well, why didn't you mention that you'd been there?"

"I'd been intrigued by those Dahl photos you had, and wanted to see the rest of the collection. I was looking for a project I could pursue on my own time. But I never discuss stuff like that. The academic world is too competitive."

Nika made it sound so logical. "Fair enough," Chloe conceded. "But there's another thing. The night before I went to Madison, I saw an embroidered Norwegian apron here on the worktable." She hesitated. Did Nika know about the apron's connection to Berget Lundquist? Since the donation had been made through the Norwegian Women's Club, possibly not.

Nika folded her arms over her chest, looking more defensive. "Yeah? So what?"

"I'd just asked you if you'd found any ethnic pieces, and you said no."

"I hadn't examined that apron yet. I didn't know it was an ethnic piece."

More logic. "OK," Chloe said. "But when I got back to Eagle on Tuesday evening, I looked all over for the apron—" Chloe gestured vaguely at the cabinets and neatly stacked storage boxes—"but it wasn't here. So … where is it?"

"Are you accusing me of stealing it?" Nika demanded.

"No," Chloe said carefully. "I am asking you a question."

"I took the apron and a couple of other pieces to Ed House so I could clean them."

"Why not just clean things here at the church?"

"Here? With no sink? And visitors all around?"

Chloe thought that through. Cleaning white textiles meant soaking them on screens in plastic trays with a bit of archival soap. After repeated rinses, the pieces were spread on grass to dry and bleach. "I see your point," she said, feeling like an idiot.

The strident chords of a pump organ suddenly came through the ceiling as the interpreter upstairs began playing for visitors. Nika pinched her lips together. "Do you know that I have an arrest record?"

Chloe's eyebrows went up. "Um, no. I did not know that."

"I thought Petty might have checked before hiring me. Well, you might as well know. When I was in high school, sometimes I went to antique stores. I was flat broke, saving every penny for college, but I just liked looking around. One day I talked my cousin into coming with me. In one shop I found this great embroidered handkerchief. I studied it for a while, then moved on. Suddenly a cop showed up, and the dealer accused me of shoplifting. He said the handkerchief was in my purse. It was."

Chloe opened her mouth, closed it again. *Shit.*

"I did not steal it," Nika said coldly. "My cousin had pinched it and slipped it into my bag."

"But—but *why*?"

"I never got a straight answer from her. Maybe she just wanted me to have the piece I liked so much. Or maybe ..." Nika shook her head. "Maybe she wanted to knock me down a peg. All she wanted to do was get pregnant and quit school. I probably talked way too much about everything I planned to accomplish."

"Perhaps it was a little bit of both."

"Maybe. I know I can be intense."

"Kind of," Chloe agreed. "But there's nothing wrong with knowing what you want and going after it."

"Maybe. But if I hadn't been so focused on building my career, I might have noticed that my fiancé was struggling." Nika abruptly shoved the textiles aside, dropped her elbows on the table, and buried her face. "If I hadn't worked so many evenings and weekends, my fiancé wouldn't have had so much time to kill in taverns."

Chloe's chest ached. What could she say to ease Nika's burden? Not a damn thing.

No ... wait. There was perhaps one thing, one small thing, she could do.

"Nika," she said. "I think one of your female ancestors actually made the ale bowl. Do you have any interest in pursuing that?"

Nika looked up, her mouth twisted with revulsion. "*God*, no."

"So you still need a project. A good one. Here's the thing. I met with Margueritte Donovan this morning. It looks like the cobblestone cottage we thought belonged to a Swiss carpenter, didn't."

"It didn't?"

"Nope. There were actually *two* small buildings on the lot. The records were misleading. The freelance curator who researched the building drew the obvious conclusions. But last week a newspaper clipping turned up that suggests that the lot was divided. Margueritte did some more digging. The cottage Old World acquired was actually owned by a Yankee woman from Vermont. Sally Jenkins. And get this: Sally Jenkins, who evidently never married, had some medical training. Her business notice in the local paper says 'Dr. S. A. Jenkins.'"

Nika stared at her, mouth slightly open.

"So, how would you like to do the research report and furnishing plan for the Jenkins House?" Chloe asked.

"*Really?*" Nika sat up straight. It was a hint of the old Nika—alert, on the hunt.

"Really."

"I would like that. Thanks. But . . . are you in a position to offer me that? Word I heard was that Ralph got the OK to fire you."

"I met with him first thing this morning. And—well, he's not going to fire me. At least not today."

"How'd you manage that?"

"I ate a good-sized helping of crow."

"That can't have been fun, you being a vegetarian."

A startled laugh hiccupped from Chloe. A smile twitched at Nika's mouth, too. It was gone in an instant. A fresh sheen of tears glazed her eyes. But it gave Chloe hope that maybe, one day, Nika would be OK.

THIRTY

THAT EVENING, CHLOE WAS surveying her dinner options—Oreos or peanut butter on crackers—when Roelke called. "Are you doing OK?" he asked.

"I'm working on it."

"Did you get fired?"

So much for small talk. "As a matter of fact, no. I am still employed."

"Hunh." He sounded thoughtful. "Well, that's good. So. Libby and I are meeting for fish at the Nite Cap Inn in Palmyra on Friday. Six o'clock. Want to join us?"

"Well ... sure," she said. "Why not."

The Nite Cap was a big cream-city brick structure, quintessential Wisconsin, with a bar and restaurant on the lower story and rooms for rent on the second. When Chloe arrived at the tavern on Friday it was jammed, noisy, and full of smoke. She spotted Roelke waving from a corner table.

"This place is nuts," she said, as she slipped into a chair across from him.

"Their fish fry is famous. I had to order so we could get a table. Libby should be along soon."

A waitress came to take drink orders. Chloe splurged on a rum and Coke. Roelke ordered a beer. "So," Chloe said, as they waited for their drinks. "I guess everything is about wrapped up."

"It looks that way. Carlisle's prints matched a couple that the Dane County boys found at Mrs. Lundquist's house, so they're considering Mr. Solberg's death a closed case as well. The assumption is that Joel broke in searching for—something he thought might help him locate the bowl."

"I am choosing to believe that Joel never intended to hurt Mr. Solberg."

"Your call." Roelke studied her. "I guess I won't yell at you for acting stupid when Carlisle cornered you at the farm. Going into the barn after the bowl, coming out from the breezeway into the open, diving at—"

"Thanks for not yelling."

"You were pretty damn accurate with those sheep shears. You could have killed either me or Carlisle—"

Chloe's cheeks burned. "I was only trying to help."

"I had things under control," he said. "But where did you learn to throw like that?"

"I played softball in college. Just intramurals, but I was pretty good." The waitress showed up with their drinks, and she took a grateful sip.

“When you dove at us, were you trying to keep Carlisle from shooting me? Or were you just trying to catch the ale bowl?”

“Well … I, um, assumed you *did* have everything under control. And Gro’s ale bowl is irreplaceable.”

Roelke rolled his eyes, then took a swig of beer. “So. Are you still feeling OK? Not, you know, depressed?”

“I’m still feeling OK.” Chloe leaned forward so she could keep her voice low. “Stop asking, all right? There’s nothing like being scared shitless to make you realize that you don’t want to die.”

He traced a line in the cold bottle’s sweat with one finger. “Then how would you like to go out sometime? Not with Libby. Not to talk about a crime.”

This was a conversation Chloe did not want to have. “We really don’t know each other very well.”

“Well, yeah,” he said. “That’s sort of the point. To get to know each other a little better.”

Shit. Where the heck was Libby? “I don’t think I’m ready for anything like that,” Chloe said, forcing herself to meet his gaze. “I’m still … sorting a lot of stuff out.”

“Is it that guy from Switzerland? Is he the one in the picture in your bedroom?”

“No. But speaking of pictures, what about the woman in the photograph *I* saw? At the police station? Above your locker?”

“Oh. No. That’s not someone I ever dated.”

The waitress appeared again, looking harried, and deposited plates of cod and walleye, plus homemade potato pancakes, coleslaw, and applesauce. Roelke was still waiting expectantly.

“Look,” Chloe tried. “I just don’t think it will work.”

“Why not?”

Because I don't trust relationships! she wanted to shout. She'd believed that Markus Meili loved her. She'd thought that Joel Carlisle was a great guy, and that Berget Lundquist was a sweet old lady. She obviously was no judge of character.

"Well?" he prodded.

"For one thing, I'm older than you."

"Ex-*cuse* me?" Roelke hooted with laughter. "Aren't you the person who scolded me for saying 'maiden name' instead of 'birth name'? And now *age* is a problem?"

Chloe smoothed a wrinkle in the tablecloth. Agreeing to come this evening had not been one of her better moves, potato pancakes or not.

Libby appeared, and slid into the empty chair. "Sorry I'm late." She turned to Chloe. "It's good to see you. You've been through the wringer."

"Kinda." Chloe stirred her drink, watching the ice cubes whirl.

"So, what were you two bickering about when I got here?" Libby asked.

Roelke smiled. "Whether or not we should go out."

"You are out, aren't you?" Libby began filling her plate.

"Oh, for God's sake," Chloe muttered.

"Chloe thinks I'm too young for her," Roelke added, sounding a little smug.

"Tell the whole bar, why don't you?"

Libby rolled her eyes. "You're both acting like seventh graders." She grabbed two cocktail napkins and slapped one on the table in front of each of them. "Here. You've both been around the block. Write down three pet peeves from past relationships. Things that you can't live with. Don't think about it!" she added, as Roelke opened his mouth. "Just do it!" Two pens appeared from the depths of her purse.

Chloe sighed, feeling cornered. Did Markus dumping her because she had a miscarriage qualify as a pet peeve? Probably not. Better to dredge up her pre-Switzerland era. Feeling Libby's frown, she picked up a pen and scribbled a list.

Roelke wrote quickly, slapped his pen down, and glared at his cousin. Libby snatched both napkins, gave them a quick scan, and handed them off.

Roelke began to read. "One: Leaving the toilet seat up." He frowned. "Isn't that a cliché?"

"Not if you find it irritating."

He returned to her list. "Two: Leaving the TV on as background noise. Three: Being too quick to shut windows and turn on the AC or heat." He regarded Chloe, gaze inscrutable. "Well, hunh."

Chloe looked at Roelke's peeves, written in a tight, slanting hand: "One: Mindless chatter. Two: Foo foo."

"What's 'foo foo'?" she asked, confused by a mental image of the malicious bunny that delighted in scooping up field mice and bopping them on the head.

"You know. Candles that smell. Teddy bears wearing lacy dresses." Roelke shuddered. "Knick-knacks."

"Got it." Chloe looked back down at the list in her hand. "Three: Pulling down the blinds before it's completely dark."

She sucked in a breath and blew it out slowly, seeing the exquisite filigree of bare black limbs against a cobalt sky. Something beneath her ribcage tightened.

"O-K," Libby said, holding up one hand. "I don't see any insurmountable problems here. I'm going to get a drink. You kids decide what you're going to do." She shoved back her chair and headed toward the bar.

Roelke rolled his beer bottle between his palms, regarding her across the table. “So. How about tomorrow? You free for the afternoon?”

Tomorrow? The *afternoon*? Whatever happened to evening dates—a bracketed time span that left plenty of room for “It’s getting late, I gotta go?” Chloe swallowed uneasily. “What do you have in mind?”

“Something fun,” he promised. “I’ll pick you up at one o’clock.”

THIRTY-ONE

Roelke was predictably prompt. As she finished braiding her hair, Chloe watched him survey the living room: a vase with a single white rosebud on top of the bookshelf, next to a framed photograph of the Swiss Alps. A stack of record albums on the floor, her dulcimer on a chair, some books on the shelves.

"This is better," he said.

"I'm ready," Chloe said. "Let's go."

They drove through Whitewater and continued west. Roelke started humming, exuding an air of actual good cheer. They were headed toward Fort Atkinson … was he taking her to hear bluegrass music at the Green Lantern? Probably not. In profile, even his jaw looked relaxed. Too relaxed for an afternoon of music he didn't like.

"So," she said. "What are we doing this afternoon?"

"We're going sky diving."

"… I beg your pardon?"

"Sky diving. You. Me."

"This afternoon?"

"Yep."

"No we aren't!"

"Yes, we are."

Chloe twisted in the seat so she could face him. "What—you can't—stop this truck!"

Roelke began to whistle.

"I mean it! Pull over!" Chloe tried to grab the steering wheel. "Take me home!"

"Stop it!" he bellowed. They swerved onto the shoulder before he muscled the truck safely back into the lane. "Jesus, Chloe!"

"Jesus yourself! I'm not going sky diving! I—I have stitches in my leg!"

"Exactly three. You'll survive."

"Now, you listen to me, Officer McKenna," Chloe snapped. "I—"

"No, you listen to me. You found out you didn't want to die. That's not the same as wanting to live."

"Of all the patronizing, arrogant, *manipulative*..." She ran out of adjectives and folded her arms, glaring out the window.

Roelke kept driving. By the time they arrived at Fort Atkinson's municipal airport ten minutes later, a steely resolve had narrowed her eyes and stiffened her spine. She'd rappelled down cliffs in her day. Belly-crawled through caves. Paddled Class-5 rapids. She could do this. She *would* do this.

Then she would hitchhike home.

Anger and pride carried her through an absurdly brief orientation provided by an enthusiastic instructor named Dave. Chloe tried to listen as Dave demonstrated the mechanics of parachutes and the tandem harness. She practiced jumping from a demo plane door just outside the hangar, learned the basic hand gestures used for in-air communication, and practiced the butt-in, arms-and-legs outstretched position she was supposed to adopt in the air. Roelke, who'd greeted Dave as an old friend, sat through the briefing with an air of wired anticipation. Clearly, Roelke had jumped from airplanes before.

"And don't forget to smile," Dave concluded. "Smiling reduces drag and turbulence in your face."

Facial turbulence. Chloe gritted her teeth. "Super," she muttered. "That's just super."

Chloe tried to ignore the nibbling fear as they climbed into the Cessna. The jumpsuit and harness she'd donned felt strange. Her stomach lurched sickly as the pilot began to taxi down the runway.

What the *hell* was she doing?

"We'll climb to 8,700 feet," the pilot shouted.

Chloe, seated directly behind the pilot, swallowed hard. Her heart was in her throat. This was *insane*! She clutched Dave's arm convulsively. "Wait!"

"You OK?" he shouted.

Chloe hesitated. She could suck it up and jump. Or, she could add a new humiliation to her ever-accumulating train of emotional baggage.

"OK?" Dave shouted again.

With every cell of her being, Chloe hoped that Roelke was regretting his heavy-handed prank. She sucked in a deep breath and looked back at Dave. "OK."

The plane continued to climb. A patchwork of farm fields spread below, and ... was that Lake Koshkonong? What if they landed in the lake? What if—

"Ready, Roelke?" Dave shouted. Roelke buckled a helmet over his goggles and grinned, the bastard. He unfastened his seat belt and eased a foot out the open door, onto the wheel. "Blue skies!" he yelled, and plunged from sight.

A surge of raw, primal panic swept away the last grains of Chloe's eroding pride.

"OK!" Dave nodded at Chloe. "Our turn."

Her limbs had stopped obeying mental commands. Dave unhooked her seatbelt and helped her stand. Once she was steady, he stood directly behind her and fastened their harnesses together.

Chloe found herself at the door of an airplane almost nine thousand feet above the earth. Wind punched her body and screamed past her ears. Her knees began to jackhammer uncontrollably. Sweat soaked her shirt. "I can't do this!" She clung desperately to the vinyl rope.

"Put your leg out!" Dave yelled in her ear.

She inched her right foot into swirling air. Her left leg still shook uncontrollably. Centuries of genetic memory screamed a cellular warning: *Wrong! Wrong! Wrong!*

"Let go!" Dave commanded. *"Do it!"*

Somehow, her fingers released the strap. Dave stepped into the air. They plummeted. Everything moved in every direction at once. Free fall.

Then muscle memory pulled Chloe into the belly-down spread eagle she'd practiced on the ground. Miraculously, she was still breathing. She felt a hard jolt when the parachute opened, slowing their 120 mph plunge toward terra firma.

They floated down balloon-like. No plane noise. No wind.

Holy Mother of God.

It took a heartbeat, or perhaps forever, to see the earth rising beneath them. Chloe tried to process information again. Tuck your arms, lift your legs ... She and Dave glided down on wet grass, both lifting their feet so they could slide to an easy, standing position.

Chloe felt her heart thudding. The scent of crushed alfalfa filled her nostrils. The world seemed amazingly, gloriously still. Dave began tugging on the clumsy harness straps and buckles.

Then she was free. Free of the harness. Free from Dave. Absolutely free. She didn't know whether to rise on her toes or sink to the ground. She compromised by bending over, hands on knees.

"Chloe?" Roelke's hiking boots appeared in her circle of vision. His hand landed on her shoulder. She shook her head, not ready for words.

"Chloe! Are you OK? Did you hurt your leg?"

With enormous effort she straightened. She searched Roelke's face—the strong jaw, the straight nose, the startling eyes. It had somehow become completely familiar.

"Jesus!" he barked. "Yell at me, cuss at me, but for Chrissakes say something!"

Chloe took his hand and squeezed. "I finally know why birds sing."

That evening she called Ethan. "I went sky diving," she announced.

"You went sky diving?"

"Yep. Roelke took me. The cop. I know it wasn't like what you do as a smoke jumper, but still…"

"It's kind of a rush, isn't it?" Ethan asked, as if confessing to a guilty pleasure.

"Yeah," Chloe said, and laughed. She gave him the details, then happened to glance at the clock. "It's late. I better go. Good-night, Ethan."

"Chloe? Anything you want to ask me?"

She wrinkled her forehead. "What?"

"Nothing." For some reason he sounded pleased. "Good-night."

———

On Tuesday afternoon, the phone rang as Chloe sat on the floor playing with the calico kitten she'd brought home from her landlord's barn. She tossed a toy mouse to her new fur ball and stretched to reach the phone. "Hello?"

"I'm off tomorrow night," Roelke said. "Can I buy you dinner?"

"Dinner would be good."

"Great. See you then."

"What time—" Chloe began, but the receiver clicked in her ear. Well, he'd call back. Chloe turned to the kitten again. "Come here, you little munchkin—"

The phone rang. Chloe grabbed it. "I can be ready by six."

Static crackled in her ear. "Hello? Chloe?"

She went very still.

"I'm at O'Hare." The man's voice sounded distant. A flight announcement sounded in the background.

Her grip on the receiver tightened.

"Chloe? I just flew in to Chicago."

The kitten leaped for a fuzzy ball, overshot the target, and executed a flawless somersault. Chloe closed her eyes.

"Are you there?" he asked. "Chloe, it's me. Markus."

THE END

ACKNOWLEDGMENTS

Almost every business named in the novel is fictional. However, I have happy memories of visiting Sasso's, in Eagle; and the Nite Cap Inn, in Palmyra, and so included them. To the proprietors: Thanks for the hospitality, way back when.

Many people helped make this book possible. Thanks to all of my OWW friends, then and now; to the Writer Chicks, for a decade of friendship and insight; and to Katie Mead and Robert Alexander, for giving me a place to write.

Huge thanks to Chief Russ Ehlers and members of the Eagle Police Department for their patience, assistance, and encouragement. I'm in awe of what you do every day.

I'm grateful to my agent, Andrea Cascardi, and to the entire Midnight Ink team, for believing in this project.

I might not be a writer today if my parents hadn't known that books are as important as food, and if my sisters hadn't shared their favorites over the years. And I couldn't make this work without the love and support of my husband, Scott Meeker—videographer, book hauler, proofreader, and all-around partner.

ABOUT THE AUTHOR

Kathleen Ernst is a novelist, social historian, and educator. She moved to Wisconsin in 1982 to take an interpreter job at Old World Wisconsin, and later served as a Curator of Interpretation and Collections at the historic site.

Old World Murder is Kathleen's first adult mystery. Her historical fiction for children and young adults includes eight historical mysteries. Honors for her fiction include Edgar and Agatha nominations.

Kathleen lives and writes in Middleton, Wisconsin, and still visits historic sites every chance she gets! She also blogs about the relationship between fiction and museums at www.sitesandstories.wordpress.com. Learn more about Kathleen and her work at www.kathleenernst.com.